THE PRODIGAL SON

ANNA BELFRAGE

D1260946

THE PRODIGAL SON

ANNA BELFRAGE

Matador
9 Priory Business Park,
Wistow Road, Kibworth Beauchamp,
Leicestershire. LE8 0RX
Tel: (+44) 116 279 2299
Fax: (+44) 116 279 2277
Email: books@troubador.co.uk
Web: www.troubador.co.uk/matador

ISBN 978 1780885 742

British Library Cataloguing in Publication Data.
A catalogue record for this book is available from the British Library.

Typeset in 11pt Bell MT by Troubador Publishing Ltd, Leicester, UK

Matador is an imprint of Troubador Publishing Ltd

Printed and bound in the UK by TJ International, Padstow, Cornwall

This book is dedicated to all those people who open their hearts to a child not of their blood and take it as their own. Where would the world be without you?

CHAPTER 1

Four shadows rose out of the darkness of the moor, darting from patch to patch of vegetation. Here and there they found cover behind a boulder, now and then they huddled together under a stunted tree, gliding noiselessly due north. It was too early for birds, so when a sharp whistle cut through the air the leading shadow set off at speed, his companions slinking after him towards a protective outcrop of stone.

"Hush!" Matthew Graham sank down, the three men accompanying him doing the same. He pointed to where a group of six riders were making slow progress on a marshy stretch of ground.

"More soldiers," he said, his voice a low hum.

"And here was I thinking they were but angels of deliverance," the man sitting closest to him said, and despite their situation Matthew smiled. The speaker moved closer to Matthew, his mouth a scant inch from Matthew's ear. "They won't find us."

"You think not?" Matthew tried to sound unconcerned but his eyes were stuck on the approaching group of soldiers, his brain scrambling to find a way out of this neat little corner. Summer dawn was only hours away and no matter that he and his companions were all cloaked and hooded in dark colours somewhere between brown and grey, they would be visible the moment they stood to run.

"Nay," Minister Peden replied comfortably. "They may look, but they won't see." With a slight nod he indicated the strands of fog that were multiplying over the wetter ground. Days of insistent heat had dried out the moor, resulting in clouds of evaporated water that reverted to fog and mist when night was at its coolest.

"At least the weather is with us," another of the men commented in a low voice.

"God, my friend," Sandy Peden corrected. "God is with us, and this is yet another sign that he hasn't forgotten us." Without another word he moved off and one by one the others followed him, shrouded in the early morning mist.

"That way," Matthew said a bit later. "If you keep to the left of yon trees you'll find a passable path that will lead you all the way to Kilmarnock."

"Thank you," the tallest of the three men said. "And be sure to convey my gratitude to your wife as well."

"Aye," Sandy grinned. "Please tell Alex how appreciative we are of your hospitality."

"Umm," Matthew said. Alex wasn't quite as enthusiastic about extending help to their Presbyterian brethren as he was. Even if she cooked and packed baskets with food, sending along blankets when she could, he knew she didn't like it, in particular not now, not since the last few arrests that had dragged at least one of their neighbours before the court to answer to charges of treasonous activities. The man had been flogged publicly.

"Truly," Sandy said, and now there was no laughter in his grey eyes. "Do thank her, Matthew. I know it costs her in fears." With that he was off, taking the lead as the three ministers made for the depths of the moor. Not until they'd dropped out of sight did Matthew set off for home.

"Where have you been?"

Matthew started when his brother-in-law popped up to block his path.

"Out," he said.

"I gather that," Simon Melville said. He frowned, taking in the sword and pistol, the long cloak that was now bundled over an arm. "This is no game."

"Hmm?"

"Never mind." Simon gestured in the direction of the yard. "You have visitors."

"Visitors? At this hour?"

"Oh, don't worry," Simon said with a certain edge. "They're not soldiers here to drag you off for questioning – not this time. It's your ex-wife, no less."

"Margaret?" Matthew came to a halt. "What might she be doing here?"

"I have no idea; mayhap she's hankering for long morning walks over the foggy moor."

"I'm doing what I must, Simon, you know that."

"What you must? You're helping them break the law! They've been ousted as ministers, they're not allowed to preach or teach, they may not perform any types of rites, and to aid and abet them is to risk the full displeasure of the powers that be."

Matthew just shrugged.

"Oh well," Simon sighed. "You'll do as you please."

"Aye."

Simon threw him a sidelong look. "She brought Ian with her."

"Ian?" Matthew increased his pace.

"She's in the yard. I don't think Alex intends to invite her inside, and even if she did, I doubt Margaret would enter. She insists she'll wait outside until she can talk with you." Simon's face broke out in a wide grin. "I don't think she helped herself by reminding Alex that any decisions are yours to take anyway, so why waste breath telling Alex what she will then have to repeat to you?"

"Nay," Matthew said, smiling faintly. "I reckon Alex didn't like that."

The two women turned towards them when they entered the yard. Of similar height and colouring, with dark, well-defined brows, high cheekbones and shapely necks, at a distance they could be taken for sisters. But where Margaret was all willowy grace, Alex was rounder of breasts and hips – assets presently accentuated by her very trim waist. She must have tightened the stays a notch or two before going out to receive their visitors. He studied his wife; silent, arms crossed over her chest and dark blue eyes never leaving

Margaret or the half-grown lad beside her, Alex looked icily impressive – and displeased. With an inward sigh Matthew went over to greet his guests.

Alex watched Matthew come towards them, long legs striding at such speed that Simon was jogging to keep up. She gave her husband a thoughtful look; yet another morning waking to an empty bed and she had a pretty good idea of what he'd been doing. It was a constant source of contention between them, his insistence that he had to help his brethren, her loud protests that it might come at too high a price. Bloody stubborn man! She gnawed at her lip and frowned.

Having Margaret show up with Ian in tow hadn't exactly improved her mood, nor did the fact that Margaret, as always, looked gorgeous. No practical skirts in brown for Margaret, oh no; dear Margaret sported a gown in a vibrant blue that complemented her eyes, her neckline was adorned by Brussels lace and on her head she wore a rakish hat of the same hue as her dress, with glistening, black hair falling in arranged ringlets well down her back. Long riding gloves in soft red leather completed the outfit, although on a day as hot as this Alex suspected they were quite uncomfortable to wear.

"Mama?" Mark tugged at her skirts. "Who's that?"

Alex smiled and brushed his hair back from his brow. Nearly six, Mark was normally his father's shadow, but the tension in the air had made him gravitate towards his mother, with his two siblings in tow.

"That's your cousin, Ian."

She was convinced Mark had forgotten the events surrounding the last time he'd seen his cousin nearly two years ago, but from the wary look in Ian's eyes she could see that he had not – and nor had any of the adults presently in the yard. Not that she blamed them; two grown men, brothers, fighting with deadly intent until their respective wives managed to step between.

"He's my son," Matthew had said on that occasion, pointing at the then nine year old Ian. "My son, and you know it, Luke Graham."

Alex threw a quick look in the direction of Ian; still a startling copy not only of Matthew but also of Mark – same dark hair highlighted by chestnut strands, same hazel eyes fringed by thick, dark lashes. The resemblance as such was not all that much of an issue, given that Luke and Matthew were brothers – or it wouldn't have been if it hadn't been for Matthew's angry outburst. Why have you brought him back, Alex thought, throwing eyebolts at Margaret. Why couldn't you stay well away from me and mine?

"I have nowhere else to go." Margaret kept round, imploring eyes on Matthew as she spoke.

Smart move, Alex fumed, because for some inexplicable reason Matthew had a soft spot the size of an elephant when it came to his ex-wife. Totally incomprehensible, given how the woman had behaved – married to the one brother while betraying him with the other.

"And I had to get away. People are dying like flies and I hope you'll allow me the use of the wee cottage yet again."

"What?" Alex took a hurried step back. "The plague? You've brought the plague?" Even this far north they'd heard of how London and the villages around it were suffering a virulent outbreak of the Black Death.

"Nay, of course not," Margaret said. "We haven't been in London proper for months. But what with the heat of the summer and the increasing number of deaths, I thought it safer to repair even further north. I can't risk my son."

Matthew's eyes strayed to Ian and Alex sighed. She could commiserate to a point with his feelings for the boy that should have been his but no longer was – due to Margaret's lying insistence that Luke had fathered her child – but Matthew's statement almost two years ago could put her children's inheritance at risk, and there were days when she had problems forgiving him for that.

Alex' eyes fluttered over to Simon Melville, who winked at her. She stuck her tongue out, making Simon grin. A thousand times he'd told her not to worry, that there was no way Ian had a claim to Hillview, not now that he was the recognised son of Luke. Besides, he'd said rather smugly, he'd drafted the documents himself, and so he could assure her there were no loopholes, none at all.

"You may stay," Matthew said, and Alex glowered at him. He should at least discuss it with her first. At times Matthew was a bloody old-fashioned man – to be expected, given that this was in fact the seventeenth century and the odd one out was she, born in 1976.

Not that it showed, she reflected, throwing a quick glance down her body. In skirts and bodice, her head neatly capped and a clean apron covering the dark material of her skirts, she was undistinguishable from most of the women of the here and now. All in all a good thing, because to shout to the world that she was from a future time would be the equivalent of tying a noose and placing it around her neck. Witches hang, and no one would listen to her protestations that she'd done nothing to transport herself from modern day Scotland to here, that it had all been due to the thunderstorm.

Her eyes flitted to the sky and she almost laughed at herself. No storm brewing, and besides, it had to be a once in a lifetime experience to live through a thunderstorm so gigantic it caused a rift in time. Once in a lifetime? It should be impossible and yet here she was, a living, breathing example of the fact that sometimes impossible things happened – as they had done to her seven years ago when time was torn apart at her feet.

Alex returned her attention to Margaret, who was beaming at Matthew. To Alex' huge irritation, Matthew smiled back.

"Thank you." Margaret dismissed the hired grooms who'd escorted them and set off in the direction of the cottage, her son at her heels.

"You'll stay away for the first few weeks," Matthew said. "As a precaution, aye?"

"Aye, a precaution. I see." Margaret paled, looking so frightened that Alex felt sorry for her.

"I'll send up Sarah later, you'll need food and such, right?" she said.

Margaret gave her a grateful look and hefted the rather insignificant bundle she was carrying.

"Aye, we left in haste."

"I can imagine." An instant of shared motherhood flew between them.

"That was generous," Simon muttered to Matthew as Alex strode away to arrange for a basket to be taken to the cottage. Matthew nodded. Not that it surprised him, because this wife of his might on occasion blow both hot and cold but was mostly a temperate warm, being in general kind and cheerful. He put out a hand to stop Rachel from whacking Jacob over the head with her wooden doll.

"Nay, Rachel! You mustn't fight with your wee brother. It's unseemly."

"He pushed me."

"He did no such thing," Matthew said, sinking down onto his haunches to give her the full benefit of his stare. "If you hit him then you mustn't be surprised when he hits you back."

Rachel gave her baby brother a sly look. At almost three Rachel was tall and sturdy for her age and topped Jacob by a head. Let him try, her face told Matthew, let him try and I'll send him flying.

"One day he'll be taller and stronger than you, and you won't want him hitting you then." He sincerely hoped his children had grown out of squabbles by the time Jacob overtopped Rachel, but eyed his daughter doubtfully. He adjusted her cap and gave her a gentle shove in the direction of Mark.

"Keep an eye on your sister," he said. Mark's face clouded and Matthew beckoned him over. "And you won't go near the cottage." Mark looked crestfallen. "You can help me carry up the basket later, but only if you watch Rachel first."

Mark sighed but took Rachel's hand, wandering off in the direction of the swing Matthew had made them.

"And you make sure she stays with you, all the time," Matthew called, receiving a despairing look in return that made Matthew smother a smile. Where Rachel got her boundless energy from was an open question, although Matthew insisted he had been a most biddable child – at least until the age of seven – so therefore it had to come from her mother.

"For my sins," Alex would sigh every now and then, making Matthew laugh out loud. Even worse, wee Rachel had her brothers firmly in hand and showed hair-raising creativity when it came to new activities, leaving a wake of destruction behind her.

"Come, you," Matthew said to Jacob and swung him up to sit on his arm. "Let's find your mama." He kissed the hair of his youngest before going off in search of his disgruntled wife.

"I couldn't do otherwise," Matthew said to Alex' back.

"Of course not," she replied, a trifle too coolly to sound sincere. She put a loaf of dark bread into the basket, added eggs, cheese, a flask of beer, half a pie, and as an afterthought a piece of currant cake. Jacob smacked his lips, waving a chubby hand in the direction of the cake.

"After dinner," Alex said. "And only if you eat all your greens."

Matthew made a face. Obliged to act the role model, these days he found himself eating large quantities of uncooked vegetables, his muttered protests along the lines that he was no cow ignored by his wife, who insisted it was good for him.

"I can carry the basket," Matthew offered once she'd finished loading it.

"I have no doubts whatsoever on that score, but you're not. Sarah will take it."

"I've promised Mark he can go with me," Matthew said, receiving a long look in return.

"Neither of you will and both of you will stay well away from them, at least to begin with. Make sure Mark knows that as well."

Matthew frowned at her peremptory tone. "You can't stop me from seeing them. I have to help them settle in."

"You go up there, Matthew Graham, and you'll be sleeping very alone at night, in the hayloft. Your choice." She hefted the heavy basket off the table and went to find Sarah.

Matthew considered chasing her up the stairs for a serious one on one conversation regarding her duties and roles as a wife, but decided to save it for later. Much later, and possibly in the hayloft…

Halfway through the afternoon, Alex decided to escape the heat by settling herself under the large ash that stood on the further side of the stables. A quick look in the direction of her youngest children showed her they were muddy and happy by the trough, and Mark would be with Matthew somewhere. She reclined against the trunk, produced her work and with a little sigh set to.

"You don't need to worry." Simon flopped down in the shade beside Alex, his light blue eyes intent on her.

"Worry about what?" Alex held up the boy's shirt she was sewing against the light. The hemline was uneven, but she decided it would do. She was sick of sewing and mending, sometimes she longed for a shopping centre with one shop after the other; GAP, H&M, M&S. She sighed and picked up the next garment in her basket. An impossible dream, given that this was 1665.

"About her, Margaret."

"I know I don't," she said. "But as to Ian… he eats him with his eyes!"

Simon hemmed in agreement.

"And it must be difficult for him – for Ian. I wonder what they've told him to explain that sorry mess two years ago. It's not as if they can wave a paternity test at him."

Simon sat up, eyes bright with curiosity. Of a need he knew her background, and he was always pestering her for details about life in the future.

"Paternity tests?"

"They take blood from the baby, the mother and the father and then they can see if it all matches." She smiled and beckoned him closer. "They say that on average one child in four is a cuckoo," she confided, grinning at his horrified expression. "I dare say it's more or less the same now."

"No!" Simon shook his head. "You can't think that married women would do something like that!"

"Have sex? Or have sex with someone other than their husband?" She laughed, her sewing forgotten in her lap.

"Hmph!" Simon lay back and stared up at the sky through the rustling leaves of the tree. "A man never knows, he never knows for sure if it's his child or not."

"No, and that's the starting point of all this sorry mess with Ian, isn't it?"

"Did he tell you?" she asked a bit later.

"No," Simon said. "But it doesn't take a genius to work out where he's been."

Alex hugged her knees. "I don't like it. From being the occasional meal, the odd night's lodging, now it's Matthew guiding them across the moor, helping them find other hideouts." She leaned her cheek against her skirts.

"I'm sure he's careful."

"Of course he is," Alex agreed, mainly to convince herself. She smiled down at Simon and poked him in the gut. "That wasn't very nice of you, to leave poor Joan all alone with your Aunt Judith." She'd only met Judith Melville once, a quarrelsome, nosy woman with no similarities whatsoever to Simon. Matthew's sister Joan on the other hand, was one of the sweetest people she knew.

"Joan doesn't mind, I think she even likes the old bat, aye? Anyway, she'll be here tomorrow."

Someone called for the mistress, and Alex got to her feet. "Now what?"

She slowed her steps halfway across the yard. "Who are they?" she asked Simon.

"Dragoons," he said, frowning. He buttoned up his coat as he walked and brushed his collar into place. By the time they were at the door, Simon Melville was all lawyer, joviality wiped from his face. He expanded his considerable girth, nodded at the officer and placed a hand at Alex' waist.

"Mistress," the officer said.

"Captain," Alex curtsied.

"We will not importune you for long," the officer continued, jerking his head in the direction of the stables. Alex' heart nosedived at the sight of her man being marched across the yard. He was struggling, his arms held in a tight grip by the two soldiers flanking him.

"What on Earth…" Alex gasped, wheeling to face the officer. Behind her Matthew cursed, his voice loud in anger. Oh God; someone had seen him on the moor last night, and now they'd cart him off and flog him for it.

"We are taking him in for questioning," the officer said.

"Questioning? About what?" She turned, eyes flying until they found Matthew's. He was not only angry, he was afraid, she could see that. Calm down, she tried to tell him telepathically, furrowing her brow in concentration. Okay, so she seriously doubted she was a new Mr Spock, but he did stop struggling, informing the soldiers he wasn't about to run anywhere so they could unhand him.

"Now, now, Mistress Graham. Surely you've heard. Fugitive preachers abound all around, and to aid them…" the officer's voice tailed off.

She widened her eyes. "Matthew? When? How?"

"Last night. We had them surrounded, three of them, and out of nowhere appeared a man." He glared in the direction of Matthew. "A capable swordsman at that, leaving one of my men badly wounded."

What? Alex forced herself not to look at Matthew. To wound a soldier… they might hang him! Her throat

11

tightened and it took considerable effort to turn to the officer and give him a little smile.

"Well, I can assure you it wasn't him," Alex said. "He was snoring his head off in bed, with me."

"If so a spot of questioning will do no harm, will it?" the officer shrugged, clearly not believing her.

"I'm going with him," Simon said.

The officer raised a brow. "I think not."

"I think aye. I'm his lawyer."

That didn't please the officer, narrow face pinching together into a frown. But he acquiesced, muttering something under his breath. Simon scurried off to see to his horse and Alex moved close enough to touch Matthew's hand, a light graze no more.

"It'll be alright," Matthew said, swinging himself up into the saddle. She heard it in his voice, how he was struggling to sound matter-of-fact. Alex wanted to say something reassuring, but her vocal cords had somehow gone numb, leaving her mute. Instead she stood beside his horse, holding on to his leg. Matthew leaned towards her, eyes lightening into a greyish green.

"I love you," he said in an undertone, which only increased her anxiety because he rarely said such things to her. Alex managed a wobbly smile and stood on her toes to caress his cheek.

"And I you," she said.

Her husband nodded and at the officer's command followed him up the lane with Simon in his wake. Not once did he look back, but Alex stood rooted to the ground for as long as she could see him.

CHAPTER 2

They manhandled Matthew into an unfurnished room, with Simon trotting behind him. The commanding officer was sitting in the single chair, to his right stood a troop of soldiers, tired, grimy men that looked as if they'd gone far too long without sleep. Mayhap they had, because it came to Matthew that these must in fact be the soldiers he'd so neatly evaded last night. He hunched together somewhat, legs bending ever so slightly in an attempt to reduce his height.

The seated officer – a chit of a lad, with fair curling hair down to his shoulders and a most impressive jaw – looked him up and down and twisted in his seat to stare at Simon, who just stared back.

"Stand up straight!" the officer barked, motioning at Matthew.

"I already am," Matthew retorted, glad of the wide breeches. He was made to turn to face the troop of soldiers.

"Is it him?" the officer asked. One of the men tilted his head to the side, frowning.

"It could be," he said, "although…"

"Could be?" Simon pounced. "Well, it could be anyone."

The soldier shuffled on his feet. "There is a likeness."

"A likeness?" Simon laughed out loud. "How?"

One of the younger soldiers took a step forward. "He's tall and the man we saw was tall – that we know for sure."

"Ah," Simon nodded. "And did he have dark hair?"

"I don't know," the young man said.

"No? Why not?"

"He was wearing a cloak."

Simon rolled his eyes, smoothed at his coat. "Not much to go on," he said to the officer, who shifted on his seat.

"Tall, a competent swordsman – and we know Mr Graham has a past as a soldier – who else could it be?" the officer said.

"You?" Simon said.

The officer flew to his feet. "What?"

"Well why not? You're of a size, and in a cloak, well…"

"What is it you're implying?" the officer barked.

"I am but making the point that it does not suffice, does it? Mr Graham insists he was at home last night, and this is corroborated by his wife, who…"

"His wife? And what else would she say?"

"Well no; there you have me," Simon conceded with a little bow. "But it is still a fact that if all your men saw was a hooded, tall man on the moor, it is not enough to place Matthew Graham there, is it?"

The officer wheeled, glared at his men, at Matthew and at his toes. "This is a serious matter," he said. "We are no longer talking of the occasional meal, are we?" He came close enough that his nose brushed against Matthew's. "This time someone has taken steel to my men, even wounded one of them."

A wee gash, Matthew was on the point of saying, but bit his tongue at the last moment. Instead he blinked, attempting to look as dense as possible.

The officer frowned, dashing a long strand of fair hair from his face. "Take him away, lock him up for the night. Who knows, it might jog his memory." He smiled – a small, cold smile that made Matthew shiver inside. They were going to hurt him.

Simon protested loudly. The officer stood his ground, repeating that he had to ascertain once and for all that Mr Graham was no threat to law and order. A shove, yet another shove, and Matthew was dragged from the room.

Merciful Lord! He gasped as yet another bucket of ice cold water was poured over him. Hands pulled him to stand, he tried to see through his swollen eye. A fist drove into his gut, another in his kidneys. Small bursts of pain all over his upper body, a fist in his face, and Matthew was unable to defend himself, could not do anything to deflect the blows, what with the two men holding him upright.

"Admit it, man," the lieutenant in charge said, leaning in to stare Matthew in his one good eye. "Admit it was you and this will stop."

Matthew just shook his head. The responding clap to his head had his brain ringing, a high pitched sound that made it difficult to hear what the wee man was saying, although he assumed it was yet another repeated 'admit it'.

After hours of this physical interrogation, Matthew was weaving on his feet. He pretended to faint time and time again, gaining himself a few minutes of precious reprieve while the soldiers set to reviving him. He let his head loll back and groaned. The lieutenant made a disgusted snort.

"For all his size he's quite the weakling," the wee officer said.

Matthew almost smiled; he could beat the lieutenant one handed should he need to.

"No," the lieutenant decided, clapping himself on his thighs. "We're done with him." A booted toe prodded at Matthew. He slumped, an unconscious mollusc on the floor.

Except that he wasn't, and the moment the door grated shut behind his tormentors he moved over to sit with his back against the furthest wall. No broken bones, no serious damage, just one bruised, aching body, a split lip, a swollen eye and a burst eyebrow. Very much on purpose, he concluded. This was merely the soldiers giving him a warning, a gentle reminder of what was in store for men who flaunted the law. He laughed hollowly; not all that gentle.

Simon must have been up with the sun. Even in his shivering, dozing state Matthew recognised his friend's voice, a loud constant haranguing as he followed whoever was guiding him across the garrison yard. The door swung open, a shaft of light made Matthew squint and Simon rounded on the lieutenant, near on spitting with anger.

"Simon," Matthew croaked, wincing when his lip split open. "It's no great matter. Just get me out of here." From the way the lieutenant was eyeing Simon, he was considering whether to lock him up as well rather than releasing Matthew.

"No great matter? Have you any notion…" Simon rushed over to steady him. "Sweetest Lord, what will Alex say?"

Matthew attempted a shrug. "Mayhap I should clean up some."

"Aye, that would be wise," Simon said. "I'll have the innkeeper heat you some water. A few hours' sleep, I think, before we ride back home." Matthew stifled a gasp when Simon's arm came round his middle but he walked as straight as he could through the yard.

A mere half-hour later he felt much better; hot food in his belly, his bruised body washed and inspected by the innkeeper's wife, a pretty lass with a gentle touch and an endless supply of herbal ointments. He was in a hurry to get back home, knowing that Alex would be worried by his continued absence, but at the mulish look on Simon's face he crawled into bed. A wee nap, no more. He yawned, closed his eyes and dropped off.

Alex was too distraught to give Joan much of a welcome when she arrived around noon. In fact, she was so immersed in her worries for Matthew, that it wasn't until Joan took off her cloak that Alex noticed her sister-in-law was pregnant.

"Why haven't you told me?"

"I wanted you to see for yourself," Joan said. "But I dare say today is not the best of days to impart such news, is it?"

Alex shook her head, eyes flying to the lane. "Not really." She made a huge effort and turned to face Joan. "But I'm so very glad for you."

Joan smiled down at her. At almost six feet she was uncommonly tall, and in general so thin as to look fragile. Now, there was a sizeable bump on her and her normally flat chest had upgraded itself to something resembling a timid B-cup.

Alex frowned. "You don't look too well." That was an understatement. Joan was pale to the point of looking ashen, with her beautiful grey eyes sunk into deep purple hollows.

"I'm tired, that's all. You shouldn't mind me," Joan said, "not all bloom like you do with the bairns."

"Have you been eating?"

Joan looked away. "I'm greensick all the time."

"No wonder you're the colour of a sheet," Alex said. "I'll fix you something with plenty of honey and eggs in it." With that she propelled Joan in the direction of the house.

"No word?" Joan sipped at the posset Alex set before her.

"No. But there wouldn't be, right? It was afternoon when they rode off."

"Mayhap." Joan drank, wiped at her mouth. "Was he? Out on the moors?"

Alex threw a wary look round the kitchen; neither Sarah nor Janey were in sight. She nodded, irritated by the admiring look in Joan's face.

"It's dangerous! What if they…" she broke off when Mark came rushing through the door.

"They're back! Da's back!"

"Well, thank heavens for that," Alex said, leaping to her feet.

Joan grabbed at her hand, met her eyes. "He does as he has to, Alex. Remember that, aye?"

"It's a risk, an unnecessary risk."

"To you, mayhap. To Matthew it's a matter of conscience and faith."

Alex came to a stop at the sight of Matthew. He gave her a rueful smile, fingers flying to his swollen face. Dear God! She moved closer, all of her itching with the need to drag him off to a secluded corner for a detailed inspection.

"They couldn't identify him," Simon said. "All they could say was that the man had been tall and shrouded in a long cloak."

"Ah. So that was it?" Obviously not, judging from Matthew's face.

"Nay," Matthew said, looking grim. "They locked me up overnight and…" He winced when he moved his arms.

"It could have been worse," Simon said. "Much, much worse."

"Oh, well; that's a comfort," Alex said. But Simon was right. Matthew might look as if he'd been trampled by the cows, but he'd suffered no serious damage – made very apparent by the fact that the first thing he did once he was off the horse was scan the skies.

"Tomorrow. We start the harvest tomorrow."

"Are you sure? Shouldn't you take it easy for some…" Her hands flew down his arms, his back. There were bruises everywhere; peeking from the neckline of his shirt, all over his face, on what she could see of his arms, and when she touched his lower back he inhaled, twisting out of reach.

"Tomorrow; and I'm perfectly hale."

"Well, sorry for asking."

"I'm fine, lass; truly." He smiled, a somewhat strained smile, and raised his hand to her cheek. "I dare not wait any longer, because if it rains now…"He shook his head.

Alex nodded her agreement, raising her eyes to the unclouded summer sky. All summer the sun had blazed down on them and the barley looked starved for rain, as did the rye and the oats. But it was ripe, however puny, standing man-high in the elongated fields.

"So, tomorrow." Without any further comments as to the events in Cumnock, Matthew set off towards the barn. Alex sighed. Sometimes this silent male thing was bloody enervating.

A fortnight or so later, Alex was so tired she considered hiding in the hayloft for the day. Instead, she was up at dawn to feed the men and then extended before her yet another stretch of never ending work.

"You must work in the field today," Matthew told her over breakfast, "you and all the lasses." He threw his head in the direction of the skies. "It'll break. I can smell it."

So could Alex; a heavy smell of brine. It made her mouth dry up and she studied the darkening horizon repeatedly during the day, lifting her face from the sheaves before going back to her work.

Sweat formed like dewdrops along her hairline, ran down her face and into her eyes. It trickled down her back and dampened the insides of her thighs, making every single piece of clothing she had on stick to her skin.

The clouds sank even closer to the ground and Matthew yelled at them to hurry up, they had to get as many of the half-dried sheaves as possible inside. Alex' back screeched in protest, her arms trembled, and still she lifted, throwing sheaves into the flat carts. Men picked up sheaves and ran towards the barn and Alex tried to do the same, but the stupid thing kept slipping through her arms, the drying stalks scratching at her face.

Overhead, the skies had begun to growl, a distant rumbling that made Alex want to rush and hide. But she didn't, of course she didn't. Instead she wiped her brow and went back to wrestling with the recalcitrant sheave.

"Here." Matthew appeared by her side. Together they lugged the sheave to the closest cart, and Matthew slapped the horse on its rump, shouting to Gavin to drive as fast as possible for the barn.

Overhead the skies exploded into a firework of lightning. Alex grabbed hold of Matthew's arm, sinking her fingers into his flesh.

"It won't happen again," he said with a small smile. "Once was improbable enough."

"You think?" she stuttered, eyes darting from him to the threatening sky and back again.

"Aye, I do; you won't be knocked from this time to another, I won't allow it."

"Good to know," she said, leaning against his solid frame. "But it almost did," she added, thinking back to an incident some years ago.

"And I stopped it from happening, didn't I?" He smiled down at her. "I'll not let you go, Alex. Ever."

The skies opened, rain fell like a sheet of water, flattening the un-harvested barley fields. Matthew took hold of her hand and ran for the house.

After a whole night's rain, the next day dawned a sullen, drizzling grey. Matthew wolfed down breakfast and rushed outside to inspect his ruined fields, although to what purpose Alex had no idea. Simon went with him, and once Alex had set Sarah and Janey to work in the kitchen she followed Joan to the parlour. She rarely sat here during daytime, preferring the warmth of the kitchen, but given the peaceful quiet of the little room maybe she should use it more often. Dark wooden floors contrasted nicely with the lighter walls, the few pieces of furniture were decorated with the odd embroidered cushion, and on one of the tables stood Matthew's precious chess set, each piece a little work of art that had taken him months to complete.

"It never looks that way when I do it," Alex said, rooting around in her basket for her present work in progress.

"Aye, well, years and years of practise," Joan shrugged, not even looking at the knitted blanket that flowered from her hands. She stopped and bent her head in the direction of Alex' half-finished stocking. "Alex! You can't go about in something like that!" She snatched the stocking from Alex' hands and proceeded to tear up most of it.

"That took me ages! And who cares, anyway? It's not as if anyone ever sees my stockings, is it?" She began rewinding the dark wool, throwing murderous looks in the direction of Joan.

"So you never wear stockings then? In your time?"

"Of course we do. But we just pop into a shop and buy them. Three for the price of two or something." Alex sighed and studied the remainder of her massacred stocking. Joan was right; she couldn't really walk around in something as badly knitted as this.

"Do you ever wish you could go back?" Joan's needles clicked on at amazing speed.

"No. Never." Alex underlined her statement with an affronted tone.

"But…" Joan began, but whatever she had planned on saying was interrupted by a series of loud, high-pitched screams.

"Rachel," Alex and Joan said simultaneously, both of them hurrying out into the yard.

Pandemonium reigned. Simon was chasing the billy goat with Mark whooping at his heels. Old Samuel was stopping the other goats from escaping their paddock, Gavin was shooing at the interested hens that seemed to be everywhere, and Matthew was holding a bawling, muddied Rachel in his arms.

"Be quiet," Alex told Rachel. "It's your own fault, isn't it?" She wrinkled her nose in distaste at the smell that emanated from her daughter. "I told you, Rachel Graham. How many times have I told you he'll butt you if you don't let him be?"

Rachel snivelled. She was fascinated by the billy goat, standing for hours by his enclosure, sometimes to feed him apples, but far more often to throw things at him and make him bleat. Today she'd apparently decided to open the gate for him so as to properly make his acquaintance which had ended with the goat sending her flying face first into the adjacent pile of manure – and serve the little missy right.

"Phew, you really stink!" Alex led Rachel towards the little river that bisected their property on its way to join the Lugar Water. "And you," she pointed at Matthew. "You stink too. So you best come along."

"Nay, I don't, I only picked her up."

"And held her in your arms, and there's something sticking to your hair."

"You best do as she says," Simon said, tongue-in-cheek. "She sounds very determined." He fell in step with them, humming something under his breath.

"And as for you, Simon Melville, you're not coming inside until you've washed," Alex said over her shoulder, already busy at the water's edge with a squirming Rachel.

"Me?" Simon made huge eyes. "Why me?"

"You caught the goat – and, let me tell you, it shows."

Simon looked down at his mud spattered shirt and grinned. "You're just wishing to see me in all my glory, Mrs Graham. You must be hungering for a peek at a real man."

"I'll give you real man," Matthew growled, stretching himself to his full six feet plus two. "Come here, you wee twat and let me show you, aye?"

Simon laughed and charged, sending both men to fall fully clothed into the water.

"Idiots," Alex said, before going back to scrubbing her daughter.

An hour or so later all the Graham children were clean and playing by the water's edge. Alex regarded them with pride; Mark and Rachel were small clones of their father, with the same somewhat olive skin, the same dark hair and the same eyes, shifting from muddy green to bright emerald depending on their mood. Jacob, however, was a throw back on his maternal grandfather, a thick thatch of blond hair topping an oval face with a skin tone just like hers – pale with pink in winter, tawny gold in summer. But his eyes were the same magical hazel as his siblings'.

"They're so beautiful," Alex said, slipping her hand into Matthew's.

"Very."

"This is where you're supposed to say they all take after their mother," Simon laughed from behind them.

"But then he'd be lying," Alex said, squeezing Matthew's hand once before letting it go. "All of them look like their father – gorgeous."

"Besotted," Simon sighed as Alex moved away. "I don't know how you do it, but you've turned that poor woman's head."

"I heard you," Alex called back over her shoulder. "Supper soon, your favourite Simon; spinach soup."

"Ugh," Simon muttered.

Supper was a loud and cramped affair, the entire household squeezed together round the kitchen table. As always Matthew sat at the head of the table, even if he did offer Simon the single chair with a rather rude referral to Simon's overall size. Not that Simon seemed bothered, calmly sliding in to sit on one of the benches.

"Girth has nothing to do with grace," he said, winking at Alex. "I dare say I can still best you on the dance floor, Matthew Graham."

Most probably, Alex grinned, because for all his general resemblance to an apple on legs Simon was by far the most graceful and tenacious dancer she'd ever seen.

Alex liked her kitchen – especially on occasions such as these, when it was full of talking, laughing people. Over the last few years she'd implemented quite a few changes, starting with how clean she kept things. The previously dark and sooty walls now received regular scrubbings, the floors were swept on a daily basis and once a week she had Sarah and Janey on their knees with a bristle brush. The small window allowed some daylight even in winter, but now, in full summer, the kitchen door was always kept propped open, and on an evening as light as this one there was no need to use the tallow candles that stood on the table, daylight spilling in through the open door.

For all that they all looked rather depressed at the sight of the dark green soup, in a remarkably short time the bowls had been emptied, her family cheering up at the sight of the pie she had Janey fetch from the pantry.

"Chess?" Matthew stood, brushed some pie crumbs off his shirt and jerked his head in the direction of the parlour.

"By all means," Simon said, "and this time…"

"When pigs fly," Matthew snorted, "but it's good that you try." He kissed Alex on his way out, murmuring that he didn't think the spinach soup had gone down well – with anyone.

"Too bad," Alex said, "I have enough left for dinner tomorrow." She laughed at his grimace and shooed him off before going over to inspect the leftovers and set the oats to soak for tomorrow's breakfast.

"It's getting worse, isn't it?" Simon was saying when Alex entered the parlour. The chess board had been shoved to the side, with both men sitting staring into the fire.

"Aye, it is." Matthew sighed and extended his long legs in front of him. "They're raising an army, Sandy says – he had it from yon Carstairs – an army that has as its single purpose to root out every single Covenanter here in the southwest."

"Good luck to them," Alex said. "That would mean more or less everyone living here." This was Presbyterian land – from here all the way to Ayr and up to Lanark.

"We'll see; it may be they've taken on more than they bargained for," Matthew said, an edge of steel to his voice.

Alex frowned; over her husband's head she met Simon's concerned eyes and made a helpless gesture. Matthew Graham was a very stubborn man and there were some principles he wasn't about to compromise on, foremost amongst them his right to hold to his faith.

Two days later Simon kissed Joan, promised to be back in three or four weeks to see how she was faring, and sat up on his placid gelding.

"You'll take care of her?" he asked Alex.

"Of course we will, she's much better off here than in Edinburgh, isn't she?" She made a slight face: Edinburgh was not a place she had any particular fondness for – at least not in its present state. Dark and damp, overcrowded and shrouded in the haze of peat smoke, it wasn't the most welcoming of cities.

"Aye, if nothing else it smells less," Joan interjected from behind her. She walked over to the horse and patted Simon on the leg. "Go. I'll be fine, and so will he." She placed a hand on her belly.

"He?" Alex asked.

"Aye, a lad," Simon grinned, "the first of many."

"As many as the good Lord gives us," Joan smiled back. Alex shook her head in exasperation and went off to find her man.

CHAPTER 3

Alex woke abruptly and for a couple of minutes she blinked at her surroundings, trying to recall where she was. The dream had been vivid and it took time to adapt to the fact that she was at home, in her bed, rather than in a berth on a small ship halfway across the Atlantic.

She stretched lazily. More than two years they'd been back home after their travels overseas, a long roll of days punctuated by the birth of Jacob, the day the new bull made a brave rush for freedom only to sink into the swampy ground of the farthest meadow and the not so long ago afternoon when Rachel decided she could fly, leaping out of the hayloft to land stunned and with a broken arm.

Sometimes Alex yearned for the years she'd spent looking for her abducted husband, a period in her life that at the time had seemed a nightmare but which in retrospect had acquired a nimbus of adventure and holiday. She knew Matthew wouldn't agree. He kept the memories of those long months of slavery on the plantation Suffolk Rose in Virginia safely locked away, but even now, more than three years since Alex had found him and bought him free, there were still nights when he woke them both with his nightmares, raging in hatred at the man who had done this to him – his own brother.

She heard her daughter's voice floating up from below. High and demanding, Alex could imagine exactly what she was on about – too much on Mark's plate, too little on her own. That girl could eat a horse for breakfast and still complain about being hungry before dinner. No wonder she ran all of them ragged.

When Alex turned to look at her husband she found him already awake, his eyes resting on her half-naked body in a way that left no doubt as to how this Sunday morning would begin. Except that she wasn't really in the mood, she was irascible this morning – over tender somehow – so she grunted and rolled away from him, only to be pulled back against his warm chest.

"You know I don't like it when you do that," Matthew said. He bit her earlobe and trailed his tongue down her exposed neck.

"I just don't feel like it," she said, knowing that would only make him more insistent. This was one of their more complicated games; the wife being taught that the husband would not be denied and that she must subjugate herself to him. It was a game they both played with enthusiasm, and by the time Matthew used his knees to spread her thighs open to him, she was tugging at him, telling him to hurry, please hurry.

"You're a very stubborn man at times," she said some minutes later, picking at his hair.

"And you must repeatedly be reminded of your wifely duties," he mock sighed, kissing her on the cheek.

"Do you think it will be today?" Alex asked, getting out of bed as naked as the day she was born. "She looks positively huge." She caught his grin and had to smile. Compared to her in the advanced stages of pregnancy, Joan looked like an underfed waif. She rolled her eyes at him, making him laugh as he settled back to watch her wash and dress.

He had once confided to her just how much he enjoyed these long Sunday mornings, looking endearingly embarrassed when he told her he collected these images of her in her morning disarray, all wild hair and nothing else. So she took her time, washing slowly, brushing her hair with slow, long strokes – well, in general giving him ample opportunity to gawk and compliment. Except that today he didn't, his eyes on the ceiling rather than on her, a concerned little wrinkle between his brows. He shifted from side to side, gnawed at his lip and threw her a look.

"What?" She met his eyes.

"I spoke to Margaret," he said.

Alex pulled on her shift. "Really? And what did she say?" She settled the linen cap atop her head, ensuring most of her hair was tucked out of sight.

"She has to hurry back to Luke."

She relaxed, focusing on the stone jars in which she kept some of her oils.

"Oh good," Alex muttered. "About time those star crossed lovers were reunited." She dipped her finger into her homemade rose scented cream and rubbed it into her hands and up her arms.

"He's written to her on several occasions," he went on, indirectly admitting that he had been talking to Margaret of other things beside leaking roofs and draughts. She sent him a dark look.

"I've met her occasionally in the woods, aye?"

Alex nodded, but she didn't believe him.

She returned her attention to her hands, doing a primitive manicure while keeping her face hidden from him. Stockings and garters, petticoats and skirts, and she swished across the room to retrieve her bodice.

"When will they set out?" Alex asked, attempting to lace the dark green bodice. It strained over her chest and a sudden insight flew across her mind. Another one! And Jacob not yet two…

"She rides out tomorrow."

It took some time for Alex to react, busy as she was with counting days, but once she did she raised his face to his.

"She?"

"Aye, I've promised to keep Ian here, for now."

Without a word she retrieved her shawl and left the room.

The night had been cold and wet. Everything glittered in the weak September sun, sheer veils of fog clinging to the long grasses that bordered the little river. Alex hurried towards the woods and the long incline that led to her favourite thinking place, the bare hilltop from which she could see her whole orderly world. She brushed against berry laden brambles and ducked under the branches of an elm, breathing deeply when she stepped into the stillness among the trees.

Behind her, the household would be coming in to sit in the kitchen to listen to Matthew read them yet another passage from the Bible, his dark, rich voice explaining the lessons to be learnt. He'd be pissed at her not being there, but frankly she didn't care. He should have asked her, he knew she found it difficult to have Ian around, even at a once remove in the little cottage. Now he was going to live in their house, with her children.

She burst into a run, stopping only when she could taste blood in her mouth, which was far too soon. She was woefully out of shape – at least compared to what she once had been. The daily karate workouts in her former life had become the occasional kata exercise, sneaking away to do it alone in the woods. And now another child… more walks, she decided, long walks.

Alex picked leaves as she ambled up the hillside, filling her apron with the yellow fronds of rowan, the muted green of oak leaves and the occasional bright red of a clambering vine. She had mingled feelings regarding a new pregnancy, but reminded herself that you reap as you sow and they were always very keen on the sowing part, she and Matthew. Well, she had no intention of telling him her news, he didn't deserve to know, at least not today. She went on with her dark, mental grumblings and the touch of a hand on her arm so surprised her she shrieked, releasing her hold on her apron so that the leaves fluttered to the ground.

"Fantastic," she said once she recognised Margaret. "The one person I really, really want to see."

"You do?" Margaret sounded surprised.

Alex sighed; sarcasm wasn't quite as widespread in this day and age as it had been in the life she came from.

"No, but it doesn't seem I have a choice, does it?"

She hadn't met Margaret properly in the two months she'd been staying here, being far too busy with the hectic days of harvest to find the time to take her rambling walks up and down the hillsides. In all honesty she hadn't wanted to see her, hating the fact that the sheer presence of Margaret made her feel diminished, a bad copy of a glorious original. Superficially, they were very alike, with similar features and colouring. Except that where Alex' hair was a normal if curly brown, Margaret's hair shone like black satin, and where Alex had a tell-tale thickening across the bridge of her nose, Margaret's was elegant and narrow. Everything about her was perfect, from those wide blue eyes to that pointed little chin.

Margaret returned her inspection, eyes travelling down Alex' body and back up again. The morning light struck Margaret in the face and Alex felt a flash of satisfaction when she saw that the skin was dry and flaky, with a discernible web of shallow wrinkles around her eyes and mouth. The grooves on either side of her mouth would with time give Margaret the depressed expression of a disgruntled pike.

"I'm glad that I have the opportunity to talk to you," Margaret said, stepping out of the ray of sun.

"I'm afraid the feeling isn't mutual," Alex bent down to retrieve some of the spilled leaves.

"Nay, I know that." Margaret was wearing an embroidered shawl over skirts in deep green, and from below the hem peeked what must be boots in red Moroccan leather. Alex eyed them enviously; her footwear was nowhere near as elegant.

"I don't like leaving Ian here, but I have no choice. You understand, no?" She looked at Alex with beseeching eyes and Alex gave her a curt nod. Margaret had no other family, Luke definitely didn't, and so, by default, they were the only kin Ian had – them and Joan.

"What will Luke think?" Alex asked, feeling an uncharitable spurt of glee at the discomfiture on Margaret's face.

"He won't like it, but I can't risk taking him back, not yet."

"You could stay a bit longer and then go. Last we heard, the number of deaths was sinking rapidly."

"You don't understand, I must go. Luke is ill."

Alex straightened up, further irritated with Matthew for not giving her the full picture.

"With the plague?"

"Nay of course not! Then he'd be dead by now."

Too bad; the world would be a much fairer place without Luke Graham in it.

Margaret's lip lifted. "You needn't worry. He won't die, I hope, but thank you for your concern."

"In that case, why not take Ian with you? If there's no risk…"

"I didn't say that, did I? Luke has the smallpox." Margaret slipped her arms tight around herself and closed her eyes briefly. "It seems the worst has passed – the physician no longer fears for his life – but he's weak, and possibly contagious. I can't very well leave him to lie alone, can I? So…"

Alex considered this in silence. Luke was in Oxford now that the king had retired out of London to avoid the plague, and Alex suspected that very little TLC would be wasted on a sick man who could infect the court with something as disfiguring and as potentially lethal as smallpox. She almost felt sorry for him, 'almost' being the key word.

"What have you told Ian?"

Margaret looked confused. "That his father is ill and he must remain here until we send for him."

"Not about that. About Matthew."

"Oh." Margaret studied the bright red fringe of her shawl intently for some minutes. "He's ours. Ian is mine and Luke's – not Matthew's." She caught Alex' eye and her mouth curved into an infinitesimal smile. "You like it that way, don't you?"

Alex most certainly did. Matthew had other children, her children, to look out for.

"But he must have asked… after what Matthew said."

"Aye, he did; for months and months he did, and Luke would sit him down and tell him how he was his son, Luke's lad, and that wasn't it Luke that had the rearing of him? Matthew had thrown him out, disowned him, so how could Ian possibly think Matthew was his father?"

Once the boy began shaving it would be enough just to see himself in the mirror to think that, Alex reflected.

"Oh, so you painted Matthew as the unfeeling ogre. Did you perhaps include some context as well?"

Margaret obviously didn't understand the word context, but she got the overall meaning and her face washed bright red.

"Nay we didn't, and for now it's best he doesn't know – it won't help him, will it?"

Alex totally agreed. What boy of eleven needed to know his mother had been a two-timing bitch, married to one brother while screwing the other?

"Matthew and I are in agreement on this."

"Oh, you are?" Alex said, cursing Matthew to hell. "And is this something you've been discussing a lot?"

"Quite often lately, aye? Just Matthew and me." It came out in a purr, Margaret's mouth settling into a pouty smile. It made Alex seethe; damn man!

As Alex turned to leave, Margaret crouched and picked up a rowan frond, extending it to Alex.

"Here; you like bitty leaves." She hung back, brows pulled together in a frown. "Matthew is playing with fire; aiding the evicted ministers will sooner or later lead to him being hanged or deported."

Alex didn't know what to say.

Margaret put a hand on her sleeve. "Luke knows; he has ears and eyes everywhere and if he can, he'll use it to bring Matthew down." She sighed and looked away. "He will neither forgive nor forget."

"Nor will Matthew." Alex tried to sound calm, but she could feel her lower lip begin to wobble and bit down hard.

"Nay, but it's Luke that has the ear of the king, and Matthew is a fool if he lets that slip his mind. There is only so much I can do, aye? When it comes to his brother Luke is difficult to reason with. So you must make Matthew see sense – if you can. Stubborn all of them, the Graham men." Halfway to the cottage Margaret turned once more. "Will you care for my son?"

Alex nodded, shook her apron free of leaves she no longer wanted and turned back home.

Matthew was irked by Alex' behaviour; run off to the woods like an irresponsible lassie, and not come back in time for the Bible reading. He saw his own irritation mirrored exponentially in her face when he stepped out to block her way as she reappeared from among the trees.

"Where have you been?"

"Walking." She attempted to sidestep him, but was snared by his arm.

"I'm talking to you."

"I'm not talking to you," she retorted, pulling herself free. "But hey, I have a suggestion, go up and have a cosy little chat with Margaret. You know, you can sit there together and reminiscence about how wonderful life was when you were newlyweds. Especially for her – after all she had variation in her bed. One day you, the other Luke."

He nearly slapped her. His hand was already flying towards her when he brought himself under control. Instead he shoved her in the direction of the house and stalked off towards the stable.

He should have told her, he knew that, but Alex was oversensitive to the issue of Margaret and so he'd chosen not to. Several times over the last few weeks he had walked with Margaret, talking for hours with her, hours when they had found their way back to some element of respect and basic liking. They had even been able to talk about Luke and his obsessive hatred of Matthew, with Margaret admitting that here, if in nothing else, Luke was somewhat warped.

One afternoon he'd worked up the nerve to ask the one question he had so often wondered about.

"Did you… did you ever love me?"

Margaret had met his eyes and shaken her head. "Not like I love Luke. And that was wrong of me, but I was but a child and you were kind and bonny to look at, and I thought Luke would never come back to me, so…" She had shrugged and smiled at him. "But you're loved now, aren't you?"

At the moment he wasn't so certain, he thought blackly, stamping up the ladder to the hayloft. At the moment he wasn't all that sure that he loved Alex either and he sank the pitchfork into the hay, working off the dangerous edge of his anger. Another gift from his beloved brother, this rage that he sometimes could barely contain. It bubbled out of him like black tar, smearing itself over his life, a residue of experienced fears and helpless anger during the long hellish months in Virginia, months when he was at times certain he would die without ever seeing either wife or son again.

"I'm sorry." Alex' head popped up, hovering above the hayloft floor. She pulled herself up and came over to where he was working. "I can't help it, just the thought of you spending any time with her makes me sick."

He threw the pitchfork to clatter against the floor and turned to face her.

"Why? Have I ever let you think she matters to me?"

"Well, yes – quite often actually. And she does, doesn't she?" She butted him in his chest with her head. "Of course she matters to you. And rationally I don't feel threatened, but emotionally I do. And before you tell me what a wee daftie I'm being, I know, okay?"

"You are a wee daftie," he said tenderly, placing his arms around her. "And I'm a big one for not telling you – and for not asking you about the lad beforehand. I know you find it difficult with Ian, but surely we can offer him a home for some weeks?"

"The nursery will be a bit crowded and I hope he doesn't mind that Jacob farts in his sleep."

"All lads fart in their sleep," Matthew laughed, "And by the way, so do you."

"Huh," Alex said, "look who's talking."

Much later, the house properly locked down and the bairns fast asleep, Matthew undressed and slid into their bed. He yawned and snuggled down beside Alex, thinking that this new concoction of hers had a most pleasing fragrance – roses and mints with a whiff of raspberries.

"Matthew?" She rolled over to face him.

"Mmm?"

"You're not doing anything stupid, are you?"

"How stupid?" In the weak light all he could see were the whites of her eyes.

"You know."

"Alex," Matthew sighed, "you can't expect me not to help."

"It might be dangerous – for you, for us."

"They need me." If it hadn't been for him and his fighting skills two preachers would have been dangling in a noose by now, but he decided not to share that with Alex, suspecting she'd be worried rather than impressed if he told her of last week's little adventure.

"But still…"

"I help them over the moss, I feed them, harbour them for a night or two. And I will continue doing it – it's the least I can do."

"And if someone finds them here?"

"They won't."

"But if they do, then what?" she insisted.

"Then…" Matthew propped himself up on an elbow and looked down at her. "They won't."

"That bad, huh?" she said, her hands closing on the linen of his shirt.

"Alex…" He brushed his nose a couple of times against hers. "I'm careful, very careful."

"Luke knows," she said.

"He does?" Matthew tried to sound unconcerned.

"That's what Margaret said."

"There's nothing he can do to harm me – he's in Oxford."

"He might tip them off," Alex said. "Who knows what contacts Luke has in the army?"

"Unless someone finds Sandy or one of the other preachers here, on my land, what can they prove? Nothing."

"Hmm." Alex sounded anything but convinced. "I don't like it."

"I know you don't." He flopped down to lie on his back, eyes on the wall.

"And?" Alex prompted.

"And that doesn't change a thing, I'll continue helping my ministers as much as I can."

Alex rolled over to face the other way.

"Alex," he tried.

She didn't reply, stiff as a board under his touch.

CHAPTER 4

Margaret rode away at dawn next morning and a silent Ian moved in, following Alex when she guided him through the house, showed him the bed where he would be sleeping with Mark and Jacob, and helped him unpack his few bits and pieces.

For the first few days Ian shrank back into the darker corners, speaking only when spoken to. His eyes followed them, seemingly sizing them all up, and at times Matthew would turn only to see Ian avert his face.

"It's disconcerting," Alex said. "He sort of flits around, like a wraith or something."

"Aye," Matthew said, his eyes drifting to the gangly lad who was sitting very much on his own out in the yard.

Despite her initial reluctance, Matthew had to admit Alex did everything she could to welcome Ian into their home. Not that it helped much; the lad escaped from them whenever he could, spending most of his days in the woods.

"It doesn't help to talk to him, he never joins us in the evening when I tell them stories and it breaks my heart to see him this alone." Alex sighed and frowned down at her knitting. "Why in the world did Margaret leave him here, with a family he barely knows?"

"She has no one else," Joan said. "You know that."

"Whatever; anyhow, after last night he probably thinks I'm the devil himself," Alex continued, making Matthew smile.

"Aye, even if cleanliness is not something generally associated with the underworld." He chuckled. "It was right fun to watch." Alex had chased after a half-naked Ian, threatening him with one dire punishment after the other unless he came back and let her finish washing him.

Alex gave him a faint smile. "What do we do with him?" she said. "How do we help him fit in and become one of us?"

"Give him time," Matthew said, "it will sort itself."

Sometimes Matthew wondered if Ian had been regularly whipped, and it was only a week or so later that he understood that the reason for Ian's shrinking existence was himself.

"Nay, that isn't true!" Mark's voice came from above Matthew, from the hayloft. "You must take it back, you mustn't say things like that about my da." Matthew smiled at his son's angry voice.

"Aye," Rachel piped up, "not about our da."

"But it's true. You're both too small to remember, but I was nine." Ian's voice froze Matthew on his way to the ladder.

"Da doesn't fight," Mark said. "He says it's wrong."

"He did then. He almost killed my father and he sliced off Father's nose years ago."

"No he didn't!" Mark sounded on the verge of tears.

There was a muted yelp and from the scuffing above his head Matthew knew his son had hit his cousin. There was a loud slap, a surprised intake of breath. Matthew stuck his head through the opening. Mark was rubbing at his cheek, and Ian looked so ashamed Matthew felt sorry for him.

"You hit him?" he asked, heaving himself onto the loft.

Ian nodded.

"Why?"

"He hit me," Ian said.

Matthew raised one brow, he raised two brows and looked from Ian to Mark and back again.

"Mark, did you?" Matthew stopped Rachel as she moved towards her cousin with a look on her face that indicated she intended at the very least to bite him.

Mark nodded.

"And why would you do something like that?"

Mark just shook his head.

"Son, I asked you a question."

Mark squirmed but continued to shake his head, eyeing his cousin from under his hair.

"You know I don't hold with fighting," Matthew said. "And even less with not having my questions answered."

Mark hunched together at the tone, but remained silent.

"So why did he hit you?" Matthew swung so suddenly in the direction of Ian that the lad overbalanced, sitting down in the hay.

"I don't know," Ian muttered. "He just did."

"Ah," Matthew looked him over. "Do you often hit bairns half your size?"

No, his nephew slash son told him, no he didn't.

"But now you did. You walloped your wee cousin and you have no idea why he hit you in the first place."

Ian scrambled to his feet but restricted himself to a slight nod; if Mark wasn't talking, nor was Ian.

"Well then, it seems you must both be punished."

Rachel opened her mouth, but Matthew put a firm finger on her lips.

"Nay, Rachel. You say nothing."

Rachel glowered at her cousin, going over to stand by her brother, her small hand sneaking into his.

"Both of you; go inside and undress, and then you'll say your prayers and go to bed. No supper." With an internal sigh he watched them troop off, all three of them, in the direction of the house.

In a gesture of solidarity with her brother, Rachel had also abstained from supper, and after a quiet meal Alex took Jacob upstairs. Given the way her apron pockets bulged she was intending to feed the lads – and Rachel – but Matthew chose to pretend he didn't notice. Instead he accompanied Joan into the parlour, giving her a brief version of the events in the hayloft.

"What can I say?" Matthew made a helpless gesture. "I can't refute that I sliced off Luke's nose, and I can't explain why without telling him the full sorry tale, can I?"

Joan patted his hand. "No you can't – not yet. But one day he'll start thinking for himself and then he'll come to you with questions."

"And I won't be able to reply," Matthew said. "I've promised Alex that I'll never tell him that he's my son. I..."

he broke off as Alex entered the room, carrying a tray with three steaming mugs.

"You what?" Alex said, setting the tray down on the table and finding herself a stool.

"I was just wondering if Joan will burst apart before the wean shows." Matthew smiled at his sister.

"Huh," Joan straightened her back with an audible pop. "It's already well over a week late. Now it best stay inside until Simon returns." She patted herself. "You hear? You stay there, aye? One more week."

"You best do as your mother says," Matthew said, placing his hand on the bulge. "You don't want her mad at you from the start."

"No, time enough for that later," Alex snorted.

Ian was not overly thrilled when his uncle took to taking him everywhere with him. From early morning to late afternoon, he tagged after his uncle, doing one task after the other as he was bid. At first he went with rancour at being used like a yard boy, but with each passing day he softened towards Uncle Matthew, and found himself talking to him, almost as much as he did with Mam. His uncle was a good listener, interjecting the odd little exclamation, even laughing out loud at some of Ian's stories from London.

"A monkey?" he chortled. "And it ate at the table like a man?"

Ian grimaced; the visiting young Earl of Rochester's monkey had eaten on the table, not at it, making Mam look at it as if she considered poisoning it.

"The king says it's a wee pest. It even bit one of the ladies once."

"Have you met the king?" Uncle Matthew sounded unimpressed. Ian threw him a cautious look. As he heard it, the king was mightily unpopular here due to religious issues, and from the look on his uncle's face, Charles Stuart was not one of his personal favourites.

"I see him now and then about court, but I've only met him properly once. It was at his coronation and I was not yet seven."

He remembered that April day for an entirely different reason. It was the day that he had first heard his parents quarrel and he had cowered under his bed as his father broke every piece of china in their home, alternating between calling Mam a whore and a traitor. At one point he had even hit her, but that had made both of them weep, with Father begging Mam to forgive him. Afterwards Ian had puzzled out why; Mam had given money to Aunt Alex, and even now, several years later, there were times when his father would curse Mam for that.

"It's your fault he didn't die!" Father had screamed, half-drunk, a few months back. "If it hadn't been for you and your meddling, Alex would never have been able to buy him free and Matthew would have died over there in Virginia – as I wanted him to."

It was all very confusing to Ian. Father hated his brother, often uttering Matthew's name as a curse. But Mam didn't, and when she'd been told by Luke to leave southern England with their son she had ridden all the way up here. "Home," she'd said, smiling down at him. "Hillview is home."

While they'd been here Ian had often seen Mam speaking to Uncle Matthew, padding on silent feet after them as they walked through the woods. He had even seen Mam touch his uncle; one part of him was offended on behalf of Father, but the other part was glad because of the pleased and surprised look on Matthew's face. Ian sneaked a look at his uncle, meeting eyes that were studying him intently. He flushed and looked away.

"Is it true?" Ian blurted one day, making Uncle Matthew loose his grip on the open sack of oats he was lifting.

"Is what true?" Matthew swept up the oats with his hand and refilled the sack.

"That you were sold as a slave."

Uncle Matthew nodded.

"And was it my father who did that to you? Who had you stolen away, sold like a beast?" He hoped his uncle would laugh and tell him not to be daft – what brother would do such – but instead Matthew sighed.

"Aye, but who told you?"

"Everyone does. They whisper it to me behind your back." Hushed conversations in which he was told just what a bastard Father was and how grateful he should be that the master could find it in him to take Ian in, given the bad blood between him and his evil brother.

Uncle Matthew set his mouth, muttering something about mean-hearted gossips.

"Why?" Ian asked with his eyes hanging off Matthew. "Why did he do that?"

"That's a question you must ask him, not me." Matthew stood and swung the bag onto his shoulder. "Come, you, we have beasts to feed."

"You do have sons of your own," Alex reminded Matthew with a nasty edge that evening. "And given that you're too engrossed with your new family addition to notice, let me inform you that Mark is feeling very excluded by all this male bonding."

"Male bonding?"

"It's what men do when they establish they belong together, you know, like slicing your thumb open and mingling your blood, or going off up the mountain to dance naked around a bonfire."

Matthew shook his head in bemusement and opened his mouth to ask some more, but Alex wasn't about to be side-tracked.

"So tomorrow you spend the day with Mark. And why not throw in some hours with Rachel and Jacob as well?" She breezed out of the room before he could protest.

He sniffed the air in her wake. She had taken a bath and used one of her scented oils, a clear signal that mayhap she was feeling somewhat ignored of late. Matthew sighed and pulled off his stockings, studying his long toes for some time. Sometimes it was exhausting to be farmer, father and husband. He washed, cleaned his teeth with a twig, masticated a sprig of mint and sank down onto the bed. He hoped she'd hurry back, or else he'd be asleep.

"Matthew!" Alex shook him hard. "The baby, you have to ride for the midwife."

"The baby?" He'd been well on his way to sleep and was still somewhat befuddled.

"Joan's!" Alex shook him again. "Hurry, okay?"

By now Matthew was up, throwing on clothes he had only recently discarded and then he was off, promising to be back within the hour.

Three hours later Alex was torn between worrying for Joan and for Matthew. What if he'd been ambushed, thrown in a ditch? The probable explanation was that the nearest midwife had been called away, so Matthew had had to ride for Cumnock. But still…

She gave her sister-in-law a concerned look. Should things be this slow? Joan was the colour of overcooked mutton, a pasty grey, and her stomach clenched and unclenched in short spasms that seemed painful but inefficient.

"We walk, Mrs Melville," she said when Joan tried to sit down. "We have to shake this baby into place."

"Into place?" Joan gasped. "It can't be more into place. Let me tell you, Simon Melville will never, ever, touch me there again."

"Pfft! All women say that."

It was well past midnight by the time Matthew returned with Mrs Wilson, who swept the room with a sharp eye, closed the window and ordered Joan to keep on walking.

"I just can't, I'm too tired."

"You'll be far more tired before you're done," the midwife said cheerily, "but then you can lie down, aye? Not before." Alex muffled a laugh at the glare Joan sent Mrs Wilson's way.

Between them, Alex and Mrs Wilson kept Joan on her feet well into dawn, but somewhere around there she paled even more, and then the waters broke, drenching Joan's long shift. Alex stared at the pinkish hue that coloured the linen and looked at Mrs Wilson. A quick shake of the head and a slight frown told Alex to shut up.

By noon Joan was lying lifeless in the bed, too weak to remain upright on the birthing stool. The midwife looked flustered, her brows frozen into a concerned frown.

"She's fully open," she whispered to Alex. "But she has no strength left and the babe needs her to help." She shook her head at the continued leaking blood. "I fear the afterbirth is letting go, and if it does, God help both mother and child."

"What can we do? There must be something we can do!" Alex stroked her sister-in-law's cheek.

"Get her upright," the midwife said. "Can you hold her, do you think?"

Joan protested, swatting at Alex, and once she was on the stool she began to scream, saying that it hurt and she wanted to go home, she didn't want to do this anymore.

"You should have thought of that before," Mrs Wilson snorted, crouching down while she gestured for Alex to straighten Joan up as much as she could. Alex held her braced against the backrest of the stool, the midwife leaned in between her legs, and at the next contraction slipped a finger round the cervix, making Joan scream even more.

"It's coming," the midwife said, holding up her bloodied fingers to Alex.

"Right, you," Alex said to Joan. "We have to get the baby out of you. Now. So at the next contraction you're going to push as hard as you can, and we'll push with you. Call for Sarah," Alex said to Mrs Wilson, "she can help as well."

It was a race against the clock, with Alex holding and shushing while the midwife and Sarah pushed and heaved at the womb, stimulating more contractions. Finally something changed; the midwife urged Joan to push once more and the floor was filled with blood, blood splattered all over Joan's legs, and the baby slid out, still and pale with the umbilical cord wrapped twice around its neck. Joan swayed on the stool, gawked at her child and slumped back, unconscious.

"Do something!" Alex looked at the midwife in panic. "Do something before she dies!" The baby was bundled into Sarah's arms and with concerted efforts Mrs Wilson and Alex half dragged, half lifted Joan to lie flat on the floor.

"There," the midwife said an hour or so later. She wiped at her face, leaving a garish streak of blood across her cheek.

"Will she be alright?" Joan looked like a waif, a white blob against the white sheets.

The midwife looked away. She had spent more than an hour stitching Joan's insides together.

"We must pray and hope."

Alex gripped Joan's hand. "If you die on me, Joan Melville, I'm going to be really, really pissed off at you."

There was a slight flutter of the bruised eyelids. "I wouldn't dare to, but I just…" Joan's mouth fell open and for a sickening instant Alex thought she had died, until Mrs Wilson pointed out that Joan was snoring.

CHAPTER 5

"Rachel Graham!"

Alex' voice froze her daughter for an instant and then the child took off, running like a hare for the safety of the stables.

"Come here, you!" Alex sprinted after her, telling her in no uncertain terms what she would do to her once she'd caught her.

Rachel shrieked, her little feet pounding towards the ladder that led to the hayloft, with her prize held high above her head. Behind her, Alex was closing the gap. One backward glance to check on her mother and Rachel went flying, landing with an audible thud on the straw strewn floor. The cake rolled out of her hands and into the pigpen, and daughter and mother could only watch as the sow devoured the unexpected treat.

"Right," Alex said, lifting her daughter to stand. "Inside with you. Now." Alex gave her daughter her most ferocious look, and with a resigned shrug Rachel followed her towards the house.

They were almost there when the sound of many horses carried through the air. Alex picked up her daughter and ran the last few yards.

"Mark! Run! You know what to do." Mark looked up the lane, back at his mother and set off, sprinting up the hill. Alex shooed Rachel and Jacob upstairs before stepping outside to face the group of dragoons that sat on their horses. All of them were new men, even the officer.

"Mistress," the officer said, tilting his head in her direction. She half curtsied, trying to remember where Matthew was today; out on the moss, cutting peat with Simon, Ian and Samuel. "Your husband?"

"He's not at home, it's just me and my children and my recently delivered sister-in-law." She couldn't help it; even in this situation the thought of baby Lucy made her smile. Alive

45

and well, despite her dramatic entry to the world, and even if Alex at times found Joan regarding her daughter with a look of disappointment in her eyes she was sure she would soon get over it.

"You'll not mind us verifying that for ourselves? Ensure you're not harbouring a fugitive or two?" He motioned for his men to dismount, jerking his head in the direction of the outbuildings.

"No, of course not," Alex said, following the two men that rode off in the direction of the mill with her eyes. Oh God; for all that Mark had a head start, he was a small boy on foot, while the soldiers were horsed. Her heart shrank into a prune when the horses were set to canter. She cleared her throat, forcing her attention back to the captain.

"Is there any particular reason why you seek my husband?"

"He hasn't sworn the Oath of Abjuration."

Alex did her best dim-witted look, giving him a simpering smile.

"The oath of what?"

The officer frowned. "Come, come, mistress, all of you know that the king requires all men to swear oaths of fealty to him and his church. A most necessary measure here, where Covenanters stand as thick on the ground as common daisies." He narrowed his eyes. "You'd be one of them yourself, I'd warrant."

"Me?" Alex said. "Not really." Out of the corner of her eye she saw the two horses disappear in among the trees, now at a more sedate trot.

"No? Well, beg my pardon for not believing you, mistress. And that absconded preacher, that… err…"

"Sandy Peden," Alex filled in. Mark should have reached the mill by now, she calculated, and if they were quick, they'd make it out in the nick of time.

"Yes, that's right. Well he doesn't help, does he? What with his insistence that there's nothing between man and God, no bishops and definitely not a royal head of church.

46

Pah! Ah well, sooner or later we'll catch him — him and anyone foolish enough to succour him."

"Not my husband," Alex said.

"No? That's not what we hear. He served in the wars, did he not? As a soldier of parliament."

Alex shrugged, succeeding in looking disinterested. "I met him seven years ago, a royalist escaping from gaol."

The captain blinked. "A royalist?"

"Convicted at the court in Ayr," she nodded. There was no need to tell him the trial had been a farce. Matthew had been falsely accused by his brother, convicted based on his brother's testimony, when all the while it was Luke, not Matthew, who was the diehard royalist.

The dragoons came back, shaking their heads. After a tense half-hour or so, the two sent off to inspect the mill returned, empty-handed. Alex' shoulders dropped an inch.

"We'll be back," the officer said as he turned his horse. "Please convey my regards to your husband." It came out with quite the edge.

"I'll be sure to." Alex curtsied and stood still until the last of the horse rumps dipped out of sight.

No sooner were they gone than she was hurrying up the hill. She met Mark making his way back down and gave him a hug.

"Are you okay?" Her son was rosy with excitement, squirming in her arms.

"We went out the back way," he said, "just as the soldiers rode up to the door."

"Oh." Alex clutched him to her.

"Mama!" He pushed at her. "He's at the oak, hiding."

As far as Alex was concerned, Sandy could bloody well stay there, but with a sigh she rose to her feet.

"We'd best go and tell him it's safe."

Mark made as if to rush off, but Alex took his hand.

"I'll come with you, okay?"

The hiding place was ingenious. Apart from Matthew, only Alex and Mark knew of its existence. While Alex was uncomfortable with lumbering her son with this kind of information, Matthew shrugged, saying that Mark had to be taught to run and warn – as he had done today.

Alex trudged after Mark down to where the millrun rejoined the river, walking along the water's edge until they reached a point opposite the old oak that hung precariously over the eroded river bank. The water was unpleasantly cold but shallow as they waded across. The platform was barely visible from below, even now in late October with the leaves more or less gone. At Mark's whistle a tousled head appeared, reappearing some minutes later on the ground.

Sandy Peden took off his mask and wig and rubbed his fingers through his thinning hair.

"They're gone," Alex said, meeting calm grey eyes. "So you can relax and go back to the room at the mill." Why not read up a bit more on the Bible, or pack your stuff together and go somewhere else altogether?

Sandy seemed to see what she was thinking, and scratched at his chest.

"Nay, I'll be leaving." He inclined his head in the direction of the moss. "A wee bit too close this time." He did look rather shaken, hands smoothing at his coat. "You've been most kind, Alexandra, but I don't want to overstay my welcome." His eyes glinted with amusement, and Alex unwillingly smiled back, thinking as she always did that she'd never met anyone with such long lashes before – long and so fair as to look almost white.

"It's just that…"

"Aye, I know," Sandy interrupted her. "And I know you have bairns to fear for."

They crossed the river and set off in the direction of the millpond, with Sandy and Mark a few paces in front of Alex. Sandy threw Alex a look over his shoulder.

"Have you been studying the texts?"

For an instant Alex had no idea what he meant, but then she remembered and felt a flare of irritation; texts to study and be tested on, making her feel like a child. This minister had repeatedly made it clear just how dissatisfying he considered her religious education – and convictions – to be, and had taken it upon himself to instruct her.

"No, I've had too much to do lately."

"You mustn't be remiss regarding your spiritual wellbeing," Sandy said.

"There's nothing wrong with my spiritual wellbeing."

"Ah no? And yet I dare say you cannot name me the books of the Holy Writ, nor even Jacob's sons, can you?"

"If I want to know I can look it up," she shrugged, and Sandy's brows sank into a bulging ridge over his eyes.

"Some things one should know by heart, I think."

"Waste of space, if you ask me," she muttered, hitching a shoulder.

"Hmm." Sandy sounded displeased, and looked over to her son. "Laddie, can you name me Jacob's sons?"

Alex rolled her eyes at how Mark shone up, hurrying over to take Sandy's hand as he recited his way through the twelve tribes of Israel. Sandy went on to tell Mark about Joseph and his dreams, about the Hebrew captivity in Egypt and Moses, the lawmaker.

"I know a song about that," Alex said, and began singing about Moses, who went down to Egypt's land to tell the pharaoh to let his people go. Both Sandy and Mark were delighted, and by the time they were back at the mill, Sandy had the verses down pat.

"...*So spoke the Lord, bold Moses said, let my people go. If not I'll strike your firstborn dead, let my people go'...*" He broke off and grinned at Alex. "It has a ring to it, aye?"

Alex nodded, wondering if she should tell him this was a song written by slaves – black slaves. Sandy surprised her by nodding seriously once he'd finished the song for the third time.

"The man who wrote it knew what it was like to be a slave."

"Yeah," Alex said. "You hear it in every '*let my people go'.*"

49

She met Matthew and Simon on the way down, and briefly recounted the events. Matthew clouded, a dark scowl settling on his features, while Simon went an interesting shade of greyish pink.

"What…" he asked, but Alex shook her head.

"Not now, not here. After supper, when we're alone."

Simon paced the parlour with his hands clasped behind his back, giving him a startling resemblance to a strutting pigeon.

"I told you the last time I was here. You must stop this, you can't put yourself at risk for men like Sandy Peden."

"Of course I can," Matthew said. "He's a friend."

Simon shook his head. "You knew him when you were young men, and aye, you share the same faith, but he's in breach of the law, a wanted man with a price on his head!" Simon slammed his hand down on the table. "You risk it all; you risk your life, your home and your family. Is that what you want, to see your family destitute with you being picked clean by the crows?"

"You're exaggerating, they wouldn't hang me." Matthew tried to sound unconcerned.

"No?" Simon knuckled at his irritated left eye. "Ah, no. They may be content with transporting you overseas. As a slave, like." Matthew frowned at him, but Simon pushed on. "Not to Virginia, Matthew, to the West Indies. And if you were badly treated in Virginia you'll have it tenfold worse in the West Indies." He wheeled to Alex. "Tell him! Tell him how men die in the sun, worked to death at the sugar plantations! Tell him, aye?"

"I already have." She shared a quick look with Matthew, who groaned inwardly. Repeatedly she raised the subject, obdurately he insisted he had to follow his conscience and help those who stood up to fight for the right to hold to their beliefs.

"I told you; Luke knows, and if Luke knows then he'll use it to have you destroyed. Not simply killed, because then

Mark inherits, but somehow charged with treason or something, with all your worldly goods befalling the king." She sounded matter-of-fact, keeping her eyes on her shoes, her skirts, anything but Matthew.

"It won't happen," Matthew said. "They'll never catch anyone here."

Alex made a face. "Well excuse me for not believing that. If it hadn't been for Mark, they'd have dragged both Sandy and you with them today."

"Aye," Simon said, "and then…" He grabbed at his throat and made strangled noises.

"It was a coincidence that they should come when Sandy was here," Matthew said. "They don't know – no one knows about me helping Sandy."

"Don't be daft! Of course someone knows, and information is always for sale – in periods of unrest especially," Simon said.

"Besides, someone told Luke." Alex said.

"I'll be more careful," Matthew said, but that was as far as he'd go. Alex pushed away from the table and left the room without a word.

"You have responsibilities," Simon said, "and first and foremost to your family – your wife, who travelled the world to bring you safely home, the bairns she's given you. They must come first. Even God would agree with that." He followed Alex out of the room, leaving Matthew to sit with Joan and the wean.

Matthew stared off through the little window, tracking Joan's reflection in the thick glass. Mostly bones and very little else, Joan tired easily, and wee Lucy was often found nursing in the arms of whatever voluntary wet nurse was at hand.

"You think I'm wrong too?"

Joan sighed. "Of course I don't; it's our faith you're protecting. But if Luke knows, and if there are dragoons riding in regularly, then you must be more than canny, take as few risks as you can." She cupped Lucy's little head.

"Simon's right; the bairns must come first." She smiled at Matthew. "And there will be one more soon."

"What?" Alex pregnant and she hadn't told him? He frowned, attempting to recollect when last she'd bled. Joan jerked her head in the general direction of the kitchen.

"You should spend some time with your wife; this last month has been very much about other people than her."

Matthew found her in the kitchen. "Will you walk out with me?"

Alex threw a look at the dark night. "Now?"

He just nodded, holding out his hand to her. He was silent when they walked across the yard, she trailing him as he closed doors, scratched Ham between the ears, and even offered a carrot to the pig.

"She doesn't need that," Alex said. "She had cake today."

Every shed he inspected before leading her to the laundry shed, a new addition to the outbuildings.

"There's a light!" Alex hissed as they got closer. "Someone's in there."

"Not yet, but soon." He swung the door open, very pleased by her exclamation of surprise.

The water in the laundry cauldron was steaming, he had lit lanterns and hung them from the roof. The new, enlarged hip bath had been scrubbed and he had brought down quilts and spread them on the broad bench that ran the full length of the small space.

"When did you do this?"

"While you were off being angry with me for being an irresponsible man." He was already undressing her, and then he helped her in, murmuring that it was about time someone washed her properly. When he began washing her hair she groaned, eyes closed as his fingers worked their way across her scalp. So much hair – so much naked skin to wash and rinse, his fingers doing the occasional detour to inspect her shapely thighs, the curve of her hip and the ticklish instep on her right foot. By the time he was done they were both very wet and very warm.

"Lie down," he said. Her skin glowed pink after his efforts with the towel. She stretched out on the bench, he kicked off his breeches and drew his damp shirt over his head and joined her, holding a flask of lavender oil. When the oil dribbled onto her stomach she shivered. He stroked her flank and goose pimples broke out all over her thighs. It made him smile, and he repeated the motion, thinking as he always did that it was odd that his woman should pimple as if cold when in reality it was heat she was feeling, her skin blushing under his touch, her pupils dilating as he increased the pressure of his hands.

"You haven't told me," he said, slowing his oiled hands over her breasts. He nudged at her darkening nipples and bent his head to kiss them. Her back arched, her breasts lifting to meet his lips.

"I thought you could find out for yourself," she said, her hands on his head as he continued further down her body. "Took you some time, though," she added, wriggling under his mouth.

Matthew stopped what he was doing and threw her a look.

"Aye well, it's been a trifle hectic." Margaret leaving, Ian moving in, Joan and the wean… all in all the last few weeks had been a bit too much. He kissed her again, tasting her properly. Salt, she was, and smooth and soft like silk. She moaned. His tongue teased her, she tugged at his hair, her thighs falling wide open.

"Now," she breathed, "I want you now."

"Oh, do you?" He kissed her pubic mound, her navel, and she squirmed, making a series of low, urgent sounds. "Matthew!" she groaned, and he took pity on her, sliding up the bench to cover her body with his.

"How far along are you?" he asked as he sank into her.

"Two months."

"Oh," he replied, concentrating on how it made him feel to be inside of her. He moved slowly, long flexing movements of his hips.

"Will it be a boy or girl, do you think?" Alex voice sounded very vague, as if the effort of holding even this desultory conversation was too much. When he slipped his hands under her and lifted her closer she made a small sound, holding still when he shifted even deeper inside of her. All the way to his root, and she sighed, crossing her legs round his hips.

"A lad," Matthew kissed her. "We must hope for a lad. One like Rachel is quite enough." He felt Alex laugh and smiled in response, thrusting into her. "But there will be time for lasses later, many, many lasses."

"You're nuts," Alex told him. "This is already number four. How many were you planning for?"

Matthew bent his head to her ear and whispered a number, making her shake with laughter.

"Totally nuts, Matthew Graham," she whispered back, and then she didn't say very much at all for some time.

She gave him a contented look afterwards, pillowing her head on his chest with a little sigh. He toyed with her hair, drawing out long, long curls that bounced back the moment he released them.

"I'll ask him to stay away, for now." Matthew choked on the words, they tore at his gullet.

"Good," Alex said, sounding relieved. "And when they come and ask you to swear the oath?"

"What oath?"

Alex raised her head. "Don't give me that; you know exactly what oath."

Aye, of course he did. He sighed and looked at her. "How can I swear an oath like that?"

Alex locked her eyes into his. "How? You just repeat the words and cross your fingers behind your back."

"That's perjury."

"No, it isn't. It's called survival. Sometimes you do things just to keep yourself and your family safe."

"It will make me a lesser man," Matthew said.

"Not in the eyes of those that matter – not in mine."

He smiled crookedly; no, not in hers. "To Sandy it will."

"Probably. But he knows you have children and he will anyway blame it on my corrupting influence."

"Corrupting influence? Aye, you could say that." He looked down to where she'd taken a firm grip of his cock. "Not that I mind." He raised a hand to brush a curl off her face.

"Of course you don't." Her hair tickled his chest, his belly and spread out across his thighs.

"Ah, Jesus," he said, when her tongue slid over his balls, the length of his cock.

"Now that Sandy would definitely not approve of," Alex said, before going back to what she was doing.

"Right now I don't care," Matthew said, holding her where she was.

CHAPTER 6

"But why?" Ian asked. "If those giant eagles could fly and fetch them from the mountain, why didn't they just carry them in? And then Frodo could have dropped the wee ring into Mount Doom much earlier."

Alex rolled her eyes; what had possessed her to try and tell them the rambling, convoluted story of *The Lord of the Rings*? Apart from the long and rather heated discussions as to whether the elves were like Scottish fairies (not, they decided), if hobbits had perhaps at one time lived on Skye (yes) and did Alex really expect them to believe Aragorn was over ninety years old (It's a fairy tale!), Alex was now tagged by Ian and Mark who wanted to know more, pestering her with detailed questions before breaking off to argue among themselves as to if it was Aragorn or Frodo who was the real hero.

At least it had proved the battering ram Alex had needed to get through to Ian, and so she replied patiently to his questions, all the while sneaking him quick looks. The pale boy of a month ago had bloomed into an active youngster and when the letter arrived requesting he be allowed to stay on further on account of Luke still doing poorly, he hadn't seemed too depressed.

"Stop!" she said. "There. Fill your basket, but make sure they're undamaged." She pointed at the rosehips in the huge briar bramble beside him.

Ian eyed the thorns and sighed. "The whole basket?"

"To the brim," Alex said, going round to do her picking on the opposite side.

"Aunt?"

"Hmm?" Alex jerked back from her agreeable daydream of a huge salad, complete with tomatoes and feta cheese.

"What happened to my grandfather?"

Alex was glad he couldn't see her, but bent down, just in case, to hide her face.

"Your grandfather?"

"Aye, Malcolm Graham."

"Why do you ask?"

Ian fell silent and as moments became minutes Alex thought that perhaps he'd retreated into one of his customary silences.

"Samuel told me he drowned," Ian finally said.

"You should really be asking Matthew this, it's not as if I was here then."

"I don't want to. Mayhap it would make him sad."

Alex smiled at the way he said it. Matthew Graham was working his magic on this young heart.

"It probably would." She peeked at him through the brambles. "You're not picking! Get on with you, we're not going home until your basket is full!"

Ian grumbled but went back to tearing off the bright red fruit.

"Yes, he drowned; in December of 1653. No one really knows what happened, but he was pulled in under the water wheel and… well, he died."

"Was he murdered?" Ian asked breathlessly.

Yeah; in all probability by your beloved father, Alex thought.

"Well it was all a bit strange. He received a message from the miller to come up because there was a problem, but the miller says he didn't send any such message. And your grandfather didn't know how to swim and was scared of water, so why would he have gotten close to the pond in the first place?" Alex wrinkled her brow in concentration. "There was something about a ring…"

"A ring?" His eager voice made her smile.

"Not one of those rings; I told you, the rings of power are just a fairy tale. No, this was a ring that he always carried but that wasn't found on his person when they pulled him out."

"Mayhap it slipped off his finger in the millrace," Ian suggested with valid logic.

"Except that he carried it on a chain around his neck, tucked away under his shirt, and according to Matthew his clothes were mostly undamaged – it was more a matter of…" She broke off. He'd been crushed, poor man, the outside looking seemingly intact while most of his bones had been pulverised. "Anyway, it was his mother's ring, three strands of gold braided together and decorated with one single blood-red stone the size of a small sea water pearl."

"A braided ring with a blood-red stone?" Ian squeaked.

"Yes." Alex peered at him through the brambles. He'd gone very pale, long arms hugging his knees tight. "What's the matter?"

"Nothing." He gave her a bright smile.

Alex shrugged. "Hips, young sir. And then if you ask nicely I might tell you some more about the battle of Helm's Deep."

Ian and Alex were a stone's throw from the house when they heard the sound of loud, angry voices floating up towards them. In the middle of the yard stood Matthew, glowering at a rotund dragoon.

"Why? I am a law-abiding man, I have no interest in…"

"Law-abiding? Well if so, Mr Graham, swearing the oath is no major matter, is it?" the soldier said. "Or do you hold convictions that stand in conflict with taking it?"

"Shit," Alex muttered when Matthew straightened up to his full height. She increased her pace, motioning for Ian to hurry along.

"I don't hold with these laws prohibiting man to follow his conscience in matters of faith," Matthew said. "They're…"

"What? No, no, Mr Graham. It is not for you to choose how things should be ordained, that is for your betters to decide."

"My betters? And who might they be?" Matthew loomed over the dragoon, who calmly held his ground.

"Your king, Mr Graham. His parliament, his officers. All of those are your betters."

Matthew scowled and Alex wheeled to face Ian.

"Lie down, pretend you're hurt. Your foot or something."

Ian fell to his knees, squealing like a dying pig.

"Not that hurt," Alex hissed, although it did seem to have the desired effect. Matthew and the officer turned to look up the hillside. She bounded down the last few yards. "Come quick, Ian has hurt himself!"

Matthew gave Alex a sceptical look, but ran off in the direction she was pointing, leaving Alex alone with the little officer.

"Sir," she curtsied, "may I perhaps offer you some beer? And your men, of course."

The dragoon cheered up at this generous offer, and by the time Matthew came back after having assured himself Ian would survive his near lethal tumble, the soldiers were far less menacing.

"Monday a week," the officer said once they were back on their horses. "At the church."

Matthew nodded and watched the troop ride off before facing her.

"You shouldn't waste beer on such."

"And you shouldn't waste breath arguing with them, it's not as if it you have much choice, it is?"

Matthew grunted something rude and colourful, among which Alex could make out whoresons and goatsuckers. Goatsuckers? It almost made her laugh.

Matthew spent the rest of the morning astride the barn roof, venting his anger on the new shingles. Now and then, he'd see Alex dart by far below, and once he even saw Joan, a hunched, grey shape that hobbled to the privy and back.

"What's ailing Joan?" Matthew asked Alex after dinner.

"I'm not sure," Alex said.

Matthew chewed his lip. Slowly but steadily Joan had been regaining her strength, and when Simon had left a week or so ago she was close to being back to normal. But since then she had begun slipping in the opposite direction, lying pale and unresponsive in her bed in between the feeding of her daughter.

"Simon says she mustn't try for another child." Matthew shook his head at the unfairness of it. Good people such as Simon and Joan should be blessed with many bairns, and now all they had was one scrawny little daughter, a wean with her father's reddish hair and her mother's wide grey eyes. Even if Simon had tried to make light of it, Matthew had heard the disappointment in his voice.

"I heard," Alex said. "How will they manage? I suppose they'll still want to have sex."

Matthew smiled at her expression; he never had sex with his Alex, he made love to her or bedded her or took her on the stairs – although that was very long ago – or had her in the hayloft. He glanced in her direction and saw she had been following his line of thought. It made his balls tighten pleasantly.

"I'd go crazy," she said, her blue eyes very intense. "You know, without…"

"Aye, but if it were a question of your life we would find other ways."

Alex groped him hard, smiling at his muffled exclamation.

"I'm sure we would," she said, and danced away.

"What's he doing here?" Alex said a few days later, her eyes shooting darts into the back of Sandy Peden, who disappeared into the house.

"Joan asked for him, so I went and found him."

"Joan? Why would she want to see him?"

"Mayhap because he's a man of God?" He wiped a hand over his face. His sister's apathy had him worried, and if Sandy could rouse her out of it, he'd be eternally grateful. "She blames herself; one bairn, and a lass at that."

Alex muttered something about living in a man's world, eyes still stuck on the door.

"He's not staying."

"Nay, of course not," Matthew hastened to say. "He knows that."

Alex tightened her shawl around her shoulders, turning to sweep their yard, the lane, the surrounding slopes with her eyes.

"Alex," he sighed, "I'm no fool. I have Gavin sitting at the top of the lane."

Sandy sat for hours with Joan and when he came out of her room so did she, gripping the minister's arm as she made her way down the stairs.

"Well done," Alex said, ushering Sandy in the direction of the kitchen. "It sort of brings to mind the tale of Lazarus."

Matthew choked on a gust of laughter.

"She wasn't dead," Sandy corrected, accepting the food she put in front of him.

"Minor difference, she's been staring at the wall for days on end – more dead than alive."

"I heard that," Joan said with a touch of asperity.

"A miracle, a miracle," Alex muttered. "Look, she moves, she talks, she even hears."

Matthew threw her a reproving look, but Alex just snorted and disappeared in the direction of the parlour, where a succession of loud noises indicated wee Rachel was doing something she shouldn't.

Matthew lifted Jacob to sit in his lap and smiled at his sister. "It is good to see you up."

"Aye, well, 'tis good to be up." She didn't sound convinced, but smiled when Sarah placed Lucy in her arms. "Will you christen her?" she asked Sandy, handing him the wean.

"He's not allowed to," Alex voice cut in. "He's been formally ejected, and mustn't perform any sacraments." She entered the kitchen, frowning at all three of them.

"He's a minister of my Kirk, and I'll much rather hide out in the moss to hear Minister Peden preach than go to Cumnock and hear a mealy mouthed representative of the Church of England offer us salvation if we just recognise the authority of the king over the church." Joan sounded more animated than she'd done for weeks, with two spots of bright red on her cheeks.

"He baptised Jacob," Matthew said, stroking back the thick, fair hair of his son.

"That was two years ago," Alex said. "Before it began to get really nasty."

Sandy smiled down at the child in his arms. "I'll be glad to baptise the wean," he said, "and if you want we can do it now." He threw a challenging look in the direction of Alex, who opened her mouth to say something but clearly thought better of it. Instead she lifted Jacob out of Matthew's lap and left the room.

"She fears for them, and for me," Matthew tried to explain, watching Alex cross the yard with all their children and Ian in tow.

"Aye well," Sandy said, "she's but a woman – weak of body and of mind."

Matthew met Joan's eyes, suppressing a smile at this description of Alex.

Once the wean had been christened, Joan took Lucy upstairs, and Matthew and Sandy sat in the kitchen, talking of this and that. Hesitantly, Matthew told him of the coming oath taking, and Sandy sat up straight.

"You can't swear that oath. It would be to renounce your faith!" Sandy looked mulish, grey eyes so sharp Matthew twisted on his stool.

"But the bairns and Alex… I can't risk them, can I?"

"It's her, isn't it? She has no concern for your immortal soul."

"She fears for us," Matthew reproved.

"She is weak of faith; we both know it. It would've been better had you wed someone like your sister, a woman who understands the sacrifices which our faith requires at times."

Matthew shook his head. "That's not fair, and…"

"You mustn't," Sandy interrupted. "How can you in conscience do something like that?"

"Something like what?" Alex asked, appearing at the door.

"It is between Matthew and me, aye?" Sandy stood. "I'll be going, daylight is fading fast and I don't want to find myself trapped halfway across the fell."

"No," Alex said, "that might be a bit uncomfortable."

"I'll walk with you," Matthew offered. He wanted to delay the inevitable confrontation with Alex, feeling her eyes burn into his back as he pulled his cloak around him and followed Sandy out into the November dusk.

"You don't like him much, do you?" Joan's voice made Alex start.

"That's not it, in many ways I find him an admirable man, but he's very black and white, and that leads to a difficult life."

"He's a good man."

Alex had no doubts about that, and at times he was even quite funny, painting an engaging picture of a God very much involved in day-to-day life.

"He always makes me feel as if I'm failing in some fundamental aspect, that somehow I'm not quite the wife Matthew deserves."

Joan sat down in the single kitchen chair and undid her shift to lay Lucy at her breast.

"He thinks you lack in piety and he worries that you won't stand by Matthew on matters of religion."

Alex wasn't quite sure how to answer that. Sandy was totally right; Alex retained a sceptical view of religion as such, and no way was she about to let anyone in her family – and that included her stubborn husband – die for their faith.

"It's a question of perspective; in Sandy Peden's book the hereafter is the most important and we must live our lives so as not to imperil the immortal soul, no matter what it might cost us or those we love."

Joan nodded in agreement.

"But you see, I don't think God agrees with him, in fact I believe it pisses him off no end if we squander the gift of life by being excessively rigid. If he didn't want us to enjoy life he wouldn't have given us eyes to see with and fingers to touch with and ears to hear all the sounds of the world with…" Alex broke off, somewhat flustered by the astounded look in Joan's eyes. "I believe we spit in God's face if we throw our lives away, and I don't think he likes that very much."

Joan shifted breasts and pursed her mouth into a funnel. "You have much more in common with Sandy Peden than you think," Joan said. "He wants to live, aye? Live and praise the Lord every day – but in accordance with his beliefs, not the Church of England's."

That sort of shut Alex up.

"What time will you be setting off?" Alex asked once Matthew got back.

"Hmm?" He dipped his bread in the soup, smiling across the table at his daughter.

"For Cumnock." Alex said with a slight edge to her voice.

"Ah." Matthew went back to his soup.

Rachel slipped from her stool to come and sit in his lap, and he blew her in the ear, making her squeal. Ears that were so like her mother's, tight and somewhat pointed and with a tendency to go pink when she was upset. Alex' ears were presently very pink and Matthew kissed his daughter before setting her back on her feet.

"Go, I must speak to your mother alone." He waited until all of them were gone, even Joan and Lucy, before turning to meet Alex' eyes. "I don't think I'll be riding to Cumnock, it will have slipped my mind. Just as it will slip my mind next time they ask as well."

"You told me you would."

Matthew shook his head. "Nay I didn't. I said swearing it would be perjury and make me a lesser man. I just can't." The hurt look in her eyes made him cringe, but he had never promised, not as such.

He expected her to remonstrate with him, but instead she got to her feet and left the room. She called for her children, promising that tonight she would begin a new exiting story, the story of four children and a lion, but only if all of them behaved and hurried into bed.

From where he sat he heard Ian and Mark argue loudly over who should sleep in the middle, and Jacob began to cry, with a muffled "Rachel!" making it clear who had been the culprit.

Around him the house settled into the November night and he made his final rounds, locked the doors and bade his sister a goodnight before entering his bedchamber. He undressed, shivering in the clammy cold of the sheets, and lay waiting for his wife. She never came. He heard her hesitating by their door and then there was the soft creak of the stairs, a sudden banging of the door. Matthew exhaled and rolled out of bed.

He knew where she'd be. Whenever Alex needed a few moments of solitude, she made a beeline for the hill. On occasion she'd spend hours there, staring out across the moor. Thinking, she'd say, I was just thinking. But why now, in the dark and the wet? Matthew cursed as he made his way through the woods. What was the stupid woman thinking of, to go rushing off into the night?

At one point he considered turning round and going back to the house, but now he was both wide awake and wet, so he pushed on, promising Alex Graham she'd have a lot to make up for once he got her back home.

He was breathing heavily by the time he made it to the top to see her silhouetted against the night, black against a lighter shade of black. He joined her and stood beside her, waiting. Alex was shivering with cold, her arms crossed over her chest. He put an arm around her and drew her towards him, wrapping his cloak round them both. She rested her head against him and from her irregular breathing he realised she was weeping.

"Alex? Ah, no, lass, don't cry." He couldn't see her properly, but managed to find her face with his hand, his thumb wiping at her eyes. "There's no need to cry, I'm here."

"For now," she sniffled. "But not for much longer."

"You don't know that," he said, feeling her stiffen against him.

"They'll insist that you take that oath – particularly as you haven't exactly been discreet these last few years regarding your convictions. And if you don't, God knows what they'll do to you. You're all I have, Matthew. I have no one else but you in this time, and still you're willing to put your life at risk for some bloody high-minded principle."

Matthew remained silent, but she seemed to have run out of things to say, at least for now.

"Some things are worth fighting for, lass."

She tore herself free and backed away. "Is that what you want me to tell your children as we walk by your displayed head? Do you think it will comfort me as I lie alone to know you died for your beliefs?"

"It won't come to that," he said.

"No? How do you know? And if they catch you with Sandy on the moss, then what? Or if they come upon you with blood on your sword after a night out helping your friends?"

"I haven't…"

"Don't lie to me!" she yelled. "You think I'm stupid? You think I don't notice when you clean your sword?" She shook her head at him. "Every night you go out on that moor you're taking a risk – a huge risk."

"I have to help as I can," he said, "they're my brethren, my friends, and…"

"But what about our children – what about me? Am I not worth something to you as well?" Her voice cracked on the last few words.

"How can you ask me that? Of course you are, I love you – all of you," he said.

"But not enough to swear the oath that will buy us all some safety, right?"

Matthew hitched his shoulders. It was a matter between him and God, and Sandy had clarified what it was he would be doing if he swore the oath with the express purpose of breaking it…

"Go away," she interrupted. "Just go away and leave me alone."

"Alex," he put his arm around her, but this time she shook it off.

"No," she said, retreating to stand several yards away. Her face was a pale oval that seemed to float, disembodied, in the dark that surrounded them.

"I must do as my conscience bids me," he tried.

"Your conscience?" She near on stuttered. "And what about your responsibilities as a father, as a husband? What does your precious conscience say about that, huh? I would die without you, you hear? I… " She broke off, wiping at her eyes.

"Ah, Alex! I would never…" Inch by discreet inch he shuffled towards her, wanting to envelop her, hold her safe against him.

"What?" she demanded. "What would you never do? Take risks? Set your beliefs before your family?"

He wasn't quite sure how to answer that. "I go canny, aye?" He made a grab for her, but she evaded his hand and pushed him, sending him stumbling backwards.

"Go! I don't want you to touch me, I don't want you to talk to me. Leave me alone. I might just as well get used to it, right?" She turned her back on him, and for a long time there was no sound but that of her unsteady breathing. Finally she cleared her throat.

"Not once have I wished myself back in my time, not one single time. But tonight I wish I had never met you, Matthew Graham, never had your children to tie me to your side."

"You don't mean that," he said, swallowing at the pain he felt at her words. "Tell me that you don't."

"I don't?" She turned to face him. "No of course I don't. But I sure wish I did."

CHAPTER 7

After persistent wheedling Matthew had gotten Alex off the hill, but she hadn't said a word to him on the way back. Once they were inside she'd gone to bed without even wishing him goodnight, maintaining as much distance from him as was possible in a bed not more than four and something feet across. In the morning when he woke, her half of the bed was empty, and when he came down to the kitchen she moved away to put the table between them.

She looked exhausted, the skin under her eyes was bruised and puffy, and he realised she'd been weeping again. Something about how she held herself made him want to sweep her into his arms and place her on his lap, rocking her until she felt safe, but she maintained a constant distance, sidestepping him whenever he tried to get close. Even the bairns noticed, with Jacob and Rachel snuggling up to their mother far more than they usually did, small hands patting at her in concern.

Alex helped Sarah clear away after breakfast, nodded to the men when they trooped by her on their way back to work. She backed away when Matthew approached her, muttered something about needing to go out, and when he held out his hand she just shook her head.

"Alex," he said. "We must talk."

"Talk? About what?"

For an instant her eyes met his, two yawning wells of deep blue, and then she had her damp cloak in her hand, her basket in the other. She rushed out the door, stumbled halfway across the yard but regained her balance, and off she went – not in the direction of the woods, but up towards the Cumnock road. No doubt to see if he went or not, he sighed, following her with his eyes until she ducked out of sight behind the elders.

For the first time in the more than seven years he'd known her, he was aware of being judged by her. There was a mental scale in her head, and what he did or didn't do today would forever determine their life together. She was making it very simple for him – his convictions or his wife. He met his sister's eyes and bowed his head.

"I have to."

"Aye, I think you do. And she's right; you'll have to sooner or later anyway. They'll use force if they have to – even Sandy knows that."

"You think?"

"Sandy is no fool, Matthew. For all his fiery words, he'll understand – and so will God."

Ham was unusually frisky, doing a series of stiff legged jumps on their way up the lane, but by the time they left Hillview behind, the horse was under control. Matthew sat easily, scanning the rolling hillocks to his right for Alex. When he saw her he raised his hand and halted the horse, waiting as she made her way across the thick heather towards him.

"Will you ride with me?" he asked once she was close enough to talk to. She nodded and held up her arms in a gesture similar to that a bairn makes when it wants to be taken up and held. He leaned towards her and helped her to sit in front of him, her wide skirts tucked tight beneath her legs to stop them from billowing like a giant puff mushroom in the wind.

"It won't hurt," she said, breaking a long stretch of silence. "It's just some words, right?"

Matthew twisted his mouth into a wry smile. "I was very young when I swore on the Solemn League and Covenant, and for me and my brothers in arms that document signified the birth of something new; a country where man was recognised as being capable of speaking directly to his God, as is taught by our Presbyterian faith."

"And somewhere there was also a clause to wipe out all popery and prelacy," Alex said. "Sounds like a most tolerant approach to fellow man."

Matthew agreed that perhaps some of the wordings had been a wee bit too harsh.

"What goes round comes round, because now the prelacy has the upper hand, right?"

"Mmm," Matthew sighed.

"What is it exactly they want you to swear to?"

"I must abjure the Solemn League and I must swear fealty to the king."

"Well that's not too bad, is it?"

Matthew looked at the sodden brown of the surrounding moor, dipped his nose to her head and drew in the smell of lavender and damp wool. Underlying it was the scent unique to her; warm and fruity, with a whiff of salt.

"I must swear to uphold all the laws of the kingdom, all of them – including the Conventicle Act and the Act of Uniformity. So every time I go off to listen to Sandy or any of the other ministers on the moss I will not only be flaunting the law, but I will also be in violation of my oath."

"Then don't go," Alex said.

"Ah, no; that you may not ask of me. You may ask that I swear the oath, that I stop harbouring my friends for the sake of our bairns. But you can't stop me from listening to the word of God from the mouth of men I love and respect." He felt her stiffen, a surprised inhalation stuck halfway to her lungs. He shook his head at her innocence. She'd thought it was only a matter of taking the oath, thereby safeguarding them all. Instead, this oath would paint him all the more effectively into a corner, because never would he renounce his beliefs.

"Promise me you'll be careful," was all she said, and her hand was like a manacle around his wrist all the way to Cumnock.

In general Alex enjoyed her excursions to their little market town, rare and welcome disruptions in her country life. Narrow houses – predominantly in stone but here and there old enough to be half-timbered – bordered the crooked and for the most part paved streets. A warren of closes and alleys connected the streets, there was a passable inn named The Merkat Cross that abutted the market place, a relatively new church and a number of shops, most of them sporting old-fashioned horizontally hinged shutters that when opened served as an extended roof and counter. Garbage and offal littered the streets and floated in the river, there was a pervading stench of unwashed humanity and ordure, but today she was far too aware of how tense her man was to do much more than wrinkle her nose.

For all that it was a weekday, men were streaming towards the church – men in dark formal wear and a set to the mouth that made Alex think of people fighting down waves of nausea. They dismounted and Matthew visibly relaxed in the presence of so many neighbours and friends, called like him to swear in front of the new Anglican reverend, the constable and the commanding officer of the garrisons in Ayr and Cumnock. Matthew nodded in silent greeting to Davy Williams from the farm closest to Hillview and took his place in the queue, leaving Alex to stand and witness from the side-lines with the few other wives that had come along.

Mrs Williams pulled her threadbare cloak even tighter around herself.

"Where will this end? Will we be forced into baptism at that half popish Church of England?"

"Shh," Mrs Brown, yet another neighbour, threw a worried look around.

"Ah, no," one of the other wives smiled. "As long as we have wee Sandy around he will be christening and marrying."

"Not burying, though," Mrs Williams said, "not if you want to lie in the kirkyard."

"We must just make sure we don't die then," Alex quipped, earning herself several disapproving stares.

Before them, their men were one by one kneeling to swear the oath, mumbling their replies almost inaudibly. It took a long time, each man being forced to repeat in verbatim a long text in which they swore fealty to the crown, abjured any previous oaths in conflict with this fealty and swore to uphold all laws of the realm. Once they were all done, the garrison commander studied them for a long time.

"All," he said in a braying voice. "All laws. To succour outlaws is to be in breach of the law, to participate in unlawful assemblies is to break the law. To forget for one moment that all power both in state and church lies vested in His Majesty, the king, is to violate the oaths you have all sworn." He heaved himself up on tiptoe and swayed menacingly towards them. "I'll be watching you. My men will be watching you – all the time." He looked each of the men in the face before nodding to the reverend, who informed them they were welcome for services the coming Sunday.

"Go with God," he added shrilly and hastened down the aisle in the wake of the striding officer.

"We always go with God," Mrs Williams muttered. "We have him with us always." There was a soft rustle of laughter from the other wives.

"Not that it will make that much of a difference," Alex commented as they rode back towards Hillview. "His soldiers are everywhere already."

"Aye, they are." Matthew frowned at nothing in particular, still shaken by the threatening tone of the officer.

"Matthew?" She tightened her hold around his waist when Ham took a few gleeful capers. "Is Sandy an outlaw?"

"Not yet, but it was a wee bit daft of him to christen all those weans over at Castlehill."

"Will it change things for him? If he's outlawed?"

Matthew laughed mirthlessly. "Change? Aye well, not as long as he isn't captured." He rode in silence for some time, wondering where poor Sandy would be sheltering today, with the wind coming almost horizontal and the clouds so low one got wet just from stepping outside. He increased the pressure of his thighs on Ham, in a hurry to get back home to warmth and food and his waiting bairns.

When they got home, they found that Joan had taken to her bed again, and at Alex' concerned questions she just smiled and assured her she would soon be alright, but that she just had to sleep, she was that tired.

"I wonder if she might be anaemic," Alex mused, frowning at the contents of her pantry. "And if she is, what do I feed her?"

"Anaemic?" Matthew had but a vague notion what that might mean, and nodded at Alex' attempted explanation.

"… so with all that blood loss…" Alex shrugged. "In my day and age they give you pills or jab you with a syringe. In this day and age, well it's all in the diet." She scrunched up her brow. "Blood sausage – and rosehips."

The enforced diet seemed to help, even if Joan grumbled at the lack of variation, and six days later she was first out of bed, sitting in the kitchen with Lucy when Alex came clattering down the stairs with four hungry children in tow.

"Better?" Alex scrutinised her sister-in-law. There was a pinkish hue to her skin and her face had lost that grim expression, as if she were permanently swallowing back on bitter bile.

"Aye, tired but better." Joan rocked Lucy and looked down at her. "She's a sweet babe. Never cries, sleeps through any kind of noise."

"She wouldn't get any sleep if she didn't," Matthew yawned from the doorway.

"Nay," Joan agreed, but there was a shade of worry in her eyes. "I fear she's deaf." She looked from Alex to Matthew in a silent entreaty that they laugh at this ridiculous statement. None of them did, instead Matthew picked up little Lucy and cradled her in his arms.

"Why would you think that?" Alex asked.

Joan stood up, found two copper pans and crashed them together behind Lucy's head. Alex and Matthew jumped, but Lucy's eyelids didn't even flutter.

"Deaf," Joan repeated and left the kitchen with the pans dangling from her hands.

"It could be worse, she could be deformed or blind or something," Alex said.

"But now she's deaf as a post," Matthew said, "and aye, it could be worse, but it's bad."

Lucy twisted in his arms, her face shifting from pink to bright red. She opened her mouth and wailed, an angry sound that had her mother at her side so quickly that Alex suspected she'd been standing on the other side of the door.

"Well, she's not mute at least." Joan brushed at the reddish hair and traced a finger across the vulnerable skull, stopping at the small, perfect little ear. "What will Simon say?" she asked and began to cry.

Simon rode in a few days later, listened in silence to his wife's news and reached an all-time high on Alex' list of favourite people when he smiled, tenderly wiped Joan's face with his handkerchief and hugged her and Lucy both.

"It'll sort itself," Simon assured her. This group hug looked uncomfortable for all of them, but neither Joan nor Simon seemed to think so, holding on very hard to each other. "And she's a bonny lass." He gazed into the wide grey eyes that were Lucy's major asset.

"Very," Alex said. No, not really, nose and ears overlarge in a pinched little face.

"She's been christened," Joan said, "Lucy Joan Judith."

"Judith?" Simon's brows rose in surprise. "Why would you name an innocent creature after that quarrelsome baggage?"

"She's your aunt, and she'll be pleased."

Simon snorted, but left it at that.

Matthew was in the barn when the bevy of soldiers rode into the manor next morning, watching with rising ire as an indignant Simon was surrounded and prodded this way and that by men on horseback.

"What do you want?" Simon snapped, hopping from one leg to the other. "Won't it keep until I've been to the privy?"

"Who are you?" the officer asked. He leaned over the neck of his horse. "You have a look of that renegade preacher about you."

"I most certainly do not!"

"No, too fat," the officer nodded, "a man living rough would not be quite so well fed. So who?"

"Simon Melville, lawyer." Simon glared at him and the officer squinted at him.

"Ah, yes; now I recognise you. We met back in July."

"We did?" Simon shrugged. "You left no impression, I'm afraid."

"Not on you, but perhaps on your... what is it, brother-in-law?"

"That too. But first and foremost friend – best friend," Simon said.

"Lucky him," the lieutenant laughed and allowed Simon to hurry off.

The officer snapped his fingers, and his men spread out over the farm, some in the house, a few in the sheds and the stables, and one off to search the barn.

"And is your husband not here today either, Mrs Graham?" Lieutenant Gower asked once Alex came outside. "Mighty strange, is it not, how he is always elsewhere when we come." He smiled down at Alex. "And yet we come by so often."

Matthew had by now had enough and came out of the barn, hammer in one hand. The wee officer was attempting to intimidate his wife, driving his horse in tight circles round Alex, who succeeded in looking quite unperturbed.

"And what may you want with me?" he called out, striding over to join them, with Ian and Mark at his heels.

"Ah, the elusive Mr Graham. And so we meet at last." The lieutenant smirked, bowing exaggeratedly.

Matthew gave him a nod, no more. "Not the first time."

"No, it isn't, is it?" the lieutenant said. "But at the time, you were... well, how shall we put it... disinclined to converse?"

"At the time I was being unjustly held and beaten – by you, as I recall."

"Unjustly?" The lieutenant laughed. "I think not."

Matthew was sorely tempted to pull the smirking fool off his horse and give him a good thrashing then and there. Instead he placed himself in front of Alex, arms crossed, and looked up at the officer.

"What can I do for you?"

Gower shrugged. "You know that, Mr Graham; always on the lookout for people that are attempting to evade the law." He patted the gleaming neck of his horse and smiled down at the household. "Like Alexander Peden."

"He isn't here."

"No, not today he isn't, but one day he will be, and then it will fare ill both for him and for you." He jerked his head at his troop and held his horse until his men were halfway up the hill. "We'll be back," he said, bowing in the direction of Alex before spurring his horse into a sedate canter.

"Not much of a surprise," Alex muttered. "It seems to me they're here more or less every other day."

"Aye," Matthew said, "much more often than elsewhere, as I hear it."

Simon reappeared from the privy, spat to the side and came over to join them.

"You've sworn the oath and yet they come. It would seem they don't trust you."

Matthew laughed softly. "It would seem so, aye."

"Without reason, of course," Simon said, giving him a penetrating look.

"Of course," Matthew lied, his eyes on anything but his wife.

Simon made a sound like a disgruntled pig. "I've told you, you're playing with fire."

Matthew bent down to pick up a discarded horseshoe and grinned. "For luck," he said airily and left them standing alone in the yard.

"Is he?" Simon asked Alex. "Does he offer them board

and bed for a night or two?"

Alex shook her head. "He has promised not to, and I believe him when he says he hasn't."

Simon rolled his light blue eyes at her.

"At least not here," she added, chewing her cheek. Margaret's cottage! Isolated and on the far edge of the woods it would make a nice little safe house, with the added benefit of being close to the moor. "I swear I'll kick his balls," she said and took off in the direction of the barn.

Matthew heard the swishing of her skirts as she made her way down the barn to where he was working on one of the walls and turned towards her.

"What exactly have you promised me?" Alex said.

He eyed her warily; there was a dangerous tone to her voice.

"Promised you? To love you and hold you, to keep you in house and food, to watch over you, to…"

"Not that! What have you promised me regarding Sandy Peden and the others?"

"Do you need to ask?"

"I just want to make sure we're in agreement," she said in a mild voice. "So?" she prompted at his continued silence.

Matthew exhaled and threw down the hammer. "I've promised not to bring them home. At least not for now."

"And home is what? The big house? The barn and the stables? "

"All of that," Matthew said in relief. "The house and the barn and all the buildings."

"All of Hillview?"

He twisted.

"All of Hillview?" she repeated.

"All of Hillview," he said, defeated.

"So if I were to go up to Margaret's cottage later this afternoon, I wouldn't find anyone there, would I?"

"Nay, you wouldn't."

"Good. And I'll check, just so you know." With that she left.

Matthew kicked at the hammer and slid down to sit. Damned woman, making him feel like a bairn of four caught with his fingers in the honey pot! Sandy was doing poorly, a nasty cough to him, and now he'd have to go up and tell him he had to leave. He groaned out loud and leaned his face into his hands.

"Here." Alex' voice startled him. A basket was placed at his feet. "I added some raspberry cordial, it helps with the cough. And I took your old cloak. I can make you a new one – there's fabric enough."

Before he had time to say anything she was gone, running from him.

CHAPTER 8

"One day it will all be mine," Mark said with evident pride. They were sitting halfway up the slope behind the house, sharing the hot biscuits Mark had lifted behind Sarah's back.

Ian let his gaze travel the grey stone of the house, the black slate roof and the weathered buildings that formed a haphazard 'U' facing the house. The yard was full of sodden, steaming linen, and here came Aunt Alex with yet another load. Given the harried look in her eyes they'd decided it was best to keep away until it was all safely done with.

"It should be mine," Ian said. "That's what my father says." Not quite; what Father said was that Hillview should've been his, not Uncle Matthew's – because Matthew should have been dead – and by definition that would have meant it coming to Ian once Father was dead.

Mark looked at him in bewilderment. "Yours? But it's Da's, and then it will be mine and my son's. From eldest son to eldest son."

Ian was bursting with jealousy; Hillview in the hands of a snotty-nosed lad five years his junior.

"Some say I'm Uncle Matthew's eldest son."

"But you're not," Mark said with a little shrug.

"No? I've even heard Uncle Matthew himself yell to the world that I'm his son." He looked away, overwhelmed by memories of bloodied faces and angry words.

Mark threw down his remaining biscuit and rushed off. Ian sighed. Mayhap he shouldn't have told him. He kicked at the discarded biscuit, scattering crumbs all over the grass.

The single benefit of spending a whole day doing the laundry was that it was blissful to sit down once it was all done. With a little grunt Alex collapsed on a stool. Her hands ached, as did her back, her thighs, her shoulders.

Rachel and Jacob were playing under the table, something promising was cooking on the hearth and here came Sarah with some herbal tea. There was a sound of running feet and Ian burst into the kitchen – alone.

"Where's Mark?" Alex looked from Ian to the door and back again. "Ian? Where's Mark?" She glanced over to where her sheets flapped in the weak November wind and sank her eyes into the boy.

Ian muttered something along the lines that he didn't know and attempted to escape.

Alex grabbed him. "You went out together and now you come back alone. So what happened? Did you have a fight?"

"Not as such. He just ran off."

"Where to?"

"Up there, somewhere," Ian replied, pointing in the direction of the mill.

Alex frowned. It was getting dark, and Mark usually never missed a meal.

"When?"

"Just before Uncle Matthew rode off with the yearling he was going to sell."

"That was hours ago!" Alex exploded, making Ian skitter away from her.

"What's the matter?" Joan came into the kitchen, with Lucy snug in a shawl at her chest.

"Mark." Alex explained and ended by throwing yet another worried look out the window. "I'll have to go and look for him. Will you keep an eye on Miss Scatterbrain and Jacob for me?"

Joan nodded that of course she would.

"He won't be far, he's just a laddie."

Nowhere! Not in the stable, not in the barn. Not up around Margaret's cottage, nor in his hideout under the blackberry brambles that only he and Alex knew about. Alex was hoarse from calling his name, and in the falling dusk her lantern spread a pathetic beam of light.

She knocked on the miller's door and Andrew opened but

said that no, wee Mark hadn't been up here, but maybe he was in the… he jerked his head in the direction of the isolated shed that Matthew had used to harbour Sandy during the summer.

Andrew walked her over: a large, handsome boy with an engaging grin and the IQ of a hamster. But no Mark there either, and Alex had to work hard to stop herself from crying, smiling a quick thanks at Andrew before hurrying off to… She stopped mid step. Surely Mark wouldn't have done something that dangerous? She eyed the swollen river with misgiving. After a month of heavy rains the millpond was overflowing into a churning millrace, spilling back with a froth of angry water into the normally placid little river.

She fell as she made her way down the river bank, sitting down hard on her rump.

"Shit," she muttered, looking at the water with dismay. Not deep, not for her, but Mark was not quite six. She took off shoes and stockings, bunched her skirts up as high as they would go and with lantern in one hand and skirts in the other waded through the cold waters towards the gnarled oak.

"Mark?" Her throat hurt with the effort. "Mark? Are you there?" There was a rustling motion over her head. "Mark? Come down son." He did, appearing by her side so suddenly that she gasped.

He was wet to well above his waist, and when Alex threw her arms around him he began to cry. She sat down and held him as close to her as she could, rubbing her hands up and down his sodden clothes.

"We have to get you out of this," she said and stood him up, stripping off breeches and stockings. She took off her shawl and wrapped it around him, took him back into her lap and rubbed him some more.

"What happened?" she asked once Mark had calmed down. He buried his face against her and refused to answer.

"Mark, tell me. Did Ian hurt you?"

Mark began crying again, and Alex shushed and patted him, telling him things would be alright, she was here, wasn't she, and no one would hurt her boy as long as she was around. Mark relaxed, his small body heavy in her hold, and she sat rocking him back and forth.

"He said he's Da's son," Mark said, and for an instant Alex was sure her heart stopped.

"Really?" She even managed to inject her voice with mild incredulity.

"He said Hillview should be his – his father told him so, that it should be Ian's." Mark took a deep breath. "Is it true? Is he Da's son?" He looked at her from under a curtain of tousled hair.

Alex hugged him close. "Listen to me, Mark Graham. Your father has two boys; Mark and Jacob. That's it. Ian must have misunderstood."

"But he said…" Mark sounded hesitant.

"What?" Alex said.

Mark looked away. "He said Da said so as well," he whispered.

Somehow Alex managed to laugh. "He did?" She laughed again, shaking her head. "Well, I'm not sure what Ian might have heard, but he got it all wrong." Alex rose and extended her hand to Mark. "Now, we have to get home and I hope you can find your way back in the dark, because I'm not sure I can."

Mark puffed up; of course he could. Alex stifled a small smile and let him lead her in the direction she had come.

They met Simon and Matthew halfway back, and Matthew rushed towards them.

"You should be spanked," Matthew said, hugging his son. "You've had your poor mama out looking for you for hours." He handed Mark to Simon. "Now you go with Uncle Simon, and it's supper and bed directly, aye?"

Mark nodded and burrowed his face into Simon's neck .

"Are you alright?" Matthew peered at Alex. She leaned against him, exhausted. She wanted to be carried as well, fed and tucked into bed.

"Tired, and wet, and very hungry, and pissed off at Ian."

And at you, she added silently, for words you slung at your brother in anger two years ago that now come back to bite us.

"Why is that?" Matthew said. "Did he harm our Mark?"

Alex gave him a short summary, feeling how he stopped breathing, holding his breath for a long time before expelling it.

"Dear Lord," he groaned. "Poor lad."

Alex wasn't certain if he meant Ian or Mark.

"You're going to have to talk to him."

"Aye," Matthew said, "it would seem I must."

Ian didn't even attempt to hide when Matthew entered the stables.

"Come here," Matthew said, and at his tone Ian moved towards him. He looked at the lad, cataloguing the evident similarities, from the hair through the eyes and skin tone to the way the chins were cleft and how both of them had a slow, wide smile. Except that neither of them was smiling now.

Ian's eyes were puffy with crying and Matthew's heart went out to him – no doubt the lad had been imagining all sorts of terrible things befalling wee Mark. With a strangled sound Ian plunked down in a heap of straw, stretching out his legs in front of him.

"Am I? Your son?" Ian wiped two thick lines of snot from under his nose. Matthew sighed and sat down beside him.

"Nay, you're Luke's son. That's what your mother says, and she should know." He could see the lad struggle with this and cleared his throat. "You were conceived in wedlock – while your mother was wed to me."

Ian's eyes widened, and Matthew twisted inside.

"To you?" Ian whispered.

Matthew nodded.

"But…" The lad swallowed. "Was she… with both of you?"

"Aye, she was. With both of us." Matthew felt terrible saying this, painting Margaret as some sort of whore.

Ian's mouth fell open. "But then you don't know, none of

you know!" He scrambled up and away.

"Ian!" Matthew had him by the shoulders and pulled him close, ignoring the flailing arms, the loud hiccupping sobs.

"Who am I?" Ian moaned, hiding his face against Matthew's shirt. "If none of you know, then who am I?"

"You're Luke's son, " Matthew repeated, ignoring how much it hurt him to say it. He cradled Ian's face between his hands and forced the lad to look at him. "It may be that we don't know for sure whether it was my seed or Luke's that planted you, but that doesn't matter, not anymore. You have a father who loves you, a mother who adores you and an uncle who loves you as well." The look in Ian's eyes made Matthew want to close his own, but he kept them open, meeting that green gaze as well as he could. "It's the caring that counts, lad, not the planting. The farmer who seeds the ground and leaves someone else to care for the growing crop can't come back and claim the harvest, it belongs to the man who tended it, no?"

Ian nodded uncertainly.

"But sometimes," Matthew went on, "sometimes the farmer who did the planting wants to claim the harvest – especially if the crop has been well cared for." He gave Ian a swift hug and smiled shakily. "You're a right bonny lad; a lad to be proud of, to love and to care for. And I would have dearly wished that you were mine, but you're not. You're Luke's. But you're my nephew, my kin. And I love you very much."

For a long time Ian neither moved nor spoke, standing very close to Matthew. At last the lad coughed and wiped his eyes.

"I love you too," he said, and darted off into the night.

Matthew sank down to sit on the floor. He hoped he'd said the right things to the lad, but it had cut him to the quick to renounce any claims to fatherhood, giving the boy permanently to Luke. "You should have been mine," he said out loud, "you were meant to be mine."

It struck him that the only man who could possibly

understand what this conversation had cost him was his brother, and for the first time in years he wished for an opportunity to sit and talk to Luke. He dismissed the notion as quickly as it had surged; Luke would sit and talk to him the day he had first nailed Matthew to his chair with a sword or two, and that was not something Matthew intended to allow to happen.

He was staring at nothing when he heard the tip tapping of clogs and lifted his head to see Alex smiling down at him.

"I don't know what you told Ian," she said, sitting down beside him. "But whatever it was you've made him very happy. He's asleep now, one arm thrown over his cousin."

"I told him he was Luke's son."

"Well, that explains it, what boy in his right mind would prefer you over that paragon of virtues?"

Matthew chuckled, toying with a strand of her hair. "I told him I love him, but that he's not mine, however much I wished he was." He closed his eyes, resting back against the wall. "I have a fine nephew and it will have to do instead."

"You have two sons as well, and soon perhaps even three."

"Not perhaps," he said, placing a hand on her belly. "This wee one is a lad." He stood up. "I'm a fortunate man. Three healthy bairns, a strapping nephew and another wean on its way." He helped her up and draped an arm over her shoulder. "And then I have a most marvellous wife. Very opinionated, mind."

"Says who? The likewise opinionated Sandy Peden?"

Matthew felt his cheeks heat at the insinuation that he had been discussing his wife with his friend and minister, but nodded.

Alex made a dismissive sound. "He's scared of women, probably had a domineering mother or something."

Matthew coughed. Mrs Peden might have been a lot of things, but domineering was not the first word that sprang to mind.

"Mrs Peden was a meek and demure woman, like you are

not." He slid his hand down to grip her buttocks. "They say regular spanking helps."

"Spanking?" Alex lifted her eyes to him. "You try and I'll knee you where it really, really hurts. Besides, you'd never be able to hold me down."

Matthew laughed and raised his brows. "You'd best not tempt me. I've told you before, that should I want to, I can always make you obey."

"In your dreams, mister," she huffed. "Pervert, you probably get a hard on just thinking of me fighting back." A deft touch of her hand made her burst out laughing and she rushed off, only to be brought up short.

"Now look what you've done," Matthew murmured, taking her hand and guiding it to his crotch. "You've woken the beast."

"Beast?" she spluttered, cupping what she could reach through the cloth. "Not much of a threat, is it?"

"Aye, the beast. So now you must make haste up to bed and take care of it."

"No way, I'm starving. Your little beast thing will just have to wait."

He shook his head. "Priorities, wife," he said. "You need to be taught a bit about them."

"I'm warning you; I'm very, very hungry, so don't blame me if I bite something off by mistake."

CHAPTER 9

November rolled into December, and weeks of fog and rain shifted to days that were crisp and dry, cold enough to make noses begin to run after just a few minutes out. The day it snowed for the first time the children capered about with their tongues extended to catch the drifting snowflakes, whilst Joan and Alex stood and watched from the kitchen door. Lucy at two months was an alert baby girl, her eyes widening when Alex scooped up some snow and placed it in her little hand. The small fingers clenched and a miniature snowball appeared.

"Strong," Alex commented. Lucy was a healthy, blooming girl. Unfortunately, Joan seemed incapable of seeing this, stuck on the fact that her daughter was deaf, and therefore, as she now confided with a sigh, probably simple – all deaf people were.

"No they're not, but it's difficult to cope without one of your senses, and that makes other people think they're stupid." Alex lifted Lucy out of Joan's arms and hoisted her into the air, making the baby squeal. "She's perfect. We'll just have to help her overcome her deafness."

The one very good thing with winter was how things slowed. Days started later and ended much sooner when the dark closed down upon them. Alex enjoyed these long, candlelit evenings spent with the children and Joan, but mostly with just Matthew in the privacy of their bedroom. Dominated by the four poster bed, it was a rather bare room – uncluttered and airy despite its size – containing a large mule chest, a stool, a table and two pewter candlesticks. The chamber pot was tucked away in a corner, there was always a pitcher of clean water and as Alex hated sleeping behind dusty bed hangings, she'd thrown them out. Sometimes they played draughts, on other occasions Alex would amuse Matthew by singing her way through one rock song after the other. At times he'd join in, singing along in his dark voice, and sometimes Alex even got him on his feet to do some dance moves, which generally resulted in her laughing her head off and him chasing her around the bed.

If Alex liked the long, dark evenings, Matthew enjoyed the late dawns. A slow, leisurely awakening, moments of undemanding proximity in the warm cocoon of quilts he shared with his wife. He moved closer, his morning erection prodding at her arse. Alex rolled towards him with a yawn and stretched. The worn linen of her shift had torn during the night and at her movement one round breast fell into full view, making him laugh.

"What?" She peered at her chest. "Oh that; I guess it's time to tear this into clouts."

"You look…" he began.

"Sexy?" she suggested with a smile.

Nay, not 'sexy', not with her sleep encrusted eyes and the imprint of her pillowcase on her rosy cheek. He tweaked her messy braid and kissed her nose. "You look like a rumpled angel," he said, "innocent and…" Young – aye, like a wee lassie woken from sleep to soon.

"Innocent?" Alex laughed. "Is that good or bad?"

Matthew tugged at her hair, releasing one long curl after the other to decorate their pillows. She stroked his head and traced the outline of his mouth. With a satisfied rumble he pillowed his head on her shoulder, her arms coming up to hold him close. No words, just a melting together, a physical nearness that filled him with such deep peace that he would gladly have remained like that for a whole day.

The scream had them breaking apart. With a bang their door opened and Mark tumbled inside. Matthew covered his half-naked wife with a quilt and turned to frown at his son, irritated at having this pleasurable moment so rudely interrupted.

"What?" He had already verified that Mark was not in any way harmed.

"Rachel, it's Rachel. She's put leeches all over Ian's… err… legs."

"She has what?" Alex sat up, holding the sheet to her chest. "Where did she get leeches?" She narrowed her eyes at Mark.

"I only wanted to show them to her – I told her to be careful with them."

"Careful," Alex said, "that's a word that doesn't exist in Rachel's vocabulary, and you know that, Mark Graham."

Matthew resigned himself to having to get out of bed and sort this situation, because something told him Rachel had planted the leeches somewhat higher up than on poor Ian's legs, and from the nursery a string of desperate little yelps continued to be heard. Alex swung her legs out of bed to go with him, but Matthew shook his head.

"Nay. You stay." He pushed her back down, kissed her and gave her a stern look. "Don't move, Mrs Graham."

"Aye, aye , sir." With a happy sound Alex burrowed deeper into their bed.

"All over his arse and privates," Matthew sighed later. "A few of them were dead when I got there." Alex shrugged; she wasn't a huge fan of leeches, she told him, the only reason she kept some was because they helped to reduce swelling around injuries.

"And how is he?"

"Complaining he has been severely weakened, but I promised you'd make pancakes for breakfast."

"Oh, you did?" She stretched and yawned. "Well, lucky you; I think we still have the eggs for it. And Rachel?"

He gave her a quick look. "Ten, one for each wee beastie. Hard enough to smart, no more." He was restrictive with corporal punishments, but when he considered them necessary he administered them without asking her opinion – a source of some contention. As he'd expected, she looked displeased. "I know you don't like it, but sometimes a sore arse is the best way to rub in a lesson."

"You think?"

"Aye." Besides, it was his duty as a father to discipline his children, but he didn't say that, knowing it would launch them into an acrimonious debate. Instead he stood up and pulled the covers off her, grinning at her protesting noise. "Get up. You have a household to fry pancakes for."

"Hey, how about someone making me breakfast for a change? Preferably served on a tray in bed."

"Someday," he promised, "but not today."

The peace of the morning was interrupted by the jangling of harnesses, and Matthew's jaws clenched when the troop of dragoons rode into his yard.

"The third time in a week, and today is Sunday."

"They probably want to make sure you're not holding a conventicle," Alex said.

Matthew said something foul under his breath and went out to meet them, followed by Alex and Joan.

"They've got Williams with them," Joan said. A battered and bruised Davy Williams was sitting his horse unsteadily, his hands tied to the saddle. Behind him sat a man Matthew had never seen before, but from his dark garb and worn demeanour he concluded this must be yet another fugitive minister.

"Please," Alex murmured, putting a hand on Matthew's tense back. "Please…"

He nodded to indicate he had heard, and when she slipped her hand into his, he splayed his fingers to braid their hands together. More for his sake than for hers, because unless she anchored him and held him back, he feared the anger in him would leak out and then there was no knowing what he would do.

"Mr Graham, a nice Sunday morn, is it not?" The officer smiled, inclining his head to Alex. "A good day to offer up a prayer to God, but as it should be done, in church, not in unlawful assembly." He threw his head in the direction of his prisoners. "Your neighbour is in breach of his oath and I fear it will cost him."

Matthew could feel himself begin to tremble, and by his side Alex shifted, leaning her warm weight against him. He tightened his hold on her fingers, heard her inhale and knew he was squeezing too hard.

"I've been requested to bring you with me," Lieutenant Gower continued, "that you may witness his punishment."

Matthew threw a look at Williams. The man was so pale the broken veins on his cheeks and nose stood out like bright red spots. Surely they wouldn't hang him, would they?

"We don't have all day," the soldier said, with a steely threat in his tone.

Matthew nodded and walked towards the stable, Alex clinging to his hand.

"I'm coming with you," she said, once they were out of hearing range. "No way are you going alone."

Matthew nodded again; not because he wanted her to come, but because he was beginning to drown in blacks and reds and only her presence could keep him somewhat sane.

It was a long and cold ride. Matthew didn't say a word, but under Alex' cloak his hand gripped hers so hard her fingers grew numb. The damned lieutenant kept up a chirpy, one-sided conversation, seemingly unperturbed by Matthew's stony silence. Alex kept her eyes on Ham's flowing mane, not wanting to see either Williams or the shivering minister behind him.

Halfway to Cumnock stood the crossroad oak, and standing in silent formation beside it were several other men. Alex hated this particular crossroads, for the same reason she hated thunderstorms. This was where she'd almost been dragged back to her time several years ago, and she studied the ground for any signs of a sudden, widening chasm. It all looked normal enough, just the dirt road and here and there a tuft of withered grass. No bottomless pit to a future she didn't want to ever return to, no funnels of bright, blinding light.

A loud yelp recalled her to the here and now. Behind her Matthew cursed when first the minister, then Williams, was pulled off the horse they were sharing. Alex didn't know what to expect, but the fact that they'd been assembled before the massive tree made her fear that perhaps the two men would hang, just like that. Williams and the unknown minister eyed the oak with trepidation.

The smirking lieutenant dismounted and stood with his hands clasped behind his back. At his nod both prisoners were manhandled to stand in front of him.

"You're in breach of a number of laws, chief amongst them the Act of Conventicle and the Five Mile Act. You…" He indicated the minister. "… You've been formally ejected from your religious office and are forbidden under pain of death to proselyte among the people of the kingdom, and yet you go from house to house spreading beliefs that stand in direct opposition to the lawful church."

The little minister straightened up at that, eyes flaming in anger. "The Church of England is naught but a whore to its erstwhile popish roots, and if you think that I'll ever accept the king as overlord of my church you have it wrong."

Lieutenant Gower ignored him and turned to Williams. "It's not much more than a month since you swore an oath to uphold the laws of this country and abjure any kind of seditious thinking." He sighed and wagged a finger. "Oaths should never be sworn lightly," he went on, his eyes travelling over the assembled men. "Because once sworn it ties you to it, and I'm charged with ensuring you uphold it."

A collective shiver ran through the group, and the lieutenant smiled – rather nastily.

"You will both be scourged here, in front of witnesses. You, Mr Williams will be levied a fine; 200 merks, payable within the month."

The shocked silence was absolute. Oh my God! Alex' brain squealed with horror. 200 merks, that was the equivalent of four year's wages, and no one – no one – had that kind of money. Not around here, anyway.

"How am I supposed to raise such an amount?" Williams said.

Lieutenant Gower shrugged. "I have no idea; sell your farm?"

"I have bairns," Williams pleaded, licking his lips. "Five, aye? How are they to live if I sell the farm from under us?"

"You should have thought of that before," the lieutenant drawled. "If you don't meet the fine within the month they'll be bonded to make up the difference."

Had Alex been closer she'd have spat in his complacent face. Probably not a good idea.

"Dearest Lord," Matthew whispered in an agonised voice. "Poor man!"

"And his family," Alex said, thinking of strong, capable Mrs Williams and her half-grown brood. The lieutenant was still talking, and from the dazed expression on the men's faces the minister's fate was as awful, if not worse, than Williams'.

"The West Indies?" the minister croaked. "But I'm a man of Scripture, I know nothing of the workings of a farm."

"I'm sure you'll be put to good use," the officer laughed, "from what I hear cane crops require very little but brute strength."

Both men were so stunned that they made no protest when their clothes were taken off them, leaving them in nothing but breeches and stockings. By the time the scourging was done, the minister had slipped into unconsciousness while Williams still stood, swaying like a drunkard when he was ordered to dress.

"Mr Graham," Lieutenant Gower said, beckoning Matthew to come closer. "Please deliver Mr Williams to his home."

"And the minister?" Alex regarded the crumpled shape with concern.

"He goes with us – he'll be staying in custody until his ship sails." He nodded at one of his men, who hurried over to drag the minister towards the horses. Just as they were leaving the lieutenant reined in his horse and looked at Williams.

"A month; January 12th, at the sheriff's court."

Mrs Williams didn't say a word when she listened to Matthew's terse account. If the sum of 200 merks made her faint inside she didn't show it, gripping her youngest boy's shoulder for support.

"How?" she said. "He hasn't been tried and convicted, and surely an officer can't just mete out punishment by himself?"

Williams sighed and leaned forward to hide his head in his arms. "It won't help to appeal."

"Nay," Matthew said in a heavy voice.

As Matthew and Alex stood to leave, Williams grabbed Matthew's sleeve.

"Who? Is there anyone you know who'll buy the farm off me?"

"Nay, not for 200 merks. I know of no one with that kind of money."

"Nor me," Williams whispered. "God help us, nor me."

"What will he do?" Alex asked once they rode off in the direction of Hillview. All the way back from the oak she'd been quiet, and the haunted look in Mrs Williams' eyes when she saw them off, thanking them for bringing her husband back home, was burning small holes of compassion through her heart.

"The only thing he can. He'll run and leave the farm to be forfeited in payment of his debt. At least that way he won't see his bairns and his wife sold into bondage." Matthew looked off in the direction of the moor. "It will be cold – but at least they'll be free."

"And poor and hungry and always scared – all because their father chose to set principles before their safety."

"Aye," Matthew replied and covered her hand with his.

CHAPTER 10

"I told you," Simon said, shaking his head at the terrible fate of the Williams family. "You're playing with fire." He was sitting as close as possible to the hearth with a plate balanced on his lap.

"Not anymore, not after seeing that." Matthew frowned at Simon. "Five times in ten days they've been here." Last time it had taken a lot of effort for Matthew to remain quiet and still while the soldiers stamped their way through his storage sheds, prodding the hay with their swords and even crouching down to inspect the space under the privy.

"Five times?" Simon looked up from his food. The four day ride from Edinburgh had seemingly whetted his appetite, and when Alex offered he eagerly held out his plate for a refill, muttering that he needed his strength back.

"Six if you count yesterday," Alex said. "But that wasn't a search, that was just the lieutenant riding by to wish us all a good day."

"Polite lad," Simon said with a gleam of laughter in his eyes. Matthew was not amused. Yon lieutenant was a cocky wee shite who took great pleasure in disrupting their life as often as possible.

"It's not right," Matthew said, "for law abiding people like us to be hounded thus."

"It's the way it is," Simon said. "No worse for you than for your neighbours."

"Oh, it's much worse," Matthew said. "Nowhere else do the soldiers descend as regularly as they do here."

"Someone has set them on us," Alex said. "These spontaneous little visits are far too well rehearsed – and increasingly nasty. I swear, if one of those morons shoves my boy again I'll…"

Joan sighed. "Luke," she said, "it has to be Luke."

Ian shrank back against the wall and took several deep breaths in an effort to make his heart stop thumping so loudly. Why would they think Father was in any way involved? He pressed his ear to the door again, listening to the low murmurs of adult voices, punctuated by the odd laugh.

Nothing more was said of Luke and Ian tiptoed back to his bed, his brain whirring as he tried to make some sense of all the new complications in his life. His uncle was perhaps his father, but at the same time he wasn't. Uncle Matthew was being harassed by soldiers and this was apparently Father's fault, and then there were those strange whispers about his faithless mother. He buried his face in his pillow, digging an elbow into Mark to make him move over.

"Did you never find the ring?" Ian asked Aunt Joan a day or so later while helping her clean Malcolm Graham's headstone.

"What ring?" Joan sounded surprised, but continued sweeping the stone free of leaves.

"The ring he always carried round his neck. Aunt Alex told me."

"Oh, his mother's ring." She patted the stone and put the small wreath she had made on it, clumsily getting off her knees. "Nay we never did, and strange that was, very strange. The chain he wore it on was short, it would never have slipped over his head. It must have come off him in the millrace, something must have snagged it – however unlikely, seeing as his shirt was whole and the lacings intact."

"What did it look like?" Ian already knew; Aunt Alex had told him, but mayhap she had it wrong.

"A dainty piece of work, too small to fit on any of his fingers. Three strands of gold braided together and a small, blood-red stone."

"Oh." Ian felt his heart sink to settle somewhere just above his balls. He kicked at a stone and sent it flying in the direction of the rowan.

"Aunt?" Ian waited until she turned to face him. "Why don't they love each other? Why is it that my father hates my uncle so?"

Joan sighed. "It's a long story. And it isn't really mine to tell."

"I must know, it's not right that I shouldn't know, because I'm stuck between them. And I love them both." Ian squared his shoulders and drew himself up straight, trying to look older than he was. "I can't ask them; Father rarely speaks of Uncle Matthew with anything but hate in his voice, my mother never mentions it at all, and my uncle, well, he says I must ask my parents." He made a wry face at that.

"You might not like what I have to tell," Joan said.

Ian looked at her for a long time. "Aye, I know that. I'm not daft for all that I have problems reading." It irked him, that wee Mark had such facility with letters, while to him they were at times incomprehensible jumbles of lines, no more.

She shook her head. "You're but a lad; mayhap when you're older."

"I'm all of eleven," Ian said, "and my uncle rode to war when he was fifteen, as did my father."

Joan made a resigned gesture. With a little exhalation she sat down on the graveyard bench, swept her shawl tight around her narrow frame and began to talk.

It was a sad story she had to tell, a tale that began the day his grandfather brought Margaret, his mam, home – a wee, bitty thing, all eyes and dark hair that took one look at Luke, slipped her hand into his and never let him go. For years it had been like that, but they grew up, and the innocent games transformed into a love affair, and when Malcolm Graham found out …

"You know how your grandfather threw Luke out, for… err.."

"Fornication," Ian whispered. "Mam told me, how she and Father loved each other, and mayhap they were too young but they couldn't help themselves, she said."

Ian didn't quite understand this. How not help oneself? And why had his grandfather been so angry? Aunt Joan hitched one bony shoulder; in retrospect Malcolm had been wrong to throw Luke out, she said, but he had been shocked to find his ward and son together, and them like brother and sister.

"So Luke rode off, and Margaret was left at Hillview – with Matthew. And where before Margaret had at most wished Matthew a good day, now she began paying court to him, a constant shadow at his heels, blue, blue eyes always turned his way."

Ian frowned; Mam throwing himself at Matthew?

"Some years on they wed, and five months later our Da was dead and Luke rode into the yard. Something snapped in Luke when he saw Matthew and Margaret together, and since then he's been driven to punish your uncle for forcing himself on Margaret." Aunt Joan broke off and gave Ian a stern look. "Matthew did no such thing. He loved your mam, was always gentle with her, but Margaret lied to Luke, painting Matthew an uncaring ogre, a vile, cold-hearted man that forced her when all she wanted to do was to wait for Luke to come home."

"Mam?" Ian shook his head.

"I told you; you wouldn't like it, to hear the truth." Joan sighed. "Margaret was always an adept liar, embroidering her little tales most convincingly, and in this particular case Luke wanted to believe her." She frowned down at her lap. "She did wrong your mam, she was wed to one brother and took the other to bed."

He just nodded; he already knew this. "Why?" He licked his lips. "How could she?"

"Ah, lad," Joan smiled. "She loved Luke. She still loves him, and he loves her." She went on to tell him of how Matthew came upon them in his bed and threw them out, divorcing Margaret on account of her adultery.

"And me?" Ian said. "What about me?"

Joan put an arm around him, drawing him close. "Matthew loved you so much, but Margaret insisted that you were hers and Luke's, not his, and Matthew feared that he might come to hate you for that, so he gave you up."

She told him how Luke had gotten Matthew convicted for treasonous royalist activities that he had never committed, and how angered he'd been when Matthew returned, alive – and with a new wife. She told him how Matthew had come upon Luke in the woods threatening Alex, and how in anger Matthew had sliced off Luke's nose. Ian gasped; he already knew this, but had never before heard how it had happened.

"Father wouldn't harm a woman!"

"You think not? He did, lad, he most certainly did." Something dark flitted over Aunt Joan's face and for some moments she was quiet, before giving him a little smile. "You've heard the rest, I reckon. How in retribution Luke had Matthew abducted and sold into slavery and Alex was obliged to go after him. Margaret helped her with money," Joan said, and Ian nodded, proud of Mam. "So now Matthew can't forgive Luke for all those years that were stolen from him, and Luke can't forgive him for having survived," she finished with a sigh.

"And how will it end?"

"I have no inkling and nor have they." She patted his cheek. "But they both love you, and that isn't a bad thing, is it?"

There was a shout from below. Alex was standing by the laundry shed, waving at Ian to come down. He made a face.

"All the time she bathes us, and it isn't enough to place us in the tub, she must oversee as well." He threw a discreet glance down at his groin.

"I dare say your Aunt Alex can handle the sight," Joan laughed. "She's used to much bigger."

Ian moved off towards the laundry shed, stopped and rushed back to hug her.

"Thank you for telling me."

"It wasn't much help, was it?" Joan smoothed his hair off his face.

Ian shrugged; at least he knew how things were, and mayhap he could someday help.

"God willing," he added and trotted off.

Next morning dawned on a day of dazzling brightness and the whole household couldn't wait to plunge through the pristine drifts of snow. Alex handed Matthew a heavily wrapped Jacob.

"Don't drop him in the snow, we might not find him again."

Matthew laughed and kissed his son. "Won't find you? Of course we will. You have a bright red cap on." Jacob pulled at the woollen cap, beaming. It even had a huge pom-pom, in blue. "A good effort," Matthew murmured to his wife. "You're getting better at it."

"Look you, you're wearing stockings I've knitted, clothes I've sewn, and your belly is full with food I've cooked. So be grateful, not sarcastic."

"Oh, I am," Matthew said, and darted outside with his children at his tail.

Halfway through the morning Jacob came back inside, snivelling and wet. His cap was askew and he garbled a long and sorry tale in which Rachel figured prominently.

"She sat on you?" Alex said, brushing the snow off him and rewrapping him in her old shawl.

Yes, Jacob nodded, and his face had been full of snow and then she had put snow down his neck.

"Right, let's go and find her, shall we? And I can hold her while you put some snow down her neck."

Jacob grinned and took her hand. They came to a standstill just outside the door and Jacob squealed at the sight of his father.

"What are you doing?" Alex eyed Matthew with interest. He had raked his hands through his hair to make it stand on end, blackened his face with what looked like soot and in his hand he carried a willow switch.

"Beware," Matthew growled, crouching back on his legs. "Beware of me. I'm the… what is it I am, lads?"

"The Balrog," Ian replied, appearing from behind a corner to pelt Matthew with a snowball.

"Aye, that's it." Matthew swung back towards his wife and leered at her. Jacob gave another squeal and buried his face against Alex' skirts. "Dangerous creature," Matthew hissed. "And now I will eat you." He pointed at Alex.

"Balrogs don't eat people, they just burn them to death," Alex laughed, backing away.

"This one definitely eats them," Matthew smacked his lips together. "A wee laddie makes for a tasty meal."

"No, no!" Jacob crawled up into Alex' arms. "Don't eat me."

"If he tries, I'll punch him, and anyway we have both Boromir and Aragorn here to beat him off. Go get him boys!"

"And me, and me!" Rachel piped up. "I'm the dwarf man, I am."

The children charged Matthew, who allowed himself to be overcome, disappearing in a flurry of snow and children. Afterwards he lay spread-eagled on the ground and complained about his aching back. Alex helped him to his feet, still laughing.

"Weakling, not all that much of a Balrog."

He tightened his grip on her hand and his eyes were so very close, the shifting green of the eddy pool in the summer when the surface was dappled with sun.

"I will eat you," he promised, his breath tickling the skin of her neck. "All night, I'll eat you."

"Words, words," Alex snorted, "I'll believe it when I see it."

He took a firm hold of her and kissed her, kissed her until she was certain she was about to die from lack of oxygen. He was still kissing her when out of the corner of her eye she saw a chestnut horse begin dancing its way down the lane towards them.

"Father!" Ian's voice squeaked up a register, and Alex froze, arms locked round her husband.

"Father, Father!" Ian had reached the horse and was hanging on to the stirrup. Luke Graham dismounted and hugged him, standing like that for a long while.

"I thought you'd forgotten me," Ian said.

"Forget my own son?" Luke sounded as unsteady as Ian. "Now why would you think I'd do that?"

Ian made an incoherent sound and rubbed his face against Luke's coat, arms tight around Luke's waist.

Matthew had gone rigid, and Alex wriggled out of his embrace to place herself in front of him, her body a shield between him and his brother. Luke released Ian and said something to him in a low voice that had Ian rushing off towards the house, before Luke turned to face Matthew. None of them said anything; there was only the barest of nods.

As tall as Matthew and with far more vivid colouring, Luke was a handsome man – even the silver prosthetic he wore in lieu of a nose enhanced rather than detracted from his looks. He was more than well-dressed, in dark velvet breeches and a matching coat, snowy linen at his throat and fur lined gloves on his hands. Over his shoulders hung a cloak that Alex eyed covetously, a lustrous grey wool lined with lamb's fleece, and here and there the sun struck silver buttons and buckles. This was a man who'd done well for himself – whether through royal patronage or actual skills was open for interpretation – but the fact remained that Sir Luke Graham cut a figure of substance and wealth far exceeding that of his elder brother.

She threw Matthew a look. In his worn breeches and shabby coat, with snow melting in his hair, soot decorating his face and damp spots on his knees, he looked a vagrant – a handsome, dishevelled hero kind of vagrant, but still. Even his Sunday best would look like peasant garb compared to what Luke was wearing – and the two silent servants looked flashier than Matthew ever could. Well; at least Matthew didn't curl his hair, she thought, taking in the deep red corkscrews that flowed over Luke's shoulders. Quite the dandy, effeminate almost.

"I see you made it through the smallpox, then," Matthew said, breaking a heavy silence.

"Aye, I imagine that makes you very happy." Luke's eyes drifted over to Alex.

She straightened up, placing a hand on her stomach, whether to protect the baby or to remind him of what he'd done to her all those years ago, she didn't really know. She shivered, blinking a couple of times to clear her head of the detailed memories of a night when Luke had lost all restraint and beaten her so badly that she'd miscarried.

Luke flushed – not at all flattering to a redhead, his skin jarring with his hair. According to Joan, Luke had expressed shame for what he'd done, but never to her or to Matthew, just as he'd never apologised for selling his brother as a slave, or for accusing him of treason, or for stealing Ian from him, or for… she broke off this train of thought. It made her angry and upset, and with Luke around one needed to keep one's cool.

He met her eyes and scratched at his silver nose. Alex suppressed an urge to spit in his face. A piece of his nose was a small price to pay for what he'd done to Matthew – to her. He broke eye contact, turning instead to Joan, who'd appeared on the door stoop with Simon at her side.

"Sister," Luke bowed.

"Brother." Joan gave him a tentative smile, but made no move to cross the few yards that separated them to greet him properly.

"What are you doing here?" Alex said. "Couldn't Margaret have come instead?" It came out very rude, but frankly, she couldn't care less. Something gleamed in Luke's green eyes, a rather smug expression settled on his face before being smoothed into a bland mask. Hmm; well, given that look Margaret wasn't ailing. She eyed her brother-in-law, turning various options over in her head. Her musings were cut abruptly short when Luke turned his full attention to Matthew.

"Hiding behind the skirts of your wife?" he jeered, and laughed when Matthew lifted Alex aside.

"I never hide from you, Luke. It's not I that club unsuspecting men into unconsciousness and have them carted onto a ship, is it? It's not I that…"

Alex gripped his arm and tilted her head in the direction of the house, where Ian had now reappeared with his few belongings. Behind him tagged Mark.

"Is that your da?" he asked Ian in a carrying whisper.

Ian nodded proudly and took Mark by the hand to lead him over to the horse.

Luke gaped; for some instants his mouth hung open before he recovered sufficiently to close it. Alex snickered, it had to come as quite a shock to see the boys together. Time and time again Luke's eyes flitted from one dark head to the other. He wet his lips, slid Matthew a look and went back to gawking at the boys – or mostly at Ian. A frown appeared on his brow, the corners of his mouth pulled downwards as his eyes travelled up and down Ian, up and down Matthew. Ian smiled, further underlining his resemblance to Matthew when a dimple appeared on his cheek. Alex studied Luke's strained, responding smile. No dimple.

Yet again Luke's eyes darted from Matthew to Ian and the look he gave the boy made Alex' stomach tighten. It's not his fault, she wanted to yell, you can't blame him for being the spitting image of the father you stole him from.

"Say your farewells," Luke said brusquely to Ian. "I want us well on our way by nightfall."

Ian hurried over to where Matthew and Alex were standing. Matthew opened his arms. Ian shuffled, clearly not sure what to do. Matthew extended his hand instead. Ian shook it and gave Alex a quick hug.

"God's speed," Matthew said. "And carry my regards to your mother, aye?"

"I will," Ian said, turning to go.

Alex stopped him with a light touch. "You're always welcome here. There's always a place in our home for you. Always, you hear?"

There was a tight set to his mouth that reminded her of Matthew when he was trying to control his feelings, so she winked at him.

"As long as you don't mind having your farting cousins in the same bed, of course."

"No leeches," Ian smiled. They both turned in the direction of Rachel.

"Well, I can't promise you that," Alex said. "God knows what she will come up with next."

Mark ran alongside the horse all the way to the top and stood for a long time waving at the receding shape of his cousin before walking down to where Matthew was standing alone now that Alex had gone inside to see to dinner.

"I'll miss him."

"Aye, so will I," Matthew said, his eyes still stuck on the spot where Ian had turned for one last wave. May the Lord keep you safe my son, he prayed. May he hold his hand over you and protect you that you grow up a good man. A small hand slipped into his and Matthew shook himself out of his thoughts, smiling down at Rachel.

"There you are lassie. Will you come help me feed the pigs?"

"Can I give them apples?" she asked, skipping beside him.

"One each, but no cake, mind."

CHAPTER 11

"I told you; we're not hiding anyone." Alex glared at the lieutenant, arms akimbo.

"And where's your husband?"

"I told you that as well," Alex sighed with exasperation. "He's in Cumnock, with our eldest son." She shifted on her feet, placing a hand on her protruding stomach. "Rachel," she snapped. "No!"

Rachel replaced the wrinkled apple and came over to join her, peeking at the soldiers from behind her mother's skirts.

"And you…" Alex moved across the kitchen to where one soldier was helping himself to her bread. "I have no recollection of offering you to partake. Thief!" she slapped at his hand, making him drop the loaf.

"Surely you won't mind offering the servants of the crown some bread?" Gower said.

"As a matter of fact I do. You poke your noses into every corner of my home on a regular basis, you push and shove at my children, you taunt my husband when he's home, and now apparently you enjoy tormenting a pregnant woman. Officers of the crown indeed! You're no credit to your master, let me tell you."

A painful grip on her arm made her wince and then she was being dragged, screaming in anger, into the cobbled yard.

"You forget your place, Mistress Graham," Lieutenant Gower said. "We're here because we know that all of you, and I mean all of you, help and abet the sworn enemies of the king. And you'll not raise your hand against one of my soldiers, nor deny him a piece of bread to still his hunger as he goes about his duty."

Alex wrested herself free. "Bully! Cowardly attacker of women. If you touch me again I'll…"

"What?" The hand was back, twisting itself into her skin. "What will you do Mrs Graham?" She slapped him hard with her free hand, noting with satisfaction how the fair skin reddened.

"Now let go of me, you lout," she said through gritted teeth. "Or I'll slap you again. Something your mother should have done when you were small to ensure you grew up respectful of women."

She gasped when he tightened his hold, swinging for him in rage. He grunted when she brought the blade of her hand down on his forearm. Right; swivel, keep hold of his arm, out with your hips, and wham! He'd fly through the air to land sprawled on the cobbles. But she had no sense of balance, not with this huge belly, and well before she'd begun to move he had clamped a second hand down on her shoulder. Alex heaved, she threw herself this way and that, but for all his slight build the lieutenant was like a tenacious badger, refusing to give an inch. There was an angry shriek and Rachel was at her side, kicking at the man who was hurting her mama.

"Tell her to stop," Gower said, "now." He cursed when Rachel's clog connected with his calf. "I'll send her flying otherwise."

"Rachel, stop. Go and mind your brother," Alex said, breathing loudly. "Go to Sarah." Rachel did as she was told, her high voice telling the lieutenant her da would belt him, aye he would, for hurting her mama. Gower laughed, tightened his grip on Alex and forced her round to face the household. Ow! Her arm!

"All of you saw this woman bear hand on me, an officer of the crown." There was a soft expectant snicker from one of the soldiers, but Gower silenced him with a look. "Twenty lashes, for opposing our work and for violence against myself and one of my men. Here. Now. "

What? The bastard was going to whip her?

"Don't you dare!" Incensed, Alex increased her efforts, ignoring the burning sensation in her arm as she twisted free of his grip. She ran. Wildly, madly, she ran for the house. He caught up with her, wrenched her to a halt, and Alex screamed, bringing her foot down on the lieutenant's toes. The slap made her reel, she staggered, both her arms were grabbed. Three men to hold her, and Alex fought like a hellcat.

"No!" Hands were tearing at her shawl. "Let me go!" Yes! One arm free. She round handed the lieutenant, there was a loosening in the hold on her left hand, she raked her nails over an unknown face. Shit! Someone kicked at her lower legs, she fell to her knees. Two hands closed on her bodice. There was a tearing sound when they ripped it off her, and Alex died with shame that she should be this undressed before them all. The lieutenant was back, his face too close to hers, and he was saying something, but she couldn't hear him, all she could hear was the loud thumping of her panicked pulse. A grip on her nape immobilised her. Someone was fumbling with the lacings on her stays, and they fell to the ground.

"No," she repeated, but it came out a whimper. Strong hands pulled her to her feet, and her breasts were visible to anyone through the worn linen of her shift. She tried to bring her arms together, shield herself, but they wouldn't let her. The lieutenant said something behind her, she heard the dull thwack of leather on leather, and then the riding crop came down on her back.

No one had ever hit her in her life before. The odd slap when she was growing up, and one very memorable slap in the early days with Matthew, but nothing like this. A sharp, slashing pain, and she hiccupped. Again, and she gulped. Aah!

"Mama! Mama!" Rachel; what the fuck was Sarah thinking of, to let her witness this? Holy Matilda! What was this? Six? Seven?

The lieutenant laughed. "Not quite as loud now, are you?" Shit! He was really enjoying this, the son of a bitch!

"Agh!" Oh God, oh God; she couldn't help it, she wailed. Number ten – or was it twelve? She bit her tongue, her mouth flooding with blood. "Stop," she begged, not caring anymore. "Please, no more."

"Twenty," Gower panted, "and one more word out of you and I'll make it twenty-five." Once again the whip came down, and Alex would have fallen if it hadn't been for the soldiers holding her upright.

"Stop!"

Yes; please stop. A flash of panic, was that Matthew? No, no, no, don't let it be Matthew, because if it is, he'll try to kill fucking Gower, and then… She gulped, raised her face. An officer was riding down the lane towards them. She squinted; a captain, followed by two men.

"This is unseemly," the captain said. "Unhand that woman now."

"She must be punished, she hit one of my men and myself," Gower said.

"Really? Why?" The captain had dismounted and was coming over to where Alex was being held.

"He took our bread," Rachel piped up. "The big man took our bread and Mama slapped him."

"Hmm," the officer said. At his look the men holding Alex let her go, and he picked up the shawl and put it over Alex' shoulders.

"I'm so sorry that this should befall you, Mrs Graham," he said. Alex recognised the voice. She turned towards him and gave him a watery smile, meeting grey eyes that she had last seen back when this was still a Commonwealth, not a Restored Kingdom.

"Captain Leslie! I'm that glad to see you." And then she burst into tears again, not so much because of the burning pain that walked up and down her back, as because of the humiliation of having been whipped, here, in her home in front of her people.

"You!" Captain Leslie waved the lieutenant over. "Get your men off this property now. And should I ever hear of your men thieving or in any way not comporting themselves as they should it will reflect badly on you."

Gower protested that they had just been doing their job, and the woman had hindered them.

"How? Did she bar your access?"

No, the lieutenant muttered, but she had berated them and then she had slapped Munro over the wrist.

"For stealing her bread."

"It was only a piece of bread," the lieutenant said.

"Her bread. Not his, so he was in fact stealing, wasn't he?"

Gower twisted, but admitted that should one be precise, well then... However, he added, drawing himself up to his full height, Mrs Graham had slapped him. And...

Leslie waved him silent. "I expect your man to be punished – for theft." As the lieutenant was leaving, Leslie stopped him. "Tell me lieutenant, did it escape your notice that Mrs Graham is heavy with child?"

"No," the lieutenant sounded sullen.

"And still you chose to whip her?" Captain Leslie's voice dripped condemnation.

It was an eternal walk to the door, even with the captain on one side and Sarah on the other. Her back; no better not think about her back, think about setting one foot before the other. Oh God it hurt! Alex blinked and blinked; don't cry, just breathe and walk.

"I've never been whipped before," Alex said, trying to smile at her saviour. "It hurts much more than I thought it would."

"I can only repeat my apologies. I can't even offer you formal redress, as many will consider Lieutenant Gower to have been in his full right to punish you. You shouldn't have slapped him, Mrs Graham, it was a foolish thing to do." He gave her an encouraging smile, grey hair falling forward to frame his face when he inclined his head towards her. "You must rest and have that back seen to. I'll set out for Cumnock to find your husband, if I can."

Alex nodded, and drew a shaky hand across her mouth. Blood, she saw, looking down at her streaked hand.

Matthew rode in a few hours later, flew up the stairs and barged into their bedchamber.

"I'll do that," he said to Sarah, who was standing with a basin of hot water, just about to wash Alex' back again. With a curtsey Sarah left the room, and Alex managed a greeting that was ignored, Matthew's hands busy uncovering her skin.

"Dearest Lord in heaven," he groaned, and from the sound of his voice Alex could imagine the state of her back.

"It isn't that bad," she said.

"He's drawn blood, misbegotten whoreson that he is!"

She could almost see the anger leaking out in puffs of steam from him.

"How many?" He traced the welts with gentle fingers, making her flinch.

"Twenty, but he stopped at twelve or something."

"Why?"

Alex didn't reply, biting back on an exclamation when he washed one of the deeper gashes. She contorted as well as she could to see the damage for herself.

"Bloody hell! Someone should do this to him, the son of a bitch."

Matthew grunted an agreement, concentrating on bandaging her.

"It will heal, right?" she said.

He pulled the shift up, turned her round to tie the drawstring, and kissed her on the nose.

"Of course it will," he said, helping her to lie down on her side. "So why?" he repeated, stroking her face.

"One of the soldiers took my bread and it made me mad." She broke off, fearing that he'd tell her this was her fault for not curbing her tongue, but he sat silent. "It sort of bubbled out, all the anger at them for charging through my home, fingering my food stuffs, drinking my beer…" Alex sighed and sat up, wincing when the skin stretched across the welts. "I sometimes forget that this is a time where the little people have no voice, where the representatives of the crown can do as they please and there's no venue of recourse. In my time I could sue the damned lieutenant for undue violence and he'd be sent down for years." She leaned her forehead against his shoulder. "Here all I can do is shut up and bear it. And I'm not that good at shutting up, am I?"

"Nay, my heart, that you're not." He rarely used endearments and Alex looked at him in surprise, meeting eyes that were soft and golden in the candlelight. "You know you are; my life, my heart."

"Yes, I do," she smiled, "just like you are mine."

He watched her like an overprotective hawk over the coming days, a hot, throbbing heat rising through his gullet every time he saw her wince or stop midway through a movement. The wee lieutenant was going to pay, he promised himself, and even more for the fear he saw in her eyes whenever something moved down the lane.

"I'm going for a walk," she said one day. "Want to come?" She gave him a little smile. "I... well, I don't like going about on my own, and it's such a nice day, isn't it?"

Matthew nodded and took her hand, swinging it back and forth. Early February and spring was already more than a promise. Tight buds swelled daily, and under their feet the nodding heads of snowdrops stuck perkily through last year's dead leaves. Soon the whole slope would be carpeted in windflowers, converting the present russet into drifts of white and green. Alex kicked at the leaves, sending them flying in sprays of brown and red, and kicked them again, hands raised as it to catch them when they fluttered back towards the ground. She bent and snapped off a snowdrop.

"Here," she said and curtsied, making him smile and bow.

"Do you think the Williams are alright?" Alex asked when they came out of the woods to stand facing the undulating moss.

"Alright? I don't think they're alright – but hopefully they're still alive." Matthew stared off towards the north. "He's branded an outlaw and all his worldly goods are forfeit, taken as payment of the levied fine." He had seen them leave; together with Tom Brown and some other local farmers he'd ridden deep into the moss and beyond to see them on their way.

To watch Davy Williams take farewell of his farm was one of the most heartrending things Matthew had ever had to witness, the man stooping to caress every stone, every plank of wood. For six generations his family had held on to the farm and now it was lost to them, forever. Mrs Williams hadn't said a word. She had hoisted stunned children to sit behind the riders, hefted tight bundles into waiting hands and then sat up behind Matthew. She'd hid her face against his back and sat like that all the way, refusing to watch as her world disappeared behind her.

"Sandy is branded an outlaw as well," he told her after some moments. "And in his case it isn't only his worldly goods but also his life that is forfeit."

"Have you seen him recently?"

He smiled at her casual tone. As long as he didn't put his family at risk by harbouring Sandy at Hillview, Alex was attempting to maintain a neutral approach to his continued support for the Covenanter cause.

"Aye I have. There's a cave where he occasionally stays, and I've spoken to him there." And a damp horrid place it was, especially as Sandy didn't dare to light a fire in case the smoke would attract unwanted attention.

"How is his cough?"

"Bad." He slipped his arm round her waist. "I want him to baptise the wean." He could see she was about to protest, her brows knitting together into a faint frown, but he held her eyes until she looked away.

"In the summer, on the fell somewhere," was all she said.

Matthew drew her even closer. He wondered if she noticed that change in herself as much as he did, but decided not to tell her that he very much liked the fact that she – at times, at least – was a most obedient wife, allowing him to lead so that she could follow.

Matthew was cautiously pleased when Captain Leslie appeared a few days later, ostensibly to inquire as to Alex' health, and after several minutes of careful overtures

Matthew relaxed in his company. After all, Captain Leslie was once a Commonwealth soldier like himself, called to ride south with General Monck in the autumn of 1659 after the collapse of parliamentary government.

They spent some hours reminiscing the battles of the Civil War, with Matthew recalling in far too much detail the massacre in the aftermath of Philiphaugh.

"I was just a lad, fifteen, and I thought war was about glory and bravery, only to find it was about fear and mud and blood – so much blood. And then they turned their swords on the innocent Irish and all I could do was watch as women and children were put to the sword. On the orders of your namesake."

"No more than that," Captain Leslie said. "And wasn't it a Graham that was defeated there?"

"Aye, James Graham, the Marquis of Montrose – not family." They shared a silent smile, sizing each other up. Last time they met, Thomas Leslie had been the commander of the small garrison in Cumnock and had in fact had Matthew hauled into custody due to his purported royalist leanings. But since that inauspicious start there had been other meetings, an odd shared tankard of beer before Leslie rode off down south, and a tentative liking had sprung up between them.

"Is it difficult?" Matthew asked, stretching to pour another tot of whisky into Leslie's pewter cup.

"Is what difficult?" Leslie sat back, sniffing with pleasure at the liquor.

"Serving the king and balancing it with your convictions," Matthew said, genuinely curious. Captain Leslie sat back, brows furrowed. He threw a look in the direction of Alex, sitting as close as she could to the candle with a shirt she was mending, and studied the cup in his hand, twisting it round and round.

"It's untenable, but I have a family to protect and support." Leslie tapped a forefinger against the table and exhaled loudly. "The principles and ideals we fought for are dead, they lie ground to dust under the feet of his returning majesty, the king, my master." He bowed ironically, making Alex laugh. "And increasingly it becomes more difficult to stand outside the accepted church. My children are vilified, my wife is shunned by the other women in our little village and yet she bears it all in silence, for my sake. My commanding officers regard me with mistrust and the younger men sigh when they are asked to serve with me. But so far I've not done anything wrong, and having been part of General Monck's closer circle still helps – but not for much longer, I fear."

"So what will you do?" Alex asked, making Leslie turn towards her.

"Do?"

"You say yourself that this won't work for much longer, right?"

Matthew smiled into his cup; Leslie was somewhat taken aback by Alex' frankness.

"My brother left six years ago," Leslie said. "For the Colony of Maryland. He writes that it's a fair land, rich and bountiful and of climes similar to ours – at least where he is, in the high country. I'm thinking of following in his footsteps." He held out his cup for a refill and gulped it down. "But once I leave I can never return, and that thought freezes my heart." He shook himself, like a large dog coming in from the rain and smiled at his host. "My brother says freedom lies to the west. It certainly doesn't lie here."

"He's right, you know," Alex told Matthew later that night. Captain Leslie had been convinced to stay the night and his loud snores penetrated both walls and doors.

"Right about what?" Matthew yawned.

"About freedom lying to the west. Maryland, Virginia and Massachusetts will be the cornerstones of the first nation ever to be ruled by free men. No king, just an elected body of men." She gingerly laid down on her back and looked at him. "Not for another century or so, but still."

Matthew yawned again and snuggled up to her, pillowing his head on her shoulder.

"Are you saying we should go there?"

"What would I possibly know? I'm just the wife, right? Such decisions are best left to the men."

He laughed at her sarcasm. "I asked you. Do you think we should go?"

"Not unless we absolutely have to. It isn't exactly an easy life to colonise a new country, is it?"

Matthew propped himself up and looked at her. "I belong here."

"I know you do, and so do I. But things change, and it might make sense to be prepared for that."

Matthew shook his head. "This is my home. We stay."

CHAPTER 12

"Go to Edinburgh? Now?" Alex gave Matthew a sceptical look. "In the middle of the spring planting?"

"Aye, there are things I must see to, urgently, and I need Simon's help."

"Why?" Alex could only think of one truly urgent matter. "Is it Luke? Has he made claims on Hillview on behalf of Ian?" That would explain why Matthew had looked so grim of late.

"No, no," Matthew said. "Nowt like that."

Alex gave him an assessing look. He didn't seem to be lying, but something had him looking tense – and mulish. She sighed. At times this man of hers had a tendency to resemble one of those crags that littered his homeland.

"And what about me?"

Matthew gave her a bewildered look. "What about you? You stay at home. You can't be riding about in your state, can you?"

"I gather that, I was rather referring to the fact that it leaves me somewhat alone, unprotected."

"Oh that," Matthew said. "Well, Captain Leslie has promised to ensure you're kept safe."

Alex became even more suspicious; very well planned, all this.

"I'll be back within a week or so, and you'll run the lads ragged. The barley fields must be turned and planted and the oat fields as well, and you must…"

"Go," she said. "Either we manage or we don't, but let's not forget who decided he had urgent legal matters to attend to all of a sudden."

He kissed her before settling himself on Ham. "And you," he said to Mark, "you're responsible for your mama. If she misbehaves you must spank her."

He laughed all the way up the lane. At the top he held in his horse and raised his hat in salute. Moments later he was gone.

Alex sighed, making mental lists of everything that had to be done. The accounts, the planting, the laundry…

"Bloody man, I bet he just felt like a break from all this." Sometimes she did as well; there were days when the sheer drudgery of this existence made her want to scream. Never a day that could be spent lazing about in bed, no fast food options, no dry cleaners, no hairdressers… She went into a long daydream involving manicures and pedicures and hours flipping through back issues of *Hello!* while someone else washed and cut her hair. Rachel's insistent tugging brought her abruptly back to the here and now.

"Sarah's crying, she fell in the kitchen."

Great, this meant she'd have to do it all herself. In her present mood she almost suspected Sarah of falling on purpose, but given that the young woman was white with pain, Alex discarded that notion. Once Sarah's arm was bandaged Alex set off towards the kitchen garden, trailed by her three children. She made a face at the as yet unturned beds; this was going to take ages!

"Mama?" Mark hesitated at the bedroom door. Matthew was strict on this being his and Alex' private space, and only rarely were the children invited in. To begin with, Alex had considered this harsh, but in a life so lacking in privacy she had come to understand and agree with Matthew's view, relishing the moment each evening when she could retire to be with him, only with him.

"Yes?" Alex beckoned him inside and continued with what she was doing, rubbing her hands with oil. Definitely necessary after her efforts in the garden.

"What happened to Da's back?"

She slowed her hands, twisting her fingers together. "What do you mean?" Matthew was sensitive about his broken skin, and the only time his children saw him naked was in summer, when the whole family would wash and swim in the little eddy pool. As the children had always seen him looking the way he did, they had never commented or even expressed curiosity about what might have happened to him. Until now.

"I saw…" Mark bit his lip. "When we were in Cumnock there was a man there." It all came out in a rush, how there'd been a man in the pillory and how his back had been bared so that everyone should see he had once been flogged, a sure sign, according to the loud soldier standing by the pillory, of having committed a gruesome crime.

"Da's been flogged, hasn't he?" Mark said in a small voice. "I've seen his back when we go swimming in the summer, but I never knew why it looked the way it did. Not until I saw the man in Cumnock."

"So now you're wondering what gruesome crime your father has committed."

Mark inclined his head in unhappy agreement.

"It's really your da's place to tell you this, and you should ask him to tell you the whole story. All I can tell you is that your father was convicted of a crime he hadn't committed and was sent to gaol for it. And being Matthew Graham, he didn't like that much, especially as he was innocent, so he was angry and loud and fought with the guards. They beat him, several times." She kissed her son and stood up. "So yes; your father has been flogged, but he's never committed a crime. Appearances aren't always what they seem, and it's a foolish man who judges people based on that alone. Remember that, honey. Now; back to bed, young man, okay?"

"Okay," Mark smiled up at her before hugging her around her expanding middle. "Goodnight, baby brother," he said, kissing the bump.

"Brother? Be careful, it might be a sister, you know."

Mark shook his head. "Da says it's a lad."

"Oh, and he would know?" Alex muttered, smiling at her son's bemused expression that indicated that of course Da knew – he knew everything.

Not much further away from home than a few miles, Matthew shared the food Alex had packed for him with Sandy.

"I just have to," Matthew shrugged.

"It's wrong," Sandy said, "and it's a huge risk, Matthew."

"I know." Matthew sat back against the damp wall of the little cave and stretched out his legs before him. "He's a nasty piece of works, and to whip a woman – pregnant at that – no, he needs a lesson."

"Hmm," Sandy voiced. "So how?"

"He's very predictable in his habits, and on Sundays, after evensong, Lieutenant Gower visits one of the working lasses – the redhead."

"Jennifer," Sandy nodded.

"You know her?" Matthew threw him a cautious look. Well, mayhap not to wonder at, even a minister must at times fall prey to the calls of the flesh.

Sandy raised his brows. "Not carnally, but aye, I know Jennifer – she's my third cousin on my mother's side." He scratched at his hair, giving Matthew a sidelong look. "Will she be at risk?"

Matthew shook his head. No, he planned on abducting the officer in the small close leading to Jennifer's room. A dark and smelly place it was, shunned by anyone not having a specific errand there.

"And if someone sees you? It's not as if you're inconspicuous." Sandy's eyes travelled over Matthew.

"I'll be in disguise." With a flourish, Matthew produced a most amazing creation.

"What in God's name is that?" Sandy said.

"A hairpiece." Matthew grinned and settled something made mostly of hen's feathers on his head. "With a hat on top and in the dark it looks verily like hair, don't you think?"

"Nay, that it does not. But neither does it look like you."

Matthew shifted on his feet. More than an hour sitting hidden in the cooper's yard had his legs cramping. It was dark, thank the Lord, dark and overcast, a chilly drizzle keeping all but the most tenacious indoors. He'd heard the church bells a while ago, and he was beginning to worry that

Gower might decide to forego sweet Jennifer, opting instead for mulled wine and pie down at the Merkat Cross Inn. He muttered a curse, adjusting his hat to keep as much of his face dry as possible. There. Bold as brass came the lieutenant, a swagger to his step as he turned into the close. He carried a lantern in his right hand, making Matthew snicker. Fool; did he perchance hope to pull his sword with his left hand, should he need it?

Matthew rose from behind the barrels and crept along the wall. So close, close enough to see the other man's exhalations despite the darkness of the night. He tightened his hold on the bludgeon. Not yet, not yet... now!

So easy; a swift clip to the head, and the lieutenant folded together. Matthew bundled him in an old cloak and stowed the unconscious man in a barrow. He picked his way through town, keeping to the shadows as much as he could.

"Who goes there?"

Matthew near on leapt out of his boots. A young voice, squeaky with fear, and out of the corner of his eye Matthew saw a soldier approaching, a mere lad no more. He didn't wait. Down one close, into an another, the iron banded wheel of the barrow clattering over the cobbles.

"Halt! I say, halt!" Heavy footsteps behind him, and Matthew increased his speed. A swerve to the right, another to the left, and Matthew rushed for the graveyard and the protective shadow of the kirk. He pressed himself to a wall and clapped a hand to his mouth to muffle his breathing. The barrow groaned. Dear God! Matthew clobbered the bundled lieutenant. Once, twice, and the shape collapsed.

"Come forth," the young voice called. "Come forth or I shoot."

At what, you daftie? At shades in the night? Matthew remained where he was, counting seconds. After what seemed an eternity he head the soldier move off, booted feet near on running over the cobbled ground as he hastened to distance himself from something he no doubt feared was a restless wraith. It took several minutes for Matthew to regain enough courage to rush the few hundred yards separating him from his horse.

Ham nickered in greeting, dancing about when Matthew slung the lieutenant over his back.

"Be still, aye?" A foot in the stirrup, astride, and off they went. Matthew tore the contraption of hen feathers from his head, suppressed an urge to whoop and urged Ham on.

A dog barked, another fell in, and Matthew swore, halting Ham so abruptly the horse skidded on his hooves. Horses, several horses coming fast, and for an instant Matthew was certain they'd seen him, but the mounted soldiers galloped by, and the bundle that was Lieutenant Gower squirmed frantically, muted sounds escaping the gag.

"Be quiet," Matthew hissed, but that only made the man increase his efforts, so Matthew hit him over the head again.

"I'm an officer of the crown," the lieutenant bleated an hour later. He was standing in only his shirt and breeches, hands tied behind his back and a noose fitted around his neck.

"I don't hold with kings," Matthew replied.

"This is murder!" the officer tried, filling his lungs as if to scream. The air was expelled in a rush when Matthew's fist drove into his stomach.

"Retribution, not murder."

"Oh God; I'm sorry for hitting her! Please... I won't tell, I promise I won't! I'll leave, yes; I'll resign my commission, but please, please..." Too late for all that; they both knew it. "Please..."

Matthew just shook his head, gagged the man and heaved him up.

"For my wife, aye?"

The officer, for obvious reasons, didn't reply; he gargled.

"There," Alex said a couple of days later, smiling at Janey. "All done."

She sank down on the bench outside the laundry shed and regarded the laden clothes lines. Item after item had been ticked off on her list, and now there was only the weekly baking to be done plus all the mending. Not today, she decided, today she was going to treat herself and the children to a long evening in the laundry shed with warm water in the bath and perhaps a story or two, while she dried them and untangled their hair. Rachel plunked down on the bench beside her, scrubbing her head against Alex' arm.

"The pig ate her babies again. She just bit them in two and swallowed them."

"Horrible mother," Alex said. "Did she eat them all?" She beckoned Jacob over, wet her finger and rubbed at a streak of dirt on his nose.

"No," Rachel held up four fingers.

"She ate four or are there only four left?"

"Four left." Rachel opened her mouth wide and made a chomping motion. "Like that, aye? One bite and then they're dead."

"I see, I wanna see," Jacob said, taking his sister's hand.

Rachel set off towards the stables, explaining over and over again that pig mothers ate their babies but human mothers mostly didn't. Alex laughed at the worried look Jacob threw her over his shoulder, turned her nose up in the general direction of the March sun, and closed her eyes. Peace and quiet, at last. The thickets further up the slope were alive with birds, their monotone winter chatter transformed into a carpet of song, and Alex relaxed further, sinking closer and closer to sleep.

"Mistress?" Janey's voice was urgent and Alex opened her eyes to see a line of soldiers riding towards her. What she really wanted to do was to leap to her feet and hurry inside, slam the door in their faces and not come out until they'd left. Instead she braced her hands against her knees and got to her feet to face them.

"Now what?" Sweat broke out along her spine, at the back of her knees and in her elbow creases. She grabbed a broom for support.

"Mistress Graham?"

Alex nodded warily.

"Captain Howard, at your service. Is your husband at home?" the officer sounded only mildly interested, scanning the well-tended fields, the yard and the soft grey stone of the house.

"No, he's not."

The brown eyes sharpened with interest, bearing down on her. "No? And where is he, if I may ask?"

None of your effing business, is it? But Alex opted for being less provocative.

"He's in Edinburgh, he's been gone for the last four days or so."

The little gleam of interest faded as quickly as it had come.

"So he was not home two nights hence?"

"No, he left already on the Saturday."

The officer looked away, beyond the house and up the wooded slope behind it.

"A fair little place," he said.

"Thank you."

"Reminds me of my home," the officer continued. "Or rather of what was my childhood home, before the Commonwealth troops burnt it to the ground."

"Oh," Alex said. "Long ago?"

"Eighteen years come June, and not a night when I don't relive that day in my dreams."

Alex had no idea what to say, disturbed by the viciousness of his tone.

"Am I to give him a message?" Alex asked as they turned to leave.

The officer shook his head. "No, there's no need. We'll be riding by next week." He held in his horse and looked down at her. "It might interest you to know Lieutenant Gower is dead – murdered."

Alex had no idea how she remained standing, fingers clenching tight around the broom.

"Dead?" she squeaked.

"Very," the captain said and clucked his horse into a trot.

She didn't move for ages. Well, she couldn't, what with how her left knee had gone all wobbly.

"What have you done, Matthew Graham?" Alex whispered, hanging on to the broom for dear life. "What in the world have you done?" Never committed a crime in his life, she'd told his son the other day, and now… She swallowed and swallowed, and she could hear the strange noises her breath made when it hitched and caught in her drying windpipe. Dragging the broom behind her, she set off for the fields.

"Samuel!" She beckoned the old man over and explained what she wanted him to do. "But be careful in how you ask things, alright?"

Samuel promised he would, saddled up the roan mare and was gone within the hour, returning just as dusk began to shift into night.

"What?" Alex grabbed at his stirrup. "What did you find out?"

"He was hanged, they say he was hanged from the crossroad oak." Samuel dismounted and looked at her with weary eyes. "They think it's Williams that did it."

Yes, of course it was; Alex weakened with relief. Williams had decided to avenge himself on the man that had stolen his life from him.

"But it can't be," Samuel went on in a flat voice. "On account of Williams being dead."

"He is?" Alex said.

"Aye, I heard it from my cousin. How Williams and his eldest bairn died out there, sickening with fever. He's been dead for some weeks."

"Oh, but that's awful!" Alex felt like crying. Poor Mrs Williams, left alone with four children. How could she possibly keep them alive? Samuel made a concurring sound, tut-tutting at this sad state of affairs.

"But if it wasn't Williams, then who?" Alex twisted her hands together. A quick shared look with Samuel and Alex could see her own suspicions mirrored in the old man's eyes. "He's in Edinburgh, he's not here."

"Aye," Samuel said, sounding unconvinced. "There are many men with grievances against the lieutenant, and Williams had extensive kin in the area." He shrugged. "We'll never know, and nor will they. But it'll become that much worse now that one of theirs has been killed." He nodded in her direction and led the horse off towards the stables. Alex stood for a long time in the dark before going back inside.

They were waiting for Matthew when he rode down the road some days later in the company of Simon. The officer nudged his horse across the road and went on to explain that there had been an unfortunate incident in the area, a murder no less, and that they had questions to pose.

"Murder?" Matthew adopted a horrified tone. "Murder of whom? My wife?"

The captain hastened to assure him that no, as far as he was aware Mr Graham's family was hale, or had been, last he saw them a few days ago.

"No, it's the murder of a servant of the crown," Captain Howard went on. "A Lieutenant Gower. You knew the man, I hear."

Matthew looked at him calmly and inclined his head in affirmation.

"Aye, I did and I won't pretend that I'm distressed by his death. He mistreated my wife some weeks back."

"Yes, I heard," the officer said. "Brought it down on herself, didn't she?"

"That's a matter of opinion," Matthew snapped.

The captain hitched his shoulders. "It does make you a most probable suspect, Mr Graham."

"Me?" Matthew injected his voice with as much incredulity he could muster. "I've been in Edinburgh."

"Aye," Simon said. "We've had deeds drawn up and witnessed a few days back."

"And you set off on Saturday?" Captain Howard said. Matthew could see him count days; Two, three days to ride to Edinburgh, some days to conduct business and three days back. The officer pulled at his lip and frowned at Ham. "A good horse – even very good; but somewhat winded at the moment."

"Cough," Matthew sighed.

"Ah," the officer nodded, did some more lip pulling. "A horse matching yours was seen the night Gower died."

Matthew looked at Ham, let his eyes travel over the officer's horse, two other horses in the troop and then back to the officer's brown gelding.

"A dark bay horse?" he said sarcastically. "Besides, my brother-in-law can vouch for me being in Edinburgh." Howard continued to block his way, looking at him with suspicion. "If you'd excuse me, I wish to hasten home."

The captain backed his horse and waved his hand to indicate the road was free. Matthew bowed and dug his heels in, making the horse snort before it bunched its legs and took off in huge strides.

It took some time for Matthew to regain control over himself. It had been an inhuman effort to maintain that outward calm while facing the inspecting eyes of the officer, and he wondered at himself for having been able to keep his hands steady on the reins. Now all of him trembled, and in the pit of his stomach a viper flung itself from side to side, forcing what little food he'd eaten today back up his gullet to block his throat. He'd killed a man, an officer no less, and should he ever be caught he wouldn't only be hanged, he'd be disembowelled and beheaded as well.

"You're sailing very close to the abyss," Simon said once he caught up with Matthew. "What in God's name have you done?"

Matthew didn't reply. The last week had been a race against time, with Ham pressed to his limit when Matthew stormed off in the direction of Edinburgh just before midnight on Sunday instead of early Saturday morning when he officially set off. But it had been worth it, he thought, shocking himself. A life taken in payment for Williams and the minister, for the petty cruelties that coloured all his neighbours' days, but most of all for Alex, for the blood-red welts on the pale skin of her back.

"Matthew?" Simon said. "You haven't been fully honest with me have you?"

"Nay, I haven't," Matthew said. "Will you still stand by me?" he asked, once he had finished retelling the events.

Simon closed his eyes in exasperation. "It's too late to ask now."

Matthew was very ashamed, dropping his head.

"And what will Alex say?" Simon said.

Matthew straightened up. "You won't breathe a word of this to Alex, never, you hear?"

Simon swore that he wouldn't. "But you must tell her. You can't keep something like this from her."

"Aye," Matthew said. "But I'll choose the when and the where with caution. And it isn't now."

Except that there was no way Matthew could evade the bright blue of Alex' eyes, scorching their way into his soul; she knew him better than he knew himself, and when she followed him across the yard into the stable he knew it wouldn't be him choosing anything, it would be her. So he took her by the hand and helped her up the ladder to the hayloft and there he sat with her on his lap and told her how Gower died. She didn't say anything once he had finished, leaning back against his chest.

"No one," she finally said. "We'll tell no one. And we'll never talk of it again."

"Never," he agreed.

CHAPTER 13

"Daniel Elijah?" Alex looked down at the wean. "Two very solemn names, don't you think? It makes him sound very religious."

"Good," Matthew said, caressing the downy head of this his latest bairn. "Quite appropriate for a future minister."

"A minister?" Alex raised a brow.

"Aye, a man of the church." Matthew had problems keeping a straight face at her dumbfounded expression.

"But what if he doesn't want to?"

"We'll make him want it." Matthew scooted closer, eyes on his nursing son. It was still a miracle to him that something so small could be so determined when it came to food. "Both of us," he added, ignoring Alex' frown.

He waited until his son had finished feeding before taking him from his mother, holding the wean in the crook of his arm.

"A wee lad, hmm?" he crooned. "Look at you, all rosy and glowing with health."

"What will the others be?" She sounded put out, clearly not taken by the notion that he should decide what direction his sons' lives would take.

He smiled. "Mark will be a farmer, and this wee one will be a minister."

"And Jacob?"

Matthew shrugged. Jacob could be so many things; strong and placid and with a good head on his shoulders, Jacob would make his own way in the world.

"Jacob? Ah, well Jacob will be happy."

"And the others won't," Alex muttered.

"Aye they will."

"And Rachel?"

Matthew rolled his eyes and made a choking sound that had Alex bursting out in laughter.

"Rachel will be a wife. God help her future husband."

May; wooded slopes clad in bright new greens, drifts of bluebells and windflowers covering the ground, the trees in the apple orchard heavy with flower and sitting there, in the shade, his wife and his newest child. Matthew remained where he was, watching how she lifted Daniel from her breast to settle him in his basket. She smiled in the direction of Jacob and Rachel, playing among the trees, and he was filled with a sensation of deep contentment. His world, his family, a small corner of paradise that belonged to him – made possible by the woman who now raised her hand in a wave. Three sons and one madcap daughter in a bit more than six years, and there would be many more, for she was healthy and fertile and both of them were still calf-sick with lust for each other.

"Here," Matthew extended the small posy of flowers he had picked.

"For me?" She looked pleased.

"Aye," he said, dropping down beside her. "Seeing as I couldn't find my honey-haired mistress." Now what had made him say something as foolish as that? She gave him a chilly look, and he felt a familiar rush of shame at the memory of Kate Jones, with her dark eyes and hair the exact shade of honey. But he'd only bedded her because he was ill and afraid he would die, all those years ago in Virginia.

"I…" he said.

"I know," she cut him off, leaning back against him. "I had a bad dream last night."

"Och, aye?" Matthew found a long stalk of grass and began nibbling at the soft, pale end. Alex settled into him and yawned.

"About Magnus; he looked awful, his head shaved, and all of him sort of shrunk together…" Her voice trailed off. "I think he's ill." She gnawed at her lip, looking quite concerned. "He's too young, not yet sixty-four."

"We can't do much for him from here," Matthew said, "and three score four is an impressive age."

"You think?"

"My da died before the age of fifty," Matthew reminded her.

Alex made an irritated sound. "Yeah; he drowned – not exactly due to old age, was it?"

"He's still dead. And besides, it's just a dream, not necessarily true."

"It's ages since I dreamt of them," Alex said, "and I almost never think of them. Not of Magnus, not of my little Isaac; slowly but safely it's all becoming a fairy tale."

"Aye, of course it is. This is your life, you belong here with me and our bairns."

"But I used to belong there."

Matthew grunted, as always uncomfortable discussing the more disconcerting aspects of his wife's life. He shifted to lie on his back, one hand on her, the other on the rim of the baby basket. Alex fiddled with his shirt, patted at his stomach, his thighs. He stretched, enjoying these slow caresses.

"Do I look old?"

He raised his head to look at her, sitting beside him. Old? His Alex? He bit back a smile. Of course she had aged since the first time he saw her, and four bairns had not slid unnoticed from between her thighs, leaving her somewhat more rounded in hips and arse. He doubted she'd fit into those odd breeches – jeans, was it? – of hers today, but to him the overall impression was more pleasing, softer somehow. He peeked at her chest; two round and shapely breasts peeked back as well as they could through linen and bodice. He lifted his hand and gave the closest one an appreciative little squeeze.

"You look lovely," he smiled, very satisfied with his little sidestep.

"But do I look old?"

"Nay, that you don't, you look younger than Joan, even than Rosie." That pleased her, he could see – Rosie was eight years her junior.

"See? Diet is important – and hygiene."

"Aye, we all know that," Matthew teased. "Teeth cleaned morning and night, baths once a week." He looked at her hopefully. "You might need some help later, no? With your oils." She all naked, the whole room suffused by the concentrated scent of lavender, his hands exploring a body he could never get enough of.

She laughed and leaned over to kiss him. "You have a dirty mind, Mr Graham, and let me remind you our son is not yet three weeks old." Her eyes were very close to his. "But I wouldn't mind some help with my oils."

"Nay; I didn't think you would."

Next morning Alex woke alone, a damp baby fretting in his basket. Daniel made small demanding sounds and Alex staggered to her feet, wondering where Matthew might be. She made a small face when she recalled it was Sunday. He'd be down in his study choosing Bible texts for today. Probably a passage she'd never heard of before, making him sigh and tell her he expected her to study it during the week. She hated it when he did that, and in protest she generally didn't read the texts, which led to some heated arguments along the lines that she, as his wife and mother of his children, must know the Holy Book well enough to impart it to the new generation.

"I can do the Old Testament part," she'd offered, "at least the general lines of it." General lines were not good enough, and now Alex was constantly being quizzed about Job and Moses, and Joshua and who was Jezebel and Ahab, leaving her head spinning as over and over again she had to admit her ignorance.

"Let's just hope no one throws you into the lion's pit," she muttered to Daniel and offered him her breast. For an instant it hurt, and then both she and baby relaxed as Daniel set himself to the important task of nursing. Alex yawned. She'd had a restless night, dreaming the same dream over and over again. Always Magnus, eyes as blue as her own dulled with pain, his long, tall frame decimated to a beanpole. He's dying, she gulped, soon he'll be dead and I'll never see him again. And despite it all she laughed – very shakily, but still. To Magnus it was the other way around; she was dead, had been drifting dust in the wind for centuries before Magnus was even born.

Very rarely did she dream of her lost life; to do so two nights in a row seemed something of an augury, and she spent the coming half-hour thinking about what might be ailing Magnus. Daniel coughed, recalling her to the here and now, and it was with some relief that she banished these thoughts of lost people in a lost future.

"Where's your da?" Alex asked Mark over breakfast, shaking her head in a silent no when Rachel stretched for the third time in the direction of the honey pot.

"I don't know, I thought he was still in bed."

Alex pursed her lips and after wrapping Daniel in his shawl went to look for her husband. In the study his Bible lay open and Alex scanned the text, smiling when she realised this was in fact a book she did know, the book of Ruth. But of Matthew there was no sign, not in the house, nor anywhere else. This was not like him, and Alex' mouth contracted into something the size of a prune as she tried to understand what this might mean. She went down to the meadows and studied the horses, but they were all there, grazing under the stand of alders that bordered the little river.

"Have you seen the master?" Alex asked Gavin, who straightened up from his contemplation of absolutely nothing. "Have you?" Alex repeated, eyes tightening when Gavin went bright red. "Gavin, I just want to know he's alright. So have you seen him?"

Gavin twisted and admitted that he had, very early, setting off in the direction of the hill. The hill... Alex looked up towards its bare head. Beyond it lay the rolling moss and with a sickening jolt in her stomach she understood where he'd gone. It was Sunday, and now that spring was here arranging a hidden prayer meeting was so much easier. But there were still dragoons all over the place, even if being on horseback was a doubtful advantage over some of the rougher patches of the moor. Alex tightened her grip on Daniel as she stared at the spot where, God willing, her husband would reappear live and well before the day was done.

Each hour was an eternity. Alex started at every sound, she sat on the bench outside the kitchen door with her eyes peeled, alternating between looking up the lane and up the slope. A glorious, warm Sunday, and she couldn't enjoy one minute of it, hating it that time crawled by as slowly as a snail in treacle. Lapwings wheeled unsteadily over the closest fields, the resident kingfisher darted by in a flurry of orange and blue, but Alex wasn't in the mood for ornithology. Morning, dinner, a long, long afternoon, and when the shadows began to lengthen she couldn't stand it any longer. With Daniel in his shawl she set off up the wooded slopes.

Alex was sweaty with exertion by the time she made it to the top of the hill. The May twilight lay purple around her and she turned to look down at her home. It all looked so peaceful, cows in the meadow, the goats bleating in their enclosure. A shriek cut through the silence, and Alex smiled in exasperation when something small pelted across the farm yard, shadowed by a larger shape. Mark out to discipline his sister, and once he caught up with her there were a number of yelps that indicated he had gotten his own back. She turned towards the moor. The air was pungent with the scent of new grass, of wild garlic and the nutty scent of the bright yellow gorse that criss-crossed the moss – deceptively beautiful at a distance, horribly thorny if you got too close.

Daniel squirmed against her chest, and Alex hefted him closer, rocking him. Matthew should be back by now, and her eyes scanned the empty expanse, trying to see something, anything, that indicated he was safe and well and making his way back to her and his home. In the falling dusk the rolling moss darkened, soft mists rising from the damp ground like floating veils. When the horses appeared out of nowhere, disembodied in the shifting light, she plunged to hide below the trees.

"Thank you. God's speed on you."

Alex recognised Matthew's voice, but remained where she was until she heard him rustling through the grass. He jumped at the sight of her.

"Alex! Why are you here?"

"Why do you think? Because I fancied a walk?" She gave him an angry look. "Where have you been?"

"You know where I've been, and I told you that I'd still continue to go when I could."

"You could've been arrested! How can you take that risk?" She put both her hands at her waist and glared at him.

"We knew what we were doing. It would be hard going for a troop of dragoons across the gorse."

"You came back by horse."

"Aye, for the last part." Matthew slipped an arm around her and drew her close. "I just had to," he said, leaning his head against hers. "I have a need of it, to hear the words of God." He used his free hand to open up a window in her shawl, and smiled down at his sleeping son, placing a long finger on the little button nose.

"Sandy will be here in three days, to christen the wean."

"As long as he comes nowhere close to the house," Alex said, stepping out of his embrace.

Matthew's jaw tightened. "He's my friend, my preacher. I'll not have you talk of him as if he were vermin."

Alex sighed. "First and foremost he's a risk; to you, to me."

He strode off down the hill and left her to follow as best as she could.

CHAPTER 14

Captain Leslie came by late in August to make his farewells, and from the eager light in his grey eyes Alex could see he had made up his mind.

"Yes," Thomas Leslie said. "I've resigned my commission and am presently selling off my worldly goods, one by one. We will set out in March of the coming year." He rolled his eyes. "So much to purchase and pack; utensils, tools, a plough for my brother, clothes and bolts of fabric to make new ones..." He smiled at the fat baby in Matthew's arms and tweaked its cheek. "You are fortunate in your children, all so healthy and strong."

"Aye." Matthew bounced Daniel on his knee. "I have a good, fertile wife."

Alex snorted, making him cast her a look. "It makes me sound like a mare – or a cow," she said, suppressing a grin at his worried expression.

"You know I don't mean it like that."

Alex just smiled, catching an admiring look from Thomas Leslie. She liked Thomas, would miss him once he was gone, even if now and then he gawked a bit too openly at her – more out of respectful admiration than lust.

"What does your wife think about all this?" Alex asked, putting away her sewing. "It must be difficult for her to uproot herself and your family."

Thomas cleared his throat and drank some of his beer. "Think? Well, I assume she trusts that I've made the right decision." He smoothed back his hair and fussed with the narrow collar that adorned his grey coat. A monochrome man, was Thomas Leslie, rarely sporting anything but grey. Maybe he was colour-blind.

"Of course," Alex said, "but you must have discussed it with her first, right?"

Leslie regarded her cautiously. "Not really, Mary leaves all such matters to me." As she should, his tone implied.

"Your wife and I must be very different," Alex commented, making Matthew choke on his drink. "If my husband were to take a decision of that magnitude over my head, I would probably be tempted to do him grave harm. Castration comes to mind." She smiled sweetly in the direction of Matthew.

"Well, my dear, I assure you my wife and you are most dissimilar."

"Fortunately. For you I mean," Alex replied.

"So is it Maryland then?" Matthew asked. Thomas nodded, explaining how his brother had been made welcome, despite the turbulent relationships between Puritans and Catholics in the colony.

"Our Puritan brethren were somewhat heavy-handed some years back," Thomas said, "burning churches throughout the colony. But now some semblance of peace exists. They have a strange decree, an Act of Toleration, a law that argues it is up to each man to follow his conscience in matters of God, and that churches of different convictions must learn to live side by side."

"How modern," Alex murmured, earning herself a warning glance from Matthew.

"Yes." Thomas gave her an odd look. "But now and then it all explodes into savagery."

"How can it matter so much?" Alex blurted. "How can men go to war, pillage, burn and destroy in the name of their God? Look at what's happening here; good, God fearing men hounded from their farms, branded as dangerous outlaws for the simple act of holding to their beliefs. And to make it all even more depressing, it's ultimately the same faith – Jesus Christ and all that stuff." Absolute silence greeted her outburst. Over Thomas' head Matthew met her eyes, doing an exaggerated eye roll.

"Well…" Thomas Leslie said, slapping himself hard on the thighs. He rubbed his legs and then looked at Alex. "You know, my dear, there are days when I think you're right. The good Lord must tear his hair as he sees us – good Christians all of us, in our own way — destroy each other. But I fear those are dangerous thoughts to voice out loud, and for your sake as well as that of your husband you must learn to be circumspect." He nodded as if in agreement with himself. "Tolerance; a virtue lacking in far too many men in this day and age…" He sighed and stood up. "I must go. I have a long ride south, and I hope to be in London before the seventh day of September. My chief asset is a draper's shop in the City, brought to me by my marriage. It is my hope the sale of that business alone will cover the full cost of transportation for my family — and some land." Alex choked back an exclamation, but if Thomas noticed he didn't say, bowing in her direction before leaving the room.

Matthew followed Thomas out into the yard.

"I wish you the best in your future endeavours, and may you and your family make it safely over to the other side."

"And you? Is it not something you've considered?"

"I've already been there. And I wasn't left with any fond memories of the place."

"No," Thomas Leslie said, sitting up on his horse. "I can imagine you would have nightmares rather."

"At times."

"Be careful, my friend," Thomas said looking down at him. "I wouldn't want to hear you've ended up dead or deported."

"I won't," Matthew said. "I have family and home to keep safe." He stretched up his hand and clasped Thomas' hand hard.

"God be with you, brother."

"And with you," Thomas Leslie replied before wheeling his horse away.

"Poor man," Alex sighed once Matthew had re-joined her. "I hope he has more assets than that draper's shop."

Matthew looked at her in bewilderment.

"It will burn," she said, "it's one of the things I definitely remember from my history lessons. In early September 1666, the whole city of London will burst into flames, leaving ash and ruin in its wake."

"Ah, no! Then how will he live? No officer's commission, no new life."

"He has a small farm," Alex said, "and he has spoken of a few other assets."

Matthew sighed. "Enough to pay the passage, and perhaps some supplies. Not enough to set him up once he reaches the colony."

"Let's hope he has a closer relationship with his brother than you do with yours," Alex said. "Not that that is saying much."

It only took a couple of days after Thomas Leslie rode away for Alex and Matthew to understand that he had been a protective influence over Hillview. From weekly, or at times only bi-weekly inspections, the soldiers now came back far more frequently, appearing sometimes from the lane, but just as often from the moor or through the water meadows. And each time they searched every building, leaving no stone unturned in their permanent hunt for outlawed ministers, foremost among them Sandy Peden.

"It's because he's a good speaker," Matthew explained to Alex one evening as they walked hand in hand down to the eddy pool for a late bath. "His sermons are whispered and repeated, and people are heartened by them." He waded out naked into the water and stood waiting for her as she shed her shift. Matthew chuckled. "It must be frustrating for the soldiers; repeatedly they've had him surrounded and then he simply vanishes. I suspect they think it's magic, while in reality it's that Sandy knows how to melt into the ground, being born and bred on that moss. He knows every hollow, every gorse stand. It makes him difficult to trap." He held out his hand to her and drew her to him, walking backwards until they were both well above their waists in water. Above them hung a yellow, heavy moon.

"Harvest moon, and this year the harvest is good, right?" Alex said.

"Aye. So far," Matthew said, stretching for the pot of soft soap. They washed in silence, helping each other with the hair before returning to the shore. Once dry, Matthew stretched out on the ground and Alex kneeled beside him.

"Will they ever catch him, do you think?" Alex asked, her hands busy working their way down Matthew's tense back. He groaned when she dug her fingers into the tendons that ran from shoulders and up through his neck.

"Aye… there… mmm, no, more to the right."

"Will they?"

"Aye they will," Matthew sighed. "Sooner or later they will. God help him then."

It used to be Alex liked Sundays. But that was before Matthew took to gallivanting about the countryside, aiming for one conventicle or the other while she remained at home, her heart in her throat for the whole day. She piled her plate with a second helping of pancakes – well, everyone was entitled to something. He needed God, and she needed comfort food – and dribbled a sizeable amount of honey over the stack. Three mouthfuls in, and Alex sighed, cocked her head in the direction of the yard and got to her feet.

"Officer," Alex was curt, her eyes on the unusually large group of soldiers in her yard.

"Is your husband at home?" Captain Howard inquired.

"I'm not sure, it depends what you mean by home. He's not in the house."

"Hmm," the officer nodded at one of his men, who rode forward. "We found this individual up by the road. Friend of yours?"

Alex' knees folded when a tall, haggard man was deposited on the ground at her feet.

"Minister Crombie!" She bent down to help him stand. "What has happened to you?"

"Alexandra Graham," Minister Crombie half croaked, half coughed. "It's a pleasure to meet you again, however constrained the circumstances." He patted her hand, regaining an element of composure as he straightened up to his full, considerable height.

"So you do know him," the captain stated.

"No, I always greet unknown men that way," Alex snapped, irritated by the smirk on the officer's face. "He wed us, eight years ago, so of course I know him."

"And since then, have you seen him?"

"Minister Crombie left the parish in late 1660, bound for Edinburgh." Minister Crombie nodded in silent agreement. "Since then I haven't seen him except for a brief visit in 1663, and I must say it worries me to see him in such state of ill health." As if on cue the minister coughed, a heavy sound that resulted in him hawking and spitting a huge globule of phlegm.

"Consumption," the captain diagnosed.

"Aye," the minister said. A slight gleam flashed through his sunken eyes. "If I'm fortunate it will mean I die here, before I am deported."

"I wouldn't think so," the officer replied laconically. "It takes a long time to cough your lungs to pieces."

Alex sent a darting glance around the yard. She'd sent Mark off the moment she saw the soldiers, and hoped he'd managed to find and warn his father before he set off in the direction of this day's hillside sermon, because something told her he would be walking straight into a trap.

The last few weeks had seen a flurry of arrests, some ending only in a beating, most resulting in fines and two in imprisonment. Behind her Daniel decided it was time for second breakfast and began to wail, a loud, insistent noise that had Alex crossing her arms to hide the fact that her breasts had begun to leak.

"By all means, take care of the child," Captain Howard said, dismounting to retrieve his prisoner. "We'll wait for your husband."

It was a long wait. Over the coming hours Alex grew increasingly nervous, and it didn't help to have the captain hovering around her like an enervating fly, his dark eyes registering her every emotion. With a superhuman effort Alex succeeded in looking mostly bland, allowing this to change into mild irritation as the day wore on, with muttered comments as to the inconsiderate nature of men in general and her husband in particular. All the time her heart was hammering inside her chest, her guts liquefying at the thought that Mark had been too late. Well; he obviously had, and Alex was torn with the double worries for her husband and her son.

"Where is he?" Captain Howard demanded.

"I don't know, he usually takes Mark for long walks on Sundays. Maybe they're fishing or hunting."

"Hmph!" Captain Howard expressed, before striding outside to talk to the messenger that came galloping down the lane.

"Where is he?" the minister asked in a low voice.

"I have no idea, he was supposed to go to the meeting, and…" She bit down on her lip, thinking that she couldn't start to cry because if she did she wouldn't be able to stop.

"He'll be fine," Minister Crombie said, patting her hand.

"You think?" Any further conversation was interrupted by the captain, who entered the kitchen with a satisfied expression on his face.

"Quite a few arrests today, I hear."

"Really?" Alex asked, going for unconcerned. But her voice betrayed her, sounding strangely cracked. For an instant she saw something akin to compassion in the officer's eyes, and she averted her face, mumbling something about having to feed the baby.

A trap. Sweetest Lord, the ground sprouted soldiers, and all around him people screamed, running this way and that like befuddled hens. A company of mounted dragoons came charging over a drier patch of ground, swords glinted in the sun, and the screaming that surrounded him intensified. Matthew grabbed hold of Sandy, boosted him over a boulder and vaulted over, landing with a curse in a thicket of brambles.

"We have to go," he said, struggling to adjust the ridiculous fair hairpiece atop his head.

"Aye, I gather that, but which way, do you think?" Sandy sounded controlled, but his hands were shaking and his mouth kept on twitching as if he were a cornered rabbit – adequate, all in all, Matthew mused wryly.

Matthew slid in under the brambles to better study the scene in front of him. The soldiers had formed a rough square and were closing in on the remnants of the meeting, swords raised. To the north, the line was straggly, and fleeing brethren and sisters rushed by the angry, shouting soldiers, making for the wetlands beyond. They could stay here, hoping that they wouldn't be found, but when he saw the dogs Matthew decided that was not a good idea.

"This way," Matthew said, and with Sandy's hand in a firm grip he broke cover.

"It's him! Peden!" There was a loud whistle from somewhere behind them, and the sound of booted feet, many feet, charging after them.

"Run!" Matthew extended his stride, dragging Sandy along. To his right, the soldiers were busy herding together a group of men. The soldiers to his left were too far away to be of any concern, and Matthew set his sights on a threesome of soldiers standing somewhat to the side. He brandished his sword, roared, and Sandy roared with him. The soldiers fell back, one of them tugged at his sword, another stumbled to his knees, and they were past, running deeper and deeper into the moor.

The ground squelched under his feet, gorse snagged at his coat, his breeches, and with Sandy like a fetter he darted this way and that, leaping over crevices, ducking under stunted trees, running, always running, despite the taste of blood in his mouth, despite the ragged sound of Sandy's breathing. Not get caught; you must not be apprehended, Matthew Graham, because if they catch you… Oh dear Lord, what will happen to Alex, his bairns?

A shout, yet another whistle, and out of the corner of his eye Matthew saw two men coming in pursuit, double mounted on a long-legged, ugly piebald.

"Over here!" Sandy tugged at Matthew, and they were on a patch of sloping ground, making for a stand of stunted trees. The ground was too dry. Lord in heaven, the horse was gaining on them! Sandy slipped, skidded for a few yards, and by the time they reached the trees the soldiers were upon them.

Sandy disappeared in a welter of limbs and garments, Matthew made a desperate attempt to rush to his aid, but was blocked by one of the soldiers, sword at the ready.

"Sit on him," the soldier called over his shoulder to his companion. "Keep him still until I've dispatched this one."

"Not quite as simple as you hope, I reckon," Matthew said.

"Ah, no?" The soldier lunged, Matthew parried. Lunge, parry, lunge, lunge, and Matthew's side burst open with pain. Keep your guard up, look him in the eye, aye? The soldier was an expert swordsman, but so was Matthew, for all that he was somewhat rusty. A misleading thrust to the right, two steps to the left and Matthew brought his blade down on his opponent's swords arm. The soldier slowed, eyes huge as he stared down at where his hand should be. Matthew muttered a hasty prayer and drove his sword into the uncovered throat. With a loud wheeze the man died.

Matthew staggered towards Sandy. The soldier lad sitting on him – aye, it was a lad, not a man – raised a white, terrified face to Matthew.

"I…" he began, trying to get to his feet. He never got any further.

Matthew's arm was shaking, blood running in rivulets over his hand and into his sleeve. A few feet away Sandy had managed to get to his knees, smoothing at his coat, his hair, his coat again.

"A lad," Matthew groaned.

"You couldn't do differently," Sandy said. "To let him live was to risk being arrested."

Matthew nodded and wiped his sword blade against the grass. So much blood… He slid a look at the dead lad. He'd never killed a mere child before, and his stomach churned.

"You're bleeding," Sandy said.

"Aye. The other one was quite the swordsman, and he got me in the side." He straightened up, squinting in the direction they'd come. He frowned; more horses, still a way off, but it was a matter of minutes before they came close enough to see them.

"Let me see," Sandy said.

"Not now. We have to get out of here." He sheathed the sword, helped Sandy back up on his feet. "And you?"

"None too bad, I have but twisted my ankle."

Matthew lugged Sandy over the rougher patches, choosing a track that led them deeper into the deceptive flatness of the moor. It was well into the afternoon when they made their way down towards the Lugar Waters.

"Someone betrayed us," Matthew said.

"Aye; it's the prize money – tempting if you're poor." Sandy stiffened, eyes on a minute speck or two on the horizon that were growing rapidly. "More soldiers."

They plunged into the river, waded through the shallows and swam towards the deep green of the further bank. Trees and thickets hung over the edge, creating adequate cover for a man or two, but the water was cold and the air in their little hiding place buzzed with hungry insects. For the better part of an hour they remained there while the horsed dragoons rode back and forth on the opposite shore, obviously nervous and irritated.

"Are they looking for us, do you think?" Sandy whispered.

"For you." Matthew's side hurt, and the makeshift bandage he'd applied earlier had slipped.

An hour or so before sunset Matthew was back at Hillview. He was tired, weakened after a whole day on the run, and it didn't much help that the wound along his flank had opened again, bleeding into his shirt and coat. He was almost off the hill when from behind a bush Mark appeared.

"Son?" Matthew drew to a surprised stop. His son was dirty and dishevelled, and from the puffy look of his face he'd been crying. "What are you doing here?"

"Mama sent me to find you," Mark said, beginning to cry again. "But I couldn't, you were already gone, and I didn't dare to go back down, and there are soldiers waiting in the yard and…"

"Shush, lad," Matthew said, wiping at his son's eyes and cheeks. "I'm here now. It'll be alright."

Alex slumped with relief when a dripping Mark appeared from under the trees, holding his father by the hand. She tightened her grasp on Daniel, who let out a muffled squawk, releasing his hold on her breast to look at her reproachfully out of eyes as blue as hers.

"Sorry," she kissed him. "Now go on, finish up." There was something wrong with how Matthew was moving, a stiffness to his gait, however well-disguised. She adjusted her clothing, handed Daniel to Sarah, and rushed out of the door, ignoring the surprised and rather disapproving looks from the assembled soldiers as she flew towards her man.

"Where have you been?" she scolded, eyes flying up and down his body to see where he was hurt.

"Fishing, up beyond the millrun."

"Aye," Mark nodded, "all day." He dropped the rods they must have borrowed from the miller to the ground.

"And the fish?" Captain Howard asked from behind Alex.

"No luck," Matthew shrugged.

"Ah," the captain said, taking in the sword that hung from Matthew's belt, the dirk, the wet clothes. "You fell in?"

"I did," Mark said, "and Da had to jump in after me."

"Ah," the captain repeated, looking unconvinced.

"Go on, get inside and change your clothes," Alex said to Mark. "And you," she added to Matthew, "you're wet all through!" She'd found the wound by now, could see the tell-tale stain on the right side of his coat. "Here." She unwrapped her shawl and swept it around him. As if by chance she stepped up close, thereby pressing against his damaged side. His arm came round her shoulders, seemingly an affectionate gesture towards his wife. In reality he was

146

using her as a prop, settling a substantial amount of his weight on her.

"Somewhat excessive," the captain commented. "To carry a sword for a day of fishing."

"Uncertain times," Matthew replied, walking towards the yard. The captain subjected Matthew to a barrage of questions, but Matthew insisted he'd been fishing – all day. He was trembling with the effort of remaining upright, and Alex couldn't very well go on clinging to him like a limpet for much longer.

"You're shivering," she said, interrupting the captain mid-flow.

"Ma'am, I'm conducting an interrogation."

"Is that what this is? Well, in that case you'll continue inside so that I can get something hot into my husband. I don't want him to die of pneumonia or something. Go on then," she chided, releasing Matthew. "Inside with you, now." And please, please walk these last few feet without stumbling. She shadowed him, keeping up a creative nagging all the way to the kitchen. "Okay?" she mumbled once he was sitting down.

"No," he muttered back, "but it'll keep." He raised a brow in warning when the captain came through the door, and Alex retreated a pace or two to allow the officer to sit.

A few minutes later the captain gave up. There was nothing to be had from Matthew, who now sat at ease in his kitchen, long legs crossed at the ankles and a mug of hot, sweetened wine in his hand. Captain Howard sat back and glared at Matthew, at Alex, in turn.

"And the minister? What of him?" He jerked his head in the direction of Minister Crombie, who was being manhandled out of the door.

Matthew looked confused. "Minister Crombie? What about him?"

"He's a friend of yours. And we apprehended him just off your land. Had he been on it, well then…"

"Plenty of men cross my land without my knowing, am I to fence it?" They eyeballed each other in silence over the table. Finally Captain Howard got to his feet, forcing Matthew to do the same and follow him outside.

"What will you do to him?" Matthew said, eyes never leaving the minister.

"He'll be taken to Edinburgh, and from there he'll find himself on a ship." The captain said.

Matthew spat and went over to the horse on which the minister was sitting.

"No," Alex moaned, eyes on her husband who was talking to Minister Crombie, the older man's hand clasped hard in his.

"He was formally outlawed a year ago, and he has repeatedly refused to take the oath or to respect the laws of the country. Surely you don't hold with lawlessness, mistress?" Captain Howard mounted his horse and frowned at Matthew and the minister.

"Not all laws are just or fair," Alex said.

"I couldn't agree more, Mrs Graham. Myself, I'm a Catholic, as were my parents and their parents before them. Not so long ago it was them that were persecuted, based on other laws."

"But then you should know…" Alex pleaded.

A small glimmer of something darted through the dark eyes of the captain.

"I know," he said, and kicked his horse hard.

No sooner were the soldiers gone than Alex dragged Matthew off to the laundry shed.

"What happened?" she asked, helping him out of shawl, coat and shirt. The shirt was wet with blood, as was the coat, but the wound itself was shallow, a long flesh wound that had done little damage to the underlying muscles or tendons, however much it had bled. Briefly he retold his day, his long mouth settling into a grim line.

"And is Sandy alright?"

He ran a light finger over the stitches up his side. "Well enough, but as for the others…" He scrubbed at his face. "What a terrible, terrible day."

"Bed," Alex said.

"Bed," he agreed.

Next morning Captain Howard was back, mouth compressed so tightly the skin around it was white.

"Two men dead! Two, you hear?"

"Nothing to do with me. I was fishing."

"Don't give me that!" The captain crowded Matthew back towards the door. Several inches shorter than Matthew, he was still a burly man. "Someone helped that accursed Peden get away – an uncommonly tall man, as I hear it, a man who slit the throat of a mere lad!"

Matthew hitched his shoulders. "Not me." Alex heard the slight quaver in his voice, saw how he wiped his right hand against his breeches and knew he was swimming in recriminations.

"Your sword," Howard said.

"My sword?"

"Yes, Mr Graham. The sword you carried yesterday, on your little fishing excursion." The captain sent his men inside the house, telling them to look everywhere for the weapon. Ten minutes later one of them returned, carrying a sword still in its scabbard. The captain took it, closed his fingers around the hilt and tugged. The sword bit into the scabbard and with a loud squeak it pulled free.

"As you can see I haven't used it much lately," Matthew said. "I mainly use it as a deterrent."

The captain inspected the blade. Alex knew for a fact it was clean but dull, with traces of rust and lint along the edges. It clattered when the captain threw it against the floor.

"I know you killed those men – just as you killed Lieutenant Gower."

"I resent your tone, captain, just as I resent your unsubstantiated accusations. I would have you leave, sir."

Captain Howard wheeled on his toes.

"I'll be back, Mr Graham." A clear threat, his steely voice indicated.

"Aye, you probably will," Matthew muttered to his back.

Much later, Matthew stowed the sword he'd retrieved from the pigpen in its normal keeping place under a floorboard by his side of the bed.

"What will happen to the ones that were arrested?" Alex asked. More than forty men and women had been taken. She sat down on her stool and let down her hair, hunting about for her brush.

"They're in breach of the Conventicle Act, apparently the single most important law to uphold in this the realm of Charles II." He studied her in the candlelight and after some time moved over and took the brush from her, pulling it through her long, curling hair. "The unwed women will be bonded overseas and we both know that means they'll never return."

Alex nodded; there was a chronic shortage of women in the colonies.

"The ministers are to be hanged, all five of them."

She didn't know what to say. Poor Minister Crombie, although she hoped he might see it as a reprieve to die here – quickly – rather than on a sugar cane field. Matthew's throat worked, his grip on the brush tightened to the point where his knuckles whitened. She took hold of his hand and pressed it to her cheek.

"I'm so sorry," she said.

He just nodded, eyes bright with unshed tears. He loved Minister Crombie and she could only imagine what it must feel like to know the minister was condemned to die so ignominiously.

"And the men?"

Matthew made a strange, guttural sound. "Fined between 150 and 300 merks each, payable within the month. And if not, they'll be shipped out as well – they and their families."

She met his eyes in the looking glass. Impossible amounts, no one had that kind of money.

"But at least the families will be kept together, right?" Alex said.

Matthew shook his head. "Nay, Alex. The bairns will be sold one by one, for periods of service up to twenty years. The women will go one way and the men another. But I'm sure they'll be made to watch as their families are torn asunder."

"Oh God," Alex whispered.

"Oh God indeed… it would seem He has forsaken us." He fell silent and concentrated on his brushing. Long strokes that made her hair crackle with static energy, smoothing it off her brow and down her back. He brushed and he brushed, and Alex sat on her stool and watched him through the mirror.

CHAPTER 15

He'd had no idea of how frightened he'd be riding on his own. What had seemed a brilliant plan when conceived in the safety of his bed was now an unhappy and fearful journey over unfamiliar terrain. Every night Ian fell asleep with his knife in his hand only to wake in the morning and find it had dropped to the ground.

It was cold sleeping outside. The bread and cheese had long since run out, and now there were only some apples left in his bag. He didn't know how much further it was, but counting on his fingers he'd been riding for near on ten days, so that should mean he was close.

He had left a week or so after the fire. The memory of the huge conflagration – a magnificent spectacle of burning houses and churches, exploding roofs and windows that fell like fiery stars towards the river – made all of him shiver with a combination of exhilaration and fear. People running, women screaming, dogs, cats, rats – a swarm of creatures plunging into the waters in a desperate attempt to evade the heat and flames. He had watched from the safety of their lodgings on the South Bank, incapable of pulling his eyes away from the horror that unfolded in front of him.

When at last the wind had died down, the charred ruins of London lay smouldering under the September sun. The stink of it filled the air, an acrid smell that made your eyes water and your mouth dry up. Soot whirled, it stuck to clothes, to hair, it fell from the sky to collect like filthy froth along the banks of the Thames. Everybody coughed, destitute people thronged the roads, pitiful creatures with no more to their name than the few garments they were wearing extended their hands and begged for pennies, for groats, for a leftover heel of bread.

A few days on Father had decided they should cut their visit to London short, muttering that there was no business to conduct given the present circumstances, so the family had returned home to the small brick manor halfway between Oxford and London.

It was when Father informed him that he was to remain at home while his parents and the babe went for an extended visit to one of his father's friends that Ian made up his mind. A day or so later he took the opportunity to slip away, leaving a note for Mr Brown, the steward, in which he explained he was riding after his father. It would have taken at least a week before they found he was gone, but by now they'd know. He wondered if they cared enough to come looking, and he turned his head into his cloak and cried because he wasn't sure they would.

Mam had greeted him with joy last December, exclaiming that he had grown, and what had they been feeding him to make him so tall and strong? But Ian was forbidden to hug her or to make too much noise. Father had explained that Mam had to rest, because the babe had to be kept safe, and surely he could count on Ian to help. The babe? Ian had looked from Father to Mam, and had felt the first coil of jealousy already then. But he'd promised that he would help as well as he could, becoming a silent shadow that spent far too much time on his own while Father hovered round Mam's bed.

Sometimes, when Father was at court or otherwise occupied, Ian spent whole days at his mother's side. He sat in Mam's bed and brushed her hair, he held the skeins of yarn for her as she wound it into balls, he read haltingly while she sewed, proud as a peacock at her vociferous praise at how well he spoke the written words. He talked, and Mam listened and sighed when he told her of how Williams had been punished for helping the unknown minister.

"No! 200 merks?"

Ian had no concept of how much money that was, but asked Mam if Father would have a problem finding it should he be fined.

"Fined?" Mam laughed. "Why would your father be fined?"

"He is also of the faith."

Mam laughed again and assured him that his father was wealthy enough to pay such a sum several times over should he have to, but that this would never be an issue as Luke Graham was high in the king's favour.

Those long spring days with Mam had been just like the old times, only him and her with all her attention focused on him, even if now and then her hand would drop to rest on her growing belly. At times she slept, her hand held in his and he worried because she looked so pale, frail and breakable, but she smiled and told him not to fret, that was the wean, aye?

He hadn't really thought so much about the babe as anything but an anonymous bump on his mother's body until the day he heard Mam and Father talk about it, none of them aware that he was sitting in the window seat.

"He thought I couldn't sire bairns of my own," Father had said. "But it seems I can." He laughed out loud and kissed Mam. "And this time I know for sure it's mine."

Ian had wanted to crawl away and die, because from the tone in Father's voice it was clear he had considerable doubts when it came to Ian himself. Not even Mam knew for sure – at least that was what she said the afternoon Ian confronted her about it, late in May.

"You must know!" he'd said. "How can you not?" Mam had gone the colour of a scalded ham and told him this was not something they were going to discuss further.

"You're Luke's son in all that matters and he loves you," she'd said, before retreating to bed, complaining all this upheaval made her stomach ache.

Ian was not so sure, not anymore. Before the wean he was convinced Father loved him, just as Uncle Matthew said he did, and he had even been able to find some comfort in the fact that his father loved him despite not knowing for sure if Ian was his. But the afternoon Father stood tall and angry in front of him, spittle flying from his mouth when he asked Ian how he dared to upset his mother now that she was heavy with child – his precious child – was the afternoon when Ian began to doubt if he was indeed as loved as he had thought. He hadn't been able to sit for a week afterwards, and was no longer allowed to either talk to or be in his mother's presence, relegated to living on the fringe of a household that orbited round the coming birth of the child.

He hated the wean; ugly and scrawny with bright red hair that shouted to the world that this was Luke Graham's son, while Ian was but a cuckoo in the nest. Mam had disappeared into a world of nursing, that horrid little creature hanging off her breast. Even once the wet nurse was installed, Mam lived her days at the beck and call of this adored new child, Luke Graham's longed for son.

"A miracle," she whispered reverently and Father would agree. And the boy thrived, smiling at his love-struck father in a way that made Luke coo and laugh. Ian had no memories of Luke ever cooing at him.

Worst of all was Mam's defection. It used to be she enjoyed his company as much as he did hers, but from one day to the other she shifted all her attention to the wean, listening distractedly to whatever he might have to say before rushing off to ensure the babe was comfortable and safe. Little Charles, named after the king and graced with the presence of His Majesty at his christening; wee Charles, apple of his father's eye... Ian sat up in the predawn darkness, too restless and cold to attempt further sleep.

He saddled up his horse, a mare that Father had bought him shortly after returning home from Hillview. It was a beautiful horse, a dark blue roan with a white tail and mane, and Ian wrapped his arms around her neck and was comforted by her warmth. Salome nickered, buffeting him with her head, and he dug into his bag for one of his few apples, feeding it to her in pieces. He hadn't taken much when he left, only some changes of clothing and something he'd wrapped in a square of silk and hidden at the bottom of the bag.

If Father ever found out he'd taken it he'd probably beat him to death, Ian swallowed, but it had seemed the right thing to do, just in case. One thing hadn't changed despite the wean, and that was Father's obsessive hatred of his brother. Ian had heard far too many threats against an absent Matthew uttered over the last few months, mostly when Father had drunk too much, but increasingly when he was sober as well.

Once on the horse, Ian shivered when the winds caught at his cloak, making it billow around him. It was raining, a sharp, driving rain that hurt his uncovered face and hands. He studied his surroundings, looking for any landmarks that could help him find his way, but with the clouds and the rain and the ice cold wind it was difficult to make out anything beyond the narrow path in front of him. Still, he was certain he was riding in the right direction, and halfway through the day he saw some stones that he thought he recognised, huge boulders that seemed to have rolled down the slope before coming to rest at a small, shallow pool.

By late afternoon he knew he was almost there. He passed the huge stand of hazels that stood just off the road to Cumnock and then he was riding up the last incline, and soon he would be home, back at Hillview. Something knotted in his stomach; mayhap they wouldn't want him either, but Aunt Alex had said that there was always a place for him here.

He held in Salome and sat in the wet and windy cold looking down at the small manor. Just as it had been when he left, snuggled against the hill behind it. There was light spilling from the kitchen window, the door opened and a tall shape stepped outside into the dusk, face raised in his direction. Ian clucked Salome into a trot.

He slowed the horse as he got closer. He swallowed once, twice, and threw back the drenched hood. There was a long, indrawn breath, and Ian tried a smile, meeting eyes just like his, in a face just like his. His uncle – or was it his father? – smiled back and opened his arms wide.

"But they must be worried sick!" Alex frowned down at Ian. He shrugged and averted his eyes, mumbling something about not being so sure about that. She set down a second helping of food in front of him and poured him another mug of milk. "Eat up first, and then we'll talk." She grinned mischievously at him. "Well; first you eat, then you wash and then we talk. You stink, Ian Graham."

"Can't it wait until tomorrow?" he asked.

Alex wrinkled her nose and shook her head. "You're going nowhere near my sheets smelling like that, so we'll be spending some quality time together in the laundry shed once you've finished your food."

"Will you be washing me yourself?" Ian squeaked.

Alex held up a pot of soap.

Ian looked at Matthew, hands coming down in a protective gesture over his crotch.

"But couldn't you, Uncle?"

Matthew shook his head. "I'm afraid this is your aunt's responsibility."

"Too right it is," Alex said, "men are lax washers." She produced a brush, some towels and jerked her head in the direction of the laundry shed. With a sigh, Ian got to his feet.

There was not one inch of him that wasn't squeaky clean once she was done with him. Ian followed her back inside, wearing one of Matthew's old shirts that flapped around him.

"Here," Alex plunked Daniel into his lap. "Hold him for me, will you? I'll see if I can find you some cake."

Ian looked at Daniel, at her. With reluctance he held the baby, arms stiff, face set in a mask of distaste.

"What? Does he need a new clout?"

Ian shook his head, and Alex ducked into the pantry. An angry holler had her reappearing like a greased rat, eyes flying from her son to Ian.

"Are you alright? And why is he crying?"

"Take him," Ian said, "just take him, aye?" When Alex hesitated he deposited Daniel roughly on the floor and turned to leave, only to run his nose straight into Matthew's chest.

"Explain," Matthew said, sitting down across the table from Ian.

"I can't abide them," Ian said, almost in tears. "I don't like weans."

"You did last time," Matthew said. "You'd sit for hours with Lucy, and you were right good with her too."

Ian dropped his eyes to the table. "That was before Charles," he said, and began to weep.

"We must send them a letter," Alex said later, holding Matthew's hand as they stood looking down at Ian, now fast asleep in the same bed as Mark and Jacob.

"Aye," he sighed. "Poor Ian."

"Yes, poor kid." Inside, she was going through a complex battle between strong maternal instincts that were telling her Ian must go, mustn't be allowed to grow into Matthew's heart, and her basic sense of compassion for a boy that had been so cruelly caught in the middle. Two letters, she decided, one to Margaret and the other one she would send to Simon, because with the advent of little Charles things might just have become one twist too complicated.

By the time Alex had finished feeding her own little tyrant – Daniel was presently in a growth mode, demanding food round the clock – Matthew was fast asleep, thrown on his back across their bed. Months of heavy harvest work combined with the heartbreak of seeing friends and neighbours carted off to gaol had left him hollowed and exhausted, and it was a long time since he'd made proper love to her – or she to him.

Alex sat down beside him and brushed his hair off his brow. There were odd strands of grey in it, and now that she looked closely she saw new lines in his face, a crease between his brows, a sharp line from nose to mouth. She kissed the corner of his mouth and he smiled in his sleep, a brief smile that flashed and was gone. She drew the sheet off him and studied his body, from his strong thighs up his concave belly to the wide chest, and there his dark hair was definitely sprinkled with grey. She let her finger touch his scars, the long puckered one that travelled from his sternum and to his right – a misdirected sword slash from very long ago – the remaining indentations on his shoulders from the months spent as a beast of burden in Virginia, and the new addition down his right flank, still a startling pink. When she placed her hand on his thigh, edging slowly upwards, his penis uncurled, lazily stretching itself to full size.

"Will I do, do you think?"

Alex met his eyes. "Oh yes," she breathed, "you do very well."

He stretched up a hand to her shift, tugging at the lacing. "It isn't fair, that you see all of me and I see nothing of you."

Alex pulled the shift over her head, sitting cross legged beside him. "Better?"

He sat up. She closed her eyes when his hand grazed her breasts. So gentle, so warm, the touch so light it made her skin prickle. She braced back against her arms, and at his insistent touch uncrossed her legs to extend them in front of her. He kneeled between them, placed his hands on her ankles and slowly moved them upwards, caressing her calves, her inner thighs. When he reached her belly he stopped, fingers spread fanlike over her skin. She covered his hands with hers. Here she had her own scars, marks left behind by their children, and he touched them gently before sliding his hands upwards to cup her breasts.

"Beautiful," he breathed, "so beautiful – and mine."

He took her nipple in his mouth and suckled.

"Ah!" She gasped, heat rushing from her breasts to her groin. He did it again and her hand fluttered up to his head, fingers threading themselves through his hair. He released her breast, placed his forehead against hers and leaned towards her, forcing her down.

Her head was loud with her pulse, his eyes were so very close and in her belly a living warmth writhed and twisted. His member prodded at the skin on her stomach when he covered her with his body. For a long time they laid like that, not moving, not talking. Brow to brow, nose brushing against nose. His warm breath tickled her cheek, her neck. A feathery sensation when he kissed her, as lightly as a butterfly landing on a rose. Again, and she extended her tongue to lick the contour of his mouth. Matthew smiled and shifted so that he was lying between her legs, his weight a tantalising promise of things to come. Inch by excruciating inch he entered her and patches of heat flew up her chest, her neck. At last; all of him inside of her. His mouth grazed her ear, his hands manacled her wrists.

"Lie still," he said, "lie very, very still."

So she did. It wasn't as if she wanted to do otherwise, not when her man was filling her every pore with his presence.

CHAPTER 16

For a moment Ian had problems recalling where he was, staring at the unfamiliar panelling on the wall. And then there were arms around his neck and high voices calling his name and all of him went warm at the riotous and loud welcome.

"Enough, then," Uncle Matthew's voice cut through the racket. "Your mama's trying to catch up on her sleep. So shush and get down to breakfast." He smiled specially at Ian. "Have you any clean clothes?"

Ian looked at his few belongings. "Clean enough I reckon," he grinned, which made Matthew shake his head.

"I assume your aunt will see you sorted, but until then wear what you have."

Matthew stuck his head into his bedchamber on his way down. Alex was still sleeping, with Daniel at her side. He smiled at her disarray. She must have fallen asleep while Daniel was still nursing, and Matthew went over to pull quilts and sheets up, stopping to brush a quick kiss across her forehead. One eye half-opened.

"More?" she murmured, her hand fumbling for his.

"You're insatiable, wife," Matthew said, pressed his lips to her palm and left her to sleep.

"I don't want to work in the kitchen garden," Mark grumbled when Matthew gave Ian and him their chores for the day. "Why can't I go with you to the mill instead?" He threw Matthew a hopeful look .

"You do as I say, both of you," Matthew said. He jerked his head in the direction of the vegetable patch. Alex needed a day or so of rest what with the wean being constantly hungry, but unless he set someone else to do it he knew she'd be out in the kitchen garden as soon as she was up.

Ian took Mark by the hand. "Come on then, if we hurry we'll be done by dinner."

Mark let himself be dragged away, his eyes bright with envy. Matthew gave him a stern look, watching the lads out of sight before settling Jacob on his shoulders and setting off up the hill, with Rachel gambolling like a spring fevered calf at his side.

Ian surveyed the kitchen garden and sighed. Work, work, everywhere work, and they would be nowhere close to being done by dinner.

"Always Rachel," Mark said. "Da always takes Rachel everywhere."

Ian smiled; that wasn't true. Mostly it was Mark who accompanied Uncle Matthew around the farm, but today wee Mark had himself convinced that all he ever got to do were the boring things, like harvesting carrots and parsnips and digging beds and spreading more manure and… Mark interrupted his whingeing, bit into a carrot and chewed in silence, kicking at the clods of wet earth.

"And Mama is always with Daniel or Jacob."

"Aye, I know how it is."

"Do you?" Mark gave him a surprised look.

Ian shrugged, wiping his dirty hands down his breeches. Dark velvet breeches, not at all suitable for this; it would drive Mam wild to see him streaking them with mud and bits and pieces of greenery. The thought pleased him, and he rubbed some more, noting the resulting stains with satisfaction.

"I have a brother," Ian said sombrely and stretched for a carrot. "Charles." He grimaced at the name.

"Only one," Mark told him. "And not a sister – you wouldn't want a sister like Rachel."

Ian considered that for a moment and gave Mark a pitying look. Rachel Graham was quite the little baggage.

"So," Mark said after a while. "What's he like? Charles?"

Ian made an indifferent sound. "He's a wean. He stinks and eats and sleeps."

Mark giggled. "Daniel stinks too, but Mama says he can't help it."

"He's ugly," Ian said, "looks like a piglet with hair. Red hair, bright red hair."

Mark agreed that that sounded very ugly. "Mayhap he'll look like your father when he grows up some," he said, "and then he'll be a right bonny lad."

Ian threw down his half-eaten carrot and stalked off.

"… and I don't understand," Mark finished, looking at his mother over the top of his mug.

Alex ruffled his hair. "It's not easy to be given a new brother. You know that, don't you?" She smiled down at her eldest, letting her hand linger on his downy cheek. "Ian's been a single child for almost twelve years, so it's even more difficult for him."

And apparently his two brainless parents hadn't taken that aspect into any consideration whatsoever. That Luke should allow himself to become besotted by this new, guaranteed his, son, she could to some extent understand, but what was Margaret thinking of?

Mark sat in thought for some time before leaning forward to pat Daniel on his head.

"I like my brothers," he said. "I even like Rachel. Sometimes," he qualified, making Alex laugh.

"It was a long awaited child, and mayhap the carrying of it was easier for her this time," Matthew said after having listened to Alex' little diatribe about Margaret's failings as a mother. He dug his spoon into the hot stew, blowing before putting it in his mouth.

"Yes, she must've had a terrible time of it last time – no idea who the father was. Poor her."

Matthew tended to be far too understanding of Margaret, making excuses for behaviour that in Alex' mind deserved a major whipping. Screwing your husband's brother in your marriage bed, standing by silently while your husband was set up as a traitor… Alex could make this list very long. Plus the woman had the temerity to look stunning. She wiped Rachel's hands and shooed her out of the door to join her brothers and cousin out in the yard.

"As you make your bed you must lie in it," she said.

Matthew frowned at her.

Alex just frowned back. "Was it?" she asked, sniffing with delight at her tea. Real tea for a change, a precious half pound Joan had sent down from Edinburgh as Alex' birthday gift.

"Was what?" Matthew wiped his bowl clean with the last piece of bread and burped.

"Difficult for her – with Ian."

"Aye, it was, and not only because of the paternity issue. Pregnancy didn't become her, and as Ian tells it, it was much the same this time as well. Nigh on seven months in bed."

"Oh dear," Alex murmured, not even attempting to sound sincere.

Matthew seemed on the point of saying something – probably rather admonishing, given the look on his face – but a high, protesting squeal made him rise and walk out into the yard instead, there to have a serious conversation with his daughter.

"It's quite unfair, isn't it?" Alex voiced much later. She yawned and pushed the accounting ledgers away from her, swivelling on her stool to face Matthew.

"Unfair? What's unfair?"

Alex dropped the last of their few coins back into the worn leather pouch and lobbed it to him. She counted, he carried – in his opinion a fair distribution of tasks.

"That the eldest boy inherits everything."

"Not everything. Land, aye, but not everything."

Alex looked round the rather bare parlour. A small table in cherry wood, a somewhat larger beautiful intarsia table that her father-in-law had made, four chairs, three of which had armrests, two stools, an oak chest, one set of hearth guards, two candlesticks in pewter and… well, that was it. Oh, and the sum total of nineteen books, of which one was illegible, two were bibles and one was in Latin. On the floor lay a rug she'd woven out of discarded clothes, and she was quite proud of the fact that she'd manage to create something that pleasing using mainly greys and browns with the odd dash of green and yellow.

"It must be that way," Matthew said. "A place like Hillview will easily support ten odd tenants and a large family in the big house, but if it's subdivided generation after generation what remains? Not a working manor, but a sad collection of smallholdings, all too meagre to support even one family."

"But it's hard on the number two and three."

Matthew shrugged. His father had been the eldest of five brothers, he reminded her, one had married a local lass, sole heiress to a small farm, two had joined fighting companies in France and the youngest, still alive and thriving, had been apprenticed to the master of the mint in Edinburgh, over time earning a comfortable living for himself and his numerous family.

"And we'll set them on their way, Daniel to school once he's of age, and Jacob we'll apprentice to a good tradesman."

"When?" Alex asked with a sinking feeling inside.

"At ten or so; a smith, I was thinking."

"Oh." No free choice there either… "But what if he wants to be an artist?"

"An artist?" Matthew's voice actually squeaked. "You can't live as an artist."

"A doctor? A lawyer?"

Matthew smiled and nodded. "Aye, if he wants to be a lawyer that can be arranged – he can clerk for Simon."

"Fantastic, the sum total of two options; smith or lawyer."

Matthew gave her a long look. "Mark has no choice at all, he's born to take over Hillview – just like I was, and my father before me."

"Well that depends, doesn't it? On if he's in fact your eldest son." She said it so matter-of-fact it took some time for Matthew to register what she'd said, and when he did he groaned.

"He is, in the eye of the law Mark is my heir."

Alex hid her eyes by bending down to pick up her next piece of mending. "And in your heart? In your conscience?" she asked, squinting as she threaded the needle.

"We've had this conversation before. It doesn't matter what I feel or think. Luke has taken him as his own."

"But that was before he had Charles." It gnawed at her, constantly she thought about it; a red-haired baby, a throwback on his sire, and what would Luke do with Ian now that he had a son he knew for sure was his?

"Ian is his son!" Matthew stood up so abruptly the chair crashed to the floor.

"Good. As long as you remember that, no matter what Luke decides to do." She swore when the needle pricked her thumb. Matthew threw himself out of the room and into the night, slamming the door behind him.

He slept in the hayloft, making a point of not entering the kitchen until most of the household had had their breakfast. Alex served him eggs and ham, placed the bread within reach and sat down by the hearth, jiggling a fretting Daniel on her lap.

"All night," she sighed, "he's been like this the whole bloody night." He grunted, keeping his eyes on the plate. Alex undid her shift and tried to settle Daniel to eat but he arched back, small arms flailing. "Suit yourself," she muttered, and went back to bouncing him silent.

He snuck her a look; she looked tired, no doubt due to the wean, but there was a set to her mouth, a line he recognised from the few previous times they'd quarrelled. She didn't like it when they slept apart, and nor did he, but this matter with Ian had his brain whirling, and he'd needed time to think – alone.

"I don't know," he said.

"You don't know what?" Alex dipped her finger into the honey jar and stuck it into Daniel's mouth, effectively cutting off his whining.

"I don't know what I'll do – or even should do – if Luke renounces him." He swallowed at the look in her eyes. "He's mine," he went on, hearing how belligerent he sounded. "And he's born in wedlock; he should inherit."

"Great. Make sure you let me know to what trade you intend to apprentice our boy then. And it best be soon, before he gets too fond of his promised future as master of Hillview." Alex slammed her hand down so hard on the table that both Matthew and Daniel jumped. "Here, take care of your son." She dumped Daniel in his arms. "Enjoy him, Mr Graham, because let me tell you I'm not about to give you anymore. Bastard!" With that she stalked off, brushing a surprised Mark aside.

For an instant Matthew considered catching up with her and dragging her screaming back into the house. How dare she speak to him like that! His fingers twitched and he clenched them hard in an effort to control this dangerous feeling. God, he wanted to... but nay, if he did that once to Alex she'd be lost to him forever, she'd never forgive him for raising his hand to her. He handed a bawling Daniel to Sarah and walked off towards the barn, kicking in the direction of the grey tabby.

Throughout the morning, Matthew worked where he could see the wooded slopes, hoping to intercept Alex when she came back down. The sun crept towards its zenith, from the kitchen came the smell of boiled fish, and still there was no sign of Alex.

"Where's Mama?" Rachel tugged at Matthew's sleeve.

"Not here, aye?" Matthew snapped, trying to block out the sounds of his hollering son. He resumed his hammering, driving in nail after nail with strong, even strokes. Sarah was walking back and forth in the yard just as he'd told her to, assuming the sound of Daniel's crying would bring Alex home. She'd been at it for some time now, and Matthew was getting angry with his irresponsible wife. What was she thinking of to leave a hungry wean like this? Some minutes later he saw Alex appear from the direction of the mill, walk over to Sarah and lift Daniel into her arms before disappearing inside. He let the hammer drop to the ground and followed her.

"I'm not talking to you." She gave him an ice cold look. "So just go." She turned away from him. Daniel was still crying, long, shaky hiccups that made him cough up milk, open his mouth to wail and then go back to eating. Matthew remained where he was, resting his shoulders against the door. She reminded him of a lioness, a dangerous female beast that crouched in defence of her young, except that this cat didn't have yellow eyes but bright blue ones that peeked at him before sliding off to rest once again on the wall.

"Can't you try to understand?"

"Of course I understand! But that doesn't help does it? The outcome will be the same for my son."

"Our son, and I said I didn't know." He ignored her stiff back and went over to sit at her feet, resting his head against her skirts. He could feel her soften, sense how she relaxed in his proximity. "You must help me, Alex. You can't leave me to handle this on my own."

"How can I help? For me the choice is self-evident."

He craned his head back to catch her eyes. "Is it?"

Alex looked away. "No," she said with a heavy sigh. "Of course it isn't."

CHAPTER 17

The man who rode in some days later was spattered with mud up to well over his knees, his horse dipping its head in exhaustion. Ian took one look and darted off, evading both Alex and Matthew before diving into the woods.

"Ah," Alex said. "The prodigal son is requested to return, but decides he doesn't want a fatted calf."

Matthew chuckled and went over to meet the traveller with Alex at his heels. Ever since their strange discussion the other day they had sidestepped the issue of Ian, concentrating instead on the remaining weeks of harvest work. But he thought about it a lot, and in the night it would happen that he lay awake with eyes stuck on the ceiling with several 'ifs' ringing in his head. If Luke were to… if he, Matthew, should… if Ian … would Alex? And what about Mark?

"Matthew Graham?" The stranger looked round the small manor with an air of condescension, plump mouth curling into an amused smile as he took in the stables, the few servants. No doubt nowhere close to Luke's grand house, Matthew thought, frowning in warning when the man's eyes lingered for far too long and with far too much familiarity on his wife. "I'm here on behalf of Luke Graham, Robert Brown, at your service." He swept off his hat and produced a letter that he handed to Matthew.

It was short and very much to the point; Ian had left his home without parental approval and was now to be returned home immediately to be firmly dealt with. Matthew's mouth tightened, but there was nothing he could do. Ian was Luke's son and must be returned.

"It's been difficult for the lad," he said to Brown, receiving a blank stare in return. "What with his brother and all."

Brown shrugged. "He's had the mistress right worried, he has. I dare say he'll receive a warm welcome, and well does he deserve it." He mimed an aching backside and grinned, his smile faltering somewhat when Alex glared at him.

"May I offer you hospitality for the night?" Matthew said. "I dare say both yourself and your horse could do with food and rest." One more day with Ian, one more evening, one more night, and then he'd never see him again, not until Ian was a grown man. It tore at him; his son, and the dear Lord help him, because, he, Matthew, couldn't.

"That's kind of you, sir, and I will gladly accept." Brown dismounted and set off towards the stables, leading his horse behind him.

"Not in my clean sheets," Alex said. "I bet he's as filthy under those clothes as he is on the outside."

"Aye," Matthew nodded, "but then he's English." Not much of a jest, but Alex pulled her lips into a faint smile before saying something about going after Ian.

"I'll go," he said.

"Oh no; you take care of your guest – make sure he understands he's sleeping in the hay, okay?" With that she was off.

Ian heard her well before she broke through the screen of shrubs that bordered the hilltop, but remained where he was, eyes locked on the undulating sea of heather in front of him; purples, pinks, here and there a dash of brown.

Aunt Alex kneeled down beside him. "Beautiful, isn't it?"

He made a strangled sound and she put her arm around him.

"It'll be alright, Ian. They love you, even if they're mad at you for running off – any parent would be. And once you've gotten used to it, you might even like having a baby brother."

He shook his head. "Half-brother, because that's what he is. And now Father will always see himself in Charles and in me he'll see Uncle Matthew." He rubbed his face against the rough fabric of his cloak, wishing yet again that Charlie had never been born. He tore at his hair; if only it had been as red as Charlie's! "And he doesn't like Uncle Matthew."

She sighed. "No, he doesn't, does he?"

"I don't want to go back, Father will be so angry at me for coming here, and Mam…" Ian drew in a long, uneven breath. "… Well Mam does as he tells her to." Father would belt him, he'd take Salome from him and then he'd be sent away to be brought up in another household.

"I think they'll mainly be glad to have you back, safe and sound – I would."

Ian shook his head. "Not them, not now that they have the wean."

"Don't be silly; yes, they seem to have lost their heads a bit over the baby, but it will pass, okay? And in your parents case, they've tried for so long, so of course they're all over Charlie." She gave him an encouraging smile, head tilted to the side.

"That's not it." He huddled into his cloak. "Before Charles I was the only son Father would ever have. Now he's no longer sure if I am his son – or if he wants me."

"Oh, Ian," Aunt Alex gave him a hard hug. "Of course he wants you. Any father would be proud of you!"

Ian tore free and stumbled to his feet. "Which one? Which one would be proud? They don't even know themselves whose son I am! Not even Mam knows, not for sure." He dragged his hand through his hair, biting down hard on the inside of his cheek to stop himself from crying. It didn't help, his vision blurred with tears. "Who am I? Where do I belong? Here? No, because Uncle Matthew has other sons. There? No, because now Father has another son as well." He took a step or two towards the moss and looked back at her. "I'm not yet twelve, but already all alone…"

Two leaps and he was out on the moss, setting off at a run. He ran as fast as his legs could carry him, jumping over stones and gorse, splashing through puddles. He ran until he stopped crying and then he ran some more, straight out into that heaving, flowering mass of pink.

Matthew brought Ian home, carrying him as if he were a small child. The boy was drenched from falling into terns and small springs, and Alex took one look at him and ordered him to bed, sitting by his side to make sure he swallowed down every last drop of the broth she brought him. Alex caressed his cheek and to her surprise the boy curled up as close as he could, face hidden in her skirts. Jesus… Alex smoothed at his hair, overwhelmed by very protective feelings towards this boy.

"I can find an excuse to keep you here for now. It won't help in the long run, but if you want me to, I'll make sure Mr Brown leaves without you tomorrow."

He nodded once, burrowed even closer.

Alex stroked him over his knobbly back. "You always belong here. Remember that, okay?" He moaned, thin shoulders shaking. Then and there he took that final leap into her heart, jostling for space with her own brood. She smiled wryly; a pushover, Alex Graham, that's what you are – at least when it comes to needy children. She sat beside him until he was fast asleep, her hand held hard in his.

"Chickenpox," Alex said. "If you want to check, be my guest. It's highly contagious and if you haven't had it as a child… well." As if on cue Daniel began to shriek, waving his arms in the air. Alex wasn't lying; Daniel's genital area was covered in the trademark blisters, travelling up his stomach and across his chest. She was, however, lying when she insisted that Ian might be coming down with it too.

"Frankly, I don't think my brother-in-law would much appreciate if his eldest son was dragged home ailing, and imagine what he'd say if the baby got infected." She eyed Daniel and turned innocent eyes on Mr Brown. "Some die, you know." A major exaggeration. Mr Brown looked flustered; the idea of travelling for eight days with a sick child clearly held little appeal.

"Chickenpox? Is it something akin to smallpox?"

"Very similar," Alex nodded. He shuddered, and Alex smiled to herself. "I'll write a letter, and I'm convinced both his parents will agree that we mustn't risk Ian's future health." She leaned forward and lowered her voice. "At his age it might affect his future… err… fertility." No, that was mumps, but apparently Robert Brown had only the vaguest concepts about illnesses in general, and he took a hasty step back from her and the crying child.

"It is for the best if I leave as soon as possible," he muttered, escaping to the other side of the table. Oh yes; the sooner the better, as far as Alex was concerned.

Alex signed the letter, blotted it and folded it together.

"There," she said, handing it to Mr Brown. And where was Matthew? He should at least say goodbye to Brown. "Have you seen the master?" she asked Sarah, but Sarah's reply was drowned in a frantic clucking, here and there interspaced by high, excited voices. "Bloody hell; now what?" Alex rushed for the hen house, with an interested Brown in tow.

The hen coop was in chaos, the hens fleeing in all directions from a determined Rachel, who seemed set on grabbing one. There were feathers everywhere; in the air, on the ground and stuck all over Rachel's hair. Jacob was in there with her, helping as well as he could, and on the outside Mark was hanging on to the latched gate, laughing his head off.

"What in the world do you think you're doing?"

If she hadn't been so angry, Alex supposed it would have been amusing to see the way her children gawked at her. The hens continued to squawk and flap, Jacob stuck his hand into Rachel's, and Mark made as if to sidle away.

"Oh, no you don't!" Her hand came down like a clamp on his arm.

"It wasn't me," Mark protested. "I'm not in there, am I?"

Rachel's mouth opened in an 'o'. She threw a reproachful look in the direction of Mark.

"You locked us in. Said we weren't coming out without a hen."

Mark twisted. "It was your fault! It was you who said you could wring a hen's neck."

"What? You dared her to kill one of my hens?" Alex scowled at Mark who shrank away. "Idiots, the lot of you. This will probably put them off laying for days, but I'll leave it to you to explain that to your father, shall I?"

An hour later a still laughing Mr Brown had bid them farewell and Alex sank down for a quick breather. Her children were confined to the kitchen bench, three pairs of hazel eyes throwing her cautious looks. Even Rachel was silent, trying out her best smile whenever Alex' gaze rested on her.

"No, mistress, he's not in the stables or in the barn, and it's only Samuel and Robbie out in the field. They say the master rode off early this morning, but they don't know where." Sarah sounded apologetic.

"Hmm." Alex regarded her children. They had to be punished, but she suspected sending them off to spend the rest of the day in their bedroom was going to be received with relief, and from the way they were looking at each other it was obvious both Mark and Rachel were counting on being let off with nothing more than a mild slap to the wrists. You wish, she thought, turning various alternatives over in her head.

Matthew came riding over the water meadows, nodded a greeting to Samuel and Robbie and handed Ham over to Gavin before making for the house. He hoped he wasn't too late to bid Ian a proper goodbye, but look as he might he couldn't find Brown's horse. Ah no; Ian was gone, and he hadn't been here to hug him one last time. He kicked at the ground and came to a halt by the hen coop. What had happened here? A fox mayhap? But there was no blood, only a flock of ruffled hens, a few of them seemingly dead. He frowned and increased his pace.

"Why are there five dead hens in the coop?" he said, making his whole family start.

"Oh, they're not dead," Alex said. "They're just suffering from shock."

"Ah." Matthew let his eyes travel over his children while Alex retold the events, struggling to keep the grin that wanted to break out under control.

"All of them were in on it," Alex said mournfully. "Well, not Daniel, but that's probably on account of him not being able to walk yet. And he has chickenpox, poor thing."

"Nor Ian," Rachel piped up. "He has the pox too."

"Ian?" Matthew turned to face Alex. "Is Ian still here?" One part of him was overjoyed, the other apprehensive.

"You heard; the poor kid has the chickenpox. I can't send him back contagious to his baby brother, can I?"

Matthew looked at her in silence, a slow smile spreading over his face. Tender-hearted, this woman of his, capable of being protective towards a lad she recognised as being a potential threat to her own son's future.

"The pox, aye?"

"Serious," she said, looking concerned. "Will probably take months of convalescence. At least that's what I wrote to Luke. Among other things…"

Matthew sighed; he could imagine those other things.

"Not to worry," Alex said, "he probably won't be able to read my handwriting."

A couple of minutes later the three elder Graham children trooped off in the direction of the henhouse.

"It must be swept and scrubbed entirely clean," Matthew called after them. "No dinner until you're done," he added before closing the door.

"Where were you this morning?" Alex patted some ground oatmeal on Daniel's irritated skin, smoothed down his smocks and set him down on a blanket.

"No clout?" Matthew smiled at the waving legs and leaned down to pinch at a rosy toe.

"Fresh air helps, I think. So, where were you?" She nodded a thank you at Sarah, and took a bite of the meat pie.

"Up on the moss. Peat, aye?"

Alex gave him a disbelieving look. He shook his head in warning and waited until Sarah left the kitchen. "Today they hang," he said softly. "All five ministers, including Minister Crombie. So I stood up there and offered up a prayer for their souls, God help them."

"With Sandy," Alex said.

Matthew nodded, ate some of his pie but shoved it away from him half-eaten. Alex scooted closer and rested her head against his shoulder. He rubbed his cheek against her head.

"Don't mind me, Alex. It's not a good day."

In response she slipped her arm around his waist and kissed his cheek.

"I'm glad you helped him stay," Matthew said, standing up with a grunt.

"Mmm? Oh, Ian. I did it for his sake. The poor kid needs someone in his corner."

"And for my sake as well." He smiled at how her cheeks reddened. "It'll be the last time I'll have with him as a lad. I don't think Luke will renounce the lad, but he'll punish him for coming running to me – Ian won't be coming back to Hillview." He sighed, bent to kiss Alex and went outside.

Ian stood with his back pressed to the wood panelling of the dark hallway. Renounce him? Could Father do that? But Mam wouldn't let him, no of course she wouldn't, because Mam loved Ian – even now with Charles in the house.

"Mam," he breathed, sliding down to sit on the floor. He missed her so much it hurt, he wanted her to laugh in his ear and tell him what a fine lad he was and how proud she was of him. Ian leaned his chin against his knees and exhaled. If only Father had come himself instead of sending Mr Brown. He closed his eyes and there in his head was his father, and he was laughing, telling Ian not to be such a daftie, for surely he knew he was loved. But Ian didn't; not right now, sitting in the dark and draughty hallway with a borrowed shirt flapping round his legs and no one in the whole world he could truly call his own. Not even Mam; not anymore, not after Charles.

CHAPTER 18

Alex reread the note before folding it together and putting it aside. Just deciphering the handwriting had been an issue, and the contents themselves didn't exactly help. A very oblique warning, but a warning none the less... Alex dug into her apron pocket for a coin or two for the messenger, a scruffy boy about Mark's age who was wolfing down the bowl of stew Sarah had served him.

"Who?" Alex held up a tarnished half-crown.

The boy's eyes widened. "A man." He extended his hand for the coin.

Alex shook her head. "Better than that."

"A soldier."

"Young? Old? Fat? Go on, what did he look like?" She flipped the coin, and the boy's eyes followed it up into the air and down.

"I don't know, he was just a soldier."

"An officer?"

He hitched his shoulders. A man with a sash on a horse had given him the letter to deliver and that was what he'd done.

"He had a scar, here." He placed his hand to cover most of the right side of his face. "Like snakeskin – and no hair."

Once the boy was gone Alex sat down and read the short message again. *Beware; an ambush can be ambushed, the attackers be attacked.* Why address it to her? She tapped at the paper. *An ambush can be ambushed...* and tomorrow some of the men fined for their participation in the disrupted meeting on the moor would be transported from Cumnock to Edinburgh, there to be bonded overseas with their families.

Alex sighed; her brave, high principled man was off to play some kind of latter day William Wallace by freeing those men, and apparently this was exactly what the soldiers were hoping he would do. And we all know how Wallace ended his days, Alex thought; hung, drawn and quartered.

Matthew read the note, read it again. They knew; somehow they'd had word of the planned ambush, and now… Sweetest Lord, it would be a bloodbath, farmers ranged against fighting men. And he'd said so, repeatedly he'd warned them, saying this was too dangerous, too risky.

"I hope you're not planning on taking part," Alex said.

"How can you think I'd do something that daft? Do you seriously think I'd put you all at risk for a gesture bound to fail?" He crumpled the paper and threw it at her feet.

"Is it? Bound to fail, I mean."

"Aye, I think so, and I will take no part. Who sent this to you?"

"I have no idea." Alex bent to retrieve the paper. "Literate at any rate, and with a scar."

"Scar? Have you seen him?"

"No, but the boy who delivered it said he was an officer, badly scarred over half of his face. Like snakeskin, he said, I suppose he means puckered, and apparently he's bald."

"Wyndham." Matthew stood stock still. "Oliver Wyndham. Now how have you managed that, you a most devout Puritan last I saw you?"

"So this is a friend of yours?"

Matthew gave her a grim look. "Not as such. But he owes me his life, like."

"He does?" Alex settled herself on an upturned bucket, looking so much like a lass waiting for a story that Matthew smiled.

"It's no tale of honour and gallantry. It's rather the sad story of two young lads, a worldly-wise whore and what can befall you if you're not careful where you leave your heart."

"Aha, a morality." Alex looked at him expectantly.

Matthew snorted, torn between amusement and irritation.

"To us she was a glamorous creature, all bared skin and ruffles with eyes the size of saucers and a wonderful mouth."

His cheeks heated at the expression on Alex' face. "Nay," he muttered, "not like you do. I… well, you were the first to…" His hand strayed to his crotch.

"And the last," Alex informed him, making him laugh.

"Oliver and I were what? Eighteen? Both far from home and always the youngest, surrounded by serious men who fought for principles and such."

"And you were only there to have a good time," Alex said, waggling her brows.

"Nay, that we weren't. But at times it's difficult to live only for duty, and especially when you are but a lad." He handed her a harness, a cloth and some grease, indicating she might as well do something useful while she sat listening. "For months we were cooped up, ordered to stay in camp, one day after the other full of the utter boredom of siege work. And the siege of Colchester was long – all summer it lasted – and it was hot. Relentless the sun shone from dull blue skies and in the city people starved and died while we sat outside and waited." All around the army camp fields had lain abandoned and untended, the air hung heavy with the stench from endless privy ditches, and over it all that constant, scorching heat.

"And she was an army whore?" Alex asked. "I didn't think Puritan morals allowed such."

"They don't," he said. "But men will be men, and months – years – away from families and wives make even the most moral of men prone to fall for the carnal itch." He smiled, shaking his head. "An angel we thought her the first time we saw her, both of us too innocent to see her for what she was. She followed the army, she and her fellow workers, and we were ripe for the plucking, all of us. Restless and itching, bored of ourselves and our comrades at arms, and these lasses sang and made eyes at us and threw long manes of hair about. They were good at what they did, they were…"

His voice trailed off and he smiled at the memories of himself, young and inexperienced and convinced he was in love with French Marie – no more French than he was, but he didn't know that at the time. And Oliver equally in love with her, and both of them certain they were the sole recipients of her true affections. Alex laughed when he told her this.

"But the lady didn't mix business with pleasure, did she?" she said.

No, she hadn't, and she'd made that very clear to both of them one night.

"We drew lots, Oliver and me, and he won and I swore to no longer importune the fair Marie, to leave the field free for him." Agreeably drunk they had made their way to the whores' end of the huge encampment, Matthew to witness as Oliver begged for her hand in marriage.

"First she laughed at him, telling him she had no patience with callow lads, but when he continued to wheedle and beg she had him thrown out, and he was so incensed by this behaviour that he grabbed a candlestick and set fire to the canvas sides of the tent." Shrieking women in different states of undress, a grim and angered madam, and poor Oliver was sent flying into the conflagration, head first. "The buff coat saved him, but when I got him out, one side of his head was one raw blister, his hair, eyebrow and eyelashes all gone." Matthew had thrown his friend over his shoulders and legged it, pelted with all kinds of hard and unsavoury objects by the angry, frightened whores.

Matthew fell silent. Oliver had been in agony for days, and the surgeon had despaired for his life and his eyesight in that order. But he lived, and where once he had been a handsome, spirited young lad he became a bitter, twisted man.

"We never spoke much afterwards. He requested transfer elsewhere and whenever we met he would avert his face and hurry off with nothing but a hasty nod." No doubt making a comparison between his own diminished state and that of his erstwhile companion, Matthew sighed.

"Apparently he still remembers you," Alex said standing up. "What will you do? I suppose you must try and warn them."

180

Matthew looked away. "Aye, I must try."

Alex watched as he saddled up Ham. "Why is he warning you, do you think? Because he owes you or because he still holds to his original convictions?"

Matthew tightened the girth and backed Ham out of his stall. "I don't know, I would hope it's because of convictions." Once outside, he swung up in the saddle and indicated the scrap of paper in Alex' hand. "Burn it."

The soldiers rode in late next afternoon. Dishevelled and dusty, they charged down the lane towards the yard with swords drawn. Jacob shrieked and hid himself against Alex' skirts, calling loudly for his da.

"Your husband, ma'am," the lieutenant barked, holding in his sweating mount. The horse frothed at the bit, and its flanks heaved, the large hoofs sliding over the cobbles. The officer swept the people in front of him with angry, bloodshot eyes, and Alex shooed her children indoors.

"Your husband! Where is your husband?" He glared at Alex, frowned at Ian who stood by her side. His eyes flew over the household, returned to Alex.

"He's in Cumnock," Alex said. She studied the officer's right leg. The breeches were dark with blood, and from the way he was sitting, she'd warrant he'd been badly hurt. Well; she wasn't about to offer first aid and a cuddly blanket.

"I think not, mistress. We both know where he's been."

"In Cumnock," Alex nodded, "all day."

He dismounted, swaying when he set the foot of his injured leg on the ground.

"I'll wait for him."

"By all means, but don't expect any hospitality."

The lieutenant was still there when Matthew rode in, accompanied by an officer and two dragoons. Well, well; Mr Wyndham himself, given his disfigured face. On one side dark, scaly skin covered everything from his brow all the way down to his jaw. The lieutenant muttered something to one of his men, eyeing Wyndham with mild dislike. It clearly didn't go down well, to see the new commanding officer riding side by side with Matthew, and in particular when the major leaned across to clasp Matthew's arm. There was a hiss to Alex' right, a vicious comment as to the need to purge the army of all erstwhile dissenters and Puritans. Alex shaded her face against the low October sun. Matthew looked tense.

"Mr Graham," the lieutenant challenged once the party drew halt. "I've reason to believe you took part in a foul ambush on my troop earlier today."

"Today?" Matthew sounded bewildered. "I've been in Cumnock since early morning." He dismounted, handing Ham's reins to Ian. "Rub him down properly."

"That's not what I hear," the lieutenant snapped.

"No?" Matthew nodded in the direction of the major. "Well then you must talk to Major Wyndham. I'm sure he'll vouch for me. After all, being interrogated by an army officer must be a valid alibi."

The lieutenant squinted at his commanding officer. "Interrogated?"

"Most certainly interrogated," the major said. "Did you think me a fool, lieutenant? A man of such staunch Presbyterian beliefs as Matthew Graham must be closely watched." He smirked as he said so.

"Oh," the lieutenant said, sounding impressed.

Oliver Wyndham was not a discreet man. Alex fumed at the way he inspected her, their home, even their children. His eyes inventoried every building, narrowed as he scanned fields and meadows, livestock and people. There was an amused look on his face as he studied her rudimentary garden – at present no more than two huge rosebushes clambering over wooden trellises – and it broadened into a derisive grin when he studied the main house. Belatedly he remembered his manners, bowed and introduced himself, and Alex curtsied, but chose not to invite him in. He did a slow turn and smiled. As the lips on the damaged side of his face didn't stretch, it was a lopsided smile, more of a grimace.

"Very different from my home down in the Cotswolds."

"I can imagine," Alex said, irritated by how his eyes had stuck on her chest.

"So grey," he muttered. "Somewhat dull to a southerner, I'm afraid."

"One uses what one has," Alex said. "And here it is stone for the most part."

"A material as recalcitrant as the Scots," the major said. Alex ignored his barbed comment, her eyes on her own personal chunk of Scottish granite. Matthew's jaws were working, his shoulders rigid.

"But even stone shatters when sufficient pressure is brought to bear on it," the major continued. "Like today." He laughed, his inquisitive eyes leaping from Alex to Matthew.

"Today?" Alex said.

"Oh yes, Mrs Graham. We crushed the rebels today, we will continue crushing them, we will persecute and plague them until they submit to His Majesty's mercy and deliver each and every one of those damned preachers to us."

The lieutenant was beaming at the major, the dragoons were grinning like halfwits. Matthew's face had gone an unhealthy dark hue, eyes a bright, dangerous green.

"They will never give them up," Alex said, choosing the pronoun with care.

"Of course you will," the major said. "Sooner or later you will."

Matthew wanted them gone. He wanted to rage and kick and ram his hand through a plank, all in a desperate attempt to get rid of the sour taste in his mouth. A right mess this was; despite his warnings, they'd gone ahead with the ambush, and as he heard it the soldiers had been taken by surprise when the hillside sprang alive and came charging towards them, huge boulders bouncing across the road. Three soldiers dead, several wounded, and ultimately nothing had been achieved – not when the troops held in reserve swung into action. More than fifteen dead, twenty or so imprisoned, no doubt to hang. He had no idea how Sandy had fared, nor Tom Brown and wee Paul….. well, he was dead, he'd seen his body on the way home. Better dead on a hillside than in a gibbet, better to fall face first into the heather than have a noose strangle your life out of you.

When Rachel rushed over he bent down to hug her and hide himself against her warm, sturdy little body, breathing in the scent of milk and honey and sun that always clung to her. He threw Wyndham a sidelong glance; what had he been playing at, dragging Matthew off the street and holding him for hours while he questioned Matthew in detail as to his whereabouts the last few weeks? And why had he insisted on accompanying him home, transforming from a most unpleasant interrogator to a friendly ex-comrade? There was something here he didn't understand, and a warning prickle at the base of his spine was telling him to tread carefully around Major Wyndham.

Ian provided part of the puzzle later that evening, sitting down beside Matthew.

"I know that man," he said.

"What man?"

"Major Wyndham."

"You do?" Matthew offered him a slice of the apple he was eating. Ian chewed in silence, accepting yet another slice.

"I've seen him with Father." He gave Matthew a long look. "They laughed a lot, aye? Laughed and drank."

Matthew nodded that he understood. "So they're friends then?"

Ian shrugged. "Mam doesn't like him, but Father has known him for several years. They were in Holland together for many months." He made a face. "He didn't recognise me. But then he wasn't looking at me, was he? He was gawking at Aunt Alex."

"Aye," Matthew nodded, "I saw that too." He took a new apple, and they sat in silence for some time. "Will you look out for your aunt? If I'm not here?" Matthew said it casually, catching Ian's eyes.

The lad smiled. "Aye, I will. But Aunt Alex can take good care of herself."

Matthew ruffled his hair and laughed. Aye, that was very true. Alex Graham was not defenceless and Oliver Wyndham might discover that at his own cost if he wasn't careful.

"I don't like him," Alex told Matthew. "I have a problem with men that allow their eyes to drift quickly off my face to lock down on my tits. Still, he did send you a warning."

Matthew settled himself on his side and gathered her to him.

"Aye, but why? And he was far from friendly earlier today." His hand found its way in under her shift, fondling her breasts. "Ian knew him, has seen him with Luke several times."

"Do you think Luke has sent him?"

"Nay; Oliver would never come here, to this far off corner of his world if he didn't have his own ends to meet." He nuzzled her along the side of her neck. "We will tread with care round that wee viper."

"Absolutely, I don't like snakes anyway."

"Ah, no?" he moved against her. Alex laughed and twisted to face him.

"That's not a snake, it's a beast, remember?"

"A very tame beast," she added a bit later.

"Tame?" Matthew bit her ear. "We'll see, Mrs Graham, we'll see."

CHAPTER 19

She was fast asleep when he left her, sometime before midnight. He just couldn't sleep, not when men he knew and liked might be languishing in jail, mayhap even dying from the wounds they'd suffered during the day. He rode Ham over the moor, keeping well off the road, and night was at its darkest when he slunk into Cumnock, a black shade that moved silently from one protective shadow to the other. He heard them well before he reached his destination; loud shrieks that spoke of pain, so much pain. His innards quivered like jellied eels, while in his head a small voice was telling him this was most unwise, and what could he do, all alone?

The entrance to the garrison yard was well guarded, a group of four soldiers standing round a brightly burning fire. However, unlike in Ayr, this was not a purpose built barracks; this was a collection of houses and sheds that the powers that be had appropriated some years back and fenced haphazardly. There was no perimeter wall, no proper munitions house. Munitions; he pursed his mouth. Aye, there he had it: if he could set the powder ablaze, it might cause the distraction he needed. But he couldn't do it alone. A high, pleading wail rose from somewhere to his right. Matthew slunk off to find help.

An hour later and they were back, four men standing in the close that ran along the back of the garrison buildings. It was quiet; no more screams, no clatter of boots on cobbles.

"They'll be in their beds by now," Matthew said in an undertone. "All but the guards." The blacksmith, Peter, nodded. He'd not been all that happy when Matthew woke him, but after a hushed conference in the smithy they'd agreed to try at least, they owed it to their brethren, one of whom was Peter's cousin. Matthew eyed the other two; he knew only one of them by name – Will – but according to

Peter they were good men, strong of faith, and both of them with relatives who'd either died or been imprisoned in the ambush.

They broke in through the wooden fence that closed the gap between stables and holding cells. One decisive jerk with the crowbar and Peter had the boards shattering, a sound that seemed far too loud in the silence of the night. One by one they slipped inside. Two made for the holding cells, Peter was to guard their retreat.

Matthew's hands were damp with sweat, the blinded lantern in his hold swung this way and that as he made his way over the yard towards the munitions store. A shed, no more, an ancient padlock on the door, no windows, but a narrow aperture along the roof on one side. He gripped the ledge and heaved himself up for a peek inside. He was in luck; barrel after barrel stood stacked in the small space.

Matthew knelt down and began his preparations. Someone laughed. Who? Where? An officer came staggering out from one of the houses, undid his breeches and pissed, continuing his conversation with the man who was standing in the door. Yet another laugh. The door creaked shut, and Matthew sank down, wiping at his brow. Had they but looked this way... but nay, he was cloaked and hooded, and in the dark it would be difficult to separate a man from a pile of sacking.

He had eight small projectiles, lengths of tightly coiled rope round a core of bundled cloth drenched in linseed oil. He began at the furthest end, as far away from the yard as possible. A couple of steadying breaths and Matthew uncovered the lantern, trying to shield what to him seemed a beacon of light with his body. He lit the first bundle. With a soft whoosh it began to burn, the fibres glowing red in the night. He lobbed it through the aperture, lit the next one, and the next one.

Sweat rolled down his spine, his hands shook. Something was beginning to burn inside the shed, he could hear the crackling sound of fire taking hold in dry wood. There; the last one lit and dropped inside, and Matthew scurried back the way he'd come. Now all they had to do was wait for the explosion and then…

Behind him there was a roar. The night exploded with light and he was thrown off his feet, near on flying for a yard or so. There was a sharp jolt of pain when he hit the ground, teeth sinking painfully into his tongue. He scrambled up onto his knees and tried to crawl away. Burning spars dropped to the ground beside him, the air was full of smoke. He wheezed, coughed and was crushed flat when something landed on his back.

"Matthew?" A hand gripped his. Matthew squeezed back, gasping with pain as he was dragged from under the debris. So much noise, so many men, soldiers pouring out of doorways in undress, horses that galloped and neighed, witless with fear, and yet in all this chaos one man had kept his head. In the light of the conflagration he saw Captain Howard standing in the middle of the yard, screaming orders. At his back he had the guards from the gate, the only men to be properly awake.

"We have to go!" Peter hissed, pulling Matthew with him. Aye, they did, but how?

"There! Who goes there?" The captain hollered, using his sword to point to where Peter was helping Matthew to his feet.

"Go," Matthew said, "leave me." They were only yards from the fence, but the four guards were covering ground rapidly.

"Nay, that I will not. Sandy will have my liver for breakfast if I leave you behind."

"But I…" Matthew could scarcely walk, let alone run. His lungs were clogged with smoke, there was blood running into his eyes, and here, God help him, came the first of the soldiers. Peter struck him over the head with the crowbar and the soldier collapsed in a heap. Will came running, and together with Peter dragged Matthew towards the gap in the fence. Dear Lord, how it hurt when they pulled him through it! Peter jammed the opening with the crowbar, and off they went. A shot went off, someone cursed, and from behind came the sounds of breaking wood.

Matthew limped and wheezed, he was half carried, half dragged, into a close, into another, up through a window, across a room where a woman screamed until Peter hushed her, out through a door, down stairs, up stairs, and all the time he could hear it; the distant screams, the angry voices of the men in their pursuit.

For near on an hour they hid in the river, flitting from one stand of reeds to the other. By the time they'd made it back to where Matthew had left Ham, approaching dawn was colouring the eastern horizon with streaks of grey.

"Did we..." Matthew croaked. Failure. He'd risked his life, their lives, and for what?

One of the men smiled. "At least seven." He described how they'd managed to breach the door to the holding cell, releasing the prisoners that could to run for the gap. His companion scuffed at the ground, muttering something about it being unfortunate the accursed captain had made directly for the makeshift prison, because if not they'd have freed most of them.

"Seven?" Matthew closed his eyes. Well that was something, he supposed, but he was too tired and too fearful to feel any elation. How on Earth would he get home? And should he go home? The soldiers ... He coughed, coughed again. His lungs hurt. Alex; he wanted his wife.

"Help me up on the horse," he said. "I'll manage on my own."

"Are you sure?" Peter sucked in his lip, looking most concerned.

Someone rustled through the nearby shrubs. "I'll see him home."

Matthew squinted in the direction of the young voice. Ian? Aye, it was, a shivering, frightened Ian, who appeared from further in the little copse, leading his mare.

"Lad? Why are you here?"

Ian just shook his head, helping Peter boost Matthew up on Ham.

"We have to go," he said. "Aunt Alex will not like it if you're not back home before daybreak."

Like it? Matthew laughed, stopped short. "Nay, I dare say she won't," he whispered. Nothing more was said. Ian whipped the horses into a mad rush for home, taking the shortcut over the moor.

She was no longer asleep. No, she was wide awake, eyes brimming with tears as she scolded him while helping him up the stairs. Matthew sagged against her, wanting to tell her that he loved her, so much did he love her, but it hurt to breathe, his head was clanging, and it was but a matter of time before the soldiers came to drag him off to hang. Look at him; sooty and damaged, the hair on one side singed, and how was he ever to get out of this alive?

"Soldiers," he mumbled. "Hang me, aye?"

"Over my dead body," she said, and no matter that he didn't quite believe her, he was comforted all the same.

Together with Ian she succeeded in getting him into their bedroom. The bed; he wanted to lie down, sleep, but she wouldn't let him. His clothes were pulled off, he was washed and washed, she muttered over the wound to his scalp, did her best to brush his hair over it. A clean shirt, and finally he was allowed to lie down. He peeked up at her. She was gnawing her lip, hands at her waist.

"What?" he croaked.

"What?" she said. "What, he asks me!" She shook her head. "I'm sorry, but this is going to hurt, okay?"

And it did; sweetest Lord, it did.

"Did you burn it?" Alex said in an undertone to Ian an hour or so later. She'd bundled clothes, boots, cloak – well, everything – and handed it to Ian, asking that he destroy it.

"Aye, all of it," he whispered back. He was all eyes, huge eyes that now and then clipped with lack of sleep. Well, no wonder, given the adventures of the night.

"And we don't tell a soul," she said. Again.

"No one," Ian swore. Again.

"Good," she nodded, eyes on the grim soldiers trotting down their lane. No major today, only that dratted captain, accompanied by a troop of six dragoons. She gave Ian a hug and painted a reassuring smile on her face. "Here goes, right?" Thank God he'd woken up, thank heavens Ian had been downstairs drinking water when Matthew snuck out of the house. And even more, thank God that he'd followed Matthew, even if it was a totally insane thing to do. She gave him yet another hug, kissed the top of his head.

"Thank you," she said.

He squirmed in her hold. "Will he... will they hang him?" He nodded in the direction of the window and the soldiers beyond.

"They'll try," Alex said. "Now, sit down and eat, okay? Pretend things are normal." She gave him a crooked smile. Normal? Bloody hell, she had a menagerie of writhing, living things in her stomach. In the yard the captain was yelling the household awake, and with a long, steadying breath she stepped outside alone.

"Captain Howard."

"Mistress." A curt nod, no more. "Your husband?"

"My husband? What do you want with him this early in the day?"

"Want with him?" The captain raised his brows. "Why, Mistress Graham, we wish to question him."

"Again? Your major was all over him yesterday."

"Yes, but that was before someone blew up our munitions building."

"What?" Alex croaked. Stupid, stupid man! "Was anyone hurt?"

The captain gave her a long look. "None too badly, fortunately. But several of the prisoners escaped."

"Ah." She shrugged. "I can't say I'm sorry."

"No, I didn't expect you to be. Now; your husband."

"He's in bed," she said. "He's sick."

"Ailing?" The captain shook his head. "Now, now, mistress, you'll not expect us to believe that, will you? He was hale and hearty yesterday."

"Some diseases strike like a bolt from heaven," she said.

"And what is ailing him"

Alex frowned, twisting her hands together. "I'm not sure; I think it may be smallpox."

"Smallpox?" The captain scratched at his bristling cheeks. Now that she'd noticed, this was not at all the normal, suave captain. No, his eyes were bloodshot, his boots unpolished and his clothes dishevelled. Well, maybe his apparel was the least of his concerns.

"I think so," she said.

"You'll not mind me looking?" he asked.

Yes, she bloody well would, but she couldn't very well say that, could she? She swallowed, but managed to shake her head.

"Mind? Of course not. But it's very contagious."

"I've had the pox," he shrugged.

Shit.

She trailed him up the stairs and opened the door to allow him entry to their bedchamber. Matthew was fast asleep, his face and the arm thrown over the pillow covered with angry, red spots, here and there small blisters. The captain took a step back.

"And these appeared overnight?"

Alex went over to smooth out a wrinkle on the sheet and adjust the ridiculous nightcap she'd crammed down on his head.

"Well, no," she said. "He felt ill last night, complained he had a headache and was cold, but these popped up this morning." Courtesy of yours truly. She shivered, knotting her hands into her apron. He'd lain perfectly still, eyes locked into hers as she tried to raise one blister after the other, mostly with the red hot muzzle of his pistol, now and then with a thimble or the pistol's little ramrod. While very few of the burns had blistered, the overall effect was pretty

192

impressive anyway, helped along by her scrubbing at them with a towel until the skin broke.

In the bed Matthew moaned. She'd fed him enough poppy syrup to sink a horse, all to make sure he looked really, really sick – which he did, eyes in bruised hollows, those horrible burns, and all of him pale. The captain stood for a moment longer, and with a muttered apology left the room. Alex sat down on the bed and hid her face in her hands.

CHAPTER 20

Even if Matthew recuperated from his ordeal in a matter of days, the coming week was sombre. So many men to lose their lives, so many families left destitute now that the man of the house was dead.

Once over her initial fright, Alex was angry with Matthew – no; she was royally pissed off at him – for having been so inconsiderate as to risk his life for something that ended up a gesture, no more. Still; what was the point of being mad at a person who was so sunk in gloom, so devastated by what was happening to people he'd grown up with, had known since he was a boy? He needed her, and anyway, she hated being angry with him, it made her itch all over. So on the fourth night after the explosion she crawled into bed, opened her arms and held him to her chest as he told her exactly what had happened and why he'd been driven to do it. All the same, it was something of a relief when Joan and Simon rode in on an unannounced visit, and then of course, there was Ian's birthday to plan for.

"Here." Mark looked embarrassed at the delighted look on Ian's face and scampered back to where his father stood.

"For me?" Ian looked from the puppy to Matthew.

"Aye, for you. You're old enough now to have a dog." Matthew smiled at Ian, slipping an arm round Alex.

Ian touched the soft, folded ears, the coarse brindle coat and laughed when the puppy nibbled his fingers, sinking sharp white teeth into his skin.

"It's a Deerhound," Mark said. "Da says they grow to be very large."

Matthew held out his hand in a rough indication making Ian's eyes widen in delight, while Alex muffled an unenthusiastic groan.

"It's not allowed in bed," she said, intercepting sly looks

between Jacob, Mark and Ian. "And if things happen you clean it up."

Ian promised he would, sinking his face into the dog's neck.

"What will you call it?" Rachel asked, crouching down to pat the puppy.

"Aragorn," Ian said, making Alex smile.

"When I get mine I'll call it Arthur," Rachel said.

"You? You won't get one." Mark sounded scornful. "That's a man's dog."

"I will too get one," Rachel glared, grabbing her father's hand. "Tell him, Da. Tell him you'll give me a bonny dog like that when I'm twelve."

"We'll see, lassie. You might want something else."

"No, I want a dog."

"Hallelujah moment," Alex muttered in sotto voce to Matthew. "Imagine the house full of teenagers *and* huge dogs." He looked confused. "Teenagers: horrible age between thirteen and nineteen, generally characterised by being obnoxious, growing at a worrying rate, discovering sex, booze and rock and roll."

"Rock and roll, aye?" Matthew murmured back. "It was a long time since you did any singing for me." He sharpened his eyes. "And there will be no… err… sex until they are wed. Well, not under my roof," he qualified, which made her grin.

If the dog had been a success, the letter from Mam was the major surprise of Ian's day. Alex waited until most of the family had disappeared to do their respective tasks before handing it to him.

"It arrived some days ago, but I thought you'd like it on your birthday."

Ian had never had a letter addressed to him in person before, and he turned the folded paper square over and over. There was a bright red Bishop's mark on it, and he squinted down at it, trying to read the date. It was a long letter, telling him how much she missed him, and how she hoped he was fully recuperated from the chickenpox. She informed him they were back in residence in their apartments at Whitehall, and that as always there was an endless stream of gossip, even if at present the mood was anything but merry, what with the aftermath of the great fire and the king's chronic financial constraints. Nor was the Dutch war any closer to a resolution, and Luke was once again to be sent as one of many negotiators to the Netherlands. Being loath to part with wife and son, Margaret was going with him, assuming Ian would be well content to remain at Hillview for the time being – probably for the best, given his recent illness. The letter ended with her assurances that she loved him very much, as did his father. He held it out to Alex.

"Horrible time of the year for a trip across the North Sea," Aunt Alex said once she'd finished reading it. "Even worse with a baby." She looked at Ian. "Do you mind?"

"Nay," he lied. All of him minded. Not once had Father ever considered it necessary to take him, Ian, along on his trips, but the red haired toad was impossible to be away from. He hoped the wean sickened and died, or perhaps he could accidentally be dropped overboard to drown. And then, well then Father would hurry back to him. Ian fisted the letter into a ball and threw it into the hearth.

Alex watched him rush outside with Aragorn in his arms and went to find Joan. The boy was at times so unhappy it hurt to watch, excluding himself from their family by his silences and tendency to walk alone through the woods. Alex suspected he cried when no one saw, but at twelve Ian was too conscious of his dignity to allow a motherly aunt to cuddle him too often, retiring into a distant approach that was extremely irritating.

Joan listened to all this in silence and sighed.

"It isn't easy for the lad, is it?" She bit off the black thread and held out Simon's enlarged coat, eyeing it critically before she handed it to her husband to try on.

"It isn't exactly easy for any of us." Alex bent down to

offer Lucy a boiled sweet. "She has the most amazing eyes," Alex smiled, straightening up.

"Aye, she does. Like her mam," Simon said, shrugging out of his everyday coat. He slid his arms into the sleeves of his black coat. "I'm surprised Luke allowed him to stay here," Simon continued.

Joan motioned for him to turn – slowly. "Aye," she said, "that must have cost Margaret a pretty fight."

"Well he's better off with us than with strangers," Alex said.

"Aye." Joan advanced on her husband, brushed at a lapel and produced a needle, stitching a loose button into place. "But Luke won't be happy."

Alex made a concurring sound: Margaret must have played with very high stakes.

"You'll do," Joan said to Simon. "Can you move your arms?"

Simon flapped his limbs. "It isn't the arms; it's the waist that expands." He looked down himself and shook his head. "I'm too short."

"Or too fat," Alex suggested, dancing away from Simon's mock punch. "Will both of you be going?" Simon's Aunt Judith had passed away and Simon was here to oversee both funeral and repartition of assets, having decided he might as well bring his family along for a visit to Hillview.

"Aye," Joan said, "if you'll care for Lucy."

Alex nodded that of course she would

"She's still too thin," Alex said to Matthew later. "And she's looking very pale, don't you think?" Something of an understatement really; Joan not only was very thin, but she also looked old, skin an unhealthy dull texture, her dark hair streaked with grey. Nor did how she was dressed help – she looked stark in the harsh mourning garb. Joan flushed when she felt their eyes on her, a surprising wave of pink washing across her face.

"Do I look strange? Is there a hairy wart on my chin?"

"Nay," Matthew said. "But you don't look well, Joan."

"It's nothing," Joan said. Her long mouth settled into a stubborn line, arms crossed over her chest. Well; if she thought that would stop this little discussion she had another think coming. Alex waited until Matthew left them before continuing with her interrogation.

"What is it?"

Joan looked at her with mild dislike. "I already said; nothing."

"Yeah; and pigs fly, fishes leap out of the water to land on our plates."

Joan smiled, ever so slightly. "It's the pain," she said. "All the time I am in pain."

After a long inventory of her herbal sachets, Alex decided that the best she could do for Joan was an infusion of St. John's wort with lavender, cloves and some valerian. She stood for some time fingering her precious flask of poppy syrup, but returned it to its place. She suspected one could become addicted to it, wasn't it a bit like heroin?

"You have to eat," Alex said, serving Joan a second helping.

"I do eat." Joan pushed the plate away from her. "I've always been thin."

"But not like this." Alex picked up Joan's hand, circling the narrow wrist with her thumb and middle finger. "You're all bones."

Joan snatched her hand back. "We're all different. Da was a tall, thin man, and I take after him."

"You do?" Alex had always assumed Malcolm Graham had looked something like her Matthew.

"He was all long, spindly legs, long thin arms and naught much else. And he had eyes like mine, grey, not hazel green like Matthew and Luke." She smiled at Matthew, who had lifted Lucy to sit on his arm, with Rachel skipping beside him as they made for the hencoop.

"I was Da's lass, just like Rachel is Matthew's ."

"He only has the one girl," Alex laughed.

"She's his lass. More his lass than yours."

Alex followed her husband and daughter out of sight.

"Yes, Rachel holds a special place in his heart – and he in hers."

Ian had initially regarded Lucy with wariness. The baby he recalled as being ugly – although not quite as ugly as Charles – was now a serious toddler with fine, straight hair of a reddish shade far from Father's deep red. To Ian's surprise he was singled out by this little girl, her hand slipping into his while her eyes fixed themselves adoringly on him or Aragorn. Occasionally she laughed, a gurgling contagious sound that made Ian laugh as well, but mostly she was a comfortable silent presence, a warm body in his lap to whom he could vent his heart and know she would never, ever tell.

"Do you think she misses it? The hearing?" Ian asked Joan one day.

"Nay, how can she? She's never heard, has she?" Joan adjusted the woollen cap on her daughter's head and cross tied the shawl over her small chest before letting her go to run unsteadily with Aragorn. "It must at times be very nice, quiet like. Only your own thoughts."

Ian considered this for some moments and nodded in agreement.

"Will she ever talk?"

"Nay. But she can make herself understood in other ways and Simon says he'll start her on her letters as soon as she can handle a quill." She walked in silence beside him for a while, twisting her head now and then to ensure Lucy was trundling along behind them.

"What's he like? Your brother?"

Ian stiffened and whistled for Aragorn, crouching down to busy himself with the dog.

"He's small and fat and has hair just like Father, and Father loves him so much more than he loves me." He raised his eyes to her. "And so does Mam," he added in an agonised whisper. "She doesn't love me anymore."

"Aye she does," Joan told him with conviction. "Margaret may have her faults, but she loves you very much." She took his hand and pulled him to his feet. "Mothers always love their bairns. Always, you hear?"

She tilted her head in the direction of the ear splitting yell that floated up from the farm behind them, rolling her eyes when Alex loudly swore that the moment she got hold of him, Jacob Graham was going to find himself hanging on to life by a very thin thread.

"We always love you, but we don't always like you," she said.

Ian laughed, comforted by her quiet assurance.

"Explain it to me again," Alex said, sitting down beside Simon. They'd taken their conversation outdoors, walking in a desultory fashion through the woods before reaching the spot where the river ran into the millpond. There was a primitive bench there, and now they were seated with the pond in front of them.

"Even if he wants to, it would be difficult for Luke to renounce the lad. He has, in front of witnesses, sworn that the lad is his. It's difficult to come back nigh on twelve years later with a change of heart. The lad has rights as well."

Alex slid her hands under her skirts to adjust her escaping stocking, pulled it tight over her calf and retied her bright red garter. Simon averted his eyes, bending down for a stick that he threw into the middle of the pond.

"Had Luke not done that, Matthew wouldn't have been able to disown the lad," Simon went on. "After all, Ian was born in wedlock, and Matthew never denied having carnal knowledge of his wife."

Eeew; just the idea of Matthew and Margaret physically exploring each other made her sick.

"So in conclusion, Luke's stuck with Ian, and Ian has rights that are protected by the law," Alex said, relieved.

"Aye, Ian has rights, but so does Luke. Luke can, should he wish it, buy Ian a commission with the army and send him off to the wars. Or he can decide his son's education is best forwarded by dispatching him to the colonies. In short, Luke decides everything in Ian's life until he reaches his majority, and he can make it most uncomfortable for the lad, should he wish to."

Alex stared at him. "But... no, Margaret wouldn't let him." Hell; she wouldn't let him! Let Luke try something like that and she'd personally disembowel him. Simon threw another stick after the first, sending it to land with a splash on the flat surface of the pool.

"Ian has some rights, but Margaret has none. She's Luke's wife, and he can do as he wishes with her and any bairns she gives him – short of killing her of course." He patted Alex' hand. "Luke's fond of the lad. He's been a good father for all the years he's had Ian, and the question of Ian's actual paternity is as unclear now as before – or perhaps even more, now that Luke has proven himself capable of siring a son." There was a slight yearning tone in his voice, a restless shift across the bench. "Luke will come for Ian, if nothing else because Margaret wants the lad back and Luke greatly loves her. He always has."

"His one saving grace," Alex nodded.

"What if..." Alex broke off. "What if Luke were to say that he's no longer sure Ian is his, and Matthew decides that he wants to recognise Ian?" But he wouldn't do that to her, not to her or to Mark – not if Ian was protected by law. He might, a small voice whispered, look at how he studies Ian, how his eyes lighten with pride when Ian walks by. In his heart Ian is his, just as much his son as Mark, Jacob and Daniel.

Simon looked at her thoughtfully. "That would complicate things, and it would require unprecedented legal work. Most complex, quite a challenge." His eyes gleamed, mouth setting in an expectant line. He shook himself, giving her a quick smile. "But this is nothing but a theoretical discussion, it'll never happen."

"No, of course not," Alex agreed, injecting her voice with as much conviction as she could muster.

CHAPTER 21

"Mr Graham."

Matthew turned at the sound of his name and sighed when he saw Oliver – Major Wyndham – bearing down on him followed by Captain Howard.

"Shit," Alex muttered. In the aftermath of that sad little rebellion that ended at Rullion Green back in late November, her husband had been persistently hounded, despite him having no connection whatsoever with the ragged band led by Colonel Wallace.

"A word?" Major Wyndham waved his hand in the direction of the Merkat Cross Inn. "Alone," he added, when Alex made as if to come with them.

"Nay, I won't leave my wife standing out in this cold."

"That's alright," Alex smiled at him. "I have some further items to purchase." She stood on tip toe and kissed his cheek. "Beware of snakes," she murmured.

She remained where she was until all three had disappeared into the inn, noting that only Matthew had to bow his head to walk in under the lintel. She hefted her basket higher and hurried off in the direction of the combined drapery and haberdashery. She wanted buttons, ribbons, linen for new shirts, and some nice dark grey broadcloth for new breeches for Matthew. She pinched at her own skirts and weighed her pouch. No, she'd have to wait; she had another winter skirt back home and the money was simply not enough – homespun would have to do. And she had to go to the apothecary; she needed camphor, willow bark and mustard seeds.

At the draper she met Mrs Brown, who drew her aside into a corner.

"Poor Jane Williams; another one dead – three bairns and a husband dead in less than a year. The remaining lad died last night, and we couldn't do anything to help." Mrs Brown sighed and adjusted her shawl. "Consumption, and with the weather we're having…" She threw a disgusted look through the door at the heavy drizzle.

"And Mrs Williams herself?" Alex asked.

Mrs Brown raised her brows at this totally idiotic question. "She isn't well, and she rarely speaks, or does anything much but sit beside her bed."

Mrs Williams had been staying quite openly with her erstwhile neighbour for the last few months. Now that the family was appropriately destroyed it would seem the crown had lost interest in punishing the poor woman further – as if there was anything more they could do to her now that her home was gone, most of her family was dead and her own health broken.

"The lasses will go into service," Mrs Brown said. "One of them in Ayr and the eldest in Edinburgh."

Alex sighed; eleven and thirteen and sent out into the world to fend for themselves. Mrs Brown shrugged; not that uncommon, was it? She drew the damp cloak tighter round her shoulders and hurried off into the rain.

Matthew sat facing the window when Mrs Brown's distinctive crouched shape crossed the open space in front of the pillory, seemingly making for the army quarters. That surprised him, but before he could dwell further on that, the barmaid set down three pewter cups and a bottle of wine on the table, returning shortly with a bowl of steaming cabbage soup and three spoons.

"We have reason to believe Alexander Peden is back in the area," Captain Howard said, sniffing at the soup.

"Alexander who?"

"Do not give us that!" Captain Howard said. "There's not one man in this accursed little town and its surroundings that doesn't know Alexander Peden."

Matthew pretended to think. "Ah! You mean Sandy. Aye, we all know Sandy." He suppressed a little smile. Sandy had been no further than ten miles away at most, utilising his network of hideouts, stretching all across the moor and the adjoining farms. Including on his own, although as yet Alex was unaware of the few nights Sandy had spent in the much improved hideout, or the little shed by the mill.

"He's an outlaw," Howard said. "A man who flaunts the authority of church and state and whose life and assets are forfeit."

"It would depend on what church," Matthew retorted.

Howard twisted his mouth into a non smile.

"It's always a question of what church, and for years it was people like my family that were persecuted by people from your church."

That shut Matthew up.

"Sandy Peden is a fanatic." Captain Howard stood up. "One day we'll apprehend him and drag him screaming to hang."

"You think? Sandy himself prophesises he'll die in bed." Matthew took a spoonful of the cabbage soup and regretted it immediately, spitting the contents onto the floor.

"And is this something he's shared with you recently, Mr Graham?" Howard said with an edge. "Seeing as that would put you in close proximity with a foresworn enemy of the king?"

"It's common knowledge," Matthew replied, stretching his booted legs in front of him. He studied the younger man in silence for some time. "I don't know what happened to your family, and I can hear in your voice it was bad, but you mustn't forget that it wasn't us up here that did it."

"No, it was soldiers. Men like yourself, Graham, who served in the parliamentary army."

"Not I, never I."

"Yes," Howard said. "That's what they always say; not me, it was someone else." Howard swivelled on his toes and walked out.

"And do you want Sandy Peden dragged to the gallows as well?" Matthew asked Oliver.

"Not particularly, no." Wyndham poured them both some more wine and regarded Matthew morosely over the rim of his cup. "What happened? Where did it all go wrong? When did our dreams of a new, better world turn into this nightmare?"

"I'm not sure. I think it all began when the king that was went back on his word, thereby reopening the fighting. You recall the siege at Colchester; men were shot point blank even after having surrendered, and the radicals urged ever harsher punishment on the royalists."

Oliver nodded. "A war between brothers, and those wounds never heal, do they?"

"Nay they don't," Matthew agreed, thinking not only of the war.

"You must be careful," Wyndham said. "Howard is a persistent man, and he's convinced you were involved in the death of those two unfortunate soldiers on the moor – and in the hanging of Lieutenant Gower."

"Aye," Matthew sneered, "there were sightings of a bay horse."

Wyndham laughed softly. "You were in Edinburgh, I'm told."

"Aye; gone the whole week."

"Mmm." Wyndham leaned forward and peered into Matthew's face. "Quite the remarkable recovery," he said, sitting back.

"Recovery?"

"From the pox. Not a scar on you, and yet Howard says you were covered in pustules." The major gnawed at his lip. "He's not convinced," he said with a shrug. " He insists it was you he saw in the yard the night the munitions shed was blown sky high."

"I was in bed," Matthew said. "Weak as a kitten."

"And that is also mighty strange. You were in the best of health when I left you late afternoon."

"Aye; it was uncommonly vicious. Near scared my wife to death, it did." He smiled; not much of an untruth, all in all.

The major downed his wine in one long gulp, eyes never leaving Matthew.

"I'll warn you if I can," Wyndham said. "But I might not always be able to."

"Why?" Matthew leaned forward. "Why would you do that for me?"

"For you?" Wyndham shook his head. "I owe you something for my life, I suppose, but I'm not doing this for you. I may sit in front of you an officer of the crown, but here…" He beat his fist against his chest. "… here the Oliver Wyndham you knew still lives. And as you may recall, that Oliver Wyndham was a pure hearted Puritan."

"Except when it came to whores," Matthew grinned.

Oliver grinned back. "Not even I am perfect."

Matthew bade Oliver good bye and went off to find his wife. Quite an eloquent performance, especially the chest beating part. Did Wyndham consider him that gullible? Matthew had not been inactive these last few weeks and was piecing together a complex portrait of a man who had once been a youth of promise and ideals but now was a husk – rotting from within.

Gambler, he heard whispered, heavily in debt and with something of a lecherous reputation. Married twice, twice widowed and with one sickly son of four, presently in the care of an aunt. He wrinkled his brow in concentration. Oliver was up to something, but for the life of him Matthew couldn't see what it was. But the fact that Luke knew Oliver, gambled and drank with him, made Matthew worry that maybe Alex was right, maybe Luke had a finger or two in this particular broth, and that was a most unnerving thought.

"I met Mrs Brown." Alex tucked her hand under his arm, shivering in the wind.

"Aye?" Matthew wanted to get home before this turned to snow, throwing a concerned eye at the leaden clouds.

"She said that only two girls remain to Mrs Williams, and she herself is in a bad way."

Matthew pressed her hand closer to him and lengthened his stride.

"I hate it when you do that," she grumbled. "You're making me run after you like a little dog."

"I want us home, wee Daniel will soon have need of you."

"Mutual need, let me tell you," Alex said, "my breasts are the size of melons."

Matthew laughed, took her by the hand and began to run towards the stables where he'd left Ham.

He had to help her off the horse when they got home. Her cloak, her skirts were encrusted in frosty sleet, her shawl was wet with molten snow, her nose was bright red with cold, and even through her tightly closed mouth he could hear her teeth chattering. When he handed her the basket she couldn't open her hand to grasp the handle, but had to suck on her frozen fingers to thaw them somewhat first.

"Je… je… je… sus," she said.

He patted her on the arse and shoved her in the direction of the house.

"Daniel; I'll wipe down Ham first."

Throughout the evening and night the snowfall intensified, the wind a constant howling.

"Amazing!" Alex stared out of the window at the unrelenting storm. "It's like a curtain of white." She stuck her hands into the sleeves of her bed jacket and shivered. "It doesn't even look like snow, it looks like falling ice." It was an hour or so until dawn and the house around them was sunk in sleep and darkness. Only here, in their room, the weak light of a single candle flared, throwing their combined shadows against the wall.

Matthew added more wood to the fire and came to stand behind her, peering out into the opaque night.

"Aye, a terrible night to be out."

Matthew tilted his head and listened. The house stood strong and solid, snug against the protective hill behind it, but he was concerned for the stable – the roof should have been replaced during autumn but he'd had neither the time nor the will. There was a thunderous crack, a loud noise that made both of them jump.

"What was that?" Alex sounded shaky. "It can't be lightning, can it?"

"Nay, of course not. But I must out and check."

"In this?" Alex gave him an incredulous look. "You'll barely make it across the yard." He was already pulling on clothes, his skin breaking out in protesting pimples at the damp wool of his breeches.

"I must check on the beasts," he said, raising his brows when she began to dress.

"If you're going, I'm going," she told him, pulling on double pairs of stockings.

They held hands as they made their way across the yard. Despite the lantern, he couldn't see a thing, and the cobbles below his feet were treacherous with ice. At one point her fingers slipped from his grasp and he had an instant of panic, seeing her swallowed forever into this swirling, impenetrable white, but then her hand was back, and he was leading them in the general direction of the stable – or where he thought the stable should be. The wind came in gusts so strong that they had to hunch and lean into it to avoid being blown away, and when he at last discerned the grey outline of the stable, his hair, his eyelashes, his brows and his coat were all layered with ice.

The stable stood, and after the storm outside it was heaven to step into its relative warmth and silence. Matthew left Alex by the door and walked through the building, inspecting doors and shutters. The loft; he clambered up, cursing loudly when he saw the leak.

"What?" she called from below. "Has the roof blown off?"

"Nay, but there's a leak. Hand me a bucket and a rake." Alex followed him up and took over the raking while he calibrated where to place the bucket, glaring at the sodden shingles above his head.

The barn was undamaged, as was the laundry shed and the smoking shed. Long before they reached the privy, he knew that this was where the damage was. Despite the wind and the snow there was a stench of ordure in the air, and when they finally could see it, he gaped. The privy was gone. Instead there was a heap of kindling, crushed by the huge oak that lay across it.

Alex tried to say something, but the wind snatched the words out of her mouth. She stood as close as she could, her lips an inch from his ear.

"I said it could be worse!"

Oh, aye; a privy was no great matter. He turned them both towards the house, shivering in his icy clothes. Alex screamed, loud enough to make him jump. She stumbled, crashed into him so heavily they both fell.

"What?" Matthew staggered to his feet, using both hands to hoist Alex back up. He fumbled for his dirk, thinking that mayhap she'd seen a wolf, hungry and mean as it came out from under the trees. She whimpered against him. He bent his head to her mouth.

"Look, look up the slope!"

Matthew squinted. Night was giving way to grey day, and the snowfall was less heavy, allowing for some visibility. All he saw was white; white on the ground, trees caked with white ice, white in the air.

"There's nothing there," he said, his mouth at her ear.

"Yes there is," she insisted, hot breath tickling the skin of his neck and jaw. "Oh God, there definitely is. Just behind the rose bushes." She attempted to burrow her way in through his clothes, all the while emitting a series of low, dissonant moans. He looked again and his arms came up to hug her to him.

"Oh dearest Lord, nay, not like that!" He was already moving in the direction of the silent shape, dragging Alex with him. "Please, no, not like this, aye?"

Mrs Williams didn't hear him. She would never hear anyone again, if it wasn't the sweet voices of the angels of heaven. She sat with her back against a tree trunk in nothing but her shift. Her hair had frozen into stiff, long strands, her skin was a mottled blue and grey and her eyes stared wide and sightless. The shift lay in icy pleats high on the thighs, and her uncovered arms hung by her sides. The naked feet were bloodied and torn, and from her right wrist hung a blue ribbon threaded through an iron wrought key.

"She was going home," Matthew said, trying to close the glassy eyes. "The poor woman was walking home to die."

CHAPTER 22

It wasn't much of a welcome party. No sooner had Simon and Joan arrived from Edinburgh before they all set off to attend the burial of Mrs Williams, with Alex filling them in on the way.

"Poor lasses," Joan said, coming over to stand by Alex.

"Yes." Her eyes followed the last remnants of the Williams family as they were led away from the grave in which their mother had just been buried, together with the boy that predeceased her by no more than a day. "Do you think she meant to?" Alex asked, wiping her hands down her skirts.

"Aye, I do, she dropped garment after garment."

The sudden thaw that followed on the ice storm had revealed a trail of discarded clothing, up the slopes and onwards towards the Brown farm.

"You do that when you get too cold," Alex said, "so that in itself doesn't signify."

"You undress when you're cold?" Joan blinked with astonishment.

Alex nodded. "As your body chills to below normal temperature the blood gets pulled back from your hands and feet and you start feeling hot. Well, that's what they say anyway." She smiled sadly and tightened her grip round Daniel. "Let's hope she died believing it was a summer day, warm and welcoming."

"Aye, let's hope." Joan's tone belied her words.

Alex scanned the small group of people for Matthew. He'd disappeared the afternoon after the storm and had been gone for several hours, waving away her questions with a curt comment that he needed to be alone. Now he stood in a small knot of men, and even from here Alex could hear the low, angry voices as they looked in the direction of the newly filled in grave. Round the men hovered Mrs Brown, waiting for her husband to take her home.

Three days to Christmas and Alex had never felt less inclined to celebrate this holiday, feeling angry with God for letting innocent people suffer on His behalf. They'd had a terrible argument about it yesterday, she and Matthew, and hadn't quite been able to make up yet, both of them throwing wary glances at each other.

"How can you think God cares?" Alex had yelled at him. "He's obviously busy with a hell of a lot of other things, isn't he? Too busy to hold a protective hand over people who have been ousted from their home because of their faith in him."

"They've been taken into his presence," Matthew attempted to argue.

"How do you know? Maybe they were predestined to suffer and die and never make it to heaven. After all that's what you believe, isn't it? That some people are chosen to live lives that may lead to heaven, while the majority, well they're just chaff, extras. And hey, God is probably somewhat blasé by now. All the people who've died on his behalf throughout the ages, it must at times make him yawn and go out to make himself some popcorn while thinking about what movie to watch. Besides, it's much better TV to watch an early Christian martyr be torn apart by lions than it is to see a poor woman freeze to death out of desperation."

"You blaspheme!" Matthew had gasped, backing away from her.

"I do? Tough; that's what you get when you marry a woman who was raised on rational thought rather than blind faith."

And that was where things stood at present; Matthew pretending to be fast asleep when she got into bed last night, she pretending she was just as heavily asleep when he rolled out of bed this morning.

"But surely…" Joan shook her head after listening to Alex' brief recap. "You can't mean that. God is always right."

"Really? To me it seems he's either very blind or extremely uncaring." She was seriously mad at God; horrible, white bearded man to sit there among his angels in eternal paradise and let the little people die for him. Alternatively, of course, God wasn't a Presbyterian and had no great fondness for them. Joan looked aghast when Alex voiced this out loud.

"Well you don't know, do you? He might be Catholic, you know. As far as I know all Christians were Catholic for the first 1500 years after Jesus, so heaven should be littered with them. Or," she added, unable to resist it, "God is Jewish. Yes, that probably makes the most sense. The Jews are his chosen people, and it was to them that he first spoke."

Joan had gone pale; without a further word she walked off.

"Oh dear," Alex muttered, "no sense of humour whatsoever."

"You forget that they were raised very strictly," Simon said, still laughing at the idea of God being Jewish. "To Malcolm, Kirk was something very serious, and his children spent much time with their nose in the Bible and being catechised."

"And look what fine examples they all turned out," Alex said caustically. "Especially the baby brother." She added saffron to the dough she was setting, mixing in honey, raisins and salt. The saffron had cost her far too much, but on seeing it at the apothecary she hadn't been able to resist it. She covered the dough with a cloth and set it to swell before turning her attentions to the ham.

"It's difficult to question truths you've grown up with," Simon said, leaning against the kitchen wall. "In the Graham home there was only the one true Kirk, and that was the Kirk of Scotland, legacy of the saintly John Knox."

"And in your home?"

Simon shrugged. "My father was a lawyer, spent his life with his nose deep in the business of his fellow men. It is somewhat disenchanting, that… My mam was a papist, a Highland lass." He chuckled. "She only agreed to me being raised in the Kirk on account of it helping Da in his business to be seen as a firm Presbyterian. But in secret she taught me both my rosary and all about the saints. " He inspected a wrinkled apple before biting into it. "Da knew, but didn't disapprove. It was his opinion that an open mind was a valuable asset – in religion as much as in other things. Not that he said that out loud, or I wouldn't have been allowed anywhere near Joan Graham."

"It's all so incomprehensible to me, I feel entirely out of context." She heaved herself up to sit on the table, dangling her legs. "I'm not even sure..." She shook her head. " There are days when I'm not sure God exists at all."

"Aye, I have such days too. But best not mention them to Joan."

Alex laughed and slid back down onto the floor. "I won't."

"Not now, not this close to Christmas," Alex said next day, looking out through the door at the three riders in the yard.

"Apparently. You stay here," Matthew said, lifting his hand to her cheek. "I'll be right back. Simon, Ian, come with me, aye?"

Together the brothers-in-law went out into the frost covered yard, with Ian hurrying after them. Joan came to stand behind Alex. It was a grim conversation, with Matthew shaking his head repeatedly. Simon took a step forward, hands in a placatory gesture, and after some minutes the lieutenant drove his horse round in a tight circle, crossed the yard in the opposite direction of the one he had come, and set his mount towards the moor, his two men falling in behind him.

"Now what?" Alex asked once they were all inside again.

Simon rolled his eyes. "They're but making the rounds, wishing us all Christmas cheer."

"We were advised to stay at home over the coming days," Matthew said in an irritated tone. "And we were reminded yet again as to the dangers of supporting confirmed outlaws or attending any unlawful assemblies." He looked worried. "They're after Sandy, a novel sort of fox hunting. "

214

"Will they find him?" Joan asked, sounding just as worried.

"Not without dogs and much luck, and Sandy is no fool. He'll have the wits to lie still." He met Alex' eyes and sat down to finish his interrupted breakfast.

"You're more concerned than you let on," Alex remarked several hours later.

"I am." He threw a look out of the window at the fading light of the December day. "He isn't well, and these last few days of icy weather have left him in bad shape. If he has to run..." Matthew shook himself. "Only one way to go; he'll have to go into the river."

"Let's hope the soldiers follow their own advice and stay home, busy stuffing their goose," Alex said, "and then let's hope they get really, really drunk – all of them – so that they leave us in peace for some days."

Matthew tried to smile; it didn't work very well.

Four young faces to kiss good night, one baby to feed and tuck into his cradle and then she slipped into bed to wait for Matthew. She could hear his voice, a dark murmur from below interspaced by Simon's higher range and occasional bursts of laughter. It made her feel safe, to lie half-asleep in her bed and hear the man she belonged with. Her man, her Matthew... she stretched out her hand to caress his pillow.

"Dear God, hold him in your hand and keep him safe," she prayed. She laughed at herself. "I know, I know. First I say I'm not sure you even exist and then I ask you for a favour. But if not for me, then for him, God. Because he's a good man and does his best – he always does his best." She curled onto her side, Matthew's pillow in her arms.

He wasn't sure she ever woke properly. He wasn't sure if he himself was awake, but he had a clear memory of bidding Simon a somewhat unsteady good night and coming into his bedroom to find his wife sleeping, his pillow held to her chest. After that it was all very fuzzy, but his cock had somehow found its way inside of her, and she was moving against him, but he could swear she was still asleep, and he was in a whisky powered dream, anchored to reality only by her body, and the warmth of her around his standing cock.

"I love you," he whispered into her hair. "I love you so very much, my bonny Alex." Easier to say when she couldn't hear it, and he mumbled it over and over again, his long body folding itself round her to keep her safe and to make sure she never, ever left him. "My Alex," he murmured, slipping his hand in under the pillow to cup her breasts. She grunted something unintelligible, but he thought he could make out his name. My own miracle, he thought dizzily, my gift from God.

"You could have woken me," Alex sounded disapproving, but the smile lurking at the corner of her mouth destroyed the effect. Matthew yawned and stretched.

"You're more biddable when you're asleep. I can do all I desire with you then." He kissed her on the cheek.

She wrinkled her nose. "Ugh! What did you do? Finish a whole cask of whisky on your own?"

"Nay," he sat up far too fast and squinted at the sudden headache that shot up from the base of his skull. "Simon helped."

"Oh dear," Alex grinned, "I can see a major hangover coming on."

Matthew slumped back in bed with a groan, covering his eyes with his arm.

"You sleep, and I'll make you some breakfast."

His stomach cramped at the thought of food. "Nay, I'll just sleep."

"Simon as well?" Alex asked Joan, who just shook her head.

"Those two and a quart, and you never know how they'll end up. They must have sat up through most of the night." She kissed Lucy on the top of her head and set her down, watching with maternal pride how her daughter hurried over to Ian.

"Thank you, Ian," Joan said, "I don't know how we manage without you in Edinburgh."

"Do you like it? Living there?" Alex asked.

Joan made a noncommittal sound, pulled back her hair into a messy knot and secured it with her hairpins.

"Well enough. Simon has plenty of work and I've found someone who may be able to help me with Lucy. A woman of our age, deaf since childhood." She kneeled down to help Ian adjust Lucy's clothing. "Go on, off with you both. And the dog."

Ian took Lucy by the hand and led her off in the direction of the stables to go and feed the pigs, with Rachel skipping beside them, rosy with excitement.

"She has a thing about the pigs," Alex sighed, smiling at the exuberance of her daughter. "She's even managed to teach one of the piglets to sit." She slid her eyes over in the direction of the pantry and the waiting Christmas ham. "Not that it helped him much," she murmured tongue-in-cheek, making Joan burst out in laughter.

Alex broke off a piece of the saffron bread, planning the day as she munched. Christmas celebration in the Graham home was mostly for her benefit, as the Scottish Kirk tended to frown on excessive celebration of this holiday. Over the years Matthew and she had developed a compromise version of the festivities, with him insisting that the reading of the Scriptures had to be the focal part of the day while agreeing to a full out Christmas feast – even if he drew the line at presents. Alex made a mental list of the foodstuffs she needed to put the final touches to, starting with the minced meat pies.

Beside her Joan stiffened, looking at her with a small crease between her brows.

"Do you hear that?"

Alex listened; a faint baying sound that made the hairs on her arms stand at attention.

"Dogs," she said, "they've brought dogs onto the moss."

When Alex entered the bedchamber Matthew was already up, dressing with haste. Down the stairs, out the door and up towards the moor, with Alex at his heels. He fumbled with his belt as he went, adjusting his scabbard and sword.

"Someone is feeding them information," Alex said, half running to keep up with him.

"Feeding them what?" He rushed up the last slope and stood panting on the flat hill top, scanning the frozen surroundings, every thicket, every stunted stand of trees as if he hoped to see Sandy pop up from behind them. The sound of the dogs was louder up here, and even if Alex couldn't see them, she could imagine them. Large and heavy, the mastiffs weren't fast, but thorough.

"Look at the size of this," she went on, waving her arms at the vast, open landscape. "And still they know to look here, on the corner abutting not only Hillview but also, more or less, the waters. He could be anywhere, and yet they keep on coming back to here – to these few square miles."

Matthew pursed his mouth, dark brows coming down to form one very straight line of anger over eyes that had gone quite cold.

"And someone told the soldiers about that failed ambush. They knew. That's why what's his name, Oliver, warned you. So who?"

"I don't know, but I aim to find out, aye?" They stood for a long time in the gusting, icy wind scanning the moss, but apart from the far off baying of the dogs they heard nothing and saw nothing – nothing at all.

CHAPTER 23

"I have to go and look for him," Matthew whispered to Alex, bending down to kiss her brow.

"Now?" Alex blinked at him, a vague shape in the dark.

"I had a dream, and I have to go and see him safe."

Alex scooted up to sit, shivering when the quilt fell off her shoulders, baring her arms to the cold night air.

"Do you want me to come with you?"

Matthew shook his head; he would cover ground much faster without her.

"Sleep, I'll be back before dawn."

"Sleep he says," she grumbled, lying back down as he tucked her in. "Sleep while your husband goes gallivanting in the dark the night before Christmas."

"Before dawn," he promised, and kissed her again.

Alex slept off and on, relaxing fully only when Matthew reappeared in the grey hours of the night. He dropped sodden clothes in a heap before he clambered into bed beside her, making her yelp at his touch.

"Matthew Graham, if you don't take your ice cold feet away from my legs I might do you some grave bodily harm, involving my knitting needle and your eye."

"Oh, aye?" He pulled her shift out of the way to warm his hands on her arse.

"Matthew!"

"I'm cold, woman, do something about it."

"Huh," she muttered, but pulled him as close as he could get. "Was he okay?"

Matthew yawned and mumbled something unintelligible that she took for a yes.

It took half the morning before Alex understood they had a new houseguest, hidden up in the attic.

"You tell her, your sister, before you tell me?" she barked at Matthew, so angry she could barely speak coherently.

"He needs help," Matthew said. "Joan can look after him."

Alex gave him a look that should have reduced him to a heap of smouldering ashes, pushed by him and stalked up to the attic to examine Sandy Peden. He looked awful, cheeks sunk into grey hollows, eyelids a dark purple. His breath came in long, unsteady rasps, and even now, after hours under quilts he was shivering. His leg was bandaged, but there was blood seeping through in places, indicating that the gash was not only long but also very deep.

"Not in our home," Alex said, turning to face Matthew. "You promised."

"He's hurt and ailing."

"I can see that, but you promised. And even worse, you didn't tell me."

"I couldn't leave him to lie like this on the moss! He'd be dead by morning."

Alex studied the pale man in silence. Maybe that would have been for the best, she thought uncharitably, feeling ashamed of herself.

"One night, that's all."

"He needs care," Matthew said. "We must help him."

"Two nights, no more," Alex compromised. She ducked beneath his arm and escaped down the stairs.

Joan bustled about, her cheeks bright with excitement as she carried up food, bandages and clothes to the hidden minister, in full view of the curious children.

"Irresponsible!" Alex said to Simon. "Do they expect children this small to hold their tongues?" She glared in the direction of her husband to whom she wasn't talking and stalked off, tagged by Rachel, who in a loud voice asked why Aunt Joan was in the attic and could she please go there too?

"Rachel, lass," Matthew's voice stopped his daughter. "Come here, I must talk to you, aye?"

"Yeah," Alex muttered under her breath. "Take the time to explain to her what you didn't bother to explain to me, you jerk." Matthew seemed to have heard, because she could feel his eyes burning into her back. Well she didn't care; she busied herself with preparing the Christmas dinner, keeping up a cheerful conversation with Simon and the children while cold shouldering Matthew completely.

Late that afternoon Alex took the tray up to Sandy, ignoring Joan's protests along the lines that this was her task. She set it down on a stool and concentrated on the nasty leg wound, making Sandy hiss when she prodded and re-bandaged the wound. It looked clean enough, so likely it would heal with time. The cough however… she rocked back on her heels and studied him, her inspection being returned like for like from watery, grey eyes.

"I know you don't like it," Sandy croaked, groping for his handkerchief. "And I wish I had no need to importune you thus." He smiled weakly. "But I do, lass. I'm not ready to die yet. Too much left to do." He closed his eyes, colourless lashes fluttering against his pale cheeks.

"Yes, I suppose being a cocklebur up the English arse is something of a vocation," Alex said, making Sandy laugh.

"I hear you think God is Catholic," Sandy said between coughs.

Alex raised a brow. "Discussing me with Joan? Or is it perhaps Matthew, looking for guidance on how to handle his difficult wife?" From the way Matthew squirmed, she had her answer. "It would've been better to talk directly to me, don't you think?" she said, before turning her back on him in a dismissive gesture.

"To answer your question, what I said was that he might be – just as he might be Jewish or Anglican. My point being that we don't know to what, if any, church he subscribes. It would be presumptuous to assume he's Presbyterian, given that the largest mass of Christianity is in fact Catholic."

Sandy struggled to sit. He fixed her with a stern look, the overall impression ruined by his running nose and red, puffy eyes.

"You can't say such. It's blasphemy."

"Not to the pope," she retorted. "To the pope it's a God given truth."

Sandy gasped. "The pope? He heads a church that has lost itself in idolatry, more concerned about trappings and riches than spiritual devotion." And, he added, she shouldn't forget that the Catholic Church was an instrument in their persecution, as was the Church of England.

Alex shrugged. "Not so long ago it was the Kirk of Scotland that was doing the persecution in the name of God." She ignored Matthew's muffled objection, keeping her eyes on Sandy.

"Not me," Sandy said.

"No? So you've never spoken out against the fiendish popish practices?"

Sandy twisted away from the look in her eyes. "We must hold to the true faith."

"That's what they say as well, and who's to know who's right and who's wrong?"

"Surely you don't mean that," Sandy spluttered. "You must bring your wife to her senses, Matthew. She's wilful, and speaks of things she has no understanding of."

"I'm sitting right beside you, so kindly address yourself to me, not him," she said.

Sandy sneezed, folding together as yet another coughing fit racked him. He waved away Matthew's hand, taking a few gulping breaths before facing Alex.

"You think too much," he wheezed. "That's unseemly in a woman. You should trust your husband's counsel on all matters spiritual and then perhaps you may hope."

"Hope for what? A place in heaven ruled by a bigoted God? No thanks."

Sandy blinked at her, his mouth falling open. Jesus! Alex reared back; he had the breath of a dead stoat.

"You speak of things you don't understand," Sandy said, "and you forget your place. You're but a helpmeet to your husband and must in all matters of any greater importance bow to his will."

"Really? And is that what he thinks as well?" Alex gave Matthew a barbed look. "Well, is it?"

"Nay, of course not," he replied with a sigh.

"That's good, seeing as I'd never consider any man to be my intellectual superior. Anyway," she went on, "now that we're having a theological discussion I might just as well come clean and tell you I have major problems with all this predestination nonsense."

"Nonsense?" Sandy's voice squeaked. He coughed and coughed, glaring at her over his sodden handkerchief.

"You can't say thus," Matthew said. "It's the truth, aye? God has preordained that some of mankind will be given eternal salvation, as indication of his mercy and justice, while the greater part will not, in just punishment of the burden of sin which all of us carry."

"Sounds very fair," Alex said sarcastically.

"Predestination is no nonsense, it's a principal tenet of faith," Sandy put in, now sufficiently recovered to be able to speak. "God extends the possibility of grace to a few chosen amongst us, and only to those."

"Well you would say so, wouldn't you? I assume you're counting yourself in among the elected few."

Even Matthew smiled at the bright red flush that rose through Sandy's face.

"I don't know," the preacher mumbled.

Alex snorted and shook her head. "Whatever... predestination takes away an element of accountability. If God has already preordained, then why bother? To me it's much more clear cut; we have free choice and can choose to shape our destinies as we want. It will be the choices we make and the actions we take that ultimately will count, not some haphazard divine lottery. That's what I believe, in any case."

Well, that shut them up. Had Sandy been a Catholic he'd have been waving a crucifix and possibly a bunch of garlic at her, so shocked did he look. And as to Matthew, to her surprise he was nodding, trying out a weak smile in her direction. Forget it; she stared him down, dumped the loaded tray on Sandy's lap and left.

"You must punish her," Sandy said. "For her own good you must beat these misconceptions out of her."

Matthew gave him an incredulous look. "Beat her? Nay, I'll never lay a hand on Alex."

"She's imperilling her immortal soul, the poor woman has her head filled with nonsense – but dangerous nonsense. What would our brethren think had they heard her speak out as she just did? She would be chastised, cast out from the Kirk."

Matthew just shook his head. "I'm fortunate in my wife, she travelled the world for me, she risked her life to find me and bring me back home." He broke off a piece of bread and chewed it. "Alexandra Ruth, that's her full name. She has more than proved herself my Ruth. I can live with her not being Martha – I don't want her to be, I want her to be just as she is."

Sandy exhaled loudly. "I'll talk to her myself then," he said in a doleful tone. "I must try and set her on the narrow path."

"You do that," Matthew replied with an encouraging nod.

It had been a horrible Christmas Day, and the evening was none the better. Battle lines were drawn across the parlour, with Simon and Alex sitting together while Joan settled herself on a stool at her brother's feet. The children flitted from one parent to the other; affected by the strained atmosphere they became loud and quarrelsome, forcing Matthew to bark at them to sit down and listen, for was he not about to read them the gospel according to Luke?

Ian sank down beside Alex when Matthew opened the Bible, leaning against her legs. He'd spent most of the day at the top of the lane scanning for soldiers, made as nervous as she was by Sandy's presence, and had over supper left his normal place beside Matthew to sit beside her instead.

She tousled his hair. Ever since the incident at the Cumnock garrison there was a special bond between them, both of them members of the let's-keep-Matthew-safe club. Not that he was making it easy for them. Her hands clenched; and if the soldiers came now? What then? She rose to her feet, interrupting Matthew halfway through the story of the birth of Jesus and without a word ushered her children up to the nursery.

She started at every sound the coming day. Repeatedly she walked up and down the lane, all of her tense with fear. When Matthew tried to talk to her, she moved away, when he came after her she wheeled and left the room. If there was someone she didn't want to see or touch or talk to, it was him, which was why she'd spent the night in the nursery with the children, ignoring him completely when he'd appeared at the door in only his shirt, asking her to stop this and come and sleep where she belonged.

She counted hours until nightfall, relaxing with relief when darkness fell. No soldiers, not this Boxing Day, and now there was only one more night to go and then he'd be gone. It made her feel small and petty to so look forward to throwing a sick and wounded man out of her house, but she had her priorities firmly in order, and on that list Sandy Peden came very much at the bottom.

Tight-arsed little man, she thought angrily, but recognised that wasn't fair. Peden had his moments of pig-headed righteousness, but he also had moments of deep spiritual insight and instinctive kindness. She spent the second night as well with her children, in a combination of protectiveness towards them and anger at her husband. Well before dawn she was up, and by the time the rest of the household woke she was already out in the yard, keeping her silent vigil.

"Is he gone?" Alex asked Simon when he joined her.

"Nay, last I saw Joan was preparing his breakfast."

"Fucking great, I said two nights, not two nights and three full days." She looked off in the direction of Cumnock. Nothing; no dust cloud, no glinting reflexes. "Will you stay? Keep an eye out?"

He nodded and pulled the cloak tighter around him. "And you?"

"Me? I have a houseguest to get rid of."

"When will he leave?" Alex asked Matthew when she entered the kitchen, "I want him out of my house now."

"But he's ill! His cough is as bad as when I brought him here."

Alex pointed up the lane. "What will you do if – no, when – a troop of soldiers materialises up there? Pick him up on your shoulders and rush for the woods? Hide him under the bed and hope they don't look there? You promised me, Matthew Graham, that you wouldn't put us at risk, and yet that is what you're doing every minute he remains in our home. Don't touch me," she snarled when he attempted to put an arm around her. "Don't try to cuddle me into acceptance. You promised."

"He's a friend in need."

Alex shook her head slowly. "He's an outlaw, and his presence here puts all of us at risk. Do you want to see us all bonded into slavery? Do you want your sons to live out what life they have as slave labour on a tobacco farm in Virginia?"

That was very underhand; a kick that hit him squarely in the balls. He jerked as violently as if she'd slapped him, his eyes shifting into a muddy green.

"You know I don't."

"And still that's what you're risking. Me abused, your children slaves and yourself a slave or hanged." She didn't like herself for saying that, not when all of him paled, an arm flung out to steady himself against the wall.

"You know…" he began, swallowing so hard she could see his Adam's apple bob up and down. He raised agonised eyes to hers. "I don't want that, but I can't leave Sandy to die." Their eyes locked and held.

"It's a question of priorities. Your family or your friend; your marriage or your friend, your life – all our lives – or his life. Take your pick, but be prepared to live with the consequences."

He said nothing for a while. She held his eyes, listening to the sound of her breathing, his breathing.

"He'll be gone by noon," he said and turned on his heel.

CHAPTER 24

They didn't know how to reach each other – or rather she didn't want to, torn into shreds that he should have broken his promise to her. To her! Words rose hot and angry up her throat at the sight of him, words that twisted her tongue into knots and were swallowed down – some things were best left unsaid. Instead, Alex escaped into the preparations for the coming Hogmanay festivities – however uninspired she felt about the whole thing.

"At least no one will leave hungry," Alex said, counting the stacked pies, puddings and cakes. "Should we really be holding this dance?" she went on, directing herself to Joan. "It could be considered unseemly."

Mrs Williams was but eight days in the ground, Matthew and she weren't talking or even touching each other, the children orbited like nervous satellites round their silent parents, Joan kept on dropping oblique comments regarding Christian duty in general and versus ministers in particular. Alex sat down to nurse Daniel. He alone of the whole family remained oblivious, smiling at his mother.

"It's too late to cancel," Joan said, "and mayhap it's what people need. A celebration among friends." She was packing foodstuffs into a basket.

"For Sandy?" Alex asked somewhat sharply.

"Aye. Matthew will be taking it to him later. We mustn't forget our friend and preacher."

There it was again, that disapproving edge, and Alex decided there and then that she'd had it.

"And if it were your children? If it were your Simon that risked hanging for the sake of friendship and faith?"

Joan's cheeks acquired a pink tone. "Some things are worth it."

"Easy for you to say," Alex snapped back. "You're not exactly risking anything, are you? It's my man who'll be carrying that basket over the moor, not you or your precious Simon. And if he's stopped? Shot? What will you tell me? That I should be glad he died because of a worthy cause? Even worse, Joan, they won't shoot him. No, they'll fine him and then we'll all be lost. Or will you put up the 200 merks?"

Joan hid her eyes, muttering that such money couldn't be found.

"No," Alex said. "I didn't think so. Bloody hypocrite." She stood up with Daniel in her arms and swept out of the room, kicking the kitchen door shut behind her.

"I hear you've quarrelled with Joan," Matthew said, sitting down on the edge of the bed.

"At present I seem to be quarrelling with everyone," Alex muttered back. Her head hurt after an aggravated discussion with Simon. It wasn't as if she'd expected Joan to take off on her own to deliver the stuff to Sandy, was it? And anyway, why shouldn't she? If she was so keen on helping Sandy bloody Peden then she could take a brisk walk across the moor just as well as Matthew could. Probably safer, given her gender.

"With me as well?" Matthew dropped his hand to rest on her hip.

"Of course with you! This is all your fault to begin with." She batted his hand off her hip and scooted up to sit against the headboard. "You promised me, and even worse... No, shut up, you listen to me, okay?" she glared when Matthew seemed on the point of interrupting. She took a big breath, took another. "How could you? How could you bring him here and not even tell me? Do you think I'd be so cold hearted as to refuse him help, given his state?"

"No, but…"

"But what? Better to sneak him in?"

"I didn't stop to think, aye? I was wet and cold, it was growing light and all I had in my head was to make it back home without being discovered. And Joan was awake, so she helped me get him up the stairs, and then, well, I knew you wouldn't like it, so…"

"So you hoped I wouldn't find out," she finished for him. "You obviously think me very stupid or unobservant."

"Of course not! I would have told you at some point."

"Yeah, if nothing else just as the soldiers came galloping down our lane." She hugged her pillow to her chest, eyes never leaving him. "You know, something along the lines '*Alex, I forgot to tell you, but we may have a wee problem.*'" She mimicked his accent to perfection, and despite the situation he smiled.

"None of you understand," Alex said. "It isn't that I don't like Sandy – even if at times he's a bit too much – it's that I'm paralysed with fear that by helping him you're damning us. To me, our children must always come first; to me you come first. But to you it seems Sandy's wellbeing is more important, and that hurts."

"That isn't true, you know it isn't true." He moved close enough to touch her, his hand closing over her ankle. "I won't do it again."

"Do what? Lie to me? Break your promises?"

"I'll not place us at risk, I'll even stop helping…" He looked crushed, saying that, and Alex gave him a long look.

"And so you'll sit on your hands and hate me for stopping you from rushing off in defence of your friends and beliefs." She shook her head. "I can't ask that of you. But I do ask that you tell me the truth – always – and that you keep our home out of it."

"I promise," he said, and at her raised brows he gave her a crooked smile. "I do, Alex. And I won't break it this time, nor will I lie to you again. I'll tell you everything."

She gave him a doubtful look, making him frown.

"My word, aye? Don't you believe me?" He leaned towards her, sinking his eyes into hers.

"I do," she said after a minute or so. "But if you break it, I'll leave."

"Leave? How leave?"

"Walk out the door, up the lane and take off." She jerked her head in the direction of several half-packed leather satchels. She'd even talked to Simon about it, but he'd looked horrified at the thought. To be honest, so was she, but there were days when all of this was just too much, long nights when she worried she wouldn't cope, couldn't live with this constant burden of fear that somehow he'd be torn away from her. She couldn't meet his eyes, and instead focused her attention on her wedding ring, turning it round and round her finger.

"I'll not break it," he said hoarsely.

"Good."

"You should make your peace with Joan," he said as he got to his feet.

"Or she with me. She's been the one dropping nasty comments the last few days."

"You're somewhat intimidating to her."

"She's the perfect Christian, not me, so if she wants to make things up then she'd better take the initiative. I won't." Don't even go there, her tone warned. With a sigh Matthew turned to leave.

"Matthew?"

He stopped by the door. "Aye?"

"I want it to be like it's supposed to be."

"So do I, lass."

She nodded and kept her eyes on the wall. With a soft thud the door closed in his wake.

Later that same day, Matthew followed the sound of shrill, happy voices, smiling when he heard Rachel insist that she could so swim, and that come summer she'd show Mark for real. Tomorrow his lass would be four, born in the Colony of Virginia on New Year's Eve. He had received her into this world, his hands had been the first to touch her, his arms the first to hold her, and he wondered if this was why he felt such a strong affinity with her. Or mayhap it was because she was so much her mother's daughter, and by watching Rachel grow he achieved a small insight into the child Alex had once been.

The laundry shed was full of young bodies in different states of undress. Ian was already in his shirt again, Jacob and Daniel both as naked as the day they were born, and Mark was busy with his stockings. Rachel was still in the tub, singing something to herself.

"Do you need help?"

Alex gave him a flustered look, shoving her hair off her damp and rosy face. She looked lovely, and suddenly he knew exactly what to do to mend things between them. He reached forward and tugged at an escaped curl, watching with interest how the tip of her ears went a promising pink.

"The idea was that I was going to sneak off for a bath all on my own," she said. "But then all of these decided they wanted to bathe."

"Not me," Ian said in a surly voice.

"No," Alex grinned at him. "But if I'm doing four I might as well do five."

In less than five minutes Matthew had the laundry shed empty of children, promising Alex she'd get the hours of peace she needed while he made sure the children were fed and put to bed. She sank down on the bench with a grunt, and sat like that for some time, waiting for the water in the cauldron to heat up. Matthew had created a system of barrels that filled with rainwater or melting snow, and these barrels were close enough to the cauldron to make the water carrying much less of a burden. Still; three pails here, another two here… her arms ached with the effort.

Alex undressed, wondering at what point Matthew intended to return. When she was in the bath or after? Her hands slid down her front, over her thighs. The enforced regime of regular morning exercise she'd implemented after Daniel's birth was having the desired effect, even if her abdominal muscles would never be the same again. She panicked regularly over getting old, because all around her she saw women younger than her collapse into something that was more old age than she'd ever seen in her own time.

Teeth dropped out, spinal columns bent into a permanent hunch...

With an inhalation she stepped into the tub. Too hot, and she hopped from one foot to the other for some time before lowering herself inch by protesting inch into the water. There, much better; she sank down deeper into the water, low enough that it should lap at her face. Her hand slid in between her legs, and she was wet and slippery but slightly cooler than the water that surrounded her. She touched herself, floating in her bath and longed for Matthew, for the strength of him inside her and the length of him on top of her.

Alex flounced into the kitchen.

"Did you have a good bath?" Matthew could see in her eyes that she'd expected something more, and it pleased him, making his privates tighten considerably. She muttered something, hung up her cloak and moved towards the staircase but was blocked by Matthew.

"Did you?"

She was only in her clean shift, and he stood close enough that he could feel the warmth radiating from her.

"Yes," she said in a breathless voice. He nodded, moving aside. Once again a flaring disappointment in her eyes. She could wait for it, he would make her wait.

All that evening he teased her; a foot snaking its way up her legs under the table, a hand that tightened hard on her hair as he passed her chair, a finger brushed along her spine. He sat across the room from where she was sewing, and he knew that all he had to do was catch her eyes and tilt his head and she'd rise and go upstairs to wait for him. It made him throb, and he found it increasingly difficult to concentrate on what Simon was saying.

His wife could play this game too, holding out the shirt she was making and telling him to stand up so that she could measure it against him. Her hands fondled him through the cloth of his breeches, and Matthew almost folded over but was held upright by her other hand on his shoulder.

"Oops," she grinned as she stuck him with a pin, very much on purpose. With a prim expression she sat back down and went on with her stitching, but he could see how her legs trembled, how her chest heaved.

Finally, Matthew could wait no more. His cock was on fire and he no longer even pretended to be listening to Simon, his eyes glued to his wife's vulnerable nape. Also on purpose, he recognised, Alex stretching and commenting on something while she pulled her hair up high onto her head, leaving neck and ears tantalisingly bare. Her eyes slid in his direction, dark in the weak light of the room. He licked his lips and raised a brow. She smiled, a slow, hidden smile that made all of her glow.

"Off with you," Simon snorted, shoving at Matthew who fidgeted at his tone, muttering something about being tired.

"Aye," Simon said. "You'll fall asleep the moment your head touches the pillow."

"I sincerely hope not," Alex said in an undertone that made Simon explode with laughter.

His hands were on her hips already on the stairs. Inside their room, he kissed her; kissed her until she was soft and malleable in his arms, shaping herself to him in whatever way he wished it. He struggled with her bodice, her stays, she tore at his shirt, his breeches. He un-gartered her stockings, kneeling to pull them off her, and backed her against the wall.

"Wait," she said, "I…"

His mouth covered hers. This was no time for talk. He sat down on the stool and pulled her towards him. She straddled him, he widened his legs and she slid down into his lap, onto his cock. He spread his thighs wider and all of him was inside her. Her inhalations came in short, quick gasps and she rose on her toes, sank back down, slowly, excruciatingly slowly. She was warm, she was moist, she smelled of rosemary and lavender, and when he bit her, none too gently, she called out his name.

"Matthew," she groaned, rising a few inches from his lap before sinking back down again. "My Matthew!" He placed his mouth against the hollow of her throat, kissing the point where her pulse leapt like an imprisoned rabbit. Her pulse; fast and strong it surged through him, blending with his own beat, a perfect syncopation. He struggled to his feet, with her still there, on him, and she wound her arms round his neck.

And then they were in bed, naked skin against naked skin, legs twisted together and it was nigh on insupportable, this burning sensation that flowed through his balls and into his cock. His hands knotted themselves in her hair, he kissed her, he bit her, she bit him back. He rose above her, she shifted from side to side, and he buried himself in her, he pushed and thrust, and still she wasn't close enough, not as close as he wanted her. Ah! Aye, there, her legs round his hips, her crotch grinding against his, and sweetest Lord, Alex, his Alex, his … Aaaah!

Like a gutted fish he lay on top of her, and it was only with a huge effort he succeeded in rolling off to lie gasping on his back. Beside him she stretched and curled up against him. Matthew smiled at her, raising his hand to caress her dark head.

"Was it like it's supposed to be?"

She nodded, pressing herself even closer to him.

"I'm glad," he breathed.

"So am I," she whispered back.

The dance was a roaring success. Edged with desperation and fear, fuelled by far too much to drink, it became a wild get together, with the fiddlers leading off on one dance after the other to the loud cheers of the people. Cakes disappeared the moment they were set down, and in one secluded corner Alex found Mark and Ian with their noses stuck far too deep into the cider.

Matthew was everywhere; on the dance floor, by the fiddlers, talking to his neighbours, carrying a fretting Daniel to allow Alex to sit and eat something in peace. Toasts were drunk, and Rachel was hoisted to stand on a table receiving a raucous round of applause on account of it being her birthday.

"If we're not careful she's going to think this is her birthday party," Alex said to Simon.

"She already does," Simon laughed. "Have you seen Joan?"

Alex pointed in the direction of where the women were congregating.

"Over there, with Lucy."

Simon sighed. "She knows you're right, that you must think first and foremost of your family. But she's equally convinced that it's our Christian duty to help Sandy Peden and the like."

"Fine; let her do it then – I won't stop her."

Tonight she wasn't going to think about any of this; not of the roaming soldiers nor of Sandy Peden, shivering all alone in a damp, cold cave. Instead she threw herself into the party, laughing and dancing. At one point she bumped into Matthew on the dance floor, was lifted in a high arc, kissed and released, and off he went to find a new partner. A few moments later he came to join her on one of the makeshift benches, handing her a mug of cider.

"I'm going up the hill later," she said.

He smiled indulgently. "Send him my regards, aye?" He looked around the teeming space. "Take Ian with you, I don't want you to walk up there alone."

"Why are we doing this?" Ian hurried after Alex, the lantern swinging this way and that in his hand.

"I always do this on New Year's Eve," Alex said. "In honour of my father." Not once since she'd been thrown through time had she missed her annual New Year's date with her father, some moments when she attempted to communicate to Magnus just how much she missed him.

"Your father? Is he dead then?"

"I'm not sure," Alex sighed, aware that this only piqued Ian's curiosity further. "He disappeared from me during a thunderstorm." Not an entire untruth, even if it was her that had disappeared from Magnus, not the other way around.

"Oh," Ian said. "How?"

"I don't know. I was knocked unconscious by a bolt of

lightning, and when I woke… well, I was here but he wasn't."

"Did it hurt?" He was walking close enough that their arms brushed against each other.

"Oh, yes," Alex said. "Not something I ever want to experience again, let me tell you." For a variety of reasons, the principal one being that she didn't want to experience yet another fall through time.

He was still there. Alex relaxed. As she stood silent and toasted Magnus she could feel his presence, see him lean towards her through the ages to kiss her on the cheek. Not dead, not dead, rang in her head, making her want to jump up and down with joy.

CHAPTER 25

Matthew took a step back into the shadows and watched Mrs Brown hurry off in the direction of the kirk. Once, even twice could be a coincidence, but this was the third time he saw her in the vicinity of the makeshift garrison buildings.

Today he'd even seen her enter, shawl pulled high over her head in a weak attempt at disguise. A go-between; less conspicuous than her red-haired husband, and a woman to boot. He didn't know for certain, he admonished himself, there might be a number of reasons for Mrs Brown visiting with the soldiers – not that he could think of any except two. Either she was informing or she was whoring, and for all that the soldiers might be desperate, Mrs Brown was no spring chicken. But wait, wasn't there a son, a lad kept under lock and key? He frowned. As he recalled the lad had been arrested last August, and if so he was either dead or bonded out by now. Strange; he couldn't recall Brown speaking of his son, at least not lately. He shrugged; mayhap it was too painful.

Any further musings on this subject were interrupted by Peter clapping him on the shoulder. As he needed a new axe head, Matthew fell into step with him, making for the smithy.

He was returning to the inn and his stabled horse when a voice rang out across the market square, calling his name. Matthew sighed in recognition. That accursed captain… He turned, wrapping the cloak tighter round him. Captain Howard and the young lieutenant were hastening across the cobbles towards him, their wide cloaks floating about them.

"Foul weather," the captain grumbled. "Rain, rain, rain and this awful wind. Why in God's name anyone would ever choose to live here is beyond me."

"Well then I suggest you leave," Matthew said. "We won't bother you, and you'll no longer bother us." He kept his eyes on the lieutenant who was strolling round him.

"What brings you to Cumnock?" the captain asked, leaning menacingly towards him.

"Business," Matthew said. "My business."

The lieutenant shoved him hard, making him land on his knees.

"You have no business that is only yours," the captain said, watching as Matthew got back onto his feet. "So why are you in Cumnock?"

"I already told you; business." Matthew's hands had clenched into fists, but he kept his voice under control, fighting back the clouds of rage that had him wanting to wheel and sink his dirk into that whelp of a lieutenant.

Captain Howard took a step back. "Take him into custody," he said to the lieutenant. "He's being obstructive."

Matthew dug his heels in. "I'm not going anywhere with you, you have no reason to detain me."

A small crowd of people were drifting in their general direction, and a low muttered agreement was heard, making the captain cast a nervous look over his shoulder.

"This is a rebel," he said, "known to have repeatedly helped outlawed men." There was a murmur of approval from the assembled people, making the captain glower at Matthew.

"You've searched my home regularly, and you've never found an outlaw there, have you?" Matthew spoke calmly, keeping his eyes on the captain while his ears strained to hear what the lieutenant was up to. Another push, this time not enough to send him to the ground, but still. Don't allow them to provoke you, he thought, that is what they want.

"We know you've hidden that accursed Peden there!" the captain said.

"You do? Where? Seeing as I haven't seen him myself."

"I have witnesses assuring me that Peden has been taken into your home."

Matthew laughed out loud. "If you had witnesses and proof to corroborate their saying then we wouldn't be here. Instead you stand here and speak untruths, accusing me of things you can't prove. And you ..." He swivelled so abruptly the lieutenant scrabbled in his haste to back away. "... do you always sneak around the back of men instead of facing them upfront? Is that how the English are taught to fight?" A snicker flew through the crowd making the lieutenant flush.

Captain Howard stepped up close. "You're coming with us for questioning, Mr Graham. Now, you may come quietly, or you may come screaming, but rest assured you will definitely be coming with us."

"Why must you be so difficult?" Oliver sighed, handing Matthew a handkerchief with which to dab at his split lip. "If you'd only come away quietly this wouldn't have happened."

"I did come away quietly, and yet this did happen. They set upon me the moment they were out of sight from the crowd." Matthew said, wincing as he sat down.

"They're frightened of you," Oliver said.

"Of me? I've never done them any harm."

"Of all of you; it's a nerve racking experience to live amongst so much silent hatred."

"We're not stopping you from leaving," Matthew said.

Oliver poured them some wine and sat down to study his prisoner. Bruised and battered, his cloak dirty and torn, Matthew emanated a silent authority that made Oliver look at him with grudging respect. Matthew Graham hadn't changed that much from the lad he once had been, no doubt he still possessed the level head and the capacity to lead which early on had singled him out for tasks requiring not only courage but a developed sense of right and wrong.

"Why am I here?" Matthew said.

"You know why; Alexander Peden. The price on his head has been raised, and it's only a matter of time before we find him. We almost did, a few weeks back, but somehow he evaded the dogs. I suppose he went into the river."

"I have no idea, but at least he hasn't floated up in my millpond."

"No, we would probably have heard had he been dead," Oliver agreed.

"Why are you here?" Matthew asked.

Oliver drained his wine and shrugged. "Alexander Peden."

Matthew snorted. "Sandy may be a lot of things, but surely he can't be considered such an enemy of the state as to merit your specific presence."

"I'm not here out of choice!"

Matthew looked him up and down. "Aye you are; you've not survived this long in the army without being adept at manipulation."

Oliver laughed. "I fear you think too much of me, Matthew." If it hadn't been for that accursed streak of bad luck he wouldn't have been here at all, but forced into earning his living by mounting debt, he'd been handed the task of cleansing the north of these loud, opinionated preachers that spoke of sedition the moment they opened their mouths. It tallied well with his private concerns, but he had no reason to share this information with Matthew.

"It's going to get much, much worse," Oliver said. "The present parliament will stop at nothing in their effort to stamp out the Covenanter movement."

"It can't be stamped out, and you know that as well as I do; some things once woken can't be put out."

Oliver nodded dourly. "*Build a man a fire and he will be warm for one day…*"

"*Set a man on fire and he will be warm for the rest of his life.*" Matthew filled in. He stood. "I have to go. If I may, of course." This said with a steely edge. Oliver regarded him for some moments before nodding. There was nothing to be gained by locking Matthew up for a night or two.

"How do you square what you're doing with your conscience?" Matthew asked Oliver as he followed him towards the gate.

"My conscience? I've told you, haven't I? I'll warn you as I can and fervently hope I never catch Peden, or any of the other preachers."

"You will," Matthew said. "Men like Captain Howard will make sure you do."

"I know." And once he did, Oliver would stand silent and watch.

Oliver walked back to his own quarters deep in thought, a coil of self-disgust winding itself tighter and tighter round his innards. What was he lending himself to? It had seemed so easy when Luke had drawn up the overall details; have Matthew arrested for sedition, fine him from home and hearth and all his debts would be forgiven. According to Luke, Matthew was heavily involved with the outlawed preachers anyway, so all Oliver had to do was make sure the levied fine was huge and that he was not condemned to death.

"Because if he dies his son gets Hillview," Luke had explained, "and that's not at all what I want." Oliver sighed; a pity about the attractive wife and the children, but what was he to do? It was the Graham family or his own home and son.

"You let him go?" Captain Howard was so surprised he forgot the customary address to a senior officer.

"I did," Oliver replied. "There was nothing to hold him for, was there?"

"But the woman! She said she'd seen Peden with Graham."

"And that would hold at a trial?" Oliver sank his eyes into the younger man, noting how Howard tried to avoid looking at the damaged side of his face. "All you achieved is to put him even more on his guard. I'll have to work that much harder to make him lower it." He pursed his mouth. "I'll warn him a couple of times, and then… well then I simply won't." He smiled complacently at the younger man. "All we need is for him to attend a conventicle and arrest him there – preferably with Peden." Or mayhap set a more subtle trap, he frowned, reminding himself that Matthew Graham was no fool. Yes, a baited trap… his mind whirred into activity.

"And then he'll hang," Captain Howard said with satisfaction.

Oliver shook his head. "No, Howard. Not hanged; deported, I think, and fined. Much worse."

"He hanged Lieutenant Gower, he should be hanged as well – for Gower and the two men he cut down on the moor."

Oliver made an impatient sound. "Conjecture, Howard."

It was dark by the time Matthew came home. Alex had been waiting for him and went out to greet him the moment she saw the horse. He dismounted, handed the reins to Gavin, and came towards her, moving with less than his normal agility.

"They've hit you!" she said, taking in his swollen mouth.

"No great matter," Matthew said, following her inside. "It's this business with Oliver that has me concerned. I don't understand, lass. It might be a coincidence that Oliver should be assigned to come to Cumnock, but the fact that he knows Luke makes it all smell of deceit. But why? How can Luke use the major against me? And why would Oliver lend himself to anything sordid to begin with?" He frowned, sitting down at the kitchen table. "I was right tempted to confront Oliver today, demand that he explain how he knows Luke, but that would not be wise. I need more information, and then I must tread with utmost care around this erstwhile friend of mine."

Alex finished her inspection of his bruises and went over to the hearth.

"Next time I see the major I might be tempted to stick my fingers into his eyes. I hate the way he looks me over."

"What? Have you seen him more than the once?"

Alex nodded and ladled up a serving of onion soup, handing him the bowl and a spoon before sitting down beside him.

"It's strange; he's been here a couple of times, but always on those searches when you haven't been home. Twice when you accompanied Simon and Joan on their way to Edinburgh."

"Why haven't you told me?"

Alex shrugged; the appearance of soldiers on her land had become so much a daily occurrence that they merited nothing but the barest of comments. Even the children would look up from what they were doing, take in the milling men and then ignore them.

The soldiers seemed to find this both boring and embarrassing, and Alex capitalised on their ambiguity by being polite and offering them beer or cider after every search. It made Captain Howard break out in bright red spots to hear his men bid her a good day when they rode off. The major, however, had laughed and conversed her, complimenting her beer, her pie, and her tits – well, not vocally, but what with the way his eyes hung off her … She gnawed at her lip. Wyndham and Luke; Luke and Matthew, Hillview. Hillview! Yes, that was it; Wyndham was here because of Hillview.

"He's here to ensure you're not hanged," Alex told Matthew in a voice that surprised even her by its matter-of-factness.

He gave her a guarded look.

"Luke doesn't want you dead, because if that happens Hillview passes to Mark, right? No, Luke wants you fined, and then he'll stand by as your home, your family and finally you are sold off to cover the price. Somehow he's twisted Wyndham's arm to ensure things go just as Luke has planned them. Very neat, don't you think? And even better from Luke's point of view is that you'll have brought it all down on yourself."

Matthew mulled this over for some time. "It fits. And Oliver warns me a couple of times and then one day he doesn't, hoping I will think it safe." He grimaced in disgust.

Alex took a deep breath. "This is the year when you don't go to one single conventicle."

"Nay, this is the year when I go even more canny. But I won't be stopped from listening to the word of God; not by my brother or by that false friend of my youth."

"And by your wife?" Alex had her heart in her mouth.

"Don't ask that of me," he said. "Please, Alex, don't."

Just like that he plunged them both into yet another killing silence, days when she evaded him, slipping like water through his fingers when he tried to corner her. In front of the bairns and the household Alex acted as if things were as they should, but once they were alone she closed down completely, escaping to her bed as soon as she could.

He tried; God knows he tried, holding long monologues where he attempted to explain that he needed this, it was like air and water to him, and of course he would be careful, mindful of every step he took. But she never replied, she just rolled over onto her side and turned her back on him. Only once did she say anything, after a night where Matthew had talked himself hoarse, giving up to subside into silence beside her.

She cleared her throat. "If anything happens to you, if they take you on the moor, I'll kill all our children and then myself. Immediately. Just so you know."

He lay stunned by her words for the rest of the night.

"You didn't mean it," he said flatly next morning, blocking her way out of the room.

Alex sat down on the bed and busied herself with her garters. "Don't tell me what I mean or don't mean."

"You wouldn't," he pleaded.

"Yes I would – I'd have to."

"But…" He shook his head. "It would be a grievous sin!"

Alex gave him a long look. "So if I kill our children and commit suicide rather than face the horrors of bonded labour that will inevitably lead to death or worse for children as young as ours, that's a sin?"

He nodded.

"And so it follows that endangering yourself in such a manner so as to force me to do this is also a sin, right?"

He groaned, dragging a hand across his face.

She stood up and moved him aside. "Touché, I think." She stopped and gripped the door jamb on her way out, keeping her back to him. "I do ask it of you, Matthew. This time I'm asking you – no, begging you – not to go near one single conventicle for the coming year."

"And what will you do if I can't promise you that?" he asked, forcing words up a windpipe that bristled with thorns.

"I don't know," she said softly. "But somehow I think our marriage will be over. At least it will never be what it used to be."

"I see," he said just as softly.

CHAPTER 26

Matthew was in a foul mood already before seeing the large troop of soldiers come down the lane. An ultimatum; Alex had placed him with his back against a wall, and even if he recognised that she did it out of fear – for him, for their children and for herself – he was foundering in waves of bright red anger that she should be making him choose between his faith and his family.

For a fleeting instant he wondered if Davy Williams had ever had these discussions with his wife, if it would have been easier had his Alex been a properly raised Christian instead of the half-heathen he still at times considered her to be. Williams was dead, he reminded himself, and so was his poor wife and most of the bairns, so it hadn't helped much, had it?

So it was in a black temper that Matthew strode over to plant himself in front of Captain Howard and his men. Very many men, and dogs as well, the huge beasts held back by thick, studded collars.

"You best keep a hold on Aragorn," he said to Ian, who had sprung up by his side. "Captain, to what do I owe this pleasure?" He pointedly looked over to where Samuel and Robbie were leading out the team of oxen. Late February was a hectic time on a farm, and he was quite convinced Captain Howard was aware of that.

"Oh, I'm sure you know why we are here," Captain Howard said. "Last night we almost cornered Alexander Peden just off the road to Cumnock, and he was seen heading this way."

"He must have come and left like a shadow in the night, for I haven't seen him, nor do I harbour him."

"Ah, Mr Graham, but that is what you would say."

With that Howard nodded in the direction of the men holding the mastiffs and the dogs were released to run free, creating pandemonium as the farm animals reacted to these new, unwelcome visitors. Howard nodded again, and his men dismounted, drew their swords and went through every building.

Torn bags of seed, casks of beer and cider upended – everywhere they went they left a wake of destruction, making Matthew knot his hands in futile ire, aware that Howard was watching his every move. Matthew hoped Alex would appear by his side and slip her hand into his, but a furtive glance over his shoulder showed her standing by the kitchen door with Daniel in her arms, and he felt abandoned by her. She knew how much it cost him to hold on to his temper, how at times he struggled with pitch black rage, and now she was leaving him to battle it on his own. "*Our marriage will be over – or at least not what it used to be,*" rang in his head.

The soldiers came back shaking their heads and the dogs were called to heel. Matthew began to relax. Soon they'd be gone and he could go back to his spring planting and his marital issues. But Captain Howard wasn't done. The officer sat on his horse, dark eyes wandering from Matthew to the stables and back again. A small smile appeared on the captain's face, it broadened into a grin.

"You," he said to one of his dragoons. "Go and get the stallion from his stall."

"Ham?" Matthew's voice rose. "Why would you take my horse?"

"Oh," Captain Howard said, "we have need of new horses."

"You won't steal my horse," Matthew said, taking a threatening step towards the captain.

The captain drew his sword. "Steal it? We'll requisition it for the crown."

"Nay, you won't." Matthew was going blind with rage. From very far away he heard Alex' voice, her tone frantic as she called his name.

He took yet another step towards the captain, and the sword flashed down. There was a shout from behind him. Ian threw himself forward and grabbed hold of the captain's arm, startling both horse and rider with his loud, angry yells. Matthew looked down at his shirt and at the blood that was welling from a long, shallow gash, and back up at the captain, who was struggling to control his mount. He heard Alex call his name again, and out of the corner of his eye he saw her hand Daniel to Sarah and come striding towards them.

"Get the lad off me," the captain snarled before sorting that by himself, sending Ian to land in a heap on the ground.

Matthew growled, the captain raised his sword again. Matthew lunged, and the captain brought the flat of the narrow blade down hard on Matthew's uncovered head. His knees buckled, pain shot like jagged bolts down his face and spine. There was a shriek, and a small shape came leaping over the ground.

"Not my da! Leave off, you nasty man. He's bleeding."

Rachel kept on screaming as she ran towards them. Like a small, avenging angel she pelted towards them, calling for her da. Her cap came off, her hair fell in untidy braids down to her shoulders and when the sun glinted on Howard's naked sword she screamed even louder, a wordless sound of equal parts anger and fear.

"Rachel!" Matthew tried to call, but it came out as a croak. "Rachel, stop, lass, stay away, lassie." He blinked in an effort to stop his head from swimming with pain and staggered towards her, arms held out to stop her. But Rachel took no notice. In her hand she brandished a stout stick and she wielded it at the horse.

"Go! Leave Da alone!" The stick connected with the horse's leg with a dull crack.

The horse neighed and reared, front legs flailing. One huge hoof came down with a sickening crunch on the little head. Matthew watched in horror as Rachel crumpled, mouth open mid-sentence, eyes shifting from bright, angry green to dull, muddy hazel in seconds. The stout little body collapsed, the head swaying like an overweight cabbage on a stalk of grass. She hit the ground with a small thud, and Matthew couldn't hear, he couldn't see anything beyond the pitiful little shape that was his daughter.

"Oh, Lord," Matthew was on his knees, his trembling hands stretched towards his unmoving lass. "Oh Jesus in heaven, my wee Rachel!" Not his lass, please Lord, not his lassie. He crawled towards her, tried to keep his eyes off her crushed skull. Two booted feet appeared in his shrinking field of vision, a man's face was lowered to his. The captain – no longer contained but pale, shivering like an aspen leaf. My lass; sweetest Lord, look at my brave, bonny lass. The captain was talking. To him? Matthew couldn't care less.

"It was not my intention," the captain said. "I swear, Mr Graham, I would not have harmed a child."

There was a keening sound in the air, a shrill sound that sliced like a honed sickle through Matthew's brain. He stumbled to his feet, moving in the direction of Alex, now flying towards them with her skirts bunched in her hands.

"Rachel!" Alex screamed, pushing Matthew to the side. "Rachel! How many times have I told you… oh, God!" She skidded to a stop and then she was lying across her daughter, gently turning her over. "Come on Rachel, this isn't funny, honey." She kissed the pale face, shook the little body repeatedly. "Rachel?" the head lolled back. "No," Alex moaned, "no, not Rachel." She fumbled with her shawl, whispered to Rachel that it would be okay, of course it would, before wrapping the bleeding head, all the while talking to her child. "See?" she said. "Much better."

When Rachel remained still and silent she gathered her daughter to her chest, she kissed her and called her name, she rocked back and forth, pleading with her to stop this play acting, to start moving again.

"Rachel, come on, Rachel." She shook her, rocked her even harder, promising her she'd get the last slice of spice cake, but please, please, Rachel stop this right now, okay?

"She's gone, Alex," Matthew said hoarsely, shaken to his core by his wife's behaviour. "She's dead."

"No!" Alex turned with blazing eyes. "She can't be! She's

a child, for God's sake. A baby, just four." She was on her feet, Rachel a limp weight in her arms, walking away from them all, telling Rachel in a shrill, quavering voice that once they were inside she'd wash her and blow on the horrible wound and then it would be alright, of course it would.

He should go after her, he should... Matthew collapsed onto his knees, staring vacantly at the ground. Arms round his shoulders. Alex? Was that his Alex? Nay; Ian. He swayed on his knees, arms coming round Ian's waist. Mayhap if he closed his eyes long enough this would go away, like a nightmare that bursts apart with the first rays of morning light. The captain knelt beside him.

"Not the girl," Howard said. "I never meant to kill the little girl."

Nay; you meant to kill me, Matthew thought fuzzily, provoking me into anger over a horse.

"Leave," Ian said, his voice harsh. "You've done enough damage for today, and I would have you gone, aye?"

Matthew raised his face. Ian let go of him and stood in front of him, arms spread out as if to shield them all with himself. Captain Howard backed away, hands raised in apology? Supplication? Matthew didn't care. On the cobbles a few feet away was a dark stain and one of the soldiers had picked up the small cap, handling it as if uncertain what to do with it. Ian walked over to him and snatched it back.

"Go!" he said, pointing up the lane. "And you leave the horse," he added, shaking the cap at the captain.

"Of course, of course we will." Was that tendril of a voice the captain's? Matthew squinted at him. The man looked devastated, near on about to burst into tears. Too late; Rachel... and Alex; oh dearest Lord, his Alex, and the look on her face as she cradled Rachel to her chest while she rocked and rocked in a desperate attempt to bring her back to life.

"I'm so sorry, Mr Graham," the captain said again. "I'm so sorry that your daughter is dead. It was never my intention."

"Go," Matthew forced the words over his lips. "You can

come back and plague us some other day. But now I want you off my land. I have a bairn to grieve and a wife to comfort and God help me, I don't know how to do that." He stared yet again at the stain left behind by Rachel, set his hands to the ground and staggered to his feet, using Ian as his prop.

"Go to Aunt Alex," Ian said. "I'll take care of the rest, aye?"

Matthew drew in a long, ragged breath and began the long walk up towards the house.

It took him an eternity to traverse his yard. People; so many people, and he heard sobs and mumbled condolences. Halfway across he stopped, looked back to where Ian still stood, a gangling lad with his arms crossed over his chest as he saw the soldiers off. He trudged on. There was a weight in his chest, a constriction that made it difficult to breathe, and when he wiped at his bloodied face he realised he was weeping. He cleared his throat, coughed a couple of times and pressed the heels of his hands into his eyes. Not now; weep he could do later, now he had to somehow comfort his wife.

When Matthew entered the house the first thing he saw was his daughter, laid out on a blanket on the kitchen table.

"She's not dead," Alex told him. "Look, she's still breathing."

To his shock he saw she was, irregular, shallow breaths that barely lifted her chest. He shifted his eyes to her head and was violently sick in the basin. Not dead… Oh, Lord, do not let her linger, do not let her mother begin to hope and then lose her yet again. He poured some water from the pitcher into his shaking hands and scrubbed them over his face before turning round.

Rachel was still breathing. The crushed mass of her head was oozing blood and other secretions to run into her hair, collecting just below her ear in a stain that seeped slowly into the blanket below her. Alex was boiling water, and Matthew saw that it was too late; his wife believed their daughter's life might be saved.

"Alex… it's… she'll die, aye?" His Rachel; his ray of sun,

his adored daughter, reduced to this, this... He groaned.

"I know." She placed a hand on Rachel's forehead. "But I can't let her lie like this, can I?"

Together they washed their child, together they combed the fine dark hair to lie in bouncing curls around the pale and immobile face, already no longer Rachel, because Rachel was never this still, not even when she slept. Together they sat, waiting as she slowly died, and together they folded her arms across the narrow chest when her heart thudded to a stop.

CHAPTER 27

Matthew threw the hammer away from him. The carefully chosen boards of pale oak lay taunting him and he raised his foot to kick one of them into splinters but stopped at the last moment. A coffin for his lass, for the bairn closest to his heart… And now bright, vibrant Rachel was to be buried in the cold, dark earth. He closed his eyes, trying in vain to block out the image of his Rachel eaten by maggots. How unbearable would it be for her mother it if was like this for him? He picked up his hammer and went back to his work.

Five days since Rachel died, five days in which the silence between him and Alex had grown. The unresolved conflict regarding his willingness to risk life for faith lay festering between them, and now with wee Rachel dead… It was his fault; he should've let them take the horse, he should have thrown himself into Rachel's path, he should…

He scratched at the sword cut. Every time it began to scab he broke it open, staining his clothes with yet another seeping line of red. If Alex saw she didn't say, sunk so deep into herself that only rarely did she seem to notice him at all. He needed her, but he didn't know how to tell her so, and he stood a mute supplicant before her but she didn't see, she didn't even look at him.

What little energy Alex had she utilised to keep up a front of normality for her children. Her insides were a dark and hollow void, and every now and then a drop of sunlight would flash through, lighting up the absolute dark before it sputtered and died. Like when Daniel crawled over to her and pulled himself up to stand, weaving proudly on his feet before he sat down with a thump, or when Mark offered her a snowdrop, mumbled a quick "I love you," and darted off. Or Ian, working so hard on being a grown up in this absence of parents, helping his younger cousins with everything he could, and still finding the time to brew her a cup of herbal tea, placing a bony arm around her shoulders.

Occasionally she was aware of Matthew and his silent, agonising grief, but she had nothing to give him, not now, not yet, so she tried to close off his pain, listening only to her own. Where Matthew escaped into the spring planting, Alex spent hours walking through the woods, sometimes with her sons, but mostly on her own, head cocked in the hope that suddenly she'd hear Rachel's high voice tell her to come quickly because the sow was doing it again, eating her babies.

Only when she was alone did she allow herself to cry, sitting for hours on the hilltop with the moss blurring in front of her eyes. It was always a relief afterwards, the grief somehow disarmed into more manageable proportions and for some time she could act normal with her boys, discuss dinner with Sarah or walk over to study the beds of her kitchen garden. And then the teeth of grief were back, tearing at her from the inside and she needed Matthew, but she didn't know how to tell him, so she'd sit and watch him from a distance, seeing how he would at times stop and falter, his shoulders rounding. Sometimes she stretched out her hand towards him and pretended that she placed it on his back, letting him know that she was, after all, still here.

Tomorrow they would bury her. Her Rachel, to lie alone in the dark, with no one to hold her hand or shush her if she was afraid. Alex didn't know how to bear it, so instead she fled away inside her mind to where Rachel was still alive, a green-eyed minx that drove her parents crazy at times, but was so tender at others. She leaned back against a tree trunk and closed her eyes. There, in her head, Rachel would always live.

"Mama?"

Alex opened one eye to see Jacob crouched in front of her. It was Jacob who was most affected of the children. Rachel and he were inseparable, spending their entire days together and now she was gone, leaving him very alone and just as confused.

"Ian says that tomorrow we're going to dig a hole up in the graveyard and put Rachel in it." Two huge eyes stared at her. "She doesn't like dark places," he said. "So I told him we won't do that, she'll be right angry with us if we do."

Alex swallowed madly. "But that is what we do. We put Rachel into a coffin and then we bury her. But to her it won't be cold or dark, to her it's all fluffy and white. She's probably somewhere up there now." She pointed at a small cloud. "See? Over there, swinging on the edge. That's Rachel and she'll always be up there, looking down at you."

Jacob strained his eyes towards the little cloud. Yes, he nodded eagerly, he could see her foot, with the striped stockings Mama had made her.

Alex kissed his hair and helped him to stand. "Let's go and find your brothers."

As they crossed the yard she heard the sound of hammering from the woodshed and hesitated. Should she go and talk to him? Hold him? Jacob tugged at her hand and she hurried after him instead.

Matthew looked down at the finished coffin and ran his hand over the smooth interior. He had sanded it repeatedly until it was soft enough for Rachel to lie on without getting splinters. Now all he had to do was fit the lid and then he was done. No, because he had to carry the coffin over to the shed, and he had to lift the stiff body into it, and then he had to nail the lid shut, sealing her off permanently from sun and light. He rubbed his hand through his hair and sighed.

"Are you alright?"

The unexpected voice made Matthew jump and he turned to find Sandy at the door. Moments later he was in his friend's arms while Sandy patted his back, telling him it was a most terrible loss, but the wee lass was with God now.

"Don't tell her mother that," Matthew said. The thought of Alex made him leap away. "You mustn't be here! If the soldiers come..."

Sandy smiled and dug around in his clothing, producing a formal looking document.

"He came and found me himself, or rather he asked that he be taken to see me."

Matthew read the document. "A safe-conduct?"

Sandy nodded. "Valid for a week. He said you might have need of me."

Matthew traced the signature at the bottom of the document.

"That was kind of him," he said grudgingly.

"Aye. It just goes to show that not all papists are rotten to the core. He also promised to ensure there were no raids on Hillview for the week I was here." Sandy coughed a couple of times. "But just in case, I won't be staying at the house."

"Nay, best not," Matthew agreed.

Alex was incensed at the sight of Sandy. Indirectly, all of this was his fault, it was him and his bloody religion that drove a wedge between her and Matthew, it was those damned convictions that led to her Rachel being dead. She stifled a sob.

"What are you doing here?" she said. "It's too much of a risk, and…"

Sandy held out a sheet of thick paper.

"Captain Howard?" The man must be wallowing in guilt, and he'd done the single thing he could think of to offer Matthew support. By doing it he was risking his career, laying in Matthew's hands a document that would damn him should it ever come to light. Alex folded the deed together and handed it back to Sandy.

"This means I can offer you open hospitality," she said politely but with very little warmth.

"Aye," the minister nodded, already at the table. Alex served him food and retreated a few paces. Sandy had grown old over the last few months, gaunt and grey-haired with a permanent cough. He was also dirty, a strong smell emanating from him that made the children shift away. No lice as far as Alex could see, but the skin was grey with grime. Not that she intended to suggest he take a bath; he would probably look at her as if she were the whore of Babylon, suspecting her of evil designs on him. For the first time since Rachel's death Alex had to suppress a bubble of genuine laughter.

Sandy burped. "I won't stay in the house, it's an unnecessary risk. It's a fine night so I'll be staying up by the oak."

Alex nodded. She'd send along an extra blanket or two, and a pillow. She stood up to fetch these and stopped when Matthew put a hand on her arm. He hadn't touched her in almost a fortnight, since well before Rachel's death, nor she him. He dropped his hand like stung at her look.

"Do you…" Matthew cleared his throat. "I have the coffin ready, will you help me place Rachel inside?"

She looked at him for a long time. This wasn't something she could leave him to do alone, so she inclined her head.

His hands were trembling so hard when he approached his daughter that Alex wanted to cry. Instead she moved over to the other side of the bench on which Rachel lay, and indicated that she was ready when he was. The body was no longer her child. Cold, beginning to bloat, it was an inanimate thing that only vaguely resembled the happy, laughing girl that populated her mind.

"Wait," Alex said when he bent to lift the lid into place. "I have something here, that I want her to have with her." She closed her hands over a little wooden carving, Matthew's gift on Rachel's fourth birthday. A promise he'd said, placing it in her small hands, a promise that one day he would give her a man's dog. But now he never would, and the least they could do was to send the beautifully carved Deerhound with her to stand over her and protect her.

Matthew uttered a small moan when he saw what she held and stumbled out of the door. Alex placed the dog beside Rachel's right hand, smoothed the hair into some semblance of order and arranged the clothes to lie tidily around the stiff limbs. The soft baby blanket was drawn up to cover her, and Alex spent a long time fussing with it so that it lay just right, snug around her child. Her Rachel... Alex cupped the cold cheek one last time, lifted the lid into place, made sure it slotted, and nailed it down. It was the least she could do for him. On the lid he had carved a heart, with a beautiful 'R' in its middle. She traced it with her finger and stooped to kiss it. Tomorrow she would pretend she wasn't here, she would stand in the little graveyard and pretend she was anywhere else but here.

But she couldn't; her eyes glued themselves to the hole, to the heaped soil beside it, and she tightened her hold on her sons. By Matthew stood Ian, close enough to touch should Matthew need it, far enough apart that he didn't impose. Even in her present state of panic Alex marvelled at the maturity of the boy, at how he'd shouldered a role that wasn't really his in the broken family of his uncle. Uncle? By his behaviour alone Ian had proved beyond any remaining doubt that he was Matthew's son. Alex looked at him, dark chestnut hair curling at the overlong tips, brows dark and straight over eyes of that magical hazel he shared with his father. Nothing at all of his mother, nowhere was there a trace of Margaret, it was all Matthew, Matthew, Matthew.

Jacob's sob recalled her to the present, and she bent to pick him up, allowing him to hide his face against her shoulder while she hid hers against his hair. She didn't watch as the earth was shovelled back into place, but however hard she shut her eyes she couldn't close out the sound.

"She lies well here." Sandy's voice interrupted Alex from where she was planting a rose by Rachel's headstone. She slid him a look, keeping her back to him.

"You think? Personally I would prefer it if she were lying in her bed at night and running through her days." She continued with her work, hoping he would have left by the time she was done, but he was still there when she got off her knees.

"You'll have more lasses," Sandy said, coming to stand beside her.

Alex slapped him. "Is that a comfort? Do you truly believe that I can replace Rachel with another child?"

Sandy rubbed at his reddening cheek, his eyes full of a compassion that she didn't want to see in them. "Nay, of course not. Rachel was Rachel; wild and bonny and with the heart of a lion, rushing to her father's defence. In many ways very like her mother."

Alex dug her fingers into the flesh of her upper arms to stop herself from crying.

"You'll never forget her, and nor will her da. All that knew her have been touched by her, by the little piece of God that lived in her."

"God!" Alex spat. "What do I care about God? He let her die, didn't he?" Shit; now she was crying again, and she was so tired of these damn tears, of how her chest hollowed out into a constant ache for her, for her Rachel.

"God does as well as he can, lass. But sometimes it might be a bit too much for him too."

Alex gave him a surprised look. "So God is fallible?"

Sandy gave her a faint smile. "Nay, not as such. But mayhap overwhelmed by events…" He regarded her in silence for a while. "She's with God now and that is not a bad thing." His smile widened. "And she'll make sure that heaven is somewhat livened up. Can you not see her, scurrying across the skies, chasing after an angel and asking why, why, why…"

Alex wiped at her eyes, half laughing, half crying at the notion of her wild, wayward girl turning the orderly existence of Heaven upside down.

"I don't want her to be with God," she said through her tears. "I want her to be here, with me. With me!" For the first time ever, Sandy touched her, holding her in a light embrace.

"I know that, aye? And so does God."

"Matthew and I had argued before all this," Alex said as they sat on the little bench under the rowan. "About God and all that stuff."

"All that stuff?" Sandy sounded disapproving. Alex nodded and gnawed at her lip.

"I told him that if he was arrested, I'd kill the children and myself rather than risk that other fate."

"That would be a terrible thing to do," Sandy said.

"In my book it's equally terrible for the father of four to risk his life and those of his children," she said. "I have no intention of witnessing my man and my babies sold into permanent servitude before being dragged off somewhere else myself." She stared off across the water meadow, tracking the narrow ribbon of water as it appeared and disappeared between stands of alders and hazels.

"Previously, all I've asked of him has been that he not put his home at risk and that he be careful. I know how important his faith is to him, and I don't want to come between him and God. But this time I'm too scared, and this time I'll insist he puts me first." Because if he dies my heart will lie in splinters on the ground, she thought. "Am I a totally depraved person, do you think?"

Sandy raised his brows. "Nay, not totally," he said drily. He patted her on her thigh. "God doesn't want us to squander our lives; he has given us life that we live it to the full, that we rejoice at the miracles he populates the world with. The perfection of a dandelion, the cold nose of a dog, the magic colours of a sunset..." He looked at Rachel's fresh grave and back at Alex. "You're within your rights to ask him, but you've placed him in a difficult position; his God or his wife."

Alex squirmed. She'd regretted her comment about their marriage the moment it had flown out of her mouth, and now it was too late to take it back.

"His wife will win – this time," Sandy concluded. "I'll talk to him."

CHAPTER 28

"I leave on the morrow," Sandy said, a couple of days after Rachel's funeral.

"So soon?" Matthew frowned down at the little wooden figurine he was carving and slashed it in two. "I can't get her face right, it's as if she eludes me, hiding herself from me."

"You're trying too hard to remember."

"I fear that I'll forget what she looked like. In my head I can see her move, I can hear her laugh, but her face, the way her eyes would narrow when she was planning something she shouldn't be doing... I know what she looked like, but I can't see her!" He picked up a new piece of wood, and notched his knife through it, creating a rough outline of a running, faceless lass. "She would still be here, if it weren't for me, she would still be alive."

He saw Sandy's grimace; for the last few days his friend had tried to move him away from this self-flagellation, but it was true, wasn't it? His lass died in his defence. His hand shook, the knife sank too deep, and Matthew swore. Sandy's hand on his arm forced him to put the piece of wood down.

"Wait some weeks and then try," Sandy said.

They walked together up to the millpond, talking in low voices about the present conflict.

"It will get worse, won't it?" Matthew said.

Sandy sighed. "Aye, I think it will. Scotland will be an unwelcoming place for many years to come. Strife, famine, more strife..." His eyes glazed over. "We'll be trod underfoot, our Highland brothers unleashed on us and we unleashed on them..." He shook himself like a wet dog. "She's right at times, your foreign wife. We've been intolerant toward others and now we're reaping what we have sown. God's punishment, one might think." He chuckled to himself. "But you must not tell her that, I wouldn't want her to think me going soft." He looked around at the greening shrubs and smiled down at an early windflower, bending down to pluck it. "God won't think less of you for staying away."

"Staying away?" Matthew looked at him warily.

"You heard; Alex told me she fears you'll be led into a trap."

Had she told him everything, her awful threat as well?

Sandy nodded that she had. "She's a woman. She sets the safety of her offspring first, as she should. Women are weak and must be protected and cared for, they aren't as spiritually resilient as a man is, and we must forgive them when they play out the single most powerful card they have; their love for us." He laughed at Matthew's face, elbowing him hard. "Aye I know; she wouldn't agree that women are weak."

"Nay, and she could prove it to you," Matthew muttered, seeing a rather entertaining image of Alex kicking Sandy hard enough to send him flying. He wondered if she still could do that; he hadn't seen her practising for well over a year. Sandy did not seem unduly worried, rather the reverse. He gave Matthew a fond look.

"She loves you."

Matthew kicked at the dried leaves underfoot, muttering that he wasn't all that sure of that – not lately.

"You're a wee fool at times. She loves you so much that a life without you would be a living death." He clapped Matthew on the back. "God will forgive; this year you'll do as she says and stay away."

Matthew felt a physical relief at his words, his shoulders dropping down from their constant tenseness for the first time in weeks.

Once they were settled on the makeshift bench by the millpond, Matthew turned the conversation to his suspicions regarding Mrs Brown.

"You think?" Sandy frowned down at the water.

"Aye I do." Too many coincidences, and then Mrs Brown slipping so discreetly through the door to the temporary barracks.

"But why?" Sandy said. "Tom Brown is a man of staunch faith. Would his wife be acting for her own reasons, do you think?"

"I don't know. You know them much better than I do, just as you know the brother."

"John? Aye, John I know very well. He wouldn't betray me." Sandy sucked in his cheeks, looking very much like a narrow faced trout. "Ah, well," he said, slapping himself on the thighs. "First we must make sure. Then we find out why." He looked rather grim. "It better be a good why."

That evening they sat in the kitchen for a long time after supper had been cleared away. The early March evening hung pale outside the window, a promise of light returning to the land.

"Beautiful, isn't it? The world is at its best at twilight, day still stands visible and the shadows of the night are merely tinting the ground. It's a hazy magical moment, an instant of quiet perfection, of balance between light and dark," Alex said, clasping her hands around a mug of chamomile tea. "When I die, I want it to be at twilight," she added in a whisper, so low Matthew had to strain his ears to hear her.

"Not yet, aye?" He wanted to take her hand, but didn't know if he dared. Instead he stood, said something about seeing to the beasts and walked outside.

"You must help your man," Sandy said as he prepared to leave. "Matthew is being eaten alive by guilt; guilt that it was for his sake she came running, guilt that he made a scene over the horse, guilt that he has failed you. And he fears that you won't forgive him."

"Forgive him?" Alex sneezed, blew her nose and tucked the handkerchief back up her sleeve.

Sandy gave her a penetrating look. "You blame him just as much as he blames himself." He bowed in her direction and stepped outside into the night where Matthew was waiting to walk with him part of the way.

Alex stood in the doorway and watched them leave, and in her depths something was telling her he was right; she did blame Matthew, and that wasn't fair.

The next morning Matthew was gone when Alex woke, and when he came in for breakfast he had a harried look in his face that stopped her from initiating any kind of conversation. He had fields to plant, and he was taking Mark and Ian along to help. Alex nodded and promised to send Sarah up with dinner to the fields.

Late in the afternoon both boys tumbled back inside, dirty and tired but with the contented expression of someone who had worked hard all day and knew himself to deserve his rest.

"And your father?" Alex asked in passing, flipping yet another pancake into the air.

"He said he would be in later," Mark said through his full mouth. "He said to tell you not to wait up."

"Ah," Alex said.

It was yet another beautiful evening when Alex walked out in search of her husband. She'd made an effort, changing to a clean bodice and combing her hair into the soft bun she knew he liked. She was nervous, wiping her palms down her skirts, and when she finally found him, in the stables, she stood for a long time in the shadows watching him. There was a slight curve to his shoulders and she felt a twinge of shame at having lumbered him with all the blame, leaving him to carry this staggering burden alone.

He was talking to Ham – at least that was what she thought at first – but once she began to listen, she heard that he was talking to himself of his wee lass, his Rachel. Her heart went out to him; Rachel was the child that always made him smile, the girl born as a confirmation that he had made it out, safe and alive, after his time as a slave on that accursed plantation, Suffolk Rose.

Her hand on his back made him jump. He tried to wipe his eyes, but she took hold of his chin, forcing him round to face her. She used her sleeve to blot his face, rested her hands on his cheeks, his hair. Her fingers smoothed their way across his brow, they touched his lips, his eyes.

"It wasn't your fault," she said, hearing just how much her voice wobbled. "Of course it wasn't. Forgive me if I've been letting you feel that it was."

He fell back against the wall of the stall and for the first time since Rachel died they stood with their arms around each other and cried for the child they'd lost, the girl who had been given such a brief allotted time on Earth.

"Bath," she said once they had stopped crying. "Bath and food."

"Food first, I think," he said, patting himself on his rumbling stomach.

They walked hand in hand back to the kitchen. He sat by the table and talked while she made him pancake after pancake. Of small things mainly, like how he'd found an abandoned fox pup on the furthest rye field, and how Ian had made him and Mark laugh by showing off Aragorn's antics. He told her that he'd seen an osprey, a huge bird floating high above the river, and at her doubtful expression huffily went on to explain that they were not that far from the sea, were they? It was relaxing, this rambling chit-chat, and when she took him by the hand and led him off towards the laundry shed it was almost like it used to be.

"Alex! Ow! Those are my balls. They're supposed to remain attached to my body." He clamped his thighs round her hand. "I'll wash myself there, why don't you busy yourself with my feet?" He stuck out a large foot and wiggled his toes. She snorted but moved over to scrub his extremities.

"You must let it scab," she said when he stood. She patted him carefully over his chest. "No more picking at it, have you got any idea how much work it is to get blood stains out?" She gave him a faint smile. "What? You think I hadn't noticed?"

He mumbled something about not being all that sure.

Alex shook her head at him, and pointed him in the direction of the closest bench.

"I spoke to Sandy," Matthew said into the blanket as she massaged his back.

"No! And there was me thinking that you spent hours and hours together in absolute silence." She dug her fingers into the trigger points along his right shoulder blade, making him hiss and tense before he relaxed back down. "I spoke to him too," she said, pouring some more oil into her hands before attacking his buttocks.

"Aah!" he groaned. "Are you sure it's supposed to hurt?"

"Wimp, lie back down or I'll show you hurt, okay?"

"Okay, okay."

She smiled; all her family used 'okay'.

"So what did he say?" she asked, once Matthew began to grunt in appreciation rather than pain.

"He said you were right to think of your family first, on account of you being but a weak woman," he said, laughing when she pinched him at the weak woman part. He flipped over, and at her nudging spread his thighs so that she could explore him there, now with a far softer hand. He raised his hand to her cheek, one finger barely touching her.

"He said I should do as you asked, on account of God not liking it when we needlessly put our lives at risk."

Alex sent a silent thanks to Sandy.

"I'd already decided," Matthew went on. "I didn't like it that you threatened me with the collapse of our marriage, but I knew you were right. I was asking too much of you, I was forgetting that you love me as much as I love you, and when I considered what I'd think if it were you risking your life…" He broke eye contact, staring at the wall instead. "Well, I wouldn't like it. Not at all." He lay in silence for some time before peeking at her.

"You can go back to your work, wife, I have no more to say, aye?" With a grunt he rolled over on his front.

Alex took her time, a slow stoking to the heat she felt building in him. By the time she was done, he could have been a giant cat, so relaxed was he under her touch. She rested her cheek on his back, smiling at the responding contented hum.

"Are you asleep?" she murmured, knowing perfectly well he wasn't, not with how his buttocks tensed when she slid her hand over them.

"Asleep? I think not." Matthew rose on his elbow. "Come here, you," he said huskily. Garment after garment dropped to the floor, strong hands slid up her naked limbs. His warm mouth on hers, his hair tickling her face, and she shifted closer to him, squishing her breasts to his chest, gluing her skin to his. They almost fell off the bench when he rolled them over, which made her gasp, him laugh. And there at last; his thighs between hers, his belly pressed to hers. She had no idea how many days it had been since last time, only that it had been far too long. Her body needed him, wanted him, loved him … She caressed his shoulders, letting her hands slide down his arms. Her man, his skin velvety to her touch, his muscles bunching under her fingers. Her man, his eyes burning into hers, his mouth hovering over hers. Some moments of absolute stillness, of relishing the size and warmth of him, and then he moved his hips. So did she, meeting his every thrust with one of her own. Deeper, harder, faster – she dug her fingers into his back.

"Alex! No, lass, I can't…"

She gripped him hard, using arms and legs to hold him deep inside of her.

"I… aah… oh God, woman!" He came, his penis so deep inside of her it must have been standing at the door of her womb. He pulled out and lay down beside her, his chest still heaving. His hand groped for hers, closing with strength on it. She squeezed back, listening to the sound of her pulse, loud and reverberating inside her head.

"We agreed, no? Still too soon," he said once he had gotten his breath back.

Alex shook her head furiously. "No." She wanted to be entirely possessed, have her body taken over by his seed and find her way back to life, burst through this bubble of numbness and loss that Rachel's death had imprisoned her in. She wanted – needed – him to fuck her senseless, leave her exhausted and sweaty and with not one single coherent thought in her head. She sat up and looked down at him.

"Make me pregnant," she said. "Please, Matthew." She traced her hand down his flat stomach, and her fingers were soft on his sex, caressing his balls, the sensitive skin behind them, the present stickiness of his cock. His hands strayed up to her breasts, to her neck, his hold closed on her nape, guiding her mouth down to his.

He had no notion as to how they made it back to their bedroom – or when. But when the first shards of sunlight spilled into their room she lay half-asleep in his arms, a warm, damp weight on his chest. What a night; his wife had given herself up to him, flaying herself open under his eyes, giving him everything he asked for and more. He owned her; her mouth, her breasts, her private parts – they were his. A total submission, a silent acceptance that it was he who was the possessor, while she was the possessed. He laughed at himself. Aye, he owned her, but she had him by his balls and by his heart, with small strong hands that held him just as enthralled to her as she was to him. His Alex; more than a wife, she was his other half, the part that made him whole. And in her womb grew yet another bairn – of that he was sure. Not a new Rachel, for how could anyone ever replace that mercurial bolt of life, but perhaps a lass. Please God, let it be a lass. He fell asleep with the high sound of Rachel's laughter ringing through his brain.

It was late when he woke to find her sitting in bed beside him, stark naked and with Daniel at her breast. Daniel smiled at him, patting him with a starfish hand before going back to his meal. Once Daniel had finished Alex made as if to slip out of bed, but Matthew stopped her with a firm grip round her wrist. He picked up Daniel and opened the door, calling for Sarah to come and take the wean. Then he closed it with a small thud and stood watching her.

"All day, I think," he said, moving towards her. "Only you and me and the bed."

"All day?"

"Aye, one full day with you in the sunlight. We can play chess."

She laughed out loud. "Is that what you want?"

"To begin with; I'll make up what other things I want as the day progresses."

"So might I," she teased, but he set a firm finger on her mouth.

"Nay, Alex. Today you do as I say." Her eyes looked up at him, bright blue in the morning sun.

"I do as you say," she repeated, and all of him went heavy with warmth and desire at the tone of her voice.

CHAPTER 29

It was one long day spent in a total state of undress with the March sun striping the dark wood of the floor with glittering blocks of light. The chess set was quickly discarded and instead they talked, at first of the easy things like how both cows were big with calf, and had Matthew noticed that Daniel could stand – if only for a few seconds.

They moved over to talk of Ian and how much he had grown over the last few days. In a burst of generosity Alex nestled close to Matthew and told him he should be proud of his eldest son.

"My son?" Matthew looked down his nose at her. "Luke's son, you mean."

Alex shook her head. "Whatever his legal status, Ian is entirely your son." She took a big breath, ignoring the image of a reproachful Mark that swam into her head. "And if you want to make that official then I'll understand and support you." Oh God, she swallowed, and now that I've said it I can never take it back.

Matthew propped himself up beside her. "And Mark?" His voice shook, and there was a sheen to his eyes that made her heart do handstands inside her chest.

"Mark will have to come to terms with it," Alex said with an outward calm that belied the turmoil inside of her. "We'll help him. Besides, he could do worse than having Ian as his brother."

Matthew collapsed to lie flat on his back and began to laugh.

"What?" She had expected a fervent thank you, a series of kisses on her cheek, not that he lie on his back and laugh and laugh.

"Don't mind me, I'm laughing because you made me happy." He grew serious. "You always do, lass. When I'm hurting you heal me, when I'm lost in the wilderness you find me and bring me home, and now that I've lost a bairn you give me another, no matter what it costs you." A long finger came up to trace her mouth, touch her cheek. He stared up at the ceiling. "Four sons…" He twisted his head to meet her eyes. "We must think this over, for Ian's sake and Mark's sake."

Matthew disappeared downstairs around noon, telling Alex she would be severely punished if she as much as put a toe on the floor while he was gone. He returned balancing a tray in one hand and with Daniel hanging from his other arm.

"He's hungry," he said, depositing their youngest son in her lap. "He eats a lot," Matthew marvelled some time later, watching with awe how Daniel emptied one round breast before attacking the next.

"They've all done, that's why they've all been so fat. A good start, I suppose." But it hadn't helped in one case, she sighed, smoothing Daniel's dark locks flat against his head. "He'll never know her, to him she will only be a story. And with time Jacob will forget her too, recalling only some small nuggets of what was a complete little human being."

"But to us she will always be real." Matthew's hand rested on hers. "Our wild child, the lass that had us shaking our heads in exasperation while our hearts burst with pride."

"Not always," Alex muttered, wiping away a tear. "Not when she locked Jacob in the privy, or when she tried to feed the pigs with my sausages." She handed him Daniel to hold. "Promise me we'll talk about her, that we'll invite her into our conversations and keep her alive for her brothers as well." She let her hand drift over Matthew's hair. Just like Rachel's, as his eyes were just like Rachel's. "Let's not kill her with our silence."

Matthew just nodded and buried his nose into Daniel's soft warmth.

Alex sneaked out of bed to find her papers and a stub of coal. She had stitched together a couple of sheets of paper into a rudimentary sketch book, and in it she drew small images of her family, filling each valuable scrap of paper to bursting before beginning on a new, pristine page. But today she folded up a glaring white square and committed to paper her man fast asleep on their bed with his son by his side.

Beside them she drew Rachel, a wild, laughing angel, her braids leaping, her eyes slitted against the afternoon sun. From her back sprouted small wings and Alex smiled through her tears, because if any one of her children would really appreciate being able to fly, it would be this one. She could almost find it in herself to forgive God for taking her. Well; no, she couldn't.

"But you can't blame God!" Matthew sounded astounded.

"Why not? Especially as a Presbyterian, who else is there to blame? He has it all preordained, right?"

"It's not quite that simple, we must all strive. And aye, God may have preordained, but his grace and mercy is boundless, so surely at times he changes his mind."

"Huh, last minute seats at a football game."

Matthew gave her a confused look.

"A child shouldn't die," Alex said. "It's wrong."

"Bairns die all the time. They die at birth and of sickness. They die in war and in famine and they die by misadventure…" He looked away briefly. "You must bow to it and trust he knows best." He pillowed his head on her lap. "I hope he does."

For the coming hour they had a heated argument regarding God and free choice, tolerance and predestination, with Matthew trying to convince her that predestination and mercy could go hand in hand, while she kept on throwing him examples of the opposite. Judas – had he ever had a choice? Luke – was he but a victim of a preordained existence?

"So what do you believe in then? If you don't believe in God?" He sounded mulish, a deep wrinkle between his brows.

"I never said I didn't believe in God," Alex corrected. "I just said that my God is less harsh, more tolerant."

Outside it was dark again, and to her surprise she was tired, despite having spent the whole day doing absolutely nothing. She finished brushing her hair, braided it, and joined him in bed, her face very close to his.

"Mostly, I believe in you," she said, smiling at how embarrassed he looked. "In you, and in us." She yawned and extended her hand to him, spreading her fingers to braid them with his. She drifted off into sleep, but when he tried to disengage himself she tightened her hold, pulling their combined hands to rest between her breasts.

"I love you," she whispered.

"I adore you," he whispered back, making her smile.

There were days when Alex woke and it took time for her to remember that things had permanently changed; Rachel was no more.

There were moments during the day when Matthew would stop what he was doing, certain that he'd heard his daughter's demanding voice, only to recall that she was gone.

Every time the soldiers rode in both Matthew and Alex stiffened with remembered anguish – and they did, frequently, but now always led by the lieutenant, never by Howard. The heart had clearly gone out of the soldiers, but they did as they were told, inspecting time and time again every shed, every nook and cranny. They stuck swords into the heaped hay of the barn, they stamped through the attic, peered into the space under the privy even though it would take a very desperate man – preferably with no sense of smell – to hide there. And all of them detoured round the spot where Rachel had died, frowning at their callow lieutenant when he brought his horse too close.

"Thrice in a week," Matthew said in an undertone to Ian, squinting in the direction of the riders making their way down to the farm.

"Those are no soldiers," Ian said.

274

Matthew shaded his eyes; the lad was right, these were ordinary travellers, mounted on excellent horseflesh. Beside him Ian gasped and then the lad was off, running like an arrow up the lane, arms extended. The person on the front horse threw back the hood, black hair spilled out to whip in the wind and Matthew echoed Ian's gasp. Margaret! He followed Ian at a more sedate pace, his heart settling in his gut. She had come for the lad, and once Ian rode out of Hillview, Matthew doubted he would ever see him again.

"And your babe?" Matthew asked, once he had greeted Margaret.

"He remains back home, with his wet nurse," she replied, turning to hug her eldest son. "You're almost as tall as I am!"

"He is as tall as you are," Matthew corrected, making Ian grin. The lad was beside himself with joy, Matthew noted, smiling when Ian snuck his hand into Margaret's before recalling that he no longer was a wee bairn but almost a man, therefore retracting his hand as if scalded. Instead he walked as close as he could to his mam, words tripping from his mouth at an alarming rate when he tried to condense six months of life into two minutes.

From where he walked behind them, Matthew picked out the odd word here and there, chief among them dog and Aragorn. Margaret shook her head and turned to Matthew with a crease between her brows.

"You gave him a dog?" She watched Ian rush off, calling for Aragorn.

"Aye, I did, I reckoned he needed something to call his own, being so far away from you." The implied criticism struck home, with Margaret's face a sudden pink.

"He rode off without permission. And then he had the pox."

Matthew raised his brows. "Nay he didn't and you knew that. He had the chickenpox as a wean."

Margaret kept her eyes on Ian, now returning at full speed with Aragorn gambolling beside him.

"It's been difficult, and Ian was better off here."

Still would be, Matthew concluded from her tone. He studied Ian; in everything a copy of himself. How would he fare at the hands of Luke, now that Luke had a son undoubtedly his own?

"Margaret," Alex sounded very aloof, inclining her head in the slightest of nods.

"Alex." Margaret shook out her purple velvet skirts ostentatiously, making Matthew muffle a chuckle. The two women were facing off, a silent contest played out with eyes and straightened spines, with bosoms and shapely waists. He had to concede Margaret was still the most attractive – beautiful, even – but Alex was quite the picture, the skin smooth and rosy, the hair gleaming with health, hair that shifted from darkest brown to strands that shone pure copper in the early April sun.

Margaret greeted the lads and looked cautiously in the direction of Alex.

"Rachel?"

Alex busied herself with Daniel, sitting him on her lap as she undid her bodice. Matthew moved over to stand beside her, a hand on her shoulder that she covered with her own.

"She's dead. She died seven weeks and four days ago," he said.

Margaret leaned forward, arms open as if to hug Alex – or him – but thought better of it and sat back.

"I'm so sorry; did she sicken?"

"No," Matthew said, unable to keep the bitterness out of his voice. "She died under the hooves of a horse – an officer's horse."

"Ah," Margaret said, "an accident."

"An accident? Aye, one could say so; an accident that occurred while the soldiers that hound us constantly were here for yet another wee visit."

Margaret looked quite stricken. "How terrible!" She placed her hand on Alex' arm. "God's will, Alex."

Stony silence met her remark.

Margaret tried out a tentative smile on Daniel, who smiled back, showing off six white teeth. "My Charlie has eight teeth," she said proudly.

"Whoopee," Alex mumbled, but Margaret launched into an eager description of her youngest son, from his dimpled knees to his perfect, bitty ears.

"He's quite big for his age," she finished, "and you should see his hair, like copper, aye?"

"We heard," Alex interjected, "just like Luke's."

Margaret beamed. "Aye, in everything he takes after his father."

"Like Ian," Alex said.

Margaret seemed on the verge of agreeing. At the last moment she collected herself.

"Ian takes after his uncle." She stood, threw Alex a poisonous look and declared she must go and find her son.

"How long is she staying?" Alex said the next day. Matthew had no idea, he told her, he was in general very confused by the visit – was it Margaret's intention to take Ian with her or not? And if it was, was it now that he should speak up?

Alex considered that for some moments. "Let's wait and see, she can't be staying long, can she? She has a baby to get back to."

Over the coming days it became apparent that Margaret was in no hurry to ride back, installing herself in the little cottage and insisting that Ian stay there with her. To Alex' immense annoyance, Matthew gravitated towards her, muttering something about needing to talk to her about Ian before disappearing for hours on end. Alex was jealous; a wild heaving, green beast of a thing that crowed and cackled inside her head.

Pretty, pampered Margaret with her expensive perfumes and well-cut clothes made Alex feel like a country bumpkin, and every morning she eyed her total of three skirts with increasing irritation. Why didn't she have something becoming to wear, something someone else had made for a change? Nor did it help that bloody Margaret was gorgeous in a way Alex definitely wasn't. She exhaled and dressed, tightening her stays as far as they would go. At least she had better tits.

Alex stopped dead on the path and shrank back against an oak. In front of her were Matthew and Margaret, and Margaret stood on her toes to pick out a dead leaf from Matthew's hair, saying something in a low voice that made him laugh. For an instant her hand caressed Matthew's cheek, dropped to rest on his arm, and there was something so natural about the gesture that Alex felt her insides contort.

She didn't know what to do; remain where she was and hope he'd take a different way home, walk up to him and ask him what the hell he was doing, letting another woman touch him that intimately, or just turn and run. He'd seen her and was coming in her direction, so Alex wheeled and walked off, as fast as she could on the muddy, slippery ground.

"Alex!"

She grabbed at a stand of hazel for support, and then she was on flatter terrain and set off at a run. He caught up with her, but was smart enough not to touch her, matching her stride instead.

"Have you been doing that a lot these last few days? You know, walking in the woods and somehow getting leaves in your hair that she has to pick off you?"

"Alex," Matthew sighed. "You know that isn't how it is."

"Then how is it?"

"We talk. About her life, mostly."

"Well that must read like a very sordid reality TV show."

"Aye it does," Matthew agreed, by now familiar with the concept. He took her hand, and led her off in the direction of the high meadows. "He's a difficult man to live with."

"Tough; she had her chance with you and blew it. I see her stroking your cheek again and she'll not be walking much for some weeks."

Matthew chuckled, giving her a sly look.

Idiot! He was enjoying this, the bastard.

"You won't," he said.

"Good."

"She thinks Ian's welcome will be harsh," Matthew said a bit later. Alex looked up from where she was cuddling a lamb.

"Has she told Ian that?"

"Nay, what purpose would it serve?" But the lad knew anyway, he said, he could see it in how Ian's face tightened whenever Margaret spoke of riding home.

"But why would Luke…" Alex voice tailed off. To see Ian now, on the brink of manhood, was to see Matthew. That would suffice; that and the rankling suspicion that Ian wasn't his to begin with. "It's all very strange. At one point in time Luke must have been certain that Ian was biologically yours as he seemingly couldn't father children, and all those years he treasured Ian as his own. And now, when by having fathered a son of his own and thereby increasing the probability that Ian might be his, he no longer knows what he feels for him."

"You forget one important aspect," Matthew said. "The new wean is the spitting image of Luke."

"But not all children look like their father and you're his uncle. Many nephews take after their uncles, I'd imagine." She chewed her lip and frowned. "No; I think this is much simpler. He's never quite believed that Ian is his – after all, he can count. And Margaret definitely knows – no matter what she says." She released the lamb and got to her feet.

"You think?"

"Absolutely. But she's lied for so long she probably believes herself by now."

"Mayhap. She's breeding again."

"She is? That was quick."

"Making up for lost time, I reckon. She didn't tell Luke before she left or he would never have let her come."

"Poor Ian," Alex said, thinking that with two children definitely his, Luke would view Ian even more askance. "Or not," she continued, eyes flashing to meet Matthew's, assuring him that her promise from some weeks back still held. He squeezed her hand in response. "So am I – with child, I mean." Her free hand drifted for an instant down her front.

"Aye, I know." There was a shade of something dark in his eyes when he looked at her; concern that it was too soon, worry that she might think this child a replacement. She drew their interlocked hands to rest on her as yet flat stomach.

"A new child; not a replacement, but perhaps a consolation."

He just nodded.

"I don't want to." Ian looked beseechingly at his mother. "I can't leave them, Mam, not now, not after Rachel." He tried to explain how Matthew needed him, how on occasion he found his uncle sitting mute by the grave and it was Ian that could sit beside him, knowing his simple presence was enough. He gnawed at his lip, surveying their surroundings. This was home now, much more than the little manor in Oxfordshire. But he didn't tell Mam that, nor did he tell her how frightened he was of standing face to face with the man who called himself his father – but he was sure she knew.

"Your father wishes you to return home," Mam said. She tried to stroke his face, but Ian scooted out of reach. She sighed, dropped her hands to her lap. "He'll be most displeased, you know that."

Ian swallowed.

"And I want you with me," Mam said, eyes shiny with tears.

"He'll send me away," Ian said. "He doesn't want me there, not now, not with Charlie." He peeked at her from under his lashes, hoping she would laugh and tell him not to be a fool, of course his father would do no such thing. Instead she looked away and Ian's stomach churned.

"Ian!" Uncle Matthew's voice rang out over the yard, and Ian jumped to his feet.

"I have to go, we're cutting the piglets today."

Mam just smiled, waving him off in the direction of his uncle. Ian took a few steps, came to a standstill and turned towards her.

"I'm staying here, I won't be riding back with you." He bored his eyes into hers and she nodded in agreement.

"It won't please Luke," Margaret confided to Matthew on the drizzling spring morning of her departure.

"Nay, it won't." He wet his lips and looked away. "But it pleases me."

Margaret inhaled noisily. "He'll come for him."

"Aye. And then we'll see."

"See? See what?"

"If Luke truly wants him back, when it stares him right in the eye that Ian is mine."

"He isn't," Margaret said.

"Aye he is; you know that, I know that. It's about time we all acknowledged it."

Margaret inhaled and opened her mouth as if to say something, but ended up emitting a loud exhalation, her eyes flying from Ian to Matthew.

"Alex won't want to," Margaret said, sounding confident.

"You think?" Matthew said, beckoning Alex to come over. He draped his arm over her shoulder and pulled her close. "She stands by me; on this issue as on all others." For an instant he felt sorry for Margaret; her eyes darkened, her mouth set into a sad little smile. But then she straightened up, arranged her features and went over to bid her son farewell. No words, no tears, just a clinging embrace, arms wound so tight round her lad it seemed they'd been welded together.

"Be a good lad," she said once she let him go. She smoothed at Ian's hair, gave him a dazzling smile and turned to Alex. "Take care of my son," she said.

"Of course I will," Alex said. "I always do."

CHAPTER 30

"I don't want to watch this!" Alex was frantic. "Please Matthew, let's go. I don't want to…"

"Here," Matthew pressed her face against his chest. "I'll tell you when it's safe to look." It was stifling in the July sun and the heat had the unwelcome effect of releasing an unsavoury stench of stale sweat, fluids and general filth from the unwashed bodies that surrounded them.

"Why can't we just leave?" Alex shoved at the people closest to them .

"Too late, the soldiers have fenced all of us in."

She struggled against his hand and stood on tip toe, frowning at the straggling line of soldiers that encircled them. Here and there Matthew caught a flash of bright steel, one of the officers was brandishing a pistol. No one would be allowed to leave, trapped between the threat of violence and the gallows.

"I'm sorry, lass," Matthew said into her hair. "I should have remembered what day it was today."

Alex peeked at the three empty spars, at the hangman who was busy with his nooses.

"Three?"

"Aye," Matthew sighed, "one outlawed preacher, one man who stabbed a soldier in defence of the preacher and a woman."

"They're going to hang a woman? What for?"

"She murdered her sister," Matthew said, hitching his shoulders. There was a commotion by the scaffold, someone screamed and Alex hid her face against his shirt.

They began with the woman, the crowd catcalling and whistling. Objects flew through the air to smack into her torn dress and one egg hit her straight in the forehead, to general cheer among the apprentices closest to the gallows. The woman looked befuddled, peering short-sightedly at the crowd, and it was only when the hangman adjusted the noose around her neck that it seemed to dawn upon her what was happening. By then it was over and she hung like a sack of barley, swinging back and forth as the rope twisted round itself.

"Good hangman," the person closest to Matthew said in an undertone. "Quick and neat."

Matthew could but agree; as hangings went this had been an easy death. Alex made a choking sound and kept her nose to Matthew's chest when the first man was guided up the ladder and hanged, as efficiently as the woman.

The mood of the crowd changed when the preacher was led forth. No jeering, no cheering, only a heavy silence that had the soldiers shifting from foot to foot. The preacher himself was calm, alternatively he was royally drunk, a mere glass away from total oblivion. Matthew kept his hand on Alex, holding her to him. All around, women were turning to their husbands, because this was something none of them wanted to see: a man of their Kirk hanged for the single offence of holding to his faith.

One of the officers was arguing with the hangman, who shook his head. There was an altercation and the hangman spat and walked off the platform, taking noose and rope with him.

"Merciful Father," the man beside them said. "That wee officer intends to hang him himself."

To hang a man quickly is an art; it requires understanding of how to calculate the fall and tighten the noose, of how the fibres in the rope function together. The officer had no such skills, and the crowd stood in agonised silence while the poor preacher slowly, very slowly, was strangled to death. Matthew couldn't breathe; he held his wife to his heart, incapable of tearing his eyes away from the man that was still twitching, still alive, eyes like pickled eggs.

"They did that on purpose, they wanted him to die like that," Alex said once it was over. He didn't reply, intent on avoiding the man that was crossing the square in their direction. Too late; Wyndham had seen them and lengthened his stride.

"Matthew! Mrs Graham," Oliver was somewhat out of breath when he caught up with them. "A word?"

"Major Wyndham," Matthew bowed.

Alex curtsied and averted her eyes from the major. "I need some buttons and a new set of shears," she said, disengaging her arm from Matthew's grip. "See you at the stables, okay?" He nodded and she stretched her lips into a semblance of a polite smile in the direction of the major before walking off.

"I should have said this earlier," Oliver said as he fell into step with Matthew. "I'm sorry about your little girl. Four, was she?"

"Aye." Near on five months in the ground, his little lass, and still it hurt just to think her name.

"Mayhap it will console the mother to have a new child to busy herself with," Oliver continued with a nod in the direction in which Alex had disappeared.

Matthew looked at him. "You think? Have you any experience of losing a bairn?"

Oliver shook his head. "Thank the Lord I don't," he said with a passion that made Matthew look at him with interest. Then he recalled that Wyndham only had the one child, and a sickly one at that.

"You got my warning?" Oliver asked in a low voice once they had been served their beers.

Matthew nodded. Always a bit too late, these warnings, for him to save any but himself, and the execution witnessed today was the fall out of a massive attack on a conventicle around Whitsun.

Fortunately, most of the participants had escaped into the waterlogged moss, but the preacher had been cornered, defended by the man who had died with him. He waited; if Oliver were to warn him of attending the conventicle planned for tomorrow then he had the final proof he needed.

Three different dates to three different people, Sandy and Matthew had decided, and depending on what Matthew heard back they'd know who it was that was feeding the authorities far too much and far too accurate information.

"Did you enjoy it?" Matthew asked, throwing his head in the direction of the gallows where the bodies still hung, revolving on their ropes. "The fifth preacher to hang in as many weeks. You must be building up quite the reputation with the powers that be." Oliver flushed, the damaged side of his face shading into a dark plum.

"They were condemned in due course, I couldn't very well intercede at the trials."

"Nay, of course not; in principle, you can do nothing once you've apprehended them, so the easy solution to your moral dilemma would be not to apprehend any." He regarded Oliver quizzically. "You said that at heart you were still the same lad I once knew and loved, a lad with ideals and convictions. I must say you hide it well."

"My hands are tied," Oliver retorted with an edge.

"Oh, aye, I imagine they are. By the army or by my brother?"

Oliver went a deathly white. "Your brother?" he said, eyes darting all over the place.

"Aye, Luke Graham. You know him, don't you?"

"Is Luke Graham your brother?" Oliver widened his eyes to the point of looking inane. "I would never have made the connection. You're very different from each other."

"Thank you, I take that as a compliment."

He wanted to sink his fist into Oliver's face, but that would end with him being carted off somewhere and he wasn't going to do anything that would place him at the mercy of this man. Instead he changed the subject, wondering if there had been any further development in the Dutch war, laughing silently when Oliver's face clouded. The Medway debacle was a raw wound, only weeks in the past, and to have the proud battleship *HMS Royal Charles* towed back to the Netherlands by the Dutch Navy rankled in the English minds.

"I'd stay home tomorrow," Oliver said in passing as they made their farewells. "Preferably with a reliable witness or two."

"Reliable?" Matthew twisted his mouth. "And that would, per definition, not be a Scot."

Oliver shrugged. "Just stay home."

He bowed and turned into the alley leading back to his quarters. Matthew watched him until he disappeared out of sight. Well, he had his answer; Tom Brown. Sandy wasn't going to like it, not one bit. Nor would the soldiers, riding all that way on the morrow only to find there was no meeting. He whistled softly to himself as he made his way back to the stables.

"Tom Brown? Are you sure?" Alex sounded disbelieving.

"Aye." He increased the pressure of his legs around Ham's flanks, making the stallion break out in a jarring trot.

"Ouuf," Alex protested. "This is very uncomfortable."

Matthew urged the horse into a canter instead, and for some minutes they submerged themselves in the primitive joy of speed, Alex whooping like a bairn as the road disappeared beneath them in huge bounds.

"What will happen to Tom and his wife?" Alex asked once they were back to a sedate walk.

"I don't know. But we'll have it out with them tomorrow."

"Tomorrow? And must you take part? It could be dangerous."

"I must," he said. "As to dangerous, I think not. The soldiers will be elsewhere." But he wasn't looking forward to it, condemning one of their own for treason.

"Are you sure it's safe?" she asked.

"Nay, which is why Ian has spent all day watching the comings and goings at the Brown farm."

"Ian?" Alex' voice soared into a treble. "But he's a boy!"

Matthew shrugged. "He is nigh on thirteen, Alex, more a man than a lad." And capable, as he had proved already back in October when Ian helped save him. He stretched with pride.

They rode in comfortable silence for the last miles, with Ham ambling along more or less on his own. The spare line of trees that bordered the road seemed to pant in the heat, leaves hanging stiff with dust. Matthew threw an irritated look at the clear sky; a soft, long summer rain, that was what his crops needed, and mayhap it would clear the heavy air somewhat.

"Every time I come back home I look for her," Alex said as Ham walked down the last slope. "I see Mark, Jacob, little Daniel and there's a gap, and I always look, but she's never there."

"Aye, I do too. And every time I get close to the pig pen I expect to see her there."

"What was it with her and pigs?" Alex laughed into his back. "From the moment she could walk it was the pigs. Especially the sow."

"Kindred souls?" Matthew suggested, laughing as well. "Pigs are intelligent creatures, and mayhap Rachel felt conversing them was somewhat more fulfilling than attempting a discussion with her brothers."

"Matthew!" Alex slapped his arm. "It makes our boys sound like imbeciles."

"Sandy will be coming by late tonight," Matthew said as he helped her off the horse. "He'll be walking in along the river. Do you want to come with me to meet with him?"

"Is it safe?"

Matthew gave her an exasperated look. "Safe enough that I ask my pregnant wife along."

"Well then I suppose the answer is yes." She took his hand and placed it against her middle. "I bet you it's a boy."

Matthew wouldn't have it. "A lass, and so far I have been right each time."

"Huh; fifty-fifty chance." But he could see she hoped he was right this time as well.

Her hand in his was slippery with nerves when they made their way through the dusky summer night. She was barefoot, as was he and they splashed into the shallows and waded in silence, with Alex waving her free hand at the night bugs that fluttered around her face.

Bats swooped down in silent arcs, cutting just in front of them, and from behind them came the distant sound of a neighing horse, making Alex flinch. Matthew steadied her and brought her to a stop. There was a largish flat stone to the side and it took some time for Alex to make out that the dark shape on top of it was Sandy, not another stone.

Sandy greeted them in a low voice, and for the coming half-hour they sat and talked, their voices inaudible to anyone not standing beside them.

Ian had come back just before they set off, to eat and report, and was already making his way back to his stake out. From what Alex could gather, his news had been unwelcome. There had been a number of sightings of soldiers during the day, soldiers that had dropped in two by two and simply not ridden off. According to Ian's calculations at least a dozen soldiers were hidden in the outhouses of the Brown farm, and Sandy and Matthew agreed that it was an elegantly sprung trap. From that first written warning to Matthew, to the repeated verbal warnings over the last few months, the intention had been to make Matthew and Sandy identify the traitor – and come after him.

"Like bait." Sandy mimed a mouse trap clapping shut.

"But that would mean they know tomorrow's meeting is a hoax." Alex said.

"Not necessarily," Sandy said. "But they know Matthew isn't a fool, and this is the sixth – no, seventh – time that intelligence has been leaked that has been known to a limited few, of which Brown is one."

"So what will you do?" Alex asked.

Sandy and Matthew looked at each other. "Nothing," they chorused.

"At least not tomorrow," Sandy said. "It's their son; one of the Brown boys was captured at that conventicle last August – the one where we were nearly caught. The lad was brought home to his stunned parents, thrown hog tied in front of a dragoon, and now he's kept alive only as long as his parents cooperate."

"They won't let him live anyway," Matthew said, sending a pebble to land with a dull splash in the water.

"Nay of course not. He stabbed a soldier, the wee daftie. But for now they hope, aye? Major Wyndham is good at spinning a tale of potential salvation."

"How do you know all this?" Alex asked.

Sandy tapped his nose. "One piece here, the other piece there."

Sandy and Matthew moved on to talk of other things while she leaned back on her arms, thinking that this would make quite a nice spot for a daytime picnic, secluded and shaded as it was. Very secluded, she thought, throwing a look up the slope. Something snagged her eye. She squinted, trying to focus. There; a flash of white in all the gloom and it was moving towards them.

There was a series of sharp cracks from further up the slope, something came crashing through the vegetation. Horses! Soldiers, oh my God, several soldiers. Matthew and Sandy acted so fast that Alex' vision blurred, and by the time the three horses splashed into the water around them all that was to be seen was Alex and Matthew, intimately entwined. Alex shrieked and pushed at Matthew, smoothing down skirts and retying her shift over her bared breasts. The lieutenant looked from one to the other, small eyes narrowed into suspicious slits.

"What are you doing here?"

"I would think that was pretty obvious," Alex said, "and we were having a lovely time, thank you very much, until you decided to scare us senseless."

The officer raised his brows. Well; he did have a point. Who in their right mind would make love on a cold stone surrounded by a cloud of midgets?

"Where is he?" The lieutenant asked, riding his horse as close to the flat stone as he could.

"Who?" Matthew did his best innocent look, eyes very round.

"That damned Peden! One of my men saw him crossing the moss towards your place."

Matthew made a big show of scanning the rock and the surrounding shrubs.

"Not here. Personally I prefer not to have a minister close by when I'm swiving my wife."

One of the mounted men snickered, making the lieutenant glare at him before turning back to Matthew.

"One day..." he hissed, spitting with precision at Matthew's feet. He rose in his stirrups, staring at the undergrowth. With a curse he spurred his horse up the steep bank and disappeared. A couple of minutes later his men had dropped out of sight and Alex unclenched her hands from her skirt.

Sandy reappeared so abruptly that Alex gasped. She raised her eyes to the tree that hung above them.

"You're some kind of monkey?"

"Aye," Sandy grinned.

Alex looked from him to Matthew, seeing the exhilaration of one mirrored in the other and was blindingly angry with both for finding anything amusing in a situation that could have ended in a catastrophe. She backed away, plunged into the water and began to run.

"Alex," Matthew was beside her in an instant, his arm around her waist. "Hush, lass, it went alright."

"But it could have gone awfully wrong," she said.

Matthew drew them both to a stop. "Nay it couldn't, I told you; I don't take risks. The slope is littered with dry branches and twigs, Sandy can scale that tree in his sleep, and if it came to the worst I would've killed them."

"All three?" Armed men on horses? Terrible odds.

"All three," Matthew said, and something in his voice made her shiver

CHAPTER 31

Ian was pale when he showed up for breakfast next morning. Over a bowl of porridge he explained that as far as he could make out there were still several soldiers on Brown's farm. Matthew nodded, drummed his fingers against the table and turned to face Alex.

"Will you come with me to Cumnock?"

"Cumnock? Again?" She had no desire whatsoever to spend a whole day riding back and forth to a somnolent Sunday town, and anyway, what would they do there? It wasn't as if Matthew intended to attend services at the Anglican Church, was it?

"Witnesses," Matthew said in a low voice. "I have no intention of being set up on account of having no one to vouch for my whereabouts."

She didn't understand. How witnesses? "But you're here, at home…" With me, she almost added, until she recalled that her testimony would carry no weight whatsoever in the here and now, she being nothing but an extension of her husband.

"… and the Brown farm is just down the road." He sighed at her continued incomprehension. "Ride with me aye?" He threw a look out of the window and back at her. "It's a beautiful day. We can pretend."

"And the children?" Alex smoothed Jacob's hair back from his brow and kissed him on the pale skin under his fringe.

"They'll be fine. Sarah will look out for them."

Half an hour later they were on their way, Alex seated in front of him.

"Why?" Alex asked, leaning back against his chest. The sun was uncomfortably warm on her skin, even through her clothes, and she was swept with longing for a pool side vacation with the smell of sun lotion in the air. Yeah; right.

Still, she could take a swim. Once they got back she was going to go for a long, private soak in the eddy pool, no children allowed.

"This wee scheme of theirs has been a long time in the making. Oliver will be most upset when it doesn't work, and God alone knows what he'll do then. And if something happens at the Brown farm, I don't want to be close," Matthew said.

Alex thought about that for a long time. "Do you think something will?" At his continued silence she craned her head back. He was looking tired, worn around the eyes, his long mouth set into a straight gash.

"Aye, along the lines of masked men entering and killing an unsuspecting Mr Brown, and when the soldiers give chase what do they find but that the tracks lead back to Hillview and there I am, a sitting duck for their accusations."

What? She sat up straight. "Kill him?" She liked Tom Brown, could only imagine what anguish he was going through as he was forced to betray his friends to keep his son alive.

"Och aye; he's expendable." He sounded sad – very sad.

"But… no! Besides, murder is a hanging offence, and that would mean that Hillview would still remain with Mark, which Luke doesn't want." She nodded, comforted by her own logic.

"Aye, but what's to stop them from hanging *and* fining me?"

"Jesus in heaven!" Alex almost fell off the horse, so upset did this make her.

Matthew slowed the horse well before the crossroad oak. The large oak drooped in the heat, and just to the right was the branch from which he had hanged Gower. He shivered, a quick prayer for forgiveness flashing through his brain – mostly for not feeling any remorse.

In his arms Alex tensed, no doubt as affected as she always was by this particular crossroads – the place where she had nearly been dragged back to her time, all those years ago. A long, guttural howl rose into the air. Ham neighed, Alex clutched at his arm.

"What was that?" Alex said.

Matthew held in his horse, reluctant to go on. Ham snorted, small ears pricked into alertness. There was something lying on the further side of the tree, half in, half out of the oak's spreading shade. Matthew took in splayed, stiff legs, the glint of metal under the hooves.

"A horse. Dead it would seem," he said. Yet another howl cut through the air, a wordless plea for help.

"Or in pain," Alex suggested.

"That's no horse," Matthew said. "That's a man."

He'd been right; it was a dead horse, and pinned below it was its rider, arms pushing futilely against the ton of horseflesh that was squeezing the life out of him. They dismounted. Matthew frowned down at one booted leg, following what little he could see of the man until he found his face. Two dark eyes met his, eyes so wide he could see the bloodshot whites that surrounded the irises.

"It's Captain Howard," Alex said.

Matthew nodded. He'd recognised the officer immediately, although this terrified man had very little in common with the normally so controlled captain. Well, with the exception of last time he had seen him.

"We have to help him." Alex put a hand on Matthew's forearm.

Aye, not much choice, was there? Not that he wanted to, the man could well die here, under his horse – a divine retribution for wee Rachel.

"Matthew!"

He sighed. "You'll have to help, I can't pull him free on my own."

Once they'd succeeded in pulling him from under the horse, Matthew propped the captain up against the gnarled trunk of the oak. Howard was so pale Matthew could see the fine blue veins that ran just below the skin at his temple.

"One broken collarbone, one mangled leg and I think you've fractured your wrist," Alex concluded after her examination. She bent his hand, he yelped. "Just checking. So, what happened?"

The captain shrugged. "I'm not quite sure. Nestor…" He broke off to look at the dead horse. "He became skittish as we approached the crossroads. Somewhat temperamental, Nestor is – was. Mayhap it was a wasp – or a viper."

"A viper?" Matthew laughed, shaking his head.

"No, probably not," the captain said. "But one moment we're trotting along, the next he's bucking and heaving, impossible to control, and then he took one giant leap, stumbled and fell, thereby breaking his neck, I'd hazard. And there was I, trapped beneath him." He rubbed at his face. "I'd have died if you hadn't come along."

"I know; terrible, isn't it, to owe your life to your purported enemies," Alex muttered and the captain went a dusky red.

Soon they were well on their way from the crossroad, with Matthew and Alex walking beside Ham while the captain sat the horse. No way was she sharing the horse with him, Alex had told Matthew when he suggested she might ride as well – not unless she broke both her legs.

"With one I'd drag myself along rather than sit that close to him," she'd said, making Matthew chuckle.

The captain looked down at them and frowned. "It's Sunday."

"Aye."

"But…" the captain's frown intensified. "You're supposed to be attending a conventicle."

"A conventicle?" Matthew shook his head. "Such things are illegal, are they not?"

A small bubble of laughter escaped from Alex' lips. After a few moments, the captain joined in.

"You should perhaps wash a bit before we get to town," Alex suggested, looking the captain up and down. He was sitting beside her on the verge, while some yards further away Matthew had disappeared behind a stand of shrubs to relieve himself.

"It won't make that much of a difference, will it?" he said, looking at his torn and dishevelled garments.

She hitched her shoulders: it wasn't really any of her business.

"Is it fun?" she asked. "You know, hunting Covenanters?"

He flushed. "They're in breach of the law."

"They are simple, good people that believe in God, just like you do."

"They?" Captain Howard looked at her with interest. "Aren't you one of them?"

Alex looked away. "My mother was a Catholic, and I dare say that some of the Presbyterian ministers I've met are very worried about my lack of commitment to their faith. Sometimes it makes things difficult – especially for him." She smiled in the direction of her husband. "He didn't much like it when I told his sister that reasonably God was Catholic rather than Presbyterian – given the overwhelming amount of Catholics."

Captain Howard stared at her. "Do you believe He is?"

Alex yanked loose a tuft of grass and pursed her mouth. "No. I don't think He cares one way or the other – He judges on actions not on denomination." She stood up and wiped her hands down her skirts. "I believe God is fair; not always kind but at least fair." She placed both hands on her stomach. "A kind God wouldn't have taken Rachel."

Captain Howard looked as if he wanted a geyser to open then and there, the heat evaporating him to smoke.

"Holy Mother of God," he groaned. "I swear I didn't mean to."

"I know you didn't, and I've forgotten to thank you."

"Thank me?"

"You sent us the one person he needed." She inclined her head in the direction of Matthew.

"Oh, that," he muttered. "It was the least I could do."

It was noon by the time they reached the garrison buildings.

"Is the major in?" Matthew asked, supporting the captain to the door.

"The major?" The captain shrugged. "I think not. He insisted on commanding today's raid on the Covenanters." He gave Matthew a shrewd look. "I dare say he'll be most disappointed at not finding you there – he had hoped to." He bowed and limped off.

"I can imagine," Alex said in an undertone to Matthew. "Who knows, maybe he'll be so frustrated he bursts a gut."

Major Wyndham was furious, stalking back and forth in the cramped, dark kitchen of the Brown's farmhouse. House? This was no house, this was a hovel, and the woman's silent weeping was making him itch. Damn! So elegantly planned, so beautifully baited and still Graham managed to evade his little trap. He'd counted on him being here, administering justice to the informants, and instead... He crashed his fist into a door and cursed.

A rivulet of sweat trickled down his back and he wasn't sure if it was the heat or fear that had him transpiring like a pig. Luke Graham had been very threatening in his last letter, and with every day Oliver saw the advent of a most unappetising future, a future in which destitution and dishonour figured to a very large degree. He looked out of the window and back at the silent Brown couple. Well, he thought, what was it the infidels used to say? If the mountain won't come to Mohammed, then Mohammed must come to the mountain. And he was doing this for his son, a small boy of five. He closed his mind to the voice of conscience reminding him that Matthew had children too, pulled his sword and turned to the fear-stricken Browns.

An hour later, Oliver Wyndham held in his horse at the top of the lane leading to Hillview. The coming half-hour was going to be most unpleasant and he hoped Mrs Graham wouldn't be too difficult to handle while Matthew was fettered, but if it came to that, he supposed a slap or two would calm her down.

The farm looked somnolent in the warm Sunday afternoon, with cows and horses grazing in the water meadows, hens scratching at the ground in the hen coop and one ancient dog stretched out in the shade of the privy. The dog lumbered to its feet, head lowered, and barked. A peaceful slice of the world, but a slice about to explode into so many shards it would never be put back together again.

"Ride on." Oliver spurred his horse and rode hard down the lane, hatless, coatless, and with his sword drawn. There was a scream, several screams. A young woman rushed for the kitchen, carrying a child while dragging another behind her. A man as crooked and bent as Methuselah appeared from behind the stables, two more men were down in the meadows, but nowhere did he see Graham's distinctive height.

"Matthew Graham?" Oliver barked, holding in his horse in front of the only humans still in the yard – two boys standing hand in hand. He frowned down at the elder of them. Hadn't he seen him before?

"My uncle isn't at home," the lad said. "He is off to Cumnock, with my aunt."

"Your uncle?" Oliver had problems keeping his mare under control. How had Matthew seen this coming? He should have been at home, and then he would've dragged him off, the evidence being found where needed. And now… Oh, Lord! What had he done?

"Aye, Matthew Graham is my uncle. I'm Luke Graham's son, and we've met before." The lad looked guilelessly at Oliver, but deep inside those hazel eyes Oliver saw a small flicker of contemptuous amusement. He was washed by a wave of anger that this boy should stand in front of him and smirk, when it was his father that was ultimately the cause of all this mess.

He tightened his hold on his sword, but behind him he heard a hissed "Sir!" and knew that while his men might turn a blind eye on the killing of two informers, they would not countenance him killing children – especially not here, where one child had already died due to the crown.

"Search the place," he said instead. "Turn the whole farm upside down. We saw, did we not, how the murderers ran off in this direction?" His men muttered an unenthusiastic agreement but dismounted all the same. Oliver raised a shaking hand to his face, wiping at sweat and blood before dropping off his horse. Think! he urged. For God's sake, think Oliver. And he was, thinking so hard his brain was overheating, but in whatever direction he turned he saw a closed door, and in his mind the space in which he stood was shrinking rapidly into something that looked uncomfortably like a hangman's noose.

He made as if to enter the house, but the elder lad blocked his way.

"Not you sir," he said. "I won't let you enter." Oliver lifted his hand to shove the boy aside and suddenly the other boy stood there as well.

"Not you," the younger one said. Two pairs of eyes, startlingly similar, stared into his, and Oliver backed away. Damnation! He was surrounded by Matthew Graham lookalikes, bright hazel eyes swimming in his head wherever he looked.

He sat down on the ground and pulled off his riding gloves. There was a soft exclamation from the younger boy and Oliver looked down at his hand, still bloodied, despite the quick wash. He closed his fist. One hour ago he had been many things, foremost among them unprincipled and in debt. Now it all paled into insignificance; he had murdered. He had killed before – often even – but in the heat of battle, not with intent in a dark, squalid kitchen. For my son, he reminded himself furiously, I'm doing this for my little Francis.

"Nothing sir." The shadow of one of the dragoons fell over Oliver.

"Well then we must keep on looking. And we must make haste towards Cumnock, lest Graham be attempting to create an alibi for himself." He rose, inflated with a new bout of self-confidence. Let him find Graham and the rest would sort itself. Yes, of course it would.

CHAPTER 32

Alex was helping Matthew saddle up Ham for the ride home when Wyndham rode into the market square, boots and breeches covered with road dust. Behind him came a dozen or so dragoons, as grimy as Wyndham was. Matthew muttered an expletive, pulled his sword free and placed Alex behind him.

"Finally!" Oliver dismounted and advanced upon Matthew, stopping only when he saw the glint of light on the uncovered blade. Wyndham shook his head.

"Attempting to resist arrest, Matthew?" The man was grinning, eyeing Matthew as if he were a coveted trophy. Not reciprocated, with Matthew's face acquiring a belligerent set to his jaw that had Alex decide it was best to take a firm grip of his coat. Oliver took another step and Matthew's sword flashed in warning.

"What are you waiting for?" Oliver beckoned at his men. "Take this man!" Four dragoons slid off their winded mounts and advanced towards Matthew, who backed away.

"Arrest me for what?" he said in a loud voice. "What is it you want to pin on me this time?"

"Pin on you? No, no Graham, this time we're talking murder."

"Murder?" Matthew licked his lips. "Murder of whom?"

"The Browns," Oliver said, "around noon, and we saw you as you left the farm running."

"Oh, no," Alex moaned.

"Did you?" Matthew said. "Well that's mighty strange. I was here at noon, and a number of people can vouch for that." He retreated, eyes flying from one dragoon to the other, always ensuring he was between Alex and the advancing men.

"I saw you there, and I'm sure more weight will be given to my sworn testimony than to the word of the odd apprentice." Wyndham made a peremptory motion with his hand. "Go on, seize him."

Four, no six, soldiers closed in on them.

"Get away, lass," Matthew said.

"No way, I can't leave you to … Ah!" A sword whizzed by her ear, she leapt back, stumbled and fell. Up; get up.

Strange how many inconsequential things one noticed in situations like these. One of the dragoons had a yawning gap between sole and upper leathers, Matthew had to change his stockings and why was there a fishing hook protruding from the lining of his coat? Matthew slipped on the cobbles, slid like a skateboarder for a yard or two. He was fighting on all sides, his sword dancing through the air, but he was hemmed in by the wall behind him, by the horse on his other side, and by her, still on her knees beside him. One of the dragoons gave her a shove, threw himself forward and Matthew disappeared from her sight.

"Matthew!" She screamed, because she couldn't see him, could only hear him, and to the side stood the smirking major. Arsehole; this was all his fault. Alex bunched her skirts up and kicked the closest dragoon. With a yelp the man fell, crashing into Matthew, who staggered back, slamming into Ham, who neighed and half reared. Shit! But Matthew was still on his feet, and the dragoon sure as hell wasn't. Right; onwards and upwards. She prepared for yet another kick. Arms grabbed her from behind, arresting her halfway through the movement.

"Hold still," the major said in her ear. You wish. Alex stamped down hard on his foot, stuck a hand in his crotch and squeezed until he squealed like a pig. She wrenched herself free from the gasping officer and launched herself into the fight.

"Alex!"

What? Where? Oh God, he was down; one of the dragoons was sitting on him, and here came another. She didn't stop to think; she rose on her toes, wheeled and crashed her foot into the breastplate. Holy Matilda, that hurt! But it stopped the poor man in his tracks, his face going bright red as he tried to breathe. His companions fell back, she grabbed the soldier sitting on Matthew by the hair and pulled. Sometimes girlie fighting is by far the best. The man yowled like a cat in heat and tried to prise off her fingers. With a grunt Matthew was back on his feet. A scratch on his cheek, blood on his arm, but all in all he seemed unharmed. He crouched, snarling. Here came the soldiers again, and now there were eight, and the look in their eyes made Alex want to break and run.

"Stop!" Despite his limp, Captain Howard covered ground quickly. Alex had never been so glad to see anyone in her whole life. "What in God's name are you doing, sir?" he asked his major, sounding extremely disapproving. The soldiers halted, looking from the captain to the major.

"Mind your own business, captain," Wyndham wheezed, clutching at his privates. "Get out of the way lest he stab you in the back. This is a desperate criminal, a coldblooded killer just come from the slaughter of two innocents in their home."

The captain looked him up and down in silence, shaking his head slowly from side to side.

"You have the wrong man, sir," he said in a ringing voice.

More and more spectators had drifted over in their direction, a loose circle of men following the proceedings with interest. Far too many were gawking at her and Alex shifted on her feet, adjusted her clothing, her hair, her lace cap, not at all enjoying being the centre of attention. Beside her Matthew drew in a long, ragged breath, lowering his sword arm to hang by his side.

"Move, captain," Oliver said, "move or regret it. That's an order."

"I can vouch for Matthew Graham's whereabouts all day. You, on the other hand, rode out very early, major, did you not? Just after dawn, if my recollection serves me right." Captain Howard let his eyes sweep the silent dragoons. "Murder is always murder and soldiers hang for that just like anybody else."

A loud murmur of approval rose from the collected townspeople.

"It wasn't us," one of the dragoons said, backing away. "It was him, the major; we were but following orders."

His companions muttered their agreement, and one by one the dragoons distanced themselves from Wyndham, leaving him to stand alone. Alex needed a stiff drink – or a chocolate bar. Given that neither materialised she snuck her hand into Matthew's. His fingers closed round hers.

"Me?" Wyndham blustered. "I've done no such thing! It was Graham! We all saw him leave at a run, did we not? I'll have any man saying differently flogged, y'hear? And that includes you, Howard!"

"Mr Graham was here," the captain said. "I'll swear to it before any court in the land." He motioned to the dragoons, and the men lowered their weapons.

Matthew returned his sword to its scabbard. "I pity you, Oliver. You began life as a person of faith and conviction and you'll end life as a man for whom nothing was holy and everything was for sale."

"Silence!" Oliver thundered. "I'm arresting you for murder Matthew Graham. Arrest him I say!" Oliver screamed, but none of his men as much as lifted a finger to comply.

"You're the one they'll lead away in chains, Wyndham. Too many witnesses, far too many." Matthew went back to tightening Ham's girth, turning his back on Oliver.

Alex heard the whoosh of air when Oliver lunged at Matthew's uncovered back and acted instinctively. A blocking movement with her arm, the impact making her wince, a quick follow up chop that made the major yelp, and then Matthew was there, wresting the knife from Oliver and throwing it to land several feet away.

"Coward," was all he said, before helping Alex up on Ham.

Captain Howard nodded to two of the soldiers and Oliver was grabbed and led away. He seemed stunned, legs dragging over the cobbles. The remaining dragoons moved off, leading their winded horses. Now that the show was over the crowd dispersed, a few of the men coming over to say something to Matthew, now and then clasping his hand.

The captain hobbled over to the horse and smiled up at Alex.

"I think you're right, Mrs Graham; God doesn't care, one way or the other."

She burst out laughing. Perfect timing for a theological discussion.

"Of course He doesn't. And whatever His denomination, you've earned yourself a seat in heaven today."

A wave of blood flew up the captain's face. "God's speed," he muttered, standing back when Matthew sat up behind her.

"And to you," Matthew said, before clucking Ham into a walk.

It was like riding in a procession. All through the narrow streets people popped their heads out to stare at them – or at her. She'd never live this down, she sighed, they'd never let her forget the day she grabbed an officer by the balls to save her husband's life. Very much worth it, all in all, even if she probably should disinfect her hand when she got home. She wiped it on her skirts, and noted that it trembled. Not only the hand, but her arm, her legs, all of her was shaking. Matthew settled her even closer to him, his thighs strong and warm, his breath tickling her cheek. She wanted him to hold her like this forever.

"I wasn't sure you still retained your fighting skills," he commented as they left Cumnock behind.

"Me neither," Alex said, "but I guess some things, once learnt, remain with you forever." And thank heavens for that; she decided then and there to implement an extension to her exercise routine A.S.A.P. – one never knew when her martial skills might come in handy.

It was late afternoon when they turned up the last stretch. What with the heat and the evening light, the landscape around them shimmered in shades of gold and burnished bronze, dust rising from the dirt road when an odd gust of wind rushed by. Two small sentinels stood waiting for them at the top of the lane, two shapes that at the sight of them began to run. Mark's face was streaked with tears, Ian looked about to cry and without a word Matthew dropped off the horse and collected both boys to his chest in a long, silent hug.

Once Ham had been taken care of, Alex produced bread and ham, beer for Matthew and Ian, and settled down to listen to Ian's description of the recent events.

"So you faced him down, just the two of you?" Matthew cleared his throat. "You're very brave, aye?"

Alex wanted to weep. Only thanks to Matthew's instincts had Wyndham's trap backfired, and even so it had been touch and go. All the long ride home they hadn't said a word, but Alex had clung to his arm with such force that when she released her grip she saw to her shame that she had left bruises on his skin.

"That was a very dangerous thing to do," Alex admonished the two young heroes. "What is it with you Graham men?" Mark's ears turned a delicate pink. Alex ruffled his hair and ordered them both to bed, promising them that tomorrow she would bake them a huge cake in recognition of their valour.

When she came up some minutes later Mark was already fast asleep in the bed he shared with Jacob and Daniel. Ian stirred on his pallet when she knelt down to kiss his brow.

"Soon we'll have to move you into a separate bedroom. Young men don't sleep with children." She was still laughing at his evident pleasure when she returned to the kitchen, where she found Matthew staring at the wall, his hand clenching and unclenching reflexively.

"Are you okay?" She came over to give him a backward hug. He hitched a shoulder, gave a rueful little shake of his head.

"It's somewhat daunting, the lengths to which my brother is willing to go to destroy me. Two people dead, no less."

"But you survived this one as well," Alex said, rubbing her cheek against him.

"Why can't he just leave me in peace? Why is it that he can't let go of this sick hatred?"

"I don't know, honey." In her private opinion Luke Graham was an obsessive jerk that would have benefited from lobotomisation, or why not a complete brain transplant with a cow.

"He has so much more than me. Sir Luke Graham no less, he's favoured by the king, is rich enough to have two homes, has a wife and a baby son and now another on its way…"

"And Ian, don't forget that he has Ian."

"Whom he stole from me!" It came out as anguished whisper. "My son, and he stole him!" He sighed and turned in her arms. "I don't want to let him go. I love the lad so that my heart breaks, and I fear that I'll tear him in two if I let him know how much I love him, but God help me, I want him here, with us. He belongs with me."

"I think Ian already knows you love him. He's known that for quite some time."

"Aye, like a nephew, not as a son," Matthew said bitterly. "It isn't enough, not anymore; I want him to know me as his father."

One small part of her was angry that this, his firstborn, should occupy such a huge place in his heart, but she recognised that he loved all his children with equal passion. It was just that welcoming Ian as a son would have such an impact on Mark, and she didn't know how to explain the whole mess to a boy that was only seven. She kissed his nose.

"I already told you; if that's what you want, then I'm with you all the way."

Ian didn't dare to move. He'd come down for a drink of water and now he had to piss instead. Pressing a shaking arm to his mouth to stop himself from making any noise, he escaped up the stairs, avoiding the treads that squeaked. He stopped outside the nursery door and sat down on the floor, filled

306

with so many whirling emotions that he couldn't clear his head.

They loved him! Both of them, he could hear it in their voices, and his heart swelled with happiness. His father – his uncle? His father! – wanted him to stay, to tell the world he was his son. And Ian wanted it too. This was where he belonged, following a man he loved as he strode from stable to field, pointing, teaching, laughing at Aragorn's antics, smiling with pride when Ian did something right. He bit back a sob; and Mam? He'd never see her again, or at least only rarely.

Ian was exhausted; not only had he not slept last night, but now his brain was a buzzing inferno of questions. After having peeked over the banisters to ensure the coast was clear he crept back down, breaking into a frantic run the moment he was out of the house. He had no idea why he was running or where, but he ran until the loud noises in his head abated and then threw himself down by the river to think.

"What are you doing here in the middle of the night?" Alex was faintly disappointed; she'd looked forward to a solitary swim in the July night, and the hunched shape by the water was a rather unwelcome intrusion on her plans.

"I couldn't sleep," Ian mumbled and shifted sideways to allow her to join him on the log.

"Me neither, it's hot, isn't it?" Plus every time she closed her eyes she saw Matthew being led away in chains by a triumphant Wyndham, or poor Mrs Brown covered in blood. They sat quietly, both of them lost in their own thoughts. Ian hunched together even further with his chin sunk into his clasped knees and sighed.

"I heard you before, when you were talking in the kitchen."

"Oh." Alex kicked at a small stone, sending it to land with a splash in the middle of the pool.

"I love them both," Ian said. "I know my father isn't always a good man, but I love him."

"Of course you do. It would be strange if you didn't. Luke has taken care of you since you were a baby."

Ian hitched a bony shoulder, hiding his face against his knees. Alex sighed; since Margaret's visit back in April they'd not had one letter, no sign of life, while Ian had written several times. She supposed Margaret was confined to her bed again, heavy with child, but still, was it too much to ask that she wrote her son now and then?

"You said Mam is breeding." It was somewhere between a question and a statement.

"She didn't tell you?" Maybe not that strange, given that it had been in the very early stages when she was here. Ian shook his head in a no.

"Do you reckon they knew?" he asked, digging his bare toes into the sand.

"Who? Knew what?"

"Them. Mam and… Luke."

Alex looked at him thoughtfully. This was the first time she'd ever heard him using her brother-in-law's name.

"That I wasn't his, that they stole me from Uncle Matthew."

"Your mother definitely, Luke perhaps. But she did it because she couldn't bear to be parted from you."

"Aye," Ian shrugged. "Mayhap. And he took me as his for her sake, not for mine."

"To begin with, but over time very much for the boy you are."

"He doesn't want me anymore," Ian said bleakly. "Not now that he has a son of his own. But…" He broke off, eyes following the silent silhouette of an owl as it sped across the clearing. "He won't give me to Uncle Matthew, not if he knows you want him to."

Alex put an arm around him and scooted closer to him. "No, probably not. But you know what? I think we'll sort it out, okay? If you want to stay here, with us, we'll fix it – it's up to you." Not that she had any idea how, but this boy belonged with her now. She stood and pulled him to his feet.

"Now, I'm going for a swim. Coming?" At his hesitation she grinned, drew the shift over her head and splashed into the water. Ian copied her, loud whoops as he made for the deep end. He lay floating while Alex swam back and forth several times before coming to stand beside him, her body modestly covered by the water.

"He said he loves me," Ian said.

"He does, very much."

Ian set down his foot on the bottom and stood with his back to her.

"I love him too." He shot out of the water, grabbed at his discarded shirt and disappeared.

Alex laid back to float. Around her the summer night stood dark and beautiful, and way, way up high she saw the weak twinkling of stars. Somehow she suspected she had just acquired a stepson and to her surprise it made her very happy.

"But if he calls me step-mama I'll whack him," she muttered to the dark.

CHAPTER 33

"Look at you," Matthew whispered in her ear. "Round like a melon." His hand spread itself fanlike over her stomach, pushing her warm, round arse against his crotch.

"Mmm," Alex creased her brow. She kept her eyes shut when he kissed his way down her cheek and neck.

"Alex... you know, no?"

"Know what? That you're an inconsiderate oaf of a man that won't let your exhausted pregnant wife sleep?" She protested when he rolled her over onto her knees, lifting her shift high enough to bare her buttocks to the cool morning air.

"Aye, an oaf," he chuckled. "But it's your fault, to lie like this, a temptress in my own bed."

"Temptress, hey?"

He was already inside her, holding her to him. "Aye. Tempting like a giant pear."

She laughed, a low gurgling sound. "You have serious problems – grave hang up issues on pregnant women. And fruit."

"Only on the one; my woman, with my bairn inside of her."

He rocked them back and forth. Her breath came in short gasps, he waited, holding back until she shivered beneath him and drove himself quickly to finish.

"I must do something about the bed," he muttered, "it sags." He hung his head over the edge and looked at the bottom. The rope frame had to be tightened, and he poked an experimental finger at the woven rush mats before flopping back down beside his wife.

From below came a babble of young voices, and they rolled away from each other to get on with the business of the day.

"You must talk to Ian," Alex said.

"Must I?" Matthew threw his stockings into a corner. Too hot. He looked at Alex, who was apparently fully dressed in only chemise, stays and skirts and frowned. "You can't go about like that."

She scowled at him. "You're only in your shirt and breeches."

"Aye," he grinned, "but I don't have these, do I?" he nudged her breasts through the thin cloth. She muttered but went to find something, making him grin even more. "Why?"

"Why what?" Alex pinned the flowered shawl into place.

"Why must I talk to Ian?"

"Because he heard us, last night." She gave him a very blue look. "I'm going to sweat like a pig in this."

"Pigs don't sweat," he said and escaped through the door to avoid the flying hairbrush.

For most of that morning Matthew was buoyed by the overwhelming sense of relief that he had escaped unscathed from yet another of his brother's nefarious schemes. He saw to his beasts, strode over to inspect the growing crops, and was ridiculously happy to be alive. Then it all struck him; Tom Brown and his wife cut down in their kitchen, the Brown lad now surely to hang – yet another family destroyed in the swelling conflict between the faith of his people and that of their overlord.

In less than a minute all energy drained out of him and he retreated to sit behind the smoking shed, staring out across the water meadows. What was life going to be like for his bairns here in the coming years? He rested his shoulders against the sun-warmed wood behind him and stretched out his legs. Around him the air hummed with the sound of bees and hundreds of small white butterflies rose, soared, and settled again on the high heads of yarrow. He exhaled; this was where he'd been born and the few times he'd thought about it he'd assumed this was where he would be buried as well, to lie close to Da and Mam up by the rowan tree. But not if he were hanged or deported…

His reverie was interrupted by one very large dog, followed by Ian, who came to a standstill at the sight of him. Matthew's throat constricted and to his sarcastic amusement he had to wipe his sweaty hands down his breeches. Nervous as a stripling… At his gesture Ian came closer, dropping down to sit beside him with legs pulled up against his chest.

"You heard, I gathered."

Ian hugged his legs closer and inclined his head.

Matthew had no idea what to say. He sneaked a look at the lad, cleared his throat, opened his mouth, cleared his throat again. His son! He felt weightless, the fine hairs along his arms were standing straight up with tension, but at least he kept himself from trembling.

"Alex rightly said it's your choice; I love you as much no matter what you decide, it's not a huge difference between an uncle and a father." He wanted to laugh out loud at that blatant lie, but he didn't, meeting eyes so similar to his and so very close.

"Da," Ian croaked after what seemed an eternity. "I want to call you Da." Matthew expelled his held breath. He laughed somewhat shakily and enveloped Ian in a bear hug.

"My son!" Matthew kissed the messy thatch of hair leaning against his shoulder. "My bonny, bonny, lad." He laughed and squeezed Ian even harder, relaxing his hold only when Ian uttered a muted "Ow."

"For now, we don't speak of it," Matthew said as they got to their feet.

Ian nodded, looking crestfallen.

"You know why. If it were me, I'd walk up to the hilltop and yell it out loud, but you're legally not my son, and we must tread carefully round this."

Round Luke, rather. If his goddamn brother were to ride in tomorrow and demand that Ian be returned to him, there would be nothing Matthew could do but acquiesce – or bring the full weight of the law down upon himself.

"And I must have time to speak to Mark," Matthew added, gnawing at his lip.

"Mark?" Ian gave him a worried look. "Will he mind if I'm no longer his cousin but his brother?"

"Not as such, but you're my firstborn."

It took some time for Ian to grasp what it was he was saying, but once he did he backed away.

"I don't want to take anything from Mark," he said in a wobbly voice. "I love Mark."

"Shush, lad, that's not your concern, it's mine."

"But Aunt Alex…" Ian shook his head. "She won't like it if Mark…"

Matthew silenced him with a hug. "She already knows. And yet it is she that has said that I must welcome you back as my son."

Ian gaped. The lad closed his mouth, opened it to say something, closed it yet again, looking very much like a landed fish.

"She did?" It came out very hoarse.

"She did."

Two brilliant eyes met his, a huge smile broke out over Ian's face. "Oh," was all he said.

"Will you mind?" Matthew asked him. "You know, with all your half-siblings?"

Ian looked at him as if he were insane. "Mind? Why would I mind?"

"Well, you don't like weans much, do you?"

Ian laughed out loud. "I don't like Charlie, but I love my wee cousins – brothers – very much." He gave Matthew a shy look. "But a lass would be good this time."

"Aye, a lass would be very nice." Matthew turned in the direction of the little graveyard. "More biddable than her sister, I hope." He tilted his head to look up at the sky. In his head he saw Rachel come rushing towards him, eyes gleaming and hair flying untidily around her head, and she was holding her arms wide for him to sweep her up in his embrace. He inhaled, and the scent that tickled his nose was that of Rachel – small and warm and smelling of honey and milk.

"So you spoke to him," Alex smiled, coming to meet him at the kitchen door. She was moving with a languid slowness that he recognised with a flutter of expectation. It must be the heat, in combination with the pregnancy, that made her undulate in his direction.

"Aye, I did." He joined the rest of the household at the table and served himself of the food.

"Don't forget the vegetables," Alex reminded him, setting down a dish of salted butter to go with the new beets and carrots. Matthew sighed and winked at his sons, receiving stifled giggles in return.

"Are you supposed to eat this?" Mark said, shoving his small helping of spinach leaves this way and that.

"It depends," Alex replied. "If you want dessert, then yes, you must. If you want second helpings of the chicken, yes, you must. If you want an extra slice of bread, yes, you must. But otherwise, no, of course not." Mark stuffed them manfully into his mouth and chewed, swallowing them down with a grimace.

"Your father loves spinach," Alex said, placing a substantial amount on Matthew's plate. "Don't you, honey?" She turned her back on him and moved over to the pantry to retrieve the dessert pie. "Same rules apply to everyone," she added, giving him a sweet smile over her shoulder.

Matthew remained behind at the table once the lads and the men left, leaning back to allow Sarah to clear the dishes.

"There's a letter for you, from Luke." Alex inclined her head in the direction of the oak chest.

"Letter? I heard no messenger riding in." Matthew held the stiff paper with as much care as if he were handling a venomous snake.

"Probably on account of you shirking work behind the smoking shed," Alex said, making him smile. "Aren't you going to open it?"

Matthew broke the seal and unfolded the paper, spending an excessive amount of time flattening out the creases before he began to read it.

"It's not a book," Alex said at his long perusal of the letter. "By now you've read it five times. What does it say?"

Matthew folded the letter together. "He wishes his son returned to him, and if the lad isn't home by the first of August he'll come for him."

"And that scares you why?"

"It doesn't frighten me. Not for myself – but it may be difficult for the lad." He frankly had no idea how to convince Luke to relinquish Ian into his care.

"Time for the light cavalry, I think," Alex said. "Write to Simon. I suppose Joan and Lucy could do with some time away from Edinburgh."

Matthew regarded her carefully. Joan and Alex had not parted on the best of terms back around Hogmanay, and the stilted if sincere letter of condolence that Joan had sent them at the time of Rachel's death hadn't helped. Alex hadn't even bothered to reply, and now it was Matthew writing Simon and vice versa, rather than the women writing each other.

"She's been very ill, all spring, Simon says."

"I know," Alex said, "and I just said. Ask them if they want to come." He stood up and looked down at her.

"I'll do it immediately."

"What will happen to Wyndham, do you think?" Alex asked, interrupting the comfortable quiet in his little office.

Matthew raised his eyes from his letter. "He'll hang, I imagine," he said with a disinterested shrug. He went back to his writing. "Why do you ask?"

"I was thinking of his son. His mother is dead, his father to hang, he is left destitute and unless his aunt can keep him…"

"Not our concern, is it?" Matthew said. "And his father didn't greatly care about the wellbeing of either yourself or our children, did he?"

She bit off the thread and inspected her work before glancing at him. "Just because he's gone it doesn't mean you're any safer."

Matthew laughed hollowly. "I know that. There's not a Covenanter alive in Ayrshire that doesn't know that." He sighed, blotted the paper and folded it together, sealing it with a blob of wax.

"I'll have Gavin go into Cumnock with it tomorrow and find someone to take it to Edinburgh."

He took her hand as they stepped out into the hot July afternoon, and together they set off in the direction of the laughing voices, finding all four lads down by the river. Daniel was crowing with delight, banging at Ian's wet head with his small hands, and in the shallow end Jacob was wading slowly along the grassy edge, dragging his legs back and forth.

"Leeches," Alex sighed. "Rachel taught him that." She pushed at him. "Go on, you're dying to get in with them."

"And you?"

"Well, Ian found it difficult in the dark, so I imagine the sight of me naked in pure daylight would leave him scarred for life." She tilted her head at him and settled herself in the shade. "I'll go for a swim later instead."

The boys shrieked with joy when Matthew joined them in the water, and even Jacob left his single-minded hunt for leeches to come rushing through the shallows.

"I can swim, Da, Ian taught me. Look, Da, I can swim." He threw himself forward, sank like a stone, but somehow paddled back to the surface, leaving a churning wake behind him.

"Well, look at you!" Matthew said. "You swim like a fish."

"Let's not exaggerate," Alex muttered, "more like a drowning monkey." A very cute little monkey, now sitting on his father's shoulders with his hair plastered to his head while Mark swam in elegant circles around them.

Ian waded out to where Matthew was, and Alex smiled at her boys. Beautiful, all of them – from Daniel with his baby fat to Ian's sinewy body. But it was to her man her eyes returned time and time again; strong and tall, all of him glowing with health and life.

Matthew turned in her direction and smiled, his eyes blazing gold in a sudden shaft of afternoon sunlight.

"I love you," he mouthed and dived into the water. And I love you, she replied silently, thanking God yet again for having given him to her.

CHAPTER 34

Joan looked terrible. A waxy pallor made her grey eyes stand like blots of ink on white paper and her hair hung dull and lifeless round her face.

"Ill?" Alex hissed to Matthew. "She looks like a corpse!"

Matthew squeezed her hand in admonishment and went over to help his sister down from the horse.

"I can do that myself," Joan said when Matthew bent down to retrieve the handkerchief she had dropped.

"I'm sure you can, but I was brought up to be polite, aye?"

Joan mumbled an excuse and turned round to receive Lucy in her arms. Not yet two, Lucy was remarkably self-possessed, regarding her boisterous boy cousins with wide, grey eyes. She twisted in Joan's arms and was set down, standing in perfect stillness when the boys moved towards her. But it was only when she saw Ian that she smiled, two dimples appearing on her cheeks.

Alex hung back at first, keeping her distance as Simon and Matthew slapped each other on the back, but after a sequence of shared looks with Joan she moved towards her.

"What's the matter with you?" Alex asked, taking Joan by the arm.

"Matter with me?" Joan shrugged free of Alex' hold.

"Oh, don't give me that. And even if Matthew may be too considerate to ask, I can tell you he's wondering and worrying too."

Joan inhaled, did a half-turn, and exhaled. "There is something wrong with my humours and my physician has recommended that I eat sparingly of dry bread and drink moderately. I'm to be bled several times a week."

Alex looked her over. "Bullshit, if anything you're undernourished, and to bleed you just makes you even more anaemic."

Joan frowned at her language. "I've consulted several physicians, and they are men of education."

Alex raised her brows. "Unlike me, you mean? Quacks, the lot of them, and now that you're here you'll eat and drink as I tell you."

Joan started to protest but Alex shook her head.

"Two weeks. And then let's see how you feel, alright?"

Joan eyed her with an mixture of respect and resentment. "You're a most overbearing person."

"I know, it's one of the things I always have very long conversations with God about." Luckily, Joan chose not to comment, however much she pressed her mouth together.

After dinner, Matthew led Simon into the privacy of his office, poured them each a whisky and sat down.

"Ian," he said, "I want him back."

Simon frowned and tented his hands, studying him for a long time.

"Are you sure?"

Matthew made an irritated noise. Of course he was sure!

"And Alex?"

"She knows what I mean to do."

"Hmm," Simon said, "and she understands it means Mark will lose Hillview?"

The bald statement made Matthew balk at the thought of explaining all of this to Mark, but the lad was only seven, and he loved Ian – anyone could see that. He'd grow out of his loss, he assured Simon, who grunted that in his experience brotherly love was one of the first casualties in disputes over inheritance – as Matthew well knew.

"I'll ensure all my sons are well set up," Matthew said.

"Oh, aye, I'm sure you will."

But the single most valuable asset in Matthew's control was the small manor and that would go unimpaired to the eldest, leaving very little for the others to share. Three – no, four – sons already.

"Are you planning many more?" For all that Simon tried,

Matthew could hear the jealousy in his voice. He shifted on his seat, looked out through the small window to where Alex and Joan were sitting in the shade.

"There will be more, I reckon. Alex is still young, and…"

"You're both willing in bed," Simon finished for him with a small grin.

"How is it with you?" Matthew asked, keeping his eyes on anything but Simon. "Do you…"

Simon choked on his whisky, coughing for several minutes. "Aye," he finally managed to say.

Wee Simon was lying through his teeth, made very obvious to Matthew by how his friend looked him straight in the eyes, those pale blue eyes of his never faltering. Well; he couldn't well push, not into matters as private as what went on in the marital bed, and from Simon's stance any further questions would be unwelcome. Instead he returned to the matter at hand.

"Will it be complicated do you think, to claim Ian as mine?"

"Aye," Simon said, "and if Luke doesn't want to renounce him, nigh on impossible." His eyes drifted to the outside, resting on Ian, who was pushing Lucy back and forth on the rope swing. "I hear Margaret is pregnant again."

"Aye, due in November. Ian had a letter from her yesterday and when he'd read it he threw it into the fire."

Matthew had been curious and used the poker to retrieve the paper, smoothing it out to read a long, gushing description of wee Charlie, and of how happy Luke was that soon there would be yet another child. There was a rather sad postscript, added in scrawled and misspelled haste, where she confessed to missing him, every day she missed her Ian, and hoped he missed her too, but what with her being bedridden, maybe it was for the best if…

"Caught in the middle," Simon said. "Poor woman."

"Aye." Matthew opened a drawer and drew out a miniature, badly singed along one side. "She included this."

It was an excellent piece of work, bringing to life the laddie who sat in long smocks decorated with lace and ribbons and smiled shyly at the beholder. Eyes glittering greens, hair that fell in soft, wavy lengths of dark red round a face that was a smaller version of Margaret's, down to the pointed little chin. In one chubby hand the boy held a rattle, in the other a silver spoon.

"Well, no doubt there. That's definitely Luke Graham's son." Simon chewed his lip. "It can't be easy for the lad," he said, waving his hand in the direction of Ian. "Now that he has this copy of himself, how can Luke look at Ian with anything but resentment at having been tricked into recognising him as his son, thereby cheating his legitimate son out of his inheritance?"

"So maybe Luke can be convinced to let Ian go, now that he has this wee lad." Matthew heard how ridiculously hopeful he sounded.

Simon snorted. "If Luke knows you want him, he'll keep him, if nothing else to spite you."

Alex regarded Ian with maternal pride when he let Lucy take his hand and drag him towards the three other boys, busy with a loud intricate game involving long sticks.

"She's a pretty little girl," Alex said, feeling a hollow ache inside of her.

Joan smiled in the direction of her daughter. "Aye she is. And stubborn like her father – not that it will be of much help." This last was said with a certain acidity.

"Help?" Alex studied her niece, who had somehow grasped that the purpose of the game was to fell Daniel to the ground and sit on him.

"No one will ever want to marry her, seeing as she's deaf."

Alex looked at Lucy but saw another girl, her little girl. "At least she's alive," she said and got to her feet.

She was sitting by Rachel's grave when the gate to the graveyard squeaked, but she didn't turn, keeping her hand on the sun warmed stone that had her daughter's name on it. Joan lowered herself to her knees beside her.

"You must miss her a lot," she said.

"Every day, almost every hour I think of her and wonder why she isn't here. When I go in to kiss them goodnight it always surprises me that she isn't in there with the others, and every time the pigs squeal I find myself thinking that Rachel is up to something again, then I remember that of course she isn't because she's dead. Dead!" Alex plucked a white rose from the bush and placed it on the headstone, brushing imaginary dirt off it first. "I hate the thought that she lies rotting in the dark, and I have these awful dreams where she's crying and holding up a half-eaten arm and asks me to do something." She crossed her arms tight over her chest.

"She's with God." Joan placed her hand on Alex' shoulder.

"Yes, that's what all of you say. Matthew, Sandy, you – even Ian." She looked over to where Matthew and Simon had come out from the house and were wandering towards the children. "It doesn't help, because she should be here, with me, not dead in the ground."

"Oh, Alex of course she should! But she isn't, not anymore, and you must trust that she is happy wherever she is." She smiled slightly. "We must hope that they have pigs in heaven."

Alex laughed at the ridiculous image of white heavenly pigs, and then began to cry instead.

"She would like that," she said through her tears.

Matthew took Simon with him into Cumnock to attend Oliver's trial, returning with a grim expression on his face. When Alex tried to talk to him, he brushed her off, saying it was nothing and that he needed some time alone.

"It's that major," Simon said to Alex, lowering himself with some effort to sit in the grass beside her. "That accursed perjurer repeated that it wasn't him, it was Matthew Graham who killed Tom Brown and his wife. He even said he'd seen it, with his own eyes."

"But no one believed him," Alex said, her eyes on where her husband had ducked out of sight.

"Nay, of course not. But it was difficult for Matthew nonetheless." Simon gave her a sad look. "They hanged the Brown lad. Not yet sixteen, and they hanged him. So now it is just the eldest lad and the two lasses. What a waste!" He shook himself, settled himself against the trunk of the nearest tree and nodded in the direction of his wife. "I don't know what you're doing, but she looks much better."

"It helps to eat, and whatever idiot suggested she be bled regularly should have his head examined or preferably bashed in." Alex finished mending the long gash in Daniel's smock and folded it together, fishing out the next garment in line from her basket.

Simon grinned. "Now why do I think Doctor Guthrie would not like to hear you say such?"

"Because he's a pompous moron?"

"Alex! He's an educated man."

"And?" She dropped her eyes to her sewing. "It would also help if you stopped going to that whore."

"Whore?"

"She knows, and strangely enough she sees nothing wrong in it." If it had been her, she'd have rammed a poker up his arse. Okay; maybe a bit excessive, but still.

"Well then you'd best not meddle," he said coldly.

"It's breaking her heart."

He exhaled, dragging angrily at the grass. "I love my wife, but I'm only thirty-eight. I can't live in celibacy and I do my best to be discreet. You shouldn't presume to judge when you don't have all the facts."

All the facts? Joan had admitted to being terrified of becoming pregnant again and apparently it had never occurred to her that one could have a pretty good time in bed without going the whole way. And now it seemed Simon was just as unenlightened …

"There are other ways, you know."

"Other ways?" He regarded her guardedly.

"You know; to… err… well, please each other." She

gathered together her mending and stood. "Talk to Matthew," she said and walked off.

"What possessed you?" Matthew barked, somewhere in between exasperation and amusement. "You left him shocked."

"I didn't tell him anything in any detail."

"Nay, that you left to me," Matthew muttered. He chuckled and shook his head. "Have you spoken to Joan? You know, about how..."

Alex squirmed and admitted that yes, she had.

"And what did she say?"

"First she said nothing, then she said nothing, after that she said absolutely nothing and then she began to laugh."

"Ah," Matthew nodded.

"And then she said no wonder I insisted so much on people washing all the time," Alex added primly, making Matthew howl with laughter.

CHAPTER 35

Matthew waited until Captain Howard had dismounted before moving over to him.

"Captain," he said extending his hand. If Howard was surprised he didn't show it, grasping Matthew's hand in his. "Your leg?"

"Better." The captain adjusted the sling on his bandaged arm. A strained silence ensued, with Matthew waiting for the captain to state his business while the captain obviously was looking for Alex. Finally Howard dug into the pocket of his long coat and brought out a folded note, handing it to Matthew.

"I refused at first, but seeing as the major pleaded, I promised I would deliver it to you in person."

"Why would Wyndham write to me?"

"I have no idea, I'm not in the habit of perusing other men's letters." Howard smiled when he saw Alex come down from the kitchen garden, a loaded basket on her arm, and raised his hand in greeting. She waved back and changed course towards them.

Howard gawked, looking like a lovesick lad – or an adoring hound, given those dark eyes of his. His eyes stuck to Alex, and Matthew wasn't sure whether to reprimand him or laugh. She was a pretty sight, his Alex, in sandals and with the sleeves of her chemise bunched with ribbons – blue ribbons that matched the embroidery on the green, sleeveless bodice.

"Captain," Alex came to a stop and set down the loaded basket. Howard bowed in her direction, looked into her basket and gave a short bark of laughter.

"Potatoes?" He picked one up. "My uncle grows them in his garden, but it's rare to see them grown this far from London."

Alex rolled her eyes. "Tell me about it, it took me years just to find someone who'd sell me some seed tubers." She smiled down at her basket. "First crop ever, so today the Graham men will be dining on potatoes and trout. I can't wait to see their impressed faces." She laughed and swung the basket back up on her arm. "Raspberries for dessert," she promised, sending Matthew a look before she strolled off in the direction of the house.

"You're welcome to stay for dinner," Matthew said to Howard. "But I must warn you – she serves much foliage and expects you to eat it."

Howard bowed and mumbled that he was much obliged.

"I take it you've resigned your commission," Matthew said, studying the other man's appearance. No officer's sash, no sword hanging at his side, and instead of boots he wore silk stockings and shoes with polished buckles. He inclined his head in the direction of the hill, suggesting that they walk, and Howard fell in beside him.

"Yes," Howard said, "it was for the best. Giving testimony against your commanding officer is not approved of in all quarters. And it was time, I think. I want to live a life less fraught with conflict than the one I've been leading lately – a better life."

"Ah," Matthew voiced.

"Could…" Howard cleared his throat. "Would it be improper of me to ask you to allow me to see your little girl's grave?" Matthew stopped for an instant before swerving to the left.

"I don't blame you. I may have done, then and there, but mostly I blamed myself. I should have let you take the horse."

Howard shook his head. "I do. Every day I blame myself. I provoked you, I did it on purpose, to allow me an excuse to drag you off."

"Aye, I know that, but I still had a choice." He stopped at the low wall and swung open the gate, allowing Howard to precede him. "I come here often in the early dawn. Before feeding the beasts I sit here and talk to my Rachel."

Howard looked down at the little headstone and extracted a small silver cross from his pocket.

"May I?" he asked.

"Aye."

Howard kneeled, dug a small hole and buried the cross, reciting a prayer in a low voice.

Matthew laughed ruefully. "Safeguarded; whether Catholic or Presbyterian, God is sure to receive her in his heaven now."

Howard straightened up to stand beside him. "All children go to heaven, of course they do."

"I hope so," Matthew said.

It was late evening of the same day and Matthew stood in the pasture, examining the breeding mare.

"Any day, lass," he said, stroking the bulging side. The horse nickered, pushed a velvet nose into his hand and blew. He found a piece of carrot and offered it to her, slapped her on the broad, brown rump and wandered over to where Ian was currying Salome, the little mare dancing about impatiently, ears laid back flat.

"Stand still." Matthew grabbed the halter and tugged hard. Salome tried to back away, but came to an obedient halt when she recognised that this man wasn't about to give in. "Daftie," Matthew crooned, rubbing the horse between the eyes. Salome stamped with her foreleg.

"Why did you invite him to your table?" Ian asked, keeping his eyes on Salome's long, white tail.

"He saved my life in Cumnock and at heart he's a decent man."

"He wasn't back in February," Ian said, moving over to comb the long mane.

Matthew bent down to inspect the hooves, running his hands over the smooth surface to ensure they were whole.

"He had no intention to kill Rachel," Matthew finally said.

"Nay, but he wanted very much to kill, or at least harm, you." Ian came over and leaned against Matthew, resting his cheek against the coarse linen shirt. "If he had, I would've killed him," he said, with such conviction in his voice that it made Matthew shiver.

"Shush," he said, hugging the lad close.

"I love you, I can't abide men that wish you harm." Ian swallowed, taking a big breath. "If my father – uncle – attempts to do you damage I'll stop him. Somehow I'll stop him, even if I have to kill him."

"Nay lad, it will not come to that," Matthew said, kissing the top of his head.

Ian tilted his head to meet his eyes and nodded gravely. "No, it won't." The lad retreated and took a couple of deep breaths. His fingers disappeared down the inside of his breeches, reappearing a few seconds later with a wee pouch. Long fingers shook as they struggled with the knot.

"He'll never forgive me for this," Ian whispered, shaking out a small glittering object that he placed in Matthew's palm. His eyes shimmered with tears and with a strangled sound he went back to his horse.

Matthew brushed a finger over the pretty piece of jewellery resting in his hand. Why had Luke kept it? Ian still had his back to him, narrow shoulders so stiff Matthew suspected he was holding his breath in an effort not to weep. Poor lad – brave lad – it had to tear him to shreds to do this. He patted Ian on the back.

"You're a son to be proud of," he said, leaving him to cry in peace.

"You just left him there?" Alex raised her brows and went back to her washing. She scooped up a new handful of fine sand and rubbed it briskly up and down her legs, strong circular motions with special emphasis on the cheeks of her bottom and the top part of her thighs.

Matthew moved closer, took some sand and did the same to her back, noting as he always did how white her skin was. The first time he'd seen her, her body had been a golden brown, all the way from her face to her feet with only some splotches of pale skin over her breasts and privates. It still horrified him to imagine a society where women wandered round in such state of undress before men other than their husbands, and he derived a considerable amount of pleasure from knowing that he was the only man who ever saw her like this, entirely naked.

"He needed to be alone," he said, retreating to sit on the log. Alex snorted and brought out a piece of soap, lathering herself everywhere before wading out to dive into the water. She swam all the way across before she came up for air, her head sleek like a seal's.

"I was right then," she said once she was back within hearing distance. "It was Luke that killed Malcolm."

"Or Margaret, but that's an option Ian hasn't considered."

She dried herself and came over to sit beside him, uncorking her stone bottle of oil. All of her skin she oiled, with him a silent but appreciative spectator.

"Your turn," she said once she'd finished. "And I'll sit and ogle you, shall I?"

Matthew chuckled and shed his clothing, picked up the soap and waded out into the deep.

"Unfair," Alex called after him. "I stayed where you could see me – all of me."

"Aye, but I have better self-control," he teased from out in the water. Obligingly he moved closer, uncovering himself well down to half-thigh.

"Nice," Alex smiled. "Looks very promising."

There was a snapping of twigs and Matthew hurriedly backed himself and his half standing cock deeper, while Alex busied herself with the drawstring of her chemise.

"Are you decent?" Simon's voice carried from the stand of alders that bordered the pool.

"Decent enough," Alex replied, looking round for her shawl. She mouthed a "later" in the direction of Matthew and stood up.

"There's a towel for you as well," she said as she passed Simon. "After all, there are certain tangible benefits to keeping clean." She evaded the stick he threw in her direction and escaped laughing towards the house.

Last night's bath seemed rather pointless after a couple of hours in the kitchen garden. Alex regarded her stained hands and arms, grabbed an empty basket and went over to join Joan, busy with the redcurrants.

"So, are things working out?" Alex said, diving further into the bushes to reap the ripe clusters. She felt like some sort of love guru, dispensing one tip after the other as to how one could, well, and… hmm… and sometimes, you know, fingers and… mouth, and why not do this…

"What things?" Joan sounded confused.

"You know, you and Simon."

"Ah."

They concentrated on filling their baskets.

"I'm not sure," Joan said, sitting back on her heels.

"Sure about what?"

"If it's right," Joan sighed.

Alex popped her head round the side to stare at her. "Right how? Don't you like making love?"

Joan went a vivid red. "A man and a woman should lie together to beget children, not for pleasure alone."

Alex darted back to her side of the bush, mainly to hide her wide, disbelieving grin.

"Your husband has needs," she said, receiving a grunt in reply, "I assume you have needs. I know for a fact that I'd go nuts if Matthew and I didn't make love regularly."

"Well you do," Joan teased. "Very regularly, it would seem."

Much more than you can imagine, Alex smiled. Last night had been very good. She stretched, her insides warming in desire at the thought of him.

"But you beget," Joan said, puncturing Alex' daydreams.

"Joan!" Alex plunked down beside her. "You can't – another child would kill you. And still you want to, don't you?"

Joan muttered that yes, she did.

"So it's easy; Simon wants to, you want to. And because you can't become pregnant you have to restrict yourself, be somewhat creative." Alex grinned at Joan's deeply embarrassed expression. "I don't think God minds."

Joan laughed and threw a handful of berries at her.

"Nay, but then you believe God might be Catholic."

"Or a woman," Alex said, ignoring Joan's loud gasp. "No one knows, do they? The dead never come back to tell us."

"You shouldn't say things like that. They might get you in serious trouble. Should a minister hear you, he would have you whipped."

"No ministers around," Alex said, "in fact, I haven't seen any for years – except in glimpses."

"Is she right?" Alex asked Matthew as they walked hand in hand up to the bare hilltop in a private celebration of their anniversary. Nine years today since she'd fallen through a gash in time to land unconscious at his feet, on the tenth of August 1658.

"Would they have whipped me?" Her back curved when she recalled Lieutenant Gower and his whip.

"They might have tried, but I wouldn't allow any man to bear hand on my wife."

No, because if they do you kill them, she gulped.

"Not even a minister of your Kirk?"

"Not even Sandy Peden himself." He smiled at her, braiding his fingers with hers. "Mind you, he'd never resort to something as crude as a whipping. No, wee Sandy would talk you to your senses – or your imminent death, whichever came first."

They reached the top and stood looking down at their home, long afternoon shadows playing over meadows and fields, patterning the orchard and the cobbled yard between the house and stable. The sheaves on the harvested fields stood in neat rows, even from here they could make out the trundling cart that was bringing in the last load for the day, the voices of the men carrying in the still evening air.

"Do you ever wish yourself back?" he asked her, drawing her to stand in front of him. He slid his hands around her waist, resting them on their unborn child.

"No," she shook her head. "How can I? But sometimes I'm very frightened, because life is so much frailer here than it is there, in the future."

"You'll live for many years more," he said, digging his chin into her head. He increased the pressure of his hands on her body, making her smile wryly. Soon she would be thirty-five, and in front of her stretched several years of fertility and thereby, per definition, more pregnancies. Not an entirely pleasant thought, but there wasn't very much she could do about it unless she planned on restricting their sexual encounters, something both she and Matthew would fail dismally at.

She turned his question around in her head. She rarely thought about her future life and with a twinge of conscience she recognised she even loved Ian more than she loved Isaac, her son in the future, because Ian was here and now, while Isaac had faded to be a vague presence in her head. But she would have loved to see them again, to sit and laugh with Magnus in his kitchen, to hold Isaac in her arms.

"I miss books," she said, "books and newspapers, to know what's happening in the world."

"Books?" He blew her in the ear. "But you haven't even managed to finish the Bible yet."

"Yes I have – almost," she protested.

He just laughed.

"I'm going to Cumnock tomorrow," Matthew informed her on the way back. "I've decided to visit Oliver."

"Why? He doesn't deserve you to." In Alex' opinion Oliver Wyndham was getting off far too easily by being hanged; he should have been transported somewhere to spend whatever remained of his life in permanent servitude.

"Nay he doesn't, but I can't erase the memory of him as he once was, wild and passionate and so full of hope for this new country we were helping build, a country governed by free men." He sounded nostalgic, and Alex squeezed his hand.

"Someday," she promised.

"Aye, but not in my time."

CHAPTER 36

"Very nice," Alex said, making Matthew twirl one more time. He complied, thinking he looked quite the gentleman in his dark blue coat with black and purple embroideries on pockets and cuffs; square lace collar, narrow breeches in matching blue and sober dark silk stockings – all of it proclaiming him to be a man of worth.

Joan peered at the stitching and pursed her mouth. "You're an excellent seamstress, this embroidery work is exquisite."

Alex made a depreciating sound. "I enjoy it, and I had a good teacher, right?"

Joan smiled and went over to help Simon with his coat, fussily arranging his collar to lie flat across his front. She frowned, wet her finger and rubbed off a stain on one of the pewter buttons and stood back to nod.

"You look right fine, the both of you."

The women trailed Matthew and Simon out into the yard, and stood waving after them as they set off. They were going to remain overnight in Cumnock, staying to witness the execution of Wyndham tomorrow, planned to coincide with a market day.

"Why does he want to see you, do you think?" Simon asked.

"I have no idea. Remorse? A last minute need to ask for forgiveness? A need to explain?" Matthew wasn't looking forward to seeing Oliver, but felt somehow obliged. "I wonder what it will have done to him to spend a month in the holding cells. I suppose they must have kept him separated from the rest – he'd find very few friends among the other inmates."

It sufficed with one look at Oliver to see that he had not been afforded the privilege of separate accommodation. Now, on

333

the eve of his execution, he had been accorded the right to a bath and a shave so as to meet his end in style and he received Matthew in the small, confined space that was to be the last room he ever slept in. Along one side was a straw filled pallet, the only piece of furniture in the cell except for the stool he offered Matthew.

"I'll stand," Matthew said. He was uncomfortable being here and had not liked the avid interest in the face of the guard who'd let him in. Something was afoot, and after a quick perusal of the little room, Matthew decided to go very canny. There was something awry in the wainscoting, a slight misalignment that had him suspecting this interview was being monitored.

"Suit yourself." Oliver sat down.

"What happened to your arm?" Matthew asked, indicating the limb Oliver was cradling.

Oliver raised red-rimmed eyes in his direction. "It broke – arms do that when they're bent the wrong way."

Aye, they did, and it was right painful, he'd assume.

"Why did you want to see me?" Matthew leaned back against the wall. Oliver didn't reply, studying Matthew intently. The coat, the white lace at collar and cuff, the well-polished shoes and even the hat, black and discreetly decorated with a dark blue band, were scrutinised.

"One could think you were going to a wedding, not a hanging," Oliver said, attempting a laugh.

"A festive occasion in any case," Matthew retorted with an edge.

Oliver yanked at his shirt and muttered something about everything being too big. Matthew looked him over; his former friend had shrunk, and the well-tailored coat hung like sacking on his bony shoulders.

"It must be easy," Oliver said. "To live in such assurance that you lead a righteous life."

"Assurance? Nay, Oliver, not that. But I try."

Oliver laughed hoarsely. "Try? To you the world was always very much black and white. Some things were right, others wrong, and there was never any doubt as to what was what. To most of us life is a jumble of grey, an endless succession of compromises between ideals we once strived for and the sordidness of reality."

"It's grey for me too, but there are some things I'd never do. Betray a former friend, for example, or kill a defenceless farmer and his wife." He spat to the side.

"So you have never killed wrongfully?" Oliver laughed in disbelief. "And the lieutenant you strung up in the crossroads oak?"

Matthew looked at him, shaking his head from side to side – a far too obvious trap.

"Aye, I've killed, and mayhap sometimes wrongfully, but it was done in battle, at war." Which neatly covered the lieutenant and the two soldiers on the fell as well.

"And the night you blew up the munitions shed?" Oliver demanded. "What then? You could have killed hundreds of men!"

"Not me; I was ill at the time," Matthew said, "with smallpox."

"From which you recuperated in a miraculously short time, with not one mark on you," Oliver said with heavy sarcasm.

"I prayed and God listened," Matthew said.

"Yes, I suppose you think he always listens to you – to you and your good friend Sandy Peden." Oliver sat forward, glaring at him.

"Not always, no. If he did, Tom Brown wouldn't be dead."

"Oh, no? And how would you have dealt with him, informer that he was?"

"Informer? Tom?" Matthew was quite satisfied with how surprised he sounded.

Oliver gave him a long look, slumped and stared down at his right hand, turning it this way and that.

"I had to," he said. "I stood to lose everything unless I… Oh God, and now my son, my Francis…" He threw a beseeching look at Matthew. "You understand, don't you?"

"And my children? My wife? My life?"

"Your life?" A spark of the old Oliver flashed over his face. "Don't give me that. You're guilty as sin when it comes to helping the damned preachers and we both know it. Admit it, man, you've been helping them all along."

"I have?" Matthew raised his brows.

The animation left Olive as quickly as it had surged. "Will you be there tomorrow?"

Matthew sighed deeply.

"Please?" Oliver said. "There's no one else up here that knew me as I once was, is there?" He gave Matthew a quick look, mouth twisting into a little smile. "I dare say you've regretted it often lately, the night you pulled me out of the fire all those years ago."

"Aye, there have been such moments," Matthew said, "but at the time…"

"You couldn't have acted differently. I know. And had it been you that had been thrown into the blaze, I'd have saved you."

"Aye," Matthew nodded, and for an instant they shared a genuine smile.

"So many years ago," Oliver sighed. "So will you? Be there tomorrow?"

"I'll be there."

Oliver just nodded. He pressed a hand to his belly, grimaced. "Go," he said, "and if you find it in you, I suspect my soul could do with a prayer or two."

Matthew produced a large flask and stood it on the floor. "Brandy, I recall you never took to whisky."

"You think I need it?"

"I would," Matthew said, bowed and left.

He found Simon waiting just outside, a worried look on his face.

"What?" Matthew asked, eyeing the two guards standing to the side.

"A word, Mr Graham?" The nasal voice came from somewhere behind him, and Matthew turned to face the commanding officer of the Ayr garrison, a Major Stapleton as he recalled it.

"About what?" Matthew asked.

"This and that," the major said, gesturing in the direction of the closest building. The guards closed in on them, indicating this was not an invitation, this was an order. "I have a witness," the major threw over his shoulder as he preceded Matthew across the yard.

"A witness?" Matthew had to struggle to sound unconcerned. Had they mayhap arrested Peter, or one of the other two, beaten the truth out of them as to what happened the night half of the garrison yard was reduced to blackened timbers and ashes?

"Yes, a man. He claims he saw you strike down those two soldiers on the moor – in cold blood, he says, and from the back."

Matthew almost laughed with relief. As he recalled it, no one had been close enough to see him, and as to him killing the two soldiers from behind, well, that was a blatant lie, so whoever had come forward had not been there.

"Me? I was fishing with my son."

"So you say, so you say." The major clasped his hands behind his back. "But then you would say that. Wyndham is convinced you're involved."

"Aye, but then he insists I murdered Tom Brown – a remarkable feat conducted over several miles, seeing as I was here at the time of the poor man's death."

"Hmm," the major said. He entered a small room, with Matthew and Simon following behind. "These are serious accusations," the major went on, sitting down behind a narrow desk. Matthew and Simon remained on their feet in front of him.

"Oh aye; but whoever that has come forth is lying."

"Really?" the major drawled. "And can you prove that?"

"No more than he can prove he saw me."

"You think?" the major smirked. He clapped his hands, and a man was escorted into the room.

"I'll handle this," Simon said in an undertone to Matthew.

"Well?" the major said to the moon faced creature standing before them.

The man took his time. He tilted his head this way and that, walked back and forth, hemmed and hawed. For a long time he stood before them, looking Matthew up and down. Finally the major cleared his throat.

"Is it him?" he said.

The man threw Matthew a triumphant look and nodded eagerly. "Yes, yes, this is the man I saw on the moor. He stabbed them in the back, he did!"

The major grinned, at which point Simon stepped forward.

"I am Matthew Graham."

It could have been amusing, if Matthew hadn't been so angered. He wanted to throttle the life out of this lying wee Englishman.

The man did a double take. "Matthew Graham?" He inhaled, licked his lips. "And as I said, it was you I saw on the moor! You!" He stabbed his finger in the direction of Simon. "It is men like you, Graham, that cost all of us in strife and suffering!"

"Oh aye? All the way down in England?" Simon inquired, and the man and the major went blood red. Simon clapped his hat on his head, bowed at the major. "I assume this farce is over." He stood on his toes, swaying towards the major, for all the world like a top on the point of overbalancing. "It would be foolish to assume that all Scotsmen are Presbyterian hotheads with no connections whatsoever. I dare say my Lord Lauderdale will not be entertained when I recount this little matter to him."

"This has nothing to do with me," the major said. "It was him who came to us, him that told us he had witnessed the slaying of our two comrades." He waved his hands at the guards. "Take him away and have him flogged."

"Me?" the false witness squeaked.

"You," the major said, "for lying. Forty lashes, I think." He stood, mouth like a narrow spout, and watched the man be dragged away before turning to face Matthew. "I remain convinced that you were involved, Graham, and I fully believe you to be an active supporter of all these accursed preachers, foremost among them that Peden. And one day…" He stopped to draw breath. "Well one day I'll apprehend you. All the time I'll be watching you; keep that in mind." He bowed slightly in the direction of Simon. "And no matter how often you sup with Lauderdale, you'll not save him then."

Matthew took a huge gulp of air once they were outside.

"Luke," he said, "that was Luke's handiwork."

"Or Wyndham's," Simon said. "Although that does seem unlikely given his present constrained circumstances." He brushed at his coat, frowned and scraped at something with his nail.

"Do you?" Matthew asked.

"Hmm?"

"Sup with Lauderdale."

Simon straightened up and grinned. "Not as such. It may be we've been in the same inn once or twice – but no need to tell the major that."

"Quite the threat." Matthew studied his brother-in-law gloomily. He had no illusions regarding the recent lack of inspections. Now that Captain Howard had resigned there would be a new energetic officer in charge and anyone fingered as a Covenanter would find his every move perused in detail – as the major had so kindly pointed out. Men had been dragged from their homes and beaten to an inch of their lives just for reading their bibles and he had problems keeping his temper in check; last time it burst from him it had cost him his daughter.

Simon listened to his little diatribe in silence, light eyes never leaving him. He cleared his throat, cleared it again.

"You have to leave; it breaks my heart to say thus, but you must go. It's but a matter of time before they trap you."

Matthew shook his head in denial. This was his home and he wouldn't be run off by a band of cut throat soldiers; soon enough it would all calm down.

"Nay, Matthew, it won't."

Matthew scowled, and Simon held up his hands in a conciliatory gesture before suggesting they repair to the inn and get royally drunk.

He woke to a horrible headache and a throat that felt as if someone had tipped buckets of ash into it. Beside him Simon snored heavily, fully dressed, and a bleary inspection confirmed that Matthew himself was still in his coat and shoes. He groaned as he sat up, running his tongue over his coated teeth. It was years since he'd drunk so much and he leaned his face into his hands, trying to stop the spinning. Simon started awake at his movements, coughed once or twice and rolled out of bed, looking disturbingly sprightly.

"Not even your lovesick wife would find you attractive today," he teased.

"Seeing as my cock is too drunk to even attempt to stand, even less find its way out of my breeches, that doesn't matter greatly," Matthew mumbled. He stood up carefully, supporting himself against the bedpost. "Ah, Jesus." He turned itching eyes in the direction of Simon. "We best make haste; he hangs soon."

Simon looked disgruntled, but nodded, leading the way down the narrow stairs.

"That wasn't pretty," Simon commented once they were safely away from Cumnock. Neither of them had said a word throughout the hanging, nor after. Matthew had thrown up on his way to the stable, not certain if it was an effect of all the drink or if it was the spectacle of a gibbering, pleading Oliver, crying that he was sorry, so sorry, but please, no, that had so turned his stomach. They'd had to drag him over to the noose, and despite his fine clothes and his newly shaved face Oliver had died without a shred of dignity.

"He deserved it," Simon said.

"Aye, but it doesn't help much, does it?"

Matthew sank into a deep sullen silence, mulling over not only Oliver's death but also what Simon had said yesterday. Leave or be destroyed... Despite all of him protesting, deep down he knew Simon was right, but he just couldn't bear it, sickening inside at the thought of leaving his home. Hillview thudded through his bloodstream, lived in his flesh, and he couldn't envision himself anywhere else. How would he survive without his woods, his fields surrounding him? Still; mayhap he should write a letter to Thomas Leslie, just in case. He glared at nothing in particular and kicked Ham into a trot.

The black mood lifted the moment he saw Alex. She was standing some way off when he rode in, raising her hand in a little wave before retreating into the shadows of the trees. He barely greeted Joan and his sons, eyes fixed on the spot where she'd disappeared.

"Here," he said to Mark, taking off his coat and hat. "Carry this inside for me." He handed Ham's reins to Ian. "You take care of the horse." And then his legs were carrying him towards his wife, all of him stirring with longing for her.

Matthew undid his shirt while he walked, stopped to kick off shoes and peel off stockings, leaving them by a tree as he continued barefoot up the slope. He ran a hand through his hair and in his breeches his member had definitely overcome any lingering effects of last night's heavy drinking, flexing against the constraining cloth. Nine years he'd known her, bedded her almost as long, and still there were moments like this when it was all startlingly new again, when his ears filled with the sound of his pulse and his breathing grew loud and irregular with need.

He had no idea where she was, but he walked on in the general direction of the mill. There was a sudden flash of white and he came to a standstill only yards from where she was standing, eyes huge, mouth slightly open. From here he could see she was trembling, and knew it was for him.

This is ridiculous, Alex berated herself, he's been gone for a day and you go all weak-kneed at the sight of him. He's your husband, for God's sake, calm down, woman! Except that she'd woken with a hunger for him, and he hadn't been there, and all day half of her had been thinking of him and the things she wanted him to do to her. Now he stood on the other side of the clearing and she was squirming inside with lust, but was rooted to the spot by his eyes, and so she just remained where she was, waiting. A dull ache sprang from a point in her lower back, spread like tendrils down into her sex, up into her womb. Like a contraction, a huge, burning contraction, and she was aware of thousands upon thousands of nerve ends, all of them shrieking for him.

At his continued silence she drew the pins from her hair and shook it out, hearing his loud intake of breath. She undid the bodice and let it drop to the ground to join her discarded straw hat and cap and shifted from one foot to the other to bring her thighs together in a soft rubbing motion that almost made her moan.

He gestured at her skirts. The look in his eyes made her clumsy, her fingers struggling with uncooperative knots, with fabric that slipped through her sweaty hold. She wriggled her hips and the heavy wool slid down her legs to puddle round her feet. It was an effort to breathe, to move. Her knees folded and dipped, her heart was pounding against her ribs, and for some reason her mouth was dry, she had to lick her lips to moisten them. The grass below her feet tickled her soles, sunlight danced through the foliage above her, touching his hair, gilding his shoulders. She raised her hands to the lacings of her shift, the thin linen an oppressive weight she had to discard. Her skin screamed for his touch, her mouth begged for his lips and there was a hollow sensation between her legs that only he could fill. The shift fluttered to the ground and she was as naked as the day she was born.

Lord, but she was beautiful, trembling like a cornered doe below the spreading branches of the oak. Matthew kicked off his breeches and advanced towards her in only his shirt, aware that his cock protruded like a prow before him. Her mouth… he wanted her mouth and then he was going to use his own, and… his cock jerked. He beckoned her to him and she stumbled, nearly falling before she righted herself.

He traced her brows, her nose, the line from her jaw to the hollow between her collar bones. He so wanted to say something, to put words to the emotions that surged through him, but all he could do was kiss her, softly at first, a bare brushing of lips that changed into an intense, hungry possession, with her as hungry as he was, her fingers closing painfully in his hair to hold him still. And then she knelt before him… he swayed, his hands on her head, eyes closed against the glare of the sun.

"No!" he backed away, "not yet… I want…" He fell to his knees beside her and now he had words, telling her she was his heart, the sun in his life, the single thing he could never do without and Alex laughed and cried at the same time, her hands on his arms, his chest.

Together they rid him off his shirt, and he held her eyes as he eased her down to lie on her back. There was the softest of exhalations when he entered her. She tightened her hold on him, he pressed his groin against hers, bracing on his arms to keep his weight off her rounded belly. Her mouth fell open, her eyes closed and she lifted her hips towards him. He was drowning in a sea of sensations; the sun on his back, the rough texture of the grass under his knees and shins, but most of all his wife, the softness of her skin, the urgency of her hold on his hips and the moist, welcoming warmth of her cleft. Heat surged through his loins, his cock twitched and roared, and Matthew came, wave after wave of bright red pleasure washing through him.

Afterwards he spooned himself around her.

"I missed you," she said, making him laugh.

"Aye, I gathered that." He nibbled her nape. "I missed you too, but then I always do."

"Liar, I bet you didn't think of me once last night."

"Too much beer," he said. Too many other things to think about, but he had no desire to ponder upon them now, so he scooted closer to her and pillowed his head on his arm.

She took his hand and lifted it to lie between her breasts, toying with his fingers. He yawned, slipping into that agreeable state halfway between wakefulness and sleep. Alex turned fully in his arms, raising her hand to his face.

"I once read in a book that making love is something you get better at with practise – a lot of practise, preferably with the same person. We're getting pretty good at this, Mr Graham."

He opened one eye and smiled. "Aye, but practise is always good, lass."

"Now?" she asked huskily.

"Now," he nodded and rose on his elbow to look at her before he lowered his head to kiss her.

Thank you, Lord for my marvellous wife, this woman that drives me to the precipice of lust and beyond, who holds me so tenderly, who loves me so entirely.

Oh God; oh God, oh God, oh God… This is my man, God, and you gave him to me.

CHAPTER 37

Three days later, Matthew was standing in the midst of his last un-harvested field when Ian came running through the rippling barley.

"He's here, Da," Ian gasped. "Fath… Luke is here! He's come to take me back, and I don't want to go, and I don't know how you can stop him, and…"

"Ian," Matthew cut him off. "We've talked this through." The lad nodded.

"So you know what to do, and so do I." He frowned at Ian. "Go on, you must make him think you're glad to see him."

As Ian wheeled to run, Matthew called him back. He studied Ian and looked at himself. In coarse linen shirts and homespun breeches of an indeterminate colour somewhere between brown and grey, they were very much alike. He leaned forward and brushed Ian's hair back, so that it fell in wild locks around his face. He ran his fingers through his own hair, and from the look on Ian's face assumed he had managed to make it stand messily.

"We walk together," Matthew said.

Luke dismounted and paced the yard, glaring in turn at Simon, Joan and Alex.

"You know why I've come," he snapped at Simon. "I'm here to take the boy back with me."

"Your son," Alex nodded, watching Luke go an interesting shade somewhere between a boiled ham and beef tartar.

"Aye," he replied, twitching at his elegant coat. He did yet another turn, walked over to talk to his men, stopped for a moment to rest his hand on one of the saddlebags his horse carried, and the ghost of a smile appeared on his face. When he turned in their direction there was a secretive look to him, lips pinched tight as if he was trying to stop himself from blabbing something. Alex felt a flutter somewhere just below her ribs. Luke Graham had something up his immaculate sleeve, that much was clear. Luke twirled on his heel, gave a short little laugh.

"What a sad, small place it is," he said to no one in particular, before wheeling to smile at Daniel, who was clutching at Alex' skirts.

"Oh aye? Then why not ride off and never come back?" Simon said.

Once again that lurking little smile, green eyes darting over to the saddlebag. "Oh, I will," Luke said, "once my business here is finished." He made an irritated noise and raised his eyes to the sun. "Where is he?" he demanded of Alex.

"Out in the fields somewhere, I'm sure he'll be back soon. Boys tend to have an inner clock when it comes to food." As if on cue Matthew and Ian appeared from behind the barn, deep in conversation.

It gave Alex huge satisfaction to see how Luke's composure shattered into undisguised shock. He blinked, looked about to knuckle his eyes but recovered, face closing into an impenetrable facade. Alex stifled a nervous laugh; no doubt he'd done it on purpose, her Matthew, because as he and Ian stepped into the yard – messy dark hair, bare legs and in more or less identical clothes – it was clear to anyone not absolutely blind this was father and son, hewn from the same block and moulded by the same hand. Luke's hands fisted, his lips thinned out.

"It hurts to realise that a cuckoo will take precedence over his beloved wee Charlie," Simon whispered in Alex ear.

"It's not funny," she whispered back.

"You think not? I myself am enjoying myself immensely. Look at him, Luke Graham speechless."

"But Ian…" Alex mumbled.

"It will sort itself," Simon said, taking hold of her hand and giving it a little squeeze.

She sincerely hoped so, because the way Luke was staring at Ian didn't bode all that well for his future should he remain in Luke's tender care.

"Father!" Ian ran towards Luke, slowed to a walk, a halt, arms held out.

"Ian," Luke replied and embraced him stiffly. "You've grown."

"Is Mam doing well?" Ian asked.

"Aye," Luke replied, "confined to bed, but doing well." He expanded his chest. "Two weans in less than two years, quite a feat, hey?"

What? He expected some sort of congratulations for having had it off with his wife? Alex patted her belly and when Luke looked her way she grinned, displaying all her sons, now gathered round her.

Matthew had by now reached them, standing a yard or so to the side. Luke turned to face him, meeting the brittle, ice cold stare with one just as hostile.

"Still alive? As yet not hanged or deported?"

"Aye, as you see. But Oliver Wyndham isn't. He hanged some days ago."

"Oliver Wyndham?" Luke sounded confused. "Someone I should know?"

"Aye, I would think so. He owed you an impressive amount of money." There was a derisive gleam in Matthew's eyes, his long mouth stretching into a smile at Luke's flush.

Whatever else the brothers were planning on saying was interrupted by the dinner bell, the family and household hurrying indoors until it was only Luke, his two servants, Matthew, Simon and Alex left outside.

"I'll bring out something," Alex said – not that she wanted to, unless it was some sort of creative stew including nightshade and a touch of hemlock.

Matthew looked at her sternly. "Nay you will not. You'll seat my brother and his men at our table."

Alex glared at him. "I don't want to eat at the same table as he does."

"Then you won't eat." Matthew stepped up close to her, taking a firm hold of her arm. "They are guests, Alex. Most unwelcome, but guests." Do as I say, his eyes told her, and over his shoulder she saw Simon nod.

It was a strained meal, putting it mildly. Almost no conversation, Luke at one end, Matthew at the other. Matthew concentrated on his food, now and then throwing a look at his brother, who did the same, however put out he seemed at the amount of vegetables.

"Now," Matthew said once the table had been cleared. "What is it you truly want?" The children had been sent outside as had the servants, and round the table remained the three adult Graham siblings, Alex and Simon.

"Want?" Luke said. "Well, that's obvious, isn't it? I'm here to take Ian home."

"I assume his mother misses him," Joan said. "They're so close – such a special bond, between a mother and her firstborn."

Luke looked as if he'd been force-fed pigswill. "Aye."

"In that case I'll help Ian pack," Alex said, getting up. She beckoned to Joan that she should come as well, and now it was only Matthew, Luke and Simon. And Ian, but in accordance with Matthew's instructions, he was standing where he could hear without being seen, in the passageway.

Matthew concentrated on his earthenware mug. To have Luke this close was proving to be quite the challenge to his self-control. For the last half-hour he'd been fighting the jet black anger that threatened to engulf his brain, urging him to pull his dirk and slit this Cain's throat, and only Simon's presence in the room stopped him from doing his brother grave bodily harm. He lifted his face to stare at Luke, who fidgeted under his eyes. Ah yes; it took but a glance to ascertain wee Luke had softened these last few years, making him no match physically for Matthew.

Luke broke eye contact and drew his saddlebag towards him.

"Do you remember, brother, the unfortunate incident more than a year ago when an officer was hanged?"

"Seeing as it happened but a few miles from here, aye I do," Matthew said.

Luke nodded, extracting a formal looking document from his bag.

"This is a sworn statement," he said, throwing it on the table. "As you can see, the person in question names you as the murderer."

Simon laughed loudly. "You must try better than that, dear brother-in-law. Rumours without substance will not lead anywhere."

"Ah," Luke smiled nastily. "This is a statement sworn by an officer. It carries some weight."

Matthew scanned the document. No proof, only a list of coincidences that pointed in his direction; his flogged wife, his open support of the Covenant movement, the fact that only on Tuesday was there a firm sighting of Matthew in Edinburgh, by one of the local judges. The undersigned had ridden the road himself and concluded that a good horse could be pushed to cover the distance to Edinburgh in something around thirty-four hours – and Graham was possessed of a very good horse. He bit back on a smile when he saw the signature. Somehow he suspected Captain Howard would no longer wish to be associated with this statement.

"Conjecture," Matthew scoffed, shoving the document in the direction of Simon. He crossed his arms over his chest and waited.

Luke leaned back until his chair balanced on two legs, eyeing him coldly.

"It doesn't take much these days, dear Brother. That document in the hands of a zealous officer will cause you much trouble. I'm sure witnesses can be found to verify that you've been seen with Peden." He leaned even further back, looking like a replete fox in a devastated henhouse. Matthew kicked the chair from under him, sending him to land on the floor.

"You're a disgusting excuse of a man," Matthew said, towering over Luke. "And I'll regret to my dying day that I didn't kill you when I had the chance."

"Well you didn't," Luke said, getting to his feet. "You lacked the balls." He bent forward and retrieved the document. "I'll give this to the commanding officer in Ayr, and then, Brother, you might find yourself in a most uncomfortable position. Perhaps not hanged, but certainly deported." He laughed and looked at Matthew. "And your family with you, Matthew."

"Bastard!"

"Tell me," Simon interrupted. "Are you planning to accuse your brother of murder, based on that?" He indicated the deed with a dismissive wave.

Luke frowned in his direction, assenting with his head.

"Murder, hmm?" Simon went on, creasing his brow. He tapped a finger against his pursed mouth and studied Luke in silence. "Then we should perhaps also talk about another murder; that of Malcolm Graham, in December 1653."

Luke had gone the colour of chalk. "Da? He died of misadventure!"

Simon shook his head slowly from side to side. "Nay, that he did not. He was lured up to the pond and there pushed, or somehow forced into the water. We have a witness recalling a scuffle, loud angry voices and a splash."

"What is it you're saying? That someone killed our father?" Luke looked from Matthew to Simon.

Matthew nodded, quite impressed by his brother's acting skills. If it hadn't been for the ring presently in his pouch, he would even have believed him.

"Well, I wasn't here," Luke said, relaxing somewhat. "I came back the day he was buried."

"Excellent timing," Matthew muttered.

"So you weren't here?" Simon repeated.

"You know I wasn't! I'd been driven from my home."

"By Da," Matthew nodded, "for your sinful behaviour with Margaret."

350

"The old fool," Luke sneered. "If only he'd listened and allowed us to wed, but no, he had to stand there and tell me I was a sinful, misbegotten creature, no son of his, and then he threw me out, promising he'd kill me himself should I ever darken his door again. He shouldn't have done that."

"Nay, he shouldn't," Matthew agreed, making Luke look at him in surprise.

"He did what he thought was right. You were both too young, and Margaret was his ward, in his mind almost a daughter – your sister." Joan came over to the table and sat down, looking from brother to brother. "I know for a fact that Matthew was nowhere close to the millpond that day, he was here, in the kitchen, repairing harness."

"And I wasn't here at all," Luke insisted.

"Are you sure?" Matthew asked, digging into his pouch.

"Of course I am!" Luke snapped. Matthew opened his hand and let a small object fall onto the table. Joan gave a loud exclamation, touching it gingerly.

"Grandmama's ring!" She looked at Matthew. "But… it was gone!"

"I found it," a low voice said from behind them.

Luke closed his eyes.

"Ian?" Joan held out her hand and Ian inched forward, maintaining a cautious distance to Luke.

"I found it," Ian repeated, "in a small casket in Father's office. It was hanging off a broken chain."

"I wasn't here," Luke insisted.

"Nay, but Margaret definitely was," Simon said, making Ian gasp.

Luke lunged across the table, making for the ring, but Matthew was too quick, snatching it back and returning it to his pouch.

"You need not fear, little brother, I won't say anything – not unless I have to."

"It isn't enough," Luke said.

"No?" Matthew laughed, holding up three fingers. "Motive, a ring in your possession that Da carried on him always, and then the witness to the struggle as such. I think it will carry quite some weight. Do you wish to put it to the test? I fear the king wouldn't be amused, would he?"

His brother was sweating, perspiration dewed his forehead, his upper lip. Well, it would, no? Matthew knew for a fact that the king had been most displeased when he received a letter a few years back, detailing Luke's sins against his brother – penned by an inspired Sandy, no less. Defeated, Luke threw the signed statement back onto the table.

"So what is it you want?"

Simon produced several papers. "First of all, you should know that the ring and a sworn statement, signed by Matthew, Joan and myself as well as Ian, will go into safekeeping. If anything happens to Matthew it will be sent to an officer of the court, with a separate letter being sent directly to His Majesty."

Luke slumped lower in his seat, his eyes glacial when he turned them on Ian.

"Secondly, you'll renounce the lad." Simon nodded in the direction of Ian.

"And you think that's a sacrifice?" Luke spat in the direction of Ian. "That's no son of mine!"

Ian jerked, his eyes dark with hurt, and Matthew rose, placing a hand on his shoulder.

"Nay, Luke, you're right. He's mine – in everything he's mine."

Half an hour later Luke was back on his horse. He'd signed Ian away, he'd signed over the princely sum of 500 pounds sterling as a lump sum compensation to Matthew – Simon's idea – and had set fire to the statement, reducing his threat to nothing but ashes.

Ian had stood mute throughout the proceedings, but had at one point opened his mouth to say that perhaps they should have a witness to all this, which had earned him an approving glance from Simon. So the literate one of Luke's men had been brought in, had listened in obvious amazement when he was told that Luke was hereby renouncing his legal rights to Ian, and had then signed the document.

My son; Matthew couldn't help it, as he stood in the yard his arm came round Ian to hug him close, thereby showing the world his son was back where he belonged – with him.

"May God grant me the pleasure of never seeing you again," Luke said in a low voice to Matthew.

"Aye, that would be for the best," Matthew replied. For an instant their eyes met and held, and then Matthew inclined his head in a stiff nod. "Please convey my regards to Margaret." He felt somewhat ashamed on her behalf; today he had reclaimed a son, today she'd lost one. Luke didn't reply. He wheeled his horse and set off up the lane.

Sandy listened as Matthew told him everything, from the sad ending of Oliver to yesterday's confrontation with Luke.

"He'll be back, of course," he finished.

"Aye; Luke Graham is a most persistent man," Sandy said. He drank some more of the beer Matthew had brought with him, belched, and bit into yet another piece of pie.

Matthew regarded the landscape spread before him. "Simon says I must leave – he says it's but a matter of time before they corner me."

Sandy finished his pie, brushed the crumbs off his worn and soiled coat and turned his grey gaze on Matthew.

"You should."

"I can't leave this, this is my home!" He looked across the bare fields and sighed. "My birthplace, the birthplace of my father and his father before him and his father... ten generations and more."

"About time for something new then," Sandy said. He nudged Matthew and pointed at Alex, who was walking through the orchard, unaware of them. "That's your home. That woman is all the home you need."

Matthew leaned back against his arms and let his eyes rest on Alex and the children that tumbled around her – all his children.

"I'm a fortunate man."

Sandy chuckled. "She may be half-heathen, wild and wayward, but aye, you're indeed blessed."

And you don't know the half of it, Matthew smiled.

CHAPTER 38

"You have to," Alex said to Matthew, "and you have to do it now."

Matthew sighed, but recognised that she was right. Mark had hovered round them the last few days, somehow understanding that things had changed, but not how.

"What do I tell him?" he groaned.

"I think you must tell him the truth."

Matthew grimaced; it seemed a lot to load on a lad not yet eight.

"He has to know," Alex said.

"Aye," Matthew agreed and got out of bed. Anyhow, he owed it to Ian.

Mark looked surprised when Matthew came to find him, suggesting they should do some fishing, just the two of them. He beamed and hurried off to find his rod, throwing a triumphant look in the direction of Ian, who was told to sweep the threshing floor.

Jacob rushed over to Matthew, saying he wanted to come too, because he didn't want to stay at home all day with only wee Daniel, and he was big enough now to go fishing, wasn't he? Matthew shook his head; today it was him and Mark.

"You like Ian, don't you?" Matthew asked once they were settled in position. The river flowed sluggish and dark below them, shadowed by alders that grew high enough to create a green tunnel. Mark was frowning down at his worm, at his hook.

"Aye," Mark replied, closing his eyes when he pushed the hook through the wriggling body.

"He'll be staying with us," Matthew said.

"Oh aye? He already is." Mark sounded rather uninterested.

"You know I was married before?" Matthew said.

Mark looked at him, shaking his head.

"To your Aunt Margaret," he continued, smiling wryly when Mark's mouth fell open into a surprised 'o'. "It wasn't a good marriage. Margaret was very much in love with your uncle, not me."

"But…" Mark frowned, clearly grappling with what Matthew had just told him. "A wife is supposed to love her husband. Like Mama; she loves you."

Matthew chuckled softly. "It isn't always like that, and your mama is an exceptional woman. Not many men find someone like that."

"I will," Mark said confidently. And his wife would have many, many babies and laugh and tell them stories and sometimes chase them round the yard when they had been naughty. He thought a bit more. "Brown eyes, I think, and her name will be Mary," he confided to his father, who didn't quite know whether to laugh or agree.

"And if you meet a bonny brown-eyed lass called Lizzie?"

Mark shrugged. "Mary."

Matthew reverted from the tangential excursion into his future daughter-in-law's name.

"While I was wed to Margaret there was a child," he said. Mark's float was bobbing up and down, and Mark was on his feet, struggling to lift the fish out of the water.

"Look!" he sang out. "A big one!"

Matthew laughed and helped him land it, waiting until he had calmed down before continuing.

"As I said, there was a child – Ian."

That got Mark's attention and he turned to face his father.

"Ian? But he's Uncle Luke's son."

"Ian was born in my marriage to Margaret, he was born as my son." Matthew inhaled loudly and looked his son in the eyes. "Ian is my son. Luke tried to steal him, but now I've gotten him back."

Mark didn't say anything. He sat looking at his float, lower lip caught between his teeth. He got to his feet.

"I want Mama," he said, sounding much younger than he was. And then he turned and ran.

Alex was singing while she stripped one line of raspberry canes after the other of its late fruit. She saw Mark come flying towards her and held out her arms, stumbling backwards when he barrelled into her.

"Oouf," Alex said, righting them both. "You're much stronger than you think." She slipped a hand under his chin and raised his face to inspect him. "So he told you."

Mark nodded and sat down at her feet. Alex sat down beside him and offered him her basket. They sat in silence, eating their way through a sizeable quantity of raspberries.

"I don't understand," Mark said in a low voice.

"Of course you don't. It's quite a mess – even if you're an adult." She tilted her head in the direction of where Matthew was coming down the hill. "It's difficult for him. You see, for very many years he's known that Ian was his boy, but Luke and Margaret tricked him. They made him believe Ian wasn't his, and so he let them take him." She smiled at him. "It's enough to see you and Ian together to see that you must be brothers, not cousins. You're both so very like him, like your father." She chewed at her cheek, trying to decide how to tell him the rest.

"Luke had a son last year."

"Charles," Mark nodded. "Very ugly, like a pig with red hair on it."

"Ah. Well, that boy now looks just like Luke, and so Luke doesn't want Ian anymore." Stretching the truth a bit, that was, but it elicited the reaction she wanted, with Mark leaping to his feet, his eyes going very green.

"How can he say that? Ian is... he is ..." He struggled to find words, but gave up. "I love Ian," he said instead, going a bright red. "Uncle Luke is a... a... horrible man to say he doesn't want him anymore."

"I couldn't agree more, but there you are. Anyway, it means your father got his son back, and that's good."

Mark sat back down and helped himself to some more raspberries.

"If…" He looked at her with huge eyes. "If Ian is Da's son, then it's him that will have Hillview, isn't it?"

Alex nodded. "Do you mind?" she asked, thinking that was an incredibly stupid question to be asking a seven year old boy.

Mark bobbed his head, keeping his eyes on his toes. "And will Da love me less?"

Alex caressed his head. "Of course not, you idiot."

He laughed shakily and moved into her embrace.

"Mark," Matthew's shadow fell over them. "Come here son," he said, crouching down.

Mark flew at him, winding his arms around his father's neck.

"I love you very much, son. You know that, don't you?"

Mark burrowed his head into Matthew's shoulder and nodded.

"And now," Matthew went on, "we have fishing to do." He set Mark down and tousled his hair. "One fish won't feed all of us, even if it was very big."

"We can always go vegetarian," Alex said, "only vegetables for dinner. Spinach, for example."

Mark and Matthew looked at each other.

"Fishing," Mark said, taking his father's hand.

"Fishing," Matthew agreed, winking at Alex.

After dinner, Ian and Mark were sent to move the cows down to the water meadows.

"I don't want to take it from you," Ian said, "you were born to it, and it doesn't feel right."

Mark shrugged. Da had explained several times why it had to be this way, and even if he felt hollow inside at the thought of not always living here, at Hillview, there wasn't much to do about it.

"You were born to it as well," he said generously. "Before me." They trudged on in silence, with Aragorn running wild circles around them both.

"Will you miss them?" Mark asked, thinking that he'd die if his mama was taken from him. And his da, but perhaps mostly his mama. Ian stopped and broke off a dried stand of cow parsley, using his fingers to disintegrate it.

"My mam," he said hoarsely. "I'll miss her."

"My mama is quite nice though," Mark said. "Soft like, and warm, and…" he was going to say pretty, but decided not to.

Ian laughed. "Aye, that she is."

"Okay?" Alex came over to where Ian was sitting. He smiled up at her and held out the little animal he was carving. She admired the cat, receiving a black look in return.

"It's not a cat, it's a fox."

"Oh," Alex said. "Well, seeing as I've never seen a fox up close, I wouldn't know, would I?"

He looked at her, not entirely mollified.

"It's Saturday," she went on, smiling at his protesting groan. "But I've decided that from now on you wash with the men. Your uncle and father are waiting." She handed him a towel and a clean shirt. "Mind you, every now and then I'll check, to make sure you're washing yourself thoroughly."

She watched them wander off towards the pool, Ian walking tall beside Matthew. Joan came to stand beside her, slipping an arm round Alex' waist.

"He's a fortunate lad, Ian, in his father but even more in his stepmother."

"Call me that again and I'll have to hurt you," Alex threatened, making Joan laugh.

"You already love him," she said.

Alex rested her head against Joan. "Very much. Which makes it much easier, let me tell you."

They stood like that for some time, and around them the evening began shifting into night. From the pool came loud laughter and protesting squeals, in the sky the moon hung like a giant Gouda cheese. Alex drew in a long breath, held it and expelled it slowly.

"Tea?" she asked, turning towards Joan.

CHAPTER 39

Over the coming months Ian merged seamlessly into their family, upgrading himself from cousin to brother so quickly it was as if he'd always been there. Just as his brothers he grumbled at the imposed hours of school work, even daring to make a face behind Matthew's back when he was told to apply himself to the set Bible texts. Mark commiserated, but at a flaming look from his father went back to his own studies, mouthing his way through the gospel.

"Maybe it's best if I teach them," Alex suggested, feeling sorry for the two eldest.

Matthew just shook his head. "We both know you're no expert."

"It depends. I could probably teach them a lot of extremely relevant things – life isn't only about religion, is it?"

"Hmph," Matthew snorted, but agreed to let her take care of some of the schooling. Which was why Alex found herself trying to recreate a map of the world from memory alone, standing back to study her effort.

"What's that?" Matthew asked, pointing at a largish blob at the bottom.

"Australia," Alex chewed her lip. "As yet not discovered, so I suppose I have to take it out."

Matthew agreed that it might be best, and listened with interest when she told him of the different continents, how they had once hung together and then split apart.

"You can see that," he said, tracing the western coast of the African continent.

The boys were somewhat less interested when Alex presented the map to them, but they all looked at her with amazement when she described how the human race had walked across the Bering strait to populate the American continent.

"So where was Eden?" Mark asked, leaning across the huge map.

"Umm," Alex said, somewhat stumped. She tilted her head and walked around the table. "Here," she said, pointing at the Mesopotamian area.

Mark hefted Daniel up to sit in his lap. "See?" he told his brother. "That's where Adam and Eve lived."

Daniel was not that interested, concentrating on his apple instead.

All through the autumn the impromptu inspections continued. There were far too many moments of tension when Alex could see Matthew was on the point of bursting, all of him stiffening with the effort to keep calm despite the overt rudeness of the soldiers.

"I told you," Simon sighed when Matthew complained loudly and in detail. "Ultimately there's no choice."

Matthew glared at him and stomped off, shrugging off Alex' concerned questions.

"What was that about?" Alex asked Simon, receiving a blank look in return. "Simon?" she said.

"Ask him," Simon snapped. He'd ridden in that same day, looking cold and dirty after three days in the saddle. He produced a sheaf of documents and stacked them beside him. "All done, Ian is now legally Matthew's son again." He threw her a guarded look, but Alex just nodded and went on with her stitching. "And the money has been paid in full," Simon went on, pulling out yet another document. "Enough to start a new life elsewhere."

Alex straightened up to look at him properly. "That's what you're arguing about."

Simon made a small face. "For months I've been telling him he has to leave. You understand, don't you? Sooner or later, he'll miscalculate. It only takes one wee mistake."

"You're preaching to the choir," Alex sighed. No wonder Matthew had been so distracted the last few weeks, escaping as much as possible to wander alone through his lands.

She went to find him, but he didn't want to talk to her about this, mumbling something about Simon exaggerating.

When Alex pushed he became irritated, telling her that he was in no mood to have a discussion about something that was entirely hypothetical.

"I'm not leaving, it will soon blow over."

"Blow over, my arse," Alex muttered to herself a couple of mornings later when yet another troop of soldiers came riding into the yard, led by a dishevelled officer wearing the tartan plaid of a Highlander.

These men were far different from the soldiers they'd seen before. Lean, with a starved look to them, heavily armed and astride a motley collection of hill ponies, they emanated an air of restless menace, as if chopping people to pieces was something they regularly did for breakfast. Well; in all probability they did, most of them no doubt having served as mercenaries in one or other European war.

Ian materialised by her side and a few seconds later Matthew crossed the yard, his face grim as he took in the soldiers.

"Papists, the lot of them, "he muttered to Alex. "With an axe of their own to grind against anyone of Presbyterian faith."

"Where is he?" the officer eyed them with indifference bordering on dislike.

"Who?" Matthew asked.

"The preacher."

Matthew shrugged. "Last I heard he was on his way north, up towards Glasgow."

The officer looked unconvinced, and ordered his men to search the premises. Matthew sighed and crossed his arms over his chest, a motionless statue oozing irritation.

"Look," Alex hissed, elbowing him. The damned soldiers were coming back out, carrying sacks of grain, casks of cider, the odd ham, quilts and even one of Matthew's shirts.

"What is this?" Matthew snapped, turning to the officer. "Are you brigands, not soldiers?"

The officer laughed, watching as his men loaded the pack ponies.

"We're paid in kind, Mr Graham. And we'll be back when we're in need of more."

"Why you …" Matthew choked.

"What?" The officer leaned towards him.

"Nothing," Alex said, "nothing at all." She clutched at Matthew, almost hanging off his arm to keep him still.

"No; I though as much." The officer grinned, eyes travelling over Alex, Sarah, Rosie, back to Sarah, a very long time on Sarah, who hunched together. The officer laughed, said something in what Alex assumed to be Gaelic to his men, who laughed as well, several eyes flashing over to poor Sarah.

One of the men said something, a high, nasal voice rising in excitement as he pointed up the slope. The officer turned keen eyes in the indicated direction and nodded.

"What?" Alex whispered to Matthew. She didn't dare to turn her head to see what they were looking at with such interest.

"I'm not sure," Matthew whispered back. "And you can let go of me. I don't intend to charge them all by myself."

"Better safe than sorry." But she let go of him all the same.

The officer dismounted. "I'm taking the dog."

What? Alex whipped round to where Aragorn was sitting halfway up the hill.

"It's the boy's dog," Alex pleaded, "please don't take him." She stood to block his way but was rudely shoved aside, stumbling heavily against Matthew. Behind her Ian wheeled and ran towards Aragorn. From in front of her came whoops of excitement and three of the soldiers charged after Ian and the dog, cheered on by their officer.

They caught up with Ian just before the woods, and Alex hung on to Matthew for dear life to stop him from running over to intercede.

"No, that's just what they want you to do." She winced at Ian's screams, but still she held on. "They'll only rough him up," she said through her tears. "But you they'll kill. Please Matthew, please…"

"I have to help him!" Matthew groaned, trying to free himself from Alex' arms.

"Da!" Ian shrieked, "Da!" A strangled yelp, a gasp from Ian, and Alex cried, but refused to let go.

"Alex, let me go, he needs me!"

Oh God, he did, she could hear it, but if Matthew were to intercede, they'd kill him, she could see it in the officer's eyes, in how avidly the men still on their horses were watching her struggle with her husband.

"I can't," she sobbed. "I can't. I…" She clung even harder, digging her heels into the ground. Why couldn't this just be over, please just take the goddamn dog and leave, you filthy bastards!

One loud scream, a bark, a snarl and a whimper when the dog was smacked over the head. Aragorn was dragged off, twisting in his makeshift lead. Ian wasn't moving, but Alex could see he was breathing, still alive.

The officer sat up, shouted something that was echoed by his men, and up the lane they went, clods of mud flying from under the hooves of their horses. Poor Aragorn; he kept on turning back, tail stuck firmly between his legs, but every time he did, the man holding him yanked on the rope.

"I couldn't do differently." Alex unclenched her hands from Matthew's clothes. He scowled at her and brushed her off, leaping up the hill to where Ian was curled into a ball.

"Jesus…" Alex stuffed her hand into her mouth and sank down into a crouch. Slowly the household unfroze, hands came down to help her stand. Sam steadied her towards the door, telling her it was fine, aye, they were gone, all of them. Fine? Alex looked up the slope to where her husband was cradling his son.

"They've been back a couple of times since," Alex told Sandy, sitting down beside him on the graveyard bench. "And they don't even pretend that they're looking for you. They just come in and help themselves to whatever takes their fancy. Bastards!" She took a deep breath and exhaled noisily. "Matthew says you're leaving."

Sandy nodded. "I must. Too many people are being put at risk by my continued presence here." He eyed her with amusement. "Will you miss me?"

She twisted away from him to hide her face. "Not much," she admitted making him laugh out loud. "It's not you, it's the constant fear."

"You don't need to explain, lass." He looked in the direction of Rachel's headstone. "You've already lost one bairn to this conflict." Sandy put a hand on her shoulder; his eyes glazed over, his mouth hung slack, and for a second or two Alex worried he might be having a stroke.

He shook himself. "This won't be the only child you'll bury."

"How do you know?" she asked, hugging her swelling belly. Who, she screamed inside, which one of my babies do you see dying? She swallowed that question down, reminding herself that Sandy Peden had no idea, no bloody idea at all – of course he didn't, no matter that he was called The Prophet.

"I just do," Sandy sighed. "I feel it in my bones, aye?"

"Has anyone ever told you it would be much better if you kept your mouth shut when you get these epiphanies of yours?"

"Och, aye, frequently. But it's not me that makes the decision whether to speak or not."

"Yeah, yeah, blame it on the Holy Ghost." She twisted her hands together. "So what else do you feel, in your bones?"

Sandy shook his head, his eyes sweeping the surrounding slopes. "You must leave, for the sake of your bairns, to give them a future they can never have here."

"Yeah, we should, given that most of Scotland will be ravaged and burnt and pillaged over the coming eighty years or so."

Sandy raised a brow at her. "You see it too?"

Alex shrugged. No she didn't see it – she knew it. Her history teacher's voice echoed in her head, repeating how Scotland had died on behalf of the Stuarts.

"Where will he go?" Alex asked Matthew, standing beside him on the hill. They could still make out Sandy's receding shape, and just before he dropped out of sight the little figure turned and waved in their direction.

"Ireland," Matthew said, taking her hand.

"And we?" she asked unsteadily. "Where will we go?"

"I don't know," he replied, shaking his head. "I have no idea."

They walked through the December woods, kicking their way through the heaped leaves that carpeted the ground. Everywhere he looked, Matthew saw a silent farewell, and it cut him to the bone to realise that he had no choice; he had to leave. He rested his hand against the trunk of a rowan, he dragged his fingers through the prickly mess of man-high brambles. All of it would be taken from him, lost forever, and he'd drift rootless through the remainder of his days. The thought made him nauseous and he tightened his grip on Alex' hand. He sighed; so loudly that Alex drew him to a stop.

"It'll be alright," she said, standing on tiptoe to brush his hair off his face. "Somehow it will be alright." She turned him in the direction of the house, and there were his sons, all four of them, their voices rising high and strong towards him. "We owe it to them," she said, slipping her arms around his waist. "They deserve a chance at life without being forever persecuted."

Just like that Matthew made the final decision, and it was like letting go of an unbearable burden to find you could straighten your back again, lift your chin and breathe. He kissed her on her cheek.

"I'll write a letter to Captain Miles and see if he can offer us berths, and then I must write another to Simon." He began walking down the last slope in the direction of their home, his hand braided with hers. "But not Virginia."

"Of course not, and anyway we have time to think this through. It's not as if we're leaving tomorrow. I'm not anyway," she puffed, "because let me tell you I have no intention of giving birth on a boat." She came to an abrupt standstill, clutching at his hand. "Oh!" she said, and then she grinned. "That's not going to be an issue, I think. If I'm not mistaken, baby Graham is about to make his entry into the world."

"Her," he corrected, "her entry." And please God, let it be a healthy bairn.

"Well, as long as it is either or," she smiled.

"Ruth?" Alex looked affronted. "I'm your Ruth." She looked down at her daughter again. "Why not something else? Like Mary or Joanna?"

Matthew kissed his daughter's downy head. "Ruth," he said. "You birth them, I name them."

"Well, that seems a very unfair distribution of labour, let's do it the other way round next time."

Matthew laughed out loud and kissed her, a long kiss. "I make them, no? And that is right hard work." He sat up and smiled down at her, brushing an escaped curl off her forehead. She looked vulnerable somehow, her eyes circled in purple, her normally so pink skin pasty. The labour had been long, and Ruth was yet another big child, nigh on nine pounds according to the impressed midwife.

"I missed you," Alex said with an edge of accusation in her voice.

"The midwife…" Matthew began, but Alex cut him short.

"I missed you, Matthew."

He took her hand and squeezed it. "I'll be there next time, no matter what the midwife says."

"Promise?" she said, tightening her hold on his fingers. Matthew nodded; next time he'd be there. She smiled and closed her eyes.

"Does she look the same?" she asked.

"They're all very alike." He ran a careful thumb over a miniature nose and a small mouth that was already blistered after a first go at nursing. He lifted the wean out of Alex' arms and sat holding her, one hand cradling the frail little head. A redhead, he smiled, a dark, vibrant red, just like his Mam.

"Nay, she looks like herself, not like Rachel."

Alex didn't reply; she was fast asleep.

Matthew placed his new-born daughter beside her and spread the quilt over them both. He sat by their side and watched them for a long time before standing up to go in search of his sons. At the door he looked back at his sleeping wife. Sandy was right; it didn't matter greatly where he went, as long as his Alex was by his side.

"I love you," he whispered.

"I adore you," she whispered back, her lashes fluttering for an instant over her cheeks.

For a historical note to this book, please visit my website, www.annabelfrage.com

For more information about the Matthew and Alex books, please visit www.annabelfrage.com

For a peek at book four, *A Newfound Land*, just turn the page.

The Matthew and Alex story continues in *A Newfound Land*

CHAPTER 1

The household was still asleep when Alex Graham snuck out of bed. Matthew grumbled, half opened an eye, and subsided back into sleep. On tiptoe, Alex traversed the room, stepping over one sleeping shape after the other. No more, she sang inside, throwing a look at the furthest wall and the as yet boarded up doorways. Matthew had promised he'd finish the extension today, and tonight they'd sleep in their new bedroom, an oasis of privacy after years living as cramped as salted herrings in a barrel.

Alex stuck her feet into her clogs and stepped outside. The sun was as yet no more than a promise on the eastern rim, the stands of grasses to her right sparkled with dew, and just by the door her precious rose was setting buds. This was their new home, a small pocket of domesticity in a wilderness that at times she found most intimidating. Not that she felt particularly threatened by the miles and miles of uninterrupted forest that surrounded her, but should anything happen they were very alone, their closest neighbours well over an hour's ride away.

When they had first arrived in 1668, not yet four years ago, this had been virgin forest, a gently sloping clearing with man-high grass and not much else. Now they had managed to carve out several sizeable fields and pastures, a respectable kitchen garden, as well as the yard she was now crossing on her way to the river. She turned to look back at the small house. The elongated wooden building with its shingled roof was already beginning to grey, acquiring an air of permanence that Alex found comforting. It spoke of roots – as yet shallow, even extremely shallow – but still, roots.

The water was so cold it numbed her toes in a matter of minutes, but Alex didn't mind. She enjoyed these early morning outings, moments when she was alone with only her thoughts for company. A brisk wash, a couple of muttered curses at just how bloody cold the water was, and she was back on the bank, dressing quickly before settling down to comb her wet hair.

In the nearby shrubs a couple of thrushes squabbled, the sun had risen enough to send a ray or two her way, and on the opposite bank a couple of deer came down to drink. So peaceful – until she became aware of the eyes. Strange that; there were eyes all over the place, but somehow one knew when another human being was gawking at you – in this case someone who was doing his or her best to stay hidden.

She returned her comb to the basket and groped until she found the knife. A sidelong glance revealed someone sitting just behind the closest stand of trees. Alex loitered, humming casually while straining her ears. Someone whispered, was hushed. She did a double take; women, not men. Without stopping to think overmuch – one of her major faults according to Matthew – she rushed for the trees.

One of the women squeaked. The other tried to run, slipped and fell.

"Sit," Alex said, waving her knife at them. They complied, huddling together under the oak. They looked bedraggled, caps askew, one with tears in her apron, both quite dirty. Escaped bond servants, Alex guessed and she recognised the monogram on one of the aprons.

"You've run away," she said.

"Please, mistress, please don't tell," the elder of them said.

Hmm. Alex was no major fan of indentured servants, but her Leslie neighbours had paid good money for these two, and would be pissed off if they weren't returned.

"He hit us," one of the girls said. "Belted us, he did."

"He did? For what?"

The elder of the girls muttered something, the younger hunched together, dark eyes never leaving Alex.

"We stole," she said.

"Stole?" The elder girl spat. "I didn't steal. I took payment."

"Payment?" Alex echoed.

The girl gave her a condescending look. "He helped himself."

"Ah." Alex was somewhat taken aback. She'd never have taken Peter Leslie for the lecherous type. "And now you're planning to do what?"

"Walk," the eldest girl said.

"To Providence?" Alex shook her head. That was well over a week's walk, and the two girls seemed to have no sense of direction as they'd walked north from the Leslie settlement, rather than south.

"No; to St.Mary's City," the younger girl said. Good luck to them; that was almost twice as far.

"You're Catholic," Alex said. No other reason to go that far – unless they'd done more than steal. The elder girl glared at her, an arm coming up protectively around the younger's shoulder.

"And what if we are?"

"I couldn't care less," Alex told her with a little smile. "But it's a very long walk – that way." She pointed south. "How are you to survive, all on your own?"

"I have a knife," the elder said.

"Whoopee," Alex muttered. She should send them straight back to the Leslies', but she already knew she wouldn't. Matthew wouldn't like it, but on the other hand, why tell him? She gnawed her lip. "I'll see what I can find for you," she said. "You'll need food and a blanket or two." The youngest girl burst into tears and clutched at Alex' skirts. "Yes, yes," Alex said, rather embarrassed by all this. She gestured into the deeper forest to their right. "Hide in there, somewhere. You'll have to stay put until you hear me whistle for you. " She shooed them off, admonished them to keep well out of sight and set off up the incline.

She was almost back at the house when her three youngest children ambushed her.

"Ouff!" Alex said when Sarah barrelled into her. Her daughter grabbed at her legs and rubbed her head against her skirts, dislodging what little remained of her night braid. The fair hair fell in soft waves around her face, making her look like a sweet angel – which she definitely was not.

"Where have you been?" Matthew said from behind her.

"I went for a swim," Alex said.

"A swim?" Sarah's reproachful blue eyes stared up at her. "Without us?"

"Aye, why didn't you say?" Ruth asked.

Because I wanted to go alone, Alex thought, smiling at her little redhead. Ruth smiled back, the hazel eyes she shared with her father and most of her siblings shifting into a light greyish green.

"We can go later," Alex said. "I probably need to give all three of you a proper scrub."

"Not me," Daniel muttered, shoving his dark hair off his brow, "I'm clean, very clean."

Alex looked at the trio; three children in three years, but since then Matthew and she had been very careful, even if at times both of them were left extremely frustrated by this. Her eyes slid over to rest on her man. Alex fluffed at her hair, catching Matthew's interested look. As far as Alex was concerned, five children – six, counting Ian – were quite enough, but she wasn't sure Matthew agreed. What the hell; she wanted to have wild and uninhibited sex with him, and damn the consequences. She saw his mouth curve and felt the blood rush up her cheeks, making him smile even wider.

"Right, you," she said to her children. "You all have chores to do."

Daniel made a face, but at Matthew's nod he and Ruth hurried off. Sarah loitered, throwing Alex a hopeful look. You wish, Alex thought, handing her three year old the egg basket.

"You look thoroughly," she said, "now that they're back to laying properly, I want them all."

Sarah set her mouth in a sulk and dragged her feet on her way to the stables.

Matthew took Alex' hand and squeezed it. She knew exactly what he was thinking. This their youngest daughter was in many ways a throwback to their eldest girl, Rachel, and both of them were very relieved that in looks Sarah did not take after their dead daughter – that would have been a bit too much.

"She'll drive her future husband to the edge of despair," Matthew said in an undertone.

She chortled. "Let's hope she calms down a bit."

They walked across the yard, him shortening his stride to match hers.

"I don't like it, that you go about alone," he said.

"I was just down there," Alex said, gesturing in the direction of the river.

"Still, I don't like it."

Alex chose not to reply, studying her house – well, cabin – instead. Two chimneys, one sticking up from the new extension, and several windows, four with horribly expensive glass panes in them that Matthew had transported up here piece by careful piece, swaddled as if they were priceless porcelain.

According to dear Elizabeth Leslie, window glass was an unnecessary luxury, but Alex didn't care about her opinion, thrilled to have light streaming into her kitchen and parlour, and now into her bedroom as well. Elizabeth… Alex threw Matthew a look. She should tell him about the girls, he didn't like it when she kept things from him. On the other hand, it made her shudder just to imagine how Elizabeth would punish her two servants for running away. Bread and water for a month, and no doubt a severe beating with that cane Elizabeth always kept close at hand.

"What is it?" Matthew said.

"Nothing."

He turned her to face him. "What?"

Alex sighed. This man of hers read her like an open book, no matter how much she tried to dissimulate. Briefly she told him of her encounter with the girls, shifting on her feet under his eyes.

"But I don't want to force them to go back," she finished. "Can you imagine how angry they'll be?"

"Escaped servants must be returned. You know I don't much hold with it," he said, swinging her hand as they covered the last few yards to the door. "It sticks in my craw, it does, to hold a fellow man as a slave, however temporarily. But that's how things are ordained here, and Peter Leslie paid good money for them. Besides, two lasses on their own in all that ..." He waved a hand at the woods.

"So what do we do?"

Matthew opened the door for her and gave Fiona, their maid, a curt nod before replying.

"For now we do nowt." He leaned close enough that his breath tickled her ear. "But if they come looking we tell them."

Alex nodded; a fair compromise and hopefully Peter would expend his efforts to the south.

The small kitchen filled with people. Mark and Jacob came from the direction of the stable, Sarah danced in to show them just how many eggs she'd found, and Daniel and Ruth were sent off to wash when they appeared dirty at the door. Eggs, ham, porridge and thick slices of rye bread were set down on the table. From the yard came Jonah, their second indenture, and after a hastily said grace everyone threw themselves at the food.

"And Ian?" Alex looked at Mark.

"I don't know," Mark said, "he may have gone hunting."

"Or fishing," Jacob suggested through his full mouth. Alex smoothed at his thick blond hair.

"Maybe," she shrugged. Ian was old enough to take care of himself.

No sooner was the table cleared than Fiona begged to be excused, whispering something about her monthlies. Alex just nodded. The last few weeks, Fiona was forever begging to be let off for one reason or the other, and this her latest excuse was wearing a bit thin. Still; mostly she did what she was told to do, and if Fiona found some sort of relief by wandering the nearby woods, so be it.

Matthew sat for a while longer at the table, conversing her as Alex went about the dinner preparations. She still had days when it shocked her just how much time she spent on something as simple as cooking. In the here and now there were no electric cookers, no microwaves, it was all open fire and heavy pots. Alex wiped her hands on her apron and leaned against the work bench.

She rarely thought about the life she'd left behind – given the circumstances she preferred not to – but every now and then she was swept with a wave of longing for her people, lost somewhere in the future. Isaac, her son; he'd be sixteen by now, and she wondered if he'd be taller than her and if he still wore his hair short. And Magnus, now pushing seventy… she couldn't quite see her father as old – to her he was an eternally middle-aged tall blond man with eyes as blue as hers.

She counted in her head; it was 2016 there in the future. Almost fourteen years ago since fate and a gigantic bolt of lightning combined to throw her more than three hundred years backwards to land stunned at Matthew's feet. Alex twisted at her wedding ring; should she ever be yanked back she was certain she'd die, of something as hackneyed as a broken heart.

She started when Matthew covered her hands with his.

"Alright?" he asked, kissing her brow.

"Yeah, I'm fine. I just had one of those flashbacks."

"Ah," he nodded. She eyed him from under her lashes. Matthew was never comfortable discussing her strange – impossible – fall from one time to the other. Heck; neither was she, it made her hair bristle. Just as she'd expected, he changed the subject.

"This afternoon I'll finish the house, tomorrow I start with the barn," Matthew said in a resigned tone, looking at what was presently a roof on stilts. He studied his callused hands and muttered that he was always one step behind, whether in the building or in the tilling. But at least there was a stable, and an assorted number of small sheds, including a well sized laundry shed, complete with a large wooden bathtub.

"No hurry, is there?" Alex said. "After all, there's nothing to fill it with as yet."

"There will be," he said, "this year the crops will be good." With that very confident statement he grabbed his hat and went outside, telling her that he'd be taking Mark and Jacob with him to clear the new field.

The boys came rushing when he called for them. Mark was already shooting up in height while eight year old Jacob was still very much a child, all downy cheeks and knobbly knees. So young, Alex reflected, watching her sons fall into step beside their father, and already most of their days were spent working side by side with Matthew. Not that they seemed to mind, both of them inflating with pride when Matthew praised them for their hard work – which he did quite often.

Alex packed her basket with some food, found a blanket in the laundry shed, draped it over her arm and made for the woods. Late April in Maryland was like a warm summer day in Scotland and Alex adjusted her straw hat as she went, before beginning her customary scanning of the ground for anything green and edible. She was sick to death of the few sad carrots in the root cellar, she wanted huge salads, ripe tomatoes, and while she was at it, why not a chocolate bar or two... Boy was she in a maudlin mood! She slowed her pace and ducked into the shade of the closest trees.

It was strange that the few times she was truly homesick it wasn't for her life in the twenty first century, it was for Hillview, the small manor in Ayrshire that they'd left one cold and drizzling March day four years ago. She'd spent weeks saying good bye, walking for hours through the woods, standing silent by the edge of the moss. Worst of all had been the last time she and Matthew had stood together in front of Rachel's grave, bowing with the pain of forever leaving behind this one tangible reminder of their daughter's brief time on Earth.

"Rachel," she said out loud. She did that sometimes; she called her dead daughter, and just by saying her name she was making sure she wasn't forgotten. Now she closed her eyes and Rachel sprang to the forefront of her mind, her hair a messy tangle down her back – just like she'd been the last day of her life, her little face contorted with fury as she flew to the defence of her beloved Da.

"Mama?" Ian materialised beside her and Alex turned away. "Are you alright?"

Alex nodded, wiping her eyes with the back of her hand before facing him.

"One of those moments." She suspected Ian had quite a few such moments himself, but he chose to keep them to himself. Alex stood on her toes and pulled out a couple of cockleburs from his hair.

"You're too tall," she grumbled, and Ian grinned and sat down, crossing his legs. Alex stood on her knees and extracted her comb from her apron pockets to comb his hair free of debris. "Where have you been? Chasing deer through the undergrowth?"

Ian mumbled something unintelligible in reply.

Alex smiled down at the back of his head and went on with what she was doing. They sank into a companionable silence, broken every now and then by the loud calling of a bird or the rustling of something moving through the forest that surrounded them.

"There." Alex sank back on her heels and returned her comb to its keeping place. "You're so like him," she said, studying her teenaged stepson, who had now gotten to his feet. A younger version of her Matthew, tall and well-built with the same hazel eyes, the same dark hair that went chestnut under the summer sun and the same generous mouth.

"Is that good or bad?" Ian teased, helping her to stand.

"Good, obviously." She bent to pick up her basket. A flurry of movement made her rear back as something mid-size and grey rushed by her.

"A wolf?" she asked tremulously.

Ian laughed, shaking his head. "Raccoon. Curious as to what's in yon basket."

"Nettle shoots," Alex said, "will make us all a very nice soup." She was very happy with her find, thinking that she'd poach some eggs to go with it. Ian eyed the contents with a decided lack of enthusiasm.

"Eat nettles? Won't it blister our mouths?"

"Of course it will. It will make all of you shut up for days and days," Alex said, elbowing him hard. "Idiot," she added, making him laugh.

"What happened to your promise to fix the hen coop?" Alex said, accepting Ian's hand when they clambered over a mossy trunk.

"I'll do it now," he said, his cheeks staining a suspicious red. Alex studied him narrowly; grasses and leaves all over his clothes, all that stuff he'd had in his hair… She smiled and hefted her basket higher onto her arm. Apparently young master Graham was discovering the pleasures of the opposite sex. She wondered if it was Jenny he'd met up in the woods – she sincerely hoped it was Jenny Leslie, given that Matthew and the girl's father were very much in agreement regarding the desirability of such a match.

Ian turned towards the house, Alex dithered; she had to find the girls.

"Are you coming?" he asked.

"Soon, I… well, I need some more nettles."

"I'll come with you." Ian held out his hand for the basket.

"I'll be fine on my own," Alex said.

He shook his head. "I'll come, aye?" Great; absolutely marvellous. Those protective genes so prominent in his father had made it down to the next generation unscathed. From the way Ian's mouth set into a line, she knew there was no point in arguing, and anyway, what did it matter if he saw the girls – he'd never tell.

"Da said you'll be staying with the Leslies when we ride down to Providence," Ian said.

Alex made a face. She was fond of both Thomas and Peter Leslie – although she should probably revise her opinion of Peter given what those girls had told her – but Mary Leslie had the intellect of a dormouse and as to Elizabeth…

"Aye," Ian said, following the train of her thoughts. "She is a bit much at times."

"Very much so," Alex agreed, thinking that Elizabeth Leslie must be an awful cross to carry for a man as mild-tempered as Peter.

A high wail had Alex almost jumping out of her skin.

"What was that?" She stooped to pick up the nettles she'd scattered all over the ground.

"I don't know," Ian frowned.

Yet another shriek, and now there was no doubt – this was a human voice, raised in fear and pain. The girls! Oh my God, and now they were being eaten alive by a bear, or were surrounded by wolves, or… Alex flew down the slope, making for the terrified sounds. Another voice; low, male. Someone laughed, harness jangled and Alex faltered. Could it be one of the Leslie brothers?

"No, please! No…" The sound was cut short.

Ian's hand closed on Alex' arm, bringing her to a halt. They crouched behind a screen of bushes, silent spectators to what was happening in the small clearing. Three men, unrecognisable in broad brimmed hats, and then there were the two girls, one of them fighting like a hellcat, while the other was gagged and hogtied, squirming like a caterpillar where she'd been thrown across a horse. To the side stood yet another man, eyes trained on the surrounding woods and musket held at the ready. Alex did a double take; she knew this man from somewhere. Thinning hair, a long narrow face with a rather prominent mouth, and dark eyes sunk into deep hollows. Yes; she had definitely seen him before, but when? Where?

"We must do something," she hissed, "those poor girls!" She made as if to stand but was arrested by Ian's hold on her hand.

"Nay," he whispered, "there's nothing we can do – not the two of us against them."

However much she hated admitting it, Ian was right.

In the clearing the screaming girl was slapped – repeatedly. The last slap was so hard her head snapped back. The man who hit her laughed, watching as his companions wrenched her hands behind her back and tied them, before sauntering over to the sentry, saying something in a low voice. He took off his hat, releasing black hair to fall like overlong bangs over one side of his face. A handsome man, his face a collection of sharp planes and angles, complemented by a square chin and a chiselled mouth. A cruel face, Alex decided – or maybe that had more to do with what she'd just witnessed him do to the poor girl. His eyes wandered over the closest bushes and Alex shrank together, thinking she had never before seen eyes so disconcerting. Irises so light so as to look almost white, the pupils like black, miniature well shafts. For some reason Alex knotted her hands together and held her breath – anything to make sure he wouldn't discover her.

The man took a step or two to the side, unlaced himself and pissed, talking with his companions over his shoulder. It was evident he was the leader, the sentry nodding at whatever it was he was saying. Alex caught the word Virginia a couple of times and focused her attention on the sentry. Why did he seem so familiar, all the way from his obsequious grin to how he stood, slightly pigeon-toed? There was a flurry of movement, the men sat up, and then they were gone, horses whipped into a canter as they set off towards the south.